The Dedalus/Ariadne Book of Austrian Fantasy:

The Meyrink Years 1890–1930

edited and translated
by
Mike Mitchell

DEDALUS/ARIADNE

Supported by the **Eastern Arts** Board

Dedalus/Ariadne would like to thank The Austrian Ministry of Culture and Education in Vienna and the Eastern Arts Board for their assistance in producing this book.

Published in the UK by Dedalus Ltd,
Langford Lodge, St Judith's Lane, Sawtry, Cambs, PE17 5XE

UK ISBN 0 946626 93 6

Published in the USA by Ariadne Press,
270 Goins Court, Riverside, California, 92507

US ISBN 0 929497 63 5

Distributed in Canada by Marginal Distribution,
Unit 103, 277 George Street North, Peterborough, Ontario KJ9 3G9

The Dedalus Book of Austrian Fantasy copyright © Mike Mitchell 1992

Printed in England by Loader Jackson, Arlesey
Typeset by Cygnus Media Services, Redhill, Surrey, UK

A C.I.P. listing for this title is available on request.

Acknowledgements

The editor would like to thank the following for permission to use copyright material:

Frau Ilse Ester Hoffe, Tel Aviv, for: Max Brod, *Die erste Stunde nach dem Tod;*
Langen Müller Verlag in F. A. Herbig Verlagsbuchhandlung, Munich, for: F. T. Csokor, *Schattenstadt, Die steinerne Frau* from F. T. Csokor: *Ein paar Schaufeln Erde,* Langen Müller, 1965; F. v. Herzmanovsky-Orlando, *Cavaliere Huscher oder Die sonderbare Meerfahrt des Herrn von Yb* from: F. von Herzmanovsky-Orlando, *Maskenspiel der Genien,* Langen Müller, 1958; Karl Hans Strobl, *Der Kopf,* from K. H. Strobl, *Unheimliche Geschichten,* Herbig, 1973; *Die arge Nonn';*
Freiherr Falk von Gagern, Vienna, for: Friedrich von Gagern, extract from *Geister: Gänger Gesichte Gewalten;*
edition spangenberg, Munich, for: Alfred Kubin, extract from Die andere Seite. Ein phantastischer Roman, (edition spangenberg, Munich, 1990);
Verlag Peter Selinka, Ravensburg, for: Paul Leppin, extract from *Severins Gang in die Finsternis;*
Paul Zsolnay Verlag, Vienna, for: Leo Perutz, *Pour avoir bien servi* from *Herr erbarme Dich meiner,* (Paul Zsolnay Verlag, Vienna/Hamburg, 1985);
S. Fischer Verlag, Frankfurt am Main, for: Franz Werfel, *Spielhof, Eine Phantasie* from *Erzählungen aus zwei Welten,* vol. 1, (Copyright 1948 Alma Mahler-Werfel; S. Fischer Verlag, Frankfurt am Main).

DEDALUS EUROPE 1992–1995

supported by
The European Arts Festival
July–December 1992

EUROPEAN ARTS
FESTIVAL
JULY-DECEMBER 1992

Dedalus as part of its Europe 1992-95 programme is combining with the Ariadne Press to make all of Gustav Meyrink's novels available in English in new translations by Mike Mitchell.

Titles so far published:

The Angel of the West Window
The Green Face

forthcoming:

Walpurgisnacht (1993)
The White Dominican (1994)
The Golem (1995)

In addition a selection of Gustav Meyrink's short stories translated by Maurice Raraty *The Opal (and other stories)* will be published in 1993.

Extracts from all of Meyrink's five novels and some of his short stories have been included in *The Dedalus/Ariadne Book of Austrian Fantasy: the Meyrink Years 1890-1930.*

THE EDITOR

Mike Mitchell is a lecturer in German at Stirling University. His publications include a book on Peter Hacks, the East German playwright, and numerous studies on aspects of modern Austrian Literature; he is the co-author of *Harrap's German Grammar*.

Mike Mitchell's translations include *The Architect of Ruins* by Herbert Rosendorfer, *The Works of Solitude* by Gyorgy Sebestyen, and Gustav Meyrink's novels *The Angel of the West Window* and *The Green Face*.

He is currently engaged on translating Gustav Meyrink's *Walpurgisnacht* and *The White Dominican* into English.

Contents

(Apart from the stories indicated, the translations are by the editor.)

The Dedalus/Ariadne Book of Austrian Fantasy

Introduction

"It is a sad but incontrovertible fact that the world stands in profound ignorance of the phenomenon of Austria." Since Fritz von Herzmanovsky-Orlando wrote those opening lines to his anarchic comic novel, *Maskenspiel der Genien* (Masque of the Spirits) at the end of the 1920s, much more has become known of Austria than "the mistakes contained in a few tourist guides published abroad". Freud was already becoming a household name even then, but the other figures who are now widely associated with the cultural florescence of the turn-of-the-century Habsburg Empire were almost unknown outside Austria: Mahler, Schoenberg, Klimt, Kokoschka, Schiele, Wittgenstein, Mach, Schnitzler, Hofmannsthal. Now the whole concept of *fin de siècle* Vienna is so well known that it is an effective tourist attraction vigorously promoted by the Austrian Tourist Board.

However, Herzmanovsky-Orlando's lament, as far as it was intended to be taken seriously (and there is a serious concern lurking deep beneath the comic-grotesque surface of his novel), does not refer to these cultural icons of a golden age that was brought to an end by the First World War. For him, the "phenomenon of Austria" was an essence, a mode of being that found expression in the Habsburg Empire, or, rather, in *his* vision of Austria as a state where the elemental forces embodied in the myths of antiquity still managed to survive behind a grotesquely bureaucratic surface. These two disparate elements are brought together in one of Herzmanovsky's pictures (he was also an artist of some stature): "Austrian customs officials supervise the birth of Venus". They are also present in the story included in this anthology, *Signor Scurri* in, for example, the soldier who, when invalided out of the army, was given "The Sea", just as others were given the more traditional barrel organ or tobacco shop.

Herzmanovsky's novel is set in an imaginary buffer state between the German, Slav and Latin areas of Europe, a concept that has reappeared on the political menu of the real world since the collapse of the Soviet Union and Yugoslavia! This state combines an anarchic vitality with the most rigidly formal of constitutions, which is based on the rules of *Tarock*, a popular Austrian card game, hence its name, Tarockania. Another more widely known fantasy version of Austria, and conceived at about the same time, is *Kakanien* (Cacania) in Robert Musil's novel, *The Man without Qualities*. The name derives from a combination of the initials *K. und K.* standing for Imperial and Royal and seen everywhere in the old Empire, and *Kacke*, crap. Musil's country might be regarded as the negative to Herzmanovsky's positive, since in Cacania the dead hand of bureaucracy tends to stifle rather than protect positive forces, although it does allow Musil to examine potential realities as a counterweight to the actual world.

A further example of these fantasy states is the Dream Realm in Alfred Kubin's novel *The Other Side*. Kubin, a friend of Herzmanovsky and a graphic artist with a particular talent for dream and nightmare figures, started preparing illustrations for *The Golem*. When Meyrink's progress on the novel halted, Kubin used the pictures he had done for *The Golem* to illustrate his own novel. Ironically, he had written the novel because he himself had been going through a difficult period when he found himself incapable of putting his ideas down on paper in drawings.

The Dream Realm is a state founded in the middle of Asia by Klaus Patera, a fabulously wealthy schoolfriend of the narrator. Its buildings have all been transported from various parts of Europe, none being later than 1860. The narrator never meets Patera, who remains a mysterious force at the centre of this kingdom where time has stopped, guarded by a punctilious and impenetrable bureaucracy. This combination of mystical force and rigid bureaucracy relates the Dream World to Herzmanovsky's and Musil's creations, though the atmosphere of Kubin's country reeks of decadence and decay. On another level, the story seems to be a nightmare journey for the narrator into his own subconscious, unsurprising in a countryman of Freud. His wanderings round the cellars of the dairy and the episode where he is chased naked through the French Quarter are good examples of this nightmare quality.

Probably the best-known literary evocation of the bureaucratic spirit is the castle in Kafka's novel of the same name. There, whatever authority resides within the castle is surrounded by an impregnable wall of bureaucracy. Yet however mean, spiteful or stupid the subordinates seem to be, those qualities do not reflect on whatever is at the centre, which remains powerful but unknowable. These features are also illustrated here in the perfect miniature, the little parable *Outside the Law*. The intimidating figure of the doorkeeper cannot diminish the radiance of the light pouring out from the door he guards so effectively. Paradox becomes an existential mode of being.

These fantasy images of Austria such as Tarockania or Cacania are not merely nostalgic recreations of the multinational Empire which was wiped from the map at a stroke in 1919, though there were also many of those. There is a quality of paradox underlying them all, and in this they hark back to the Monarchy's increasingly desperate search, as the nineteenth century proceeded, for a unifying *idea* to justify a state which held together so many disparate nationalities. Immediately after the 1848 revolution a distinguished historian, J. G. Helfert, had pointed out that for most citizens of the Empire there was a distinction between *Heimat*, the region to which they felt an emotional tie, and *Vaterland,* the state to which they owed loyalty, and he proposed a vigorous programme of education to inculcate an attachment to the *fatherland.* As far as they were ever carried out, Helfert's ideas did not have any great success; until the end of the Empire the loyalties of its subjects were focused mainly on the *person* of the Emperor, rather than on the country he represented. This ambiguity the inhabitants felt as to where they actually belonged, can perhaps best be seen in the fact that the state had no real name. Although commonly referred to as 'Austria' that was only the name of two tiny medieval dukedoms that form the north-eastern corner of the present state. Its official designation was: *The Kingdoms and Countries represented in the Imperial Diet.* Not a name to engender a strong feeling of belonging.

The contrast between the ceremonial splendour of the centuries-old Habsburg Empire, with the apparently permanent

Francis Joseph at its head, and the shifting sands of increasingly disaffected nationalities on which it was based, has something baroque about it, and, indeed, the baroque is an important part of Austria's cultural heritage. Baroque art has a splendour which is undermined by the fact that its all too palpable physicality is not important in itself, but as a symbol of a transcendental, spiritual world. Life is not something independent, self-sufficient, but merely a pale image of another, more real world. Life, in the words of the title of Calderon's play which the Austrian Grillparzer also used, is a dream.

To the baroque inheritance and the awareness, often unconscious, of the insecurities beneath the glittering surface of Imperial society must be added the researches of a school of psychologists, of which Freud is only the best-known, which laid bare the powerful urges and desires beneath the surface respectability of the personality. And it was in Vienna that Ernst Mach, a scientist whose name has been perpetuated in the term for the speed of sound, concluded, when he was looking for a solid foundation on which to base his science, that the self as an independent, ordering entity was "irretrievably lost". The literature which sprang from this background was one which casts doubt on the apparently solid surface of reality, which questions the meaningfulness of human activity, which is always ready to admit that the opposite might just as well be true. It is a literature that is a fertile ground for fantasy.

It is this which distinguishes Austrian literature from German. A culture which emphasises the potential as much as the real, which has a taste for the humour of paradox, is one which does not take a too earnest view of itself. German literature takes itself, the world and the supernatural far more seriously. There was a fashion, in the first twenty years or so of this century, for literature of the supernatural in the manner of E. T. A. Hoffmann and Edgar Allan Poe in which some Austrian writers, in particular Karl Hans Strobl, were prominent. But more characteristic Austrian fantasy tends to emphasise the puzzling coincidences, parallels and paradoxes of this world, revealing it as less solid than we would think. A good example of this is Leo Perutz. He was a mathematician, and his novels are finely calculated equations of chance, coincidence and mystery. It is a style which is less well-suited to the restricted length of the short story, but *Pour avoir bien servi* has a typical twist at the end which turns its whole basis inside out, revealing the apparently clear relationships as a construction of the narrator's imagination.

As part of Austria's baroque heritage death, too, is seen not as the end, the negation of life, but rather as a continuation in another sphere. Dying is often seen not as an abrupt event, but a gradual transition of which the character and the reader gradually becomes aware. A good example of this is Csokor's *Shadowtown* where the characters only gradually become aware they are dead and where death is like "a safe, dark cave, which will protect me as I fall asleep". In Hofmannsthal's *Sergeant Anton Lerch,* the whole, subtle transformation of mood through the day is a prelude to Lerch's unexpected and unexplained death. In Max Brod's story the 'first hour after death' is a period of adjustment to a continuation of existence on a more spiritual level. The personification of death in the extract from Rilke's novel, *The Notebooks of Malte Laurids Brigge,* is not a mere literary device. For Rilke, the depersonalisation of death was the ultimate sign of the loss of individual substance in life, which he experienced particularly strongly in Paris.

In Kafka's story, *Gracchus the Huntsman*, death is an intermediate state, neither the one thing nor the other, as the hero's funeral barge "went the wrong way", leaving him "on the great staircase leading up ... sometimes at the top, sometimes down below, sometimes to the right, sometimes to the left, always in motion." But this is the state in which most of Kafka's characters find themselves: Gregor Samsa is a man who has metamorphosed into an insect, but still retains human feeling; Josef K. has been arrested but does not know what he is accused of, nor by what law; K believes he has been appointed surveyor to the castle, but cannot convince the administrators of the fact; the man from the country in *Outside the Law* spends his life outside the Law, hoping to be granted entrance, and the country doctor in the story of the same name does not belong in the country area he serves. This sense of not belonging doubtless had its roots both in Kafka's relationship with his father and in his situation as a Germanised Jew in the increasingly Czech city of Prague, but in his writings it is raised to an existential plane. (The cryptic references to his own name in the names Kafka gave to his characters has frequently been commented on; *kavka* in Czech and *graculus*, in Latin, related to 'Gracchus', both mean 'jackdaw', for example.) These stories, which have been called "parables from which the first term is missing", present man as a displaced person in the scheme of eternity. For many readers they express the *condition humaine* of the twentieth century and this doubtless explains Kafka's worldwide popularity since the end of the Second World War.

Like a number of the writers included in this anthology – Brod, Leppin, Perutz, Rilke and Werfel – Kafka was born in Prague which, in the early part of this century, came to rival Vienna and Berlin as a centre of German literary life. But the figure with whom Prague, with its brooding castle, crowded ghetto and mysterious atmosphere, is most closely associated is Gustav Meyrink, who went to live there as an adult. An elegant dandy around whom legends naturally accumulated (he once supposedly challenged the whole of the officers' corps to a duel), he began writing while recovering from tuberculosis in 1901. His popularity was established by his short stories, in many of which his fantasy has a sharp satirical edge, attacking all kinds of narrow-mindedness, especially military, religious and scientific.

Wetherglobin is a good example of his satire. It is much harsher than might appear to the English or American ear, since the military had considerably greater power and social prestige in both Austria and Germany prior to the First World War. During the war, Meyrink was attacked for the kind of opposition to militarism and mindless patriotism that can be seen in *Wetherglobin*. Earlier, Arthur Schnitzler had been stripped of his rank as an officer of the reserve for his story *Lieutenant Gustl* by one of the 'courts of honour' that are an incidental target of Meyrink's satire.

Extracts from Meyrink's novels have been included to demonstrate his range. The first, and best-known of them, *The Golem*, was serialised in a periodical in 1913. Set in the Jewish ghetto, it has a dream-like atmosphere as the main character seems to sleep-walk his way through a series of grotesque and mysterious events to a mystical union with Miriam, the daughter of the synagogue archivist, Hillel. The extract chosen begins among typically decadent café society and then, as the hero falls into a cataleptic state, moves into another world under Hillel's guidance. His next novel, *The Green Face*, also chronicles a spiritual search ending in a mystical marriage; parallel to this ending is the destruction of Amsterdam in a natural cataclysm of apocalyptic proportions which reveals Meyrink's considerable gifts as a stylist. The end of *Walpurgisnacht* is similarly apocalyptic, but this time the apocalypse is political in origin, although translated into another dimension by the presence of occult forces. The story confronts the withered representatives of the Habsburg establishment, living a self-enclosed life in the castle above Prague, with the violent forces of the nationalist and proletarian Czech revolution; both are destroyed in the final clash.

Meyrink became increasingly concerned with the occult. He spent much time investigating, and often exposing, mediums; at the same time he edited a number of occult texts and, despite his frequent disappointment in the practitioners, clearly believed in the existence of occult forces. Some of this knowledge is used in all these novels, but it is the main focus of *The White Dominican*, which is set in a spiritualised version of the Bavarian town of Wasserburg am Inn. The occult is also important in his last novel, *The Angel of the West Window*, but that has a historical setting and the story of John Dee to give it a structural backbone which *The White Dominican* lacks. Bartlett Greene is Meyrink's own invention, apart from the name, and illustrates again the power of his writing, this time in the macabre-horrific vein, which can also be seen to good effect in such stories as *Dr. Cinderella's Plants* and *The Ring of Saturn*.

Paul Leppin was a disciple of Meyrink and the figure of Nicholas, who flits in and out of *Severin's Road into Darkness*, is a tribute to him. The Prague of Paul Leppin's short novel owes much to Meyrink; however, in spite of the subtitle of *A Prague Ghost-Story*, which it is suspected the publisher imposed on it, it is more the decadent Prague of Loisitchek's inn in *The Golem* than the city of the supernatural. The evocation of atmosphere is the attraction of this book, atmosphere which is as much in the hero's mind as in the city outside. His 'road into darkness' is the result of a kind of spell cast by a girl who is an embodiment of the decadence of Prague, but it is also a spell that finds a willing accomplice in Severin's own lust.

It is worth pointing out that Prague as a city of decadence and mystery, where the Golem walks or a whore becomes a kind of succubus, draining the hero of energy, is a German image. For the Czechs of the period Prague was the vital symbol of a people who were about to take what they regarded as their rightful place in history.

Brod and Werfel belong to the next generation of writers, which made Prague the most important centre of Expressionism in the Monarchy. Although both later abandoned the exaggeratedly expressive style, they remained concerned with a renewal of the spiritual side of man which was fundamental to Expressionism and which informs both the stories in this anthology. Brod's brilliant *The First Hour after Death,* first published in 1916, goes beyond Expressionism in its addition of humour to satire and spirituality. It creates a future world which has been at war for so long it is regarded as the natural condition of mankind. The apostle of this acceptance, the Minister, is confronted with the spirit of a being from another sphere, whose punishment for his sins is to be sent for an hour to our – lower – world. What makes the story particularly attractive is that the ghost, who temporarily converts the Minister away from his rationalistic relativism, is a comic figure who has great difficulty adapting to the physical conditions of this world.

At the beginning of his career Werfel was primarily a poet, and there is something of the expansive gestures of the writer of *Der Weltfreund* (The World-Friend) in the texture of *The Playground.* There is also something post-Freudian about its dreams within dreams, especially the first section recreating the hero's relationship with his father. What Werfel takes from Freud is not, however, psychological analysis so much as archetypical relationships which he transforms into poetic symbols.

The central section, on love/sex, is probably a working-out of some of the guilt Werfel felt at his relationship with Alma Mahler-Gropius, who was pregnant with his child before she left Gropius in 1920, the year in which *The Playground* was first published.

Much closer to Freud was the oldest writer represented in this anthology, Arthur Schnitzler. He trained as a doctor (his father's profession) and continued to practise for some years after his initial success as a writer. His interest in psychology was scientific as well as literary (he had been an assistant in the clinic of Freud's teacher, Theodor Meynert); Freud, six years his senior, even felt a superstitious thrill at the similarity between them. In a letter congratulating Schnitzler on his sixtieth birthday, he wrote:

> I have plagued myself over the question how it comes about that in all these years I have never sought your company ... The answer is this much too intimate confession. I think I have avoided you from a kind of awe of meeting my 'double' ... whenever I get deeply interested in your beautiful creations I always seem to find behind their poetic sheen the same presuppositions, interests and conclusions as those familiar to me as my own.

Schnitzler's style is, in general, a finely nuanced social and psychological realism, so that the suggestions of the supernatural in the two stories in this anthology are slightly unusual. However, in both stories these suggestions are used to highlight the psychological analysis, rather than out of sensationalism. The hero of *Flowers* feels the ghost of his former lover is taking possession of him through the flowers that came to him after her death. In fact, it is his belated pangs of conscience for his heartless treatment of her that give the memory its hold over him. His release from the spell when his healthy, uncomplicated current mistress throws the withered stalks out of the window has much of the moral ambiguity that abounds in Schnitzler's work. Life wins over death, health over sickness, but also, so it seems, egoism over moral sensitivity.

Schnitzler was the first writer to make successful use of interior monologue throughout a story (in *Lieutenant Gustl*) and in general he allows his characters to reveal themselves rather than presenting them through authorial analysis. (This can of course be seen at best in his plays, for example *La Ronde*.) *Flowers* is written in a kind of diary form; *The Prophecy*, which contains a genuine supernatural event, or at least one that is unexplained, is narrated by a writer who bears much similarity to Schnitzler. The interest, however, is in the hero who tells his story to the writer. There is suspense at to whether the prophecy will come true and as to *how* it will come true, but the strange events are also the means by which Herr von Umprecht reveals, quite unknowingly, his own shallow self, his arrogance, his selfishness and his casual anti-semitism. In spite of a further twist at the end that undermines the credibility of the narrator, that remains the chief thrust of the story.

Schnitzler's characters tend to live for the moment. Ethical values which suggest a longer-term commitment usually crumble when faced with immediate demands. In some young writers of the generation that followed Schnitzler and Freud, writers who appeared in the 1890s, this developed into an extraordinary sensitivity to mood and atmosphere, which threatened to dissolve the personality into nothing more than the focus for a multitude of separate impressions, which was all that was left of the 'self' in Ernst Mach's philosophy. Rilke's early poems are products of this subjective impressionism, which in his *New Poems* of 1907-8 he attempted to overcome by concentrating on objects from the world outside. *The Papers of Malte Laurids Brigge* is a product of that period of what has been called the 'crisis of subjectivity', when Rilke learnt, from his association with Rodin, for whom he acted as secretary for a time, to 'see' the external world, rather than the reflection of his own soul in it.

The main representative of this 'impressionism' in this anthology is Hugo von Hofmannsthal. He astonished the Viennese with his delicate, almost perfect lyrics published in the early 1890s when he was still at school. They reproduce moments of intense harmony with the beauty of the world, a beauty which he was aware was fragile, that could easily be shattered by contact with social and political realities, with ugliness and squalor. The problem of this aesthetic mode of existence runs through his delicate verse plays, which show a clearer awareness that it might come into conflict with the demands of ethical values than one finds in Schnitzler, who appears to record the problem without taking sides. Around the turn of the century Hofmannsthal went through a crisis of confidence in the ability of language to express what he really wanted to say, caused to a certain extent by his own facility, which is almost paradigmatic of twentieth-century European intellectuals' difficulties with language. He then concentrated on the writer's public function, writing for the theatre, of which his libretti for Strauss were an offshoot, and founding the Salzburg Festival, intended as a focus for the artistic and spiritual life of the nation.

His short story, *Sergeant Anton Lerch*, was written in 1899, three years before the *Chandos Letter,* in which he described his crisis of language. Although the hero of the story is not one of the aesthetes of Hofmannsthal's early verse plays who shut themselves off from the world outside, there are parallels in the intensely experienced inner world and the squalor outside. Lerch sets off with his cavalry troop on reconnaissance during the Italian campaign of the year of revolution, 1848. An apparently trivial incident during what appears to be a highly successful patrol turns his thoughts away from reality and into a day-dream of a future where he can mould his life to his own, rather crude, desires. From then on the narrative hovers with remarkable sensitivity between the real and the unreal until the Sergeant comes face to face with his own double. His death at the end (summarily executed for insubordination) is crude reality breaking in on a state of mind which he cannot or will not relinquish; it is left to the reader to decide the balance of day-dream, trance or supernatural, but that is one of the factors which make the story so powerful.

This impressionism continued to be an important part of Austrian literature into the twentieth century. It is part of the attraction of *The Golem*, and in Paul Leppin it is allied to a

21

decadence in which his heroes are the victims of their own sensibilities. They become immersed in sea of impressions in which their own lusts and what arouses them merge indistinguishably. Rational reflection and strong emotions only surface occasionally, to sink back wearily beneath the waves of sensation. Although the overall mode of Werfel's *The Playground* is different, the initial picture of its hero, Lucas, as he experiences a "dislocation within him and in the way in which he saw the world" is not dissimilar to Hofmannsthal's Sergeant Lerch.

As well as these writers, who represent the main streams of literature in Austria in the period before and after the First World War, there were a number who used the supernatural and macabre in a more direct manner as a means of arousing horror. The best known of these, Karl Hans Strobl, was probably as responsible as anyone for the spread of the influence of Edgar Allan Poe in the German-speaking world. Between 1900 and 1920 he initiated something of a fashion in the ghost/horror story, at which many writers tried their hand. Strobl himself brought out numerous anthologies and collections of his own stories. He is generally not seen as a serious writer, but *The Head*, which presents incidents during the French Revolution from the point of view of a head which has been cut off from its body by the guillotine, is a masterpiece of the macabre genre. The other story by Strobl included in the anthology appears to be a standard ghost story in which the demolition of an old convent arouses spirits which trouble the architect in charge. But the focus gradually changes and forces the reader to look at the psychology of the hero: is the story a description of a haunting, or of a man going mad? Paul Busson was another once popular writer who used elements of the supernatural, including folk beliefs, in his novels. The short story, *Folter's Gems,* published in 1919, is a good example of the influence of Edgar Allan Poe.

Perhaps the best example of this type of story, however, is Franz Theodor Csokor's *The Kiss of the Stone Woman* (*Die steinerne Frau*), written in 1915. Csokor was a dramatist, the main representative of Expressionism in Vienna, who wrote a small number of short stories. *The Kiss of the Stone Woman* is his only foray into the Gothic; although there is a play he wrote about the same time (*Die Stunde des Absterbens* – The Hour of Dying) which has elements of E. T. A. Hoffmann about it, the story was probably written as a stylistic exercise or in the hope of being able to sell it. What raises it above the others is the trace of Expressionism in the style. His deliberate choice of active vocabulary, especially verbs, for what are really static objects – trees, houses, churches etc – invests the whole setting with a dynamism and sense of threat which is not unlike the effect of distorted backgrounds used in the German Expressionist films of the time (e.g. *The Golem* or *The Cabinet of Dr Caligari*).

To round off the picture there are a few short extracts from Franz Blei's satirical *Great Bestiary of Modern Literature,* which portrays most of the well-known literary figures of the time as animals, usually imaginary ones, and from Friedrich von Gagem's *Geister: Gänger Gesichte Gewalten* (Spirits: Ghosts Visions Forces). This is a large compilation of incidents involving the supernatural or the uncanny. Many are taken from published sources, but others appear to have been supplied by his many aristocratic relations, friends and acquaintances.

POSSESSED SOULS

Flowers

Arthur Schnitzler

I've just spent the whole afternoon wandering round the streets, with white snowflakes floating down, slowly, noiselessly, and now I'm back home, and the lamp is burning, and my cigar is lit, and my books are beside me, and everything is ready for me to enjoy a cosy evening ... But it's all to no avail, I can't stop my thoughts continually coming back to the same thing.

She had long since been dead for me, hadn't she? ... Yes, dead, or even, as I put it to myself with the rather childish grandiloquence of the betrayed lover, 'worse than dead' ... And now, since I learnt that she is not 'worse than dead', no, simply dead, like all the others out there, lying beneath the earth whenever spring is here, and whenever the sultry summer comes, and whenever the snow is falling as today ... dead without any hope of returning – since then I have realised that she did not die for me a moment sooner than for everyone else. Grief? No. It is only the usual frisson we feel when someone that once belonged to us sinks into the grave while their whole being is still quite fresh in our minds, down to the light in their eyes and the sound of their voice.

There was certainly much sadness when I discovered she had been unfaithful to me; ... but how much else there was as well! My anger and sudden hatred and disgust with life and – yes, that too – my hurt pride. I only gradually came to realise I felt grief as well. But then I could relieve it with the comforting thought that she was suffering too. I still have them all, all those dozens of letters, sobbing, begging, pleading for forgiveness; I can read them whenever I want! And I can still see her in that dark English dress with the little straw hat, standing on the street corner in the twilight whenever I came out of the house ... and watching me walk away ... And I can remember her at that last meeting, standing there with her big, wondering eyes and round, girlish face, that had become so pale and haggard ... I didn't even shake hands with her when she left, when she left for the last time. And

I watched her from that window as far as the street corner and then she disappeared, for ever. Now she can never return ...

It's the purest chance I know about it at all. It could have been weeks, months before I heard. I haven't seen her uncle for a good year now, he only rarely comes to Vienna, and I met him this morning! I had only spoken to him a few times before. The first time was that skittles evening when she and her mother had come along as well. And then the next summer; I was with a few friends in the garden of that restaurant in the Prater, the *Csarda* it was called. And her uncle was sitting at the next table with two or three other old gentlemen, in unbuttoned mood, almost merry, and he raised his glass to me. And before he left, he came over and told me, as if it were a great secret, that his niece had a crush on me! And in my half-tipsy state I found it odd and funny, piquant almost, that the old man should be telling me that there, to the sound of the cymbalom and the shrill violins – me, who knew it only too well, who still had the taste of her last kiss on my lips .. And then this morning! I almost walked straight past him. I asked after his niece, more out of politeness than interest ... I didn't know what had become of her; the letters had stopped coming a long time ago; only flowers she still sent regularly, reminders of one of our most blissful days; once a month they came; no message with them, mute, humble flowers ... And when I asked the old man, he was quite astonished: You didn't know that the poor child died a week ago? It gave me quite a start. Then he told me more. That she had been ailing for some time but had been bed-ridden for scarcely a week ... And what was wrong with her? ... "Some emotional disorder ... anaemia ... The doctors never really know."

I stood there for a long time at the spot where the old man had left me; I was worn out, as if I had just made some great effort. And now I feel as if I should regard this day as marking the end of an era in my life. Why? – Why? It is not something that concerns me closely. I no longer had any feelings for her, I hardly ever thought of her any more. Writing all this down has done me good: I am calmer. I am starting to enjoy the comfort of my home. It's pointless to go on tormenting myself with thinking about it ... There'll be someone, somewhere who has more cause for mourning today than I have.

I have been out for a walk. A fine winter's day. The sky was so pale, so cold, so distant ... and I am very calm. The old man I met yesterday ... it seems as if it were weeks ago. And when I think of her, her image appears in my mind's eye in strangely sharp, complete outline; only one thing is missing, the anger that until very recently accompanied the memory. It has not really sunk in that she is no longer in this world, that she is in a coffin, buried ... I feel no pain at all. Today the world seemed quieter. At some point I realised that there is no such thing as joy or sorrow; no, we twist our faces in expressions of desire or grief, we laugh and cry and invite our souls to join in. Just now I could sit down and read profound, serious books and would soon penetrate all their wisdom. Or I could stand looking at old pictures that used to mean nothing to me, and I would respond to their dark beauty. And when I call to mind people who were dear to me and whom death has taken away, my heart does not ache as it usually does: death has turned into something pleasant; it walks among us and means us no harm.

Snow, white snow piled high in all the streets. Little Gretel came to see me and suggested it was time we finally went out for a sleigh ride. So there we were, out in the country, flying along the smooth bright tracks with a jingle of bells and a pale grey sky above us, flying along between gleaming white hills. And Gretel leant against my shoulder, watching the long road stretching out before us with bright eyes. We went to an inn that we knew well from the summer, when it was surrounded by greenery, and now looked so different, so lonely, so completely unrelated to the rest of the world, as if we had to discover it afresh. And the stove in the lounge was glowing so hot that we had to move the table well away, because little Gretel's left cheek and ear had gone quite red. I just had to kiss the paler cheek! Then the drive back, in the semidark already. How Gretel snuggled up to me and held both my hands in hers. Then she said, "Today I've got you back again." Without having to think about it at all, she had found the right words, and it made me happy. Perhaps the crisp, frosty air out in the country had relaxed my senses, for I felt freer and easier than I had during the last few days.

Once again recently, while I was lying half asleep on the sofa, a strange thought crept over me. I felt as if I was cold and hard. Like someone standing without tears, without any capacity for feeling even, beside the grave into which a loved one had just been laid. Like someone who has become so hard that not even the shudder at an early death can placate him ... Yes, implacable, that was it ...

It has gone completely, completely. Life, pleasure and a little love has swept away all those silly ideas. I'm back amongst people once again. I like them, they're harmless, they ramble on about all sorts of cheerful matters. And Gretel is an adorable, loving girl, and so beautiful when she stands there by the window with the sunbeams glistening in her blond hair.

Something strange happened today ... It's the day she used to send me flowers every month ... And the flowers arrived, as if ... as if nothing had changed. They came with the early morning post in a long, slim, white box. It was still very early; my eyes and my brain were still drugged with sleep. I was already opening the box before I became fully aware of what it was ... I almost jumped with fright ... and there they were, tied up with a delicate gold thread, carnations and violets ... They lay there as if they were in a coffin. And as I picked up the flowers, my heart shuddered. I know why they still came today. When she felt her illness coming on, perhaps even a presentiment of her approaching death, she sent her usual order to the florist's. She did not want me to go without her tender gesture. Certainly that must be the explanation of the package; it is quite natural, touching even ... And yet, as I held them in my hand, the flowers, and as they seemed to tremble and droop, I could not help but feel, against all reason and determination, that there was something ghostly about them, as if they came from her, a greeting from her ... as if she still wanted to tell me, even now, when she was dead, of her love and her – belated – fidelity. Oh, we do not understand death, we never understand it; creatures are only truly dead when everyone else has died who knew them ... Today I handled the flowers in a different way than usual, more tenderly, as if I could hurt them if I held them too tight, as if their gentle souls might start to whimper softly. And looking at them now on the desk in front of me in their slender, dull green vase, I seem to see them bow their blossoms in melancholy thanks. With their fragrance I inhale the whole sorrow of a futile yearning, and I believe they could tell me something, if we could understand the language of all living, not just all speaking, beings.

I refuse to fall under their influence. They are flowers, nothing more. Greetings from the other side, but not a call, not a call from the grave. They are flowers and some shop-assistant in some florist's tied them up mechanically, wrapped a little cotton-wool round them, put them in the white box and posted them off. And here they are, what is the point of brooding over them?

I spend a lot of time in the open air, take long walks by myself. When I am with other people I feel no real relationship with them, the links have all torn. I even notice it when my dear, blond girl is sitting in my room chattering on about ... that's just it, I have no idea what she's talking about. When she leaves, the very moment she has gone she is so distant from me; as if she were far away, as if she had been swept away for good by the current of humanity, as if she had disappeared without trace. It would hardly surprise me if she never came back.

The flowers are in their vase of shimmering green glass, their stalks reach down into the water and their fragrance fills the room. They still give off a scent, even though they have been in my room for a week and are slowly starting to wither. And I have come to understand all sorts of nonsense that I used to laugh at, I can understand people holding conversations with natural objects ... I can understand people waiting for an answer when they talk to clouds and springs; here I am, staring at these flowers and waiting for them to start to speak .. No, no, I know that they are speaking all the time ... even now ... that they are constantly speaking, sorrowing, and that I am close to understanding them.

How happy I am that the frozen winter is coming to an end. There is already a hint of the approach of spring floating in the air. Time passes in a strange way. I live my life as usual, and yet I sometimes feel as if the outlines of my existence were less sharply defined. Even yesterday is blurred, and everything that lies just a few days in the past takes on the character of a hazy dream. It keeps on happening when Gretel goes, and especially when I don't see her for a couple of days, that I feel as if it were an affair that is long since over. When she comes it is from so far away! Of course, once she starts chattering on, everything is back to normal and I have a clear sense of immediacy, of life. And the words then are almost too loud, the colours too bright; and just as the darling girl vanishes into some indefinable distance the moment she leaves me, so abrupt, so fiery is her presence. Moments of brightness, of vibrancy, used to leave an after-image, an echo within me; now sound and light die away at once, as if in a dim cave. And then I am alone with my flowers. They are already withered, quite withered. Their fragrance has gone. Up to now Gretel has ignored them; today for the first time her gaze rested on them a while, and I sensed the question rising within her. Then, suddenly, some hidden qualm seemed to stop her asking it; she said not a single word more, but took her leave of me and went.

They are slowly losing their petals. I never touch them; if I did they would crumble to dust between my fingers. I feel an inexpressible sadness that they have withered. Why I have not the strength to put an end to the ridiculous spell they cast, I don't know. They are making me ill, these dead flowers. Sometimes I can't stand it any more; I rush out. And then in the middle of the street a thought grips me, I have to come back, have to check that they are all right. And then I find them in the same green vase I left them in, tired and sad. Yesterday I stood there and cried, as one would cry at a grave, and I wasn't even thinking of the girl from whom they actually came. Perhaps I'm wrong, but it seems to me as if Gretel too feels the presence of something strange in my room. She has stopped laughing when she comes to visit me. She doesn't talk so loud, not in that fresh, lively voice I was used to. Also I am tormented by a constant fear that she might ask me; I know that I would find any question intolerable.

She often brings some needlework, and when I am working at my books, she sits quietly at the table, sewing or crocheting, patiently waiting for me to put the books away, stand up, come over to her and take her needlework out of her hands. Then I take the green shade off the lamp she was sitting by, and the whole room is flooded with warm, soft light. I don't like it when it's dark in the corners.

Spring! My window is wide open. Late in the evening I was looking down into the street with Gretel. The air around was soft and warm. And when I looked towards the street corner, where the lamp casts a faint light, there was suddenly a shadow. I could see it and I couldn't see it ... I knew I was not seeing it ... I closed my eyes. And suddenly I could see through my closed lids; there was the wretched figure, standing in the faint light of the lamp, and I could see her face with an eerie clarity, as if it were illuminated by a yellow sun, and I saw her pale, careworn face with her large, wondering eyes ... Then I walked slowly away from the window and sat down at my desk; the candle was flickering in a breath of wind that came from outside. And I sat there motionless; for I knew that the poor creature was standing, waiting at the street corner; and if I had dared to touch the dead flowers, I would have picked them out of the vase and taken them to her ... Those were my thoughts, perfectly lucid thoughts, and yet at the same time I knew they were irrational. Then Gretel too came away from the window and stood for a moment behind my chair, and brushed my hair with her lips. Then she went, leaving me alone ...

I stared at the flowers. They are hardly flowers any more, just bare stalks, thin and pathetic ... They are making me ill, driving me mad. And it must be plain to see; otherwise Gretel would have asked me; but she feels it too, she sometimes flees as if there were ghosts in the room. Ghosts! They exist, they do exist! Dead things playing at life. And if flowers smell of decay as they wither, it is only a memory of the time when they were blooming and fragrant. And dead people return as long as we do not forget them. What does it matter if she can no longer speak – I can still hear her! She doesn't appear any more but I can still see her! And the spring outside, and the bright sun streaming over the carpet, and the scent of fresh lilac coming from the nearby park, and the people walking past below who are no concern of mine, is that life? I can close the curtains, and the sun is dead. I can ignore all those people, and they are dead. I close the window, the fragrance of the lilacs is not wafting around me any more, and the spring is dead. I am more powerful than the sun and the people and spring. But memory is more powerful than I am, it comes when it will and there is no escape. And these brittle stalks in the vase are more powerful than all the lilac scent and spring.

I was bent over these pages when Gretel came in. She has never come so early before. I was surprised, amazed almost. For a few seconds she stood in the doorway; I looked at her without saying hello. Then she smiled and came closer. She had a bunch of fresh flowers in her hand. Without a word she came up to the desk and laid the flowers before me. The next moment she grasped the withered ones in the green vase. It felt as if someone were squeezing my heart, but I was incapable of saying anything; and as I was about to stand up to grab the girl by the arm, she looked at me with a laugh. Holding her arm aloft as she carried the withered flowers, she rushed round the desk to the window and simply threw them out into the street. I felt as if I ought to follow them ... But there was the girl, leaning against the window-sill, her face towards me. And the sun was streaming over her blond hair, the warm, living sun ... And a rich scent of lilac coming from across the road. I looked at the empty green vase standing on the desk; I was not sure how I felt; freer, I think, much freer than before. Then Gretel came over, took her little bouquet and held it up to my face: cool, white lilac ... such a healthy, fresh scent, so soft, so cool, I wanted to bury my face in it. Laughing, white, kissing blooms: I knew the spell was broken. Gretel was standing behind me running her hands wildly through my hair. You fool, you darling fool, she said. Did she know what she had done? I took her hands and kissed them ... And in the evening we went out into the open air, out into the spring. I have just come back with her. I lit the candle; we had a long walk and Gretel was so tired that she has nodded off in the armchair by the stove. She is very beautiful as she smiles in her sleep.

Before me is the lilac in the slender green vase; down below in the street – no, no, they disappeared from there long ago. The wind has already scattered them with all the other dust.

Severin's Road into Darkness

Book Two: The Spider

Paul Leppin

I

Summer had slowly returned. Imperceptibly, one week after another had slipped past Severin's life without shaking his heart out of the exhaustion in which it had lain since the end of the winter. On that evening when he had shed tears of despair in Zdenka's room in the Old Town Square, he had not believed there was such a thing as peace. And now there was a wondrous tranquillity inside him, sharpening his senses, enfolding him as he smiled at the world like someone who had recovered from a serious illness. A tender alertness awoke within him, through which he observed the thousand tiny details of life around like a foreigner to whom everything is new and who is forever astonished. Every day the dawn woke him from a long and even sleep, and the sun had risen outside his window, hot and shining, when he opened his eyes and then shut them, dazzled; or the warm rain, that he loved so well, pattered against the wall of his room, filling the air outside with sweet odours. He was together with Zdenka all the time now.

He felt afraid whenever a memory of the winter caught him unawares, and his love sought help from her. It was with a childlike reverence that he enjoyed her companionship, which, as in earlier days, led them on Sundays to various places of recreation in the city and suburbs. They sat together in beer-gardens, listening to concerts given by military bands, which would play a pot-pourri of pieces by Verdi and Wagner, hits from Viennese operettas and the Reserve Officer's Dream. The leaves of the chestnut trees spread like a green fanlight above them and cast bobbing patches of sunlight onto the table-cloths, to which dampness and the smell of clothes-pegs still clung. Severin fixed his gaze on Zdenka's beautiful face and placed his cigarette between his lips with the lethargy of a convalescent. He found the voices of the people chatting at the neighbouring tables soothing. In the scraps of conversation that reached him he could hear the well-ordered, cosily stifled rhythm of a life to which he abandoned himself contentedly.

That year, or so it seemed to him, the city had been particularly transformed by the summer. His body still responded to the throb of its blood, but it no longer frightened him. In the afternoons, before he met Zdenka from the office where she worked, he would wander through the sunny streets. He would watch the men as they sprinkled the roads, delighting in the little fountains that spurted up from the damaged hosepipes and the colourful rainbows glinting through the fine spray. The acacias were in bloom along the Francis Embankment. Severin sat on a bench at the edge of the river bank. Below him flowed the Moldau and a sailing boat was slowly drifting down towards the mills. A swarm of fantastically shaped clouds crossed the sky, blotting out the sun for a while.

It was a scene Severin knew from his childhood. Then he had sometimes sat under the acacias on the embankment with his father, waiting for Aunt Regina. A musty memory raised its sleepy head in his mind and before his inner eye appeared the dark, ground-floor apartment, where his aunt had lived with the old lady. He had always liked going there to visit her. Behind the white tulle curtains had stood a weather-house with a little man carrying a red tin umbrella outside the door. The old lady was ill, cancer was eating up her frail body. She leased a small tobacco shop on Bethlehem Square, a wooden kiosk in the angle of the houses where she sat during the day selling cigars. In the sitting room, which she shared with Aunt Regina, there was always a strange mixture of smells, of fusty air from the cellar and withered Corpus Christi wreaths, of incense and the dry aroma of her stock of tobacco. For Severin it all had a special attraction, filled with a quiver of childish surmise. It was from his aunt's room, which was crowded with consecrated candles and pictures of saints, dog-eared hymn-books and crosses of coral, that his soul had taken home the first flickerings of the fervour which had haunted his childhood.

A little of this fervour stirred within Severin once more. He saw the Lesser Town on the other side of the river, and Charles Bridge with the priests of the religious orders in their long cassocks crossing it in pairs like school-children. There was something of the atmosphere of the feast of St. John Nepomuk left on the breeze, as it wafted calmly across the water and swept up the withered petals of the Moldau acacias at his feet. On the bridge the wooden trestle with the glass lamps was still standing before the statue of the martyr where each year the country people came from their villages to honour their patron saint. Severin remembered the fever of expectation that had accompanied the feast day of the Czech saint. On St. John's Eve he had gone with his father to the river bank where the flood of people had been piling up for hours. When darkness fell there had been a firework display and the thin rockets had shot straight up into the sky with a soft crackling noise. Down below, the boats floating on the river were hung with lights and the peasants on the bridge were praying before the statue of St. John Nepomuk.

Severin had not been inside a church for years. His youthful fire had been consumed in blind and casual enthusiasms. He was in the grip of a weariness which he allowed to carry him aimlessly from one day to the next and from which the old, long-forgotten yearning of his boyhood soul now rose to the surface. From the scent of the acacias and the river air, the afternoon sun had brewed a warm haze with a hint of decay which excited him. An orphanage was taking a walk along the embankment path and the girls, all dressed the same, were whispering to each other. They were accompanied by a nun enveloped in her habit; for a brief second the young eyes beneath the cowl looked across at Severin. They were grey and pious eyes with a star glittering in the middle, just as Aunt Regina's had been.

Uncertain what to do, he stood up and searched through his pockets for a cigarette. Opposite him the sign of the Bible Society was gleaming in the sun. Once, during the school holidays many years ago, he had bought a copy of the Scriptures there for a few coppers. He had not kept it for long; it had disappeared, as did most of the books he possessed. It only came back to mind because he felt a longing for the records of the

Testaments, heavy and dark with age, and for the bright wisdom of the Evangelists.

Some children were playing in the sand by the monument to Emperor Francis. A white-bearded old man with a green eye-shade and a misshapen pair of spectacles was selling sticky sweets and Brezels, twisted bread sticks covered in salt crystals or poppy seeds. Severin bought the rest of his stock and shared it out amongst the children. The old man went off with an empty basket and a pleased look on his face; the servant girls on the benches nudged each other and giggled.

Severin was moved by a soft and blissful emotion which was interwoven with the long-faded objects of his school-days. His thoughts cautiously felt their way back into that world, to the naive magic of the school chapel, to his feeling of shyness whenever his fingertips touched the cool communion cloths. The music of the May services began to resound within him, when the organ united with the hymns to the Virgin and outside, where the lime tree grew beside the open church window, a bird warbled, loudly and with a throbbing throat.

He had crossed the bridge and doffed his hat to the golden crucifix. Before he realised where he was, he was standing outside the portal of St. Nicholas' in the Lesser Town Square. Its green dome glittered above the roofs, and the sun fell on the steps up to the door with a burning, dazzling light. The stone faces of the bishops watched him out of the richly hued gloom, and his steps echoed from the pillars. The church was empty apart from a woman in black kneeling not far from the door. When he entered she turned round, and he recognised the nun from the embankment. Her face was white and her eyes burnt beneath the cowl. Severin knelt next to her and said the 'Salve Regina' aloud. And he felt as if a startled smile crossed her lips behind her folded hands.

II

Together with her new friend, Karla had opened a wine-bar near the centre of the town. By the German University, with the students in their colourful caps standing beside the huge wooden doors, began a maze of winding alleys. Cool air came from the entries of the houses that stretched between the streets, and from the craftsmen's workshops the smell of damp felt and mouldy leather. Sometimes pedlars who had brought mushrooms or fresh berries to the city would spend the night beside their baskets under the tree-lined arcades of the fruit and vegetable market. During the day there was a bustle of activity, people crowded the narrow pavements, junk dealers cried out their wares in lilting tones and carts rumbled over the bumpy cobbles. At night the noise went into hiding behind the murky windows of the little dance halls, except when a drunken group passed by, or a policeman, surrounded by a circle of curious onlookers, dealt with a drunken brawl.

A fiery arc-lamp hung outside the wine-bar in the dark alley-way. Coming round the corner between the badly lit houses, the light was blinding and the muted sound of a piano came from the door. In decorating the rooms, Karla had consulted the fruitful and elegant taste of young Nicholas, who was to be found there every evening. To this Karla's love of unbridled discord had given a particular, provocative beauty, which corresponded to her personality and which she could not do without. The first time he entered, Nicholas shook his head reflectively. The deep tones of the wallpaper were drowned by the blazing scarlet of the door-hangings, and Karla had had the fancy of embroidering a bizarre and restless pattern of blood-red hearts all over his beloved black velvet table-cloths and sofa-covers. But this expression of untutored temperament was infectious and compelling. And in the evening, when Karla stood in the glare of the electric lamps, wearing a savage, gypsy-like evening gown which showed off her beautiful breasts and arms, her recalcitrant hair bound with a chain, the wine foaming in the cut-glass goblets tasted all the sweeter and the music had a wonderful, bewitching sound.

But the most exquisite attraction, the one that lured the people there, was Mylada. No one knew where the girl came from, she had never been seen in Prague before, but Karla had discovered her somewhere. She sat in the wine-bar every evening, her thin face never reddened by the drink. She wore a simple green dress that was like a thin petticoat, revealing her small, pointed breasts. Within a few weeks all the men had fallen in love with her. She had a manner that no one could resist, that seduced the most taciturn of men into conversation and drew out even the most reserved. Her bright eyes, which sometimes clouded over when she was speaking, could captivate the ponderous, intoxicate the fickle and overwhelm the debauched. She was a new and provocative star in the torpid nightlife of the city. Karla had engaged her as a singer, and now and then she would sing a song for the customers in her high voice, accompanied on the piano: German music-hall songs which were popular at the moment, Czech folk-songs such as young men would play on their harmonicas outside East End doors in the evening. But her attraction had nothing to do with these songs.

The unexpected crush of customers made Karla's wine-bar fashionable. A shrill revelry raged there from night until early morning, screaming, stamping and roaring with laughter. Outside in the street, where the arc-lamp burnt, passers-by would stop and then slip enviously into the shadows. When they had passed the bar, the sweet and sickly verve of the Viennese music called them back and drew their hands to the door-knob. The joie de vivre that was roistering riotously in three-four time from within dug its claws into the lonely and dragged them into the circle of light. And many of Karla's old friends turned up, who had not been together since Dr. Konrad's death. Ruschena, the blonde, came, bringing a fat, pockmarked painter along with her. She sat in a corner, supping the vinegary Austrian wine he bought her and gazing into space with a bored smile. It was usually midnight before Nicholas appeared. He came from his evening round of dinners and parties in white tie and silk waistcoat, and Karla immediately put a white-stoppered bottle of champagne in the ice-bucket for him.

It was at the end of a very hot day that Severin went with Zdenka to the dark alley for the first time. A grumbling storm was building up over the city and they were both tired. Zdenka was hungry and thirsty, so Severin suggested they should try Karla's. He had seen her adverts in the papers and heard people at the office talking about Mylada. It was still early evening and the wine-bar was empty. Only old Lazarus was squatting in a corner, drunk. He recognised Severin and waved to him. Next to him Mylada was sitting in her green dress, patiently listening to his chatter. Her bright eyes subjected Zdenka to a cool scrutiny and gave her companion a brief glance. Severin stared, spellbound, at her small, thin face. When he had come in and found the bookseller there he had been gripped by a startled reluctance to stay. Now he was sitting, quiet and transformed, at his table, responding in disbelief to the heavy, tremulous throb of blood in his heart as he watched Mylada. He was puzzled by a strange, oddly familiar expression in her eyes. Zdenka fell into an embarrassed silence when she noticed his furrowed brow and did not dare to disturb him. Only when Karla entered and, delighted to see him there, came over to shake his hand, did he wake from his trance and come back to his senses. She sat beside him on the sofa and began to whisper to him about Lazarus. Every evening after he had closed up his shop he came here and got drunk. But he did not stay for long. When the first customers began to appear after the theatres had finished, he went home.

And Karla told him how sometimes when he was drunk he would talk nonsense and cry.

"Sometimes he throws his arms around, like a bird trying to fly and caws like a raven. And then sometimes he screams for his daughter ..."

Severin went pale. As in a vision he saw in his mind the evening when he had met the Jewess in the dark street and she had sent him packing. He could not remember her words any more, but he could see her body, distended by pregnancy, and he trembled. He stood up and went over to the drunken bookseller.

"Good evening, Lazarus", he said. "How is Susanna?"

His voice was hoarse with fear, and at the same time he was surprised he had the courage to ask.

The old man stared into his wine without moving his head.

"She came back from the foundling hospital today ..."

Then, after a long pause, during which the three women

looked at each other and held their breath,

"But the child is dead, Master Severin ... dead as a doornail ..."

And Lazarus laughed until the tears ran down his gaunt cheeks.

III

The summer became more delightful and tender the more it approached its end. Every day the sky spread out its immaculate cover and the sun shone down gently. Severin spent his holidays in the city. The mornings, which he could now spend strolling where he pleased, were a delight he had long had to go without. At times the mood of his school holidays, miraculously clear, would seep through the years which had been annihilated by numbing office work, and then all the thoughts of the treadmill crushing his miserable life and of the events of the previous winter would blow away like thin cobwebs. In the early hours, when he was released from sleep, he would stretch his limbs and spend another hour in bed. Reflectively, he watched the rings that the light falling though the meshes of the curtains made on his bedroom door, and felt freed from a burden. Then he washed and went out into the street. He climbed the hill where, from the vineyard terraces one could look down on the valley of Nusle. New, chalk-white buildings gleamed in the sunshine below and the air was filled with the roar of the distant railway trains. Somewhere nearby in his childhood had been a small, over-grown garden where he had looked for pebbles and snails' shells and in the spring daisies had grown in the unkempt grass. Beside the Children's Hospital, the dome of Karlov Church peeped out at him like an enormous brown onion and on the other side of the valley rose the new water tower in the fields of Pankrác which always looked to him as if someone had cut it out of a picture book he had possessed as a child. The morning was transparent and shone over the houses. In a factory the whistle of a siren started up and its melancholy voice continued to sound long afterwards in his ear, like a monotonous, avant-garde song.

It was in these morning hours that he first came to appreciate the multifaceted life of the city. Beside him and behind spread its thousand streets, and when he climbed the slope over there he could see the Moldau flowing past the ramparts of the Vysherad fortress with the reflections of the sunlight floating on its waters like glowing fires. The grass was sprouting from the crumbling gun embrasures of the rampart walls. Severin thought back to the evenings when he had stood, heavy-hearted and filled with unease, in the maze of houses, quivering with fear and premonitions. The city, as it lay before him, dipping its towers in the morning light, seemed to be more beautiful and yet to have retained its marvels.

On the way home he usually went into some church which had its door open. Since that afternoon in the Lesser Town, there was always something urging him to stand a while in the darkness of the side altars where the earnest-looking statues leant in their niches and the sanctuary lamp burnt in a red glass bowl. He would sit down on a bench and rest for fifteen minutes. At that hour it was rare that anyone else should visit the church, only an occasional old woman shuffling with short steps across the tiles. Severin absorbed the silence like someone who had long been accustomed to noise. In the half-light of the corner he had withdrawn into, his thoughts spun a continuous unbroken thread and entwined his heart in a tangled childhood world. The images of the morning returned as a dream-vision with the waves of the river and the low gables of Hradcany Castle in the dappled air and the blare of the steam-whistle in the valley. Sometimes he was disturbed by a noise when a woman, who had come in quietly, knelt down and started to pray before he turned round. Then he would peer over his shoulder and scrutinise her face.

He gradually came to realise that he was looking for the nun with the starry eyes. On a whim, without foundation as far as he knew, he had christened her Regina and had ended up believing that was her name. He recalled how he had met her under the acacias on the embankment. Some abrupt and unfathomable connection made him think of Mylada.

In such hours he drew up an account for himself of the days on which Zdenka's love had protected him. He experienced everything that had happened to him since then for a second time. What old Lazarus had said came to mind, and futile and cruel tears reminded him of his child. Bit by bit he came to realise that this summer's idyll was a delusion. The sleepy weariness of his heart had made him believe that solace and true happiness had come to stay. But the evil forces still lived there, they proliferated in secret, while he was smiling and kissing Zdenka's lips, and they ate into him like a corrosive acid until his soul was an open sore. Something had disturbed the flickering shadow within him from which he had fled during the winter, and which he recognised again in the dark of the empty church. He did not know whether it was Regina or Mylada, and, strangely, the memories of both intertwined to form a single figure. Susanna's plight was a sign for him that his feet were treading an ominous and ill-fated path. Wherever it led, sorrow and misfortune appeared behind him and joy withered along its track. Concern for Zdenka seized him, and however much he twisted and turned in its claws, he could not free himself from them. And in his frightened love for her he discovered, with an icy shiver, that he took a bitter pleasure in the fact that he held her life in his hands and could crumple it.

When Severin left the church and was back in the open air he shook his head at such fancies. The midday sun flowed like warm honey through the streets and by the wall a blind man was standing with his hat in his hand, blinking. Over the roofs hung the delicious, late-summer heat-haze, that rose from the stubble-fields outside the town. Severin stroked his forehead with his fingers. He continued on his uncertain way and the pleasant numbness of the last few weeks relaxed the tension within him. Sometimes the trill of a canary came from the open window of a ground-floor apartment and from the third floor of one house the scratching of a violin. A humming noise came through the air from a long way off, a metallic ringing that grew stronger and stronger. The midday bells were beginning to sound out from the towers.

IV

Nathan Meyer loved to keep his life hidden from people. Since he had opened the wine-bar in the dark alley together with Karla he had never joined the customers downstairs. He kept his room locked, where he lived among books and pamphlets carelessly scattered over the floor, and he only left it at night, when the other occupants of the building were in bed and he was sure of meeting no one on the stairs. He must have been around forty years old, but his short-cropped hair and smooth-shaven face made him appear much younger. Little was known about his past. His father had owned a large brewery in Russia and had left him a handsome fortune on his death. For years he had lived on the interest on his capital without feeling the need for any kind of activity. His predilection for solitude met with no resistance from his temperament, which was prickly and not softened by any kind of good-naturedness. Some unknown chance had brought him together with Karla, but had had little effect on his way of life. In the apartment they shared his door remained closed to her most of the time. Thus the few people with whom he had some kind of passing relationship found the enthusiasm and persistence, with which Nathan suddenly pursued the idea of setting up a wine-bar, astonishing and difficult to understand. Perhaps the stimulus had come from Karla, her active mind seeking something to occupy it in the unbearable monotony of their relationship. But he welcomed her idea with a fanaticism which even Karla, who knew better than anyone else what energies he wasted in his life of idle contemplation, was at a loss to explain. It was he who had tracked down Mylada, rubbing his hands as he insisted she would be a success. But once everything was under way and the business made a promising start, he returned to his old habits and showed no further interest in it.

At least it appeared to be so. For there was no one to see the contented smile on his thin lips when at night the music from the wine-bar could be heard in his room. The window was open, and Nathan Meyer was sitting at his desk, his head raised, listening. The quiet alley trapped all noises between the high walls of its houses and carried them up to his room. He heard glasses clinking in the bar below and Mylada's thin laughter inflaming the men. He heard the shrill and ecstatic voices of people getting drunk on wine and conversation. On his smooth face appeared an expression of satisfaction, and he nodded. On some evenings there came from below an uproar lasting for minutes on end, the hiss and gurgle of unbridled lust bubbling over and turning somersaults in its inability to contain itself. Torrid chords on the piano sounded through the noise and heavy hands ran their fingers through the keys, extracting rapturous melodies, waltzes and marches. Then Nathan Meyer would take his hat and coat from the wardrobe and go down the stairs. Unseen and unrecognised he would wait beside the wine-bar, counting the customers who disappeared through its doors. The arc-light painted a bright circle in the darkness of the alley and illuminated the faces of the guests as they entered with its glaring white beam. For just a second Nathan could see the souls of the people as, dazzled, they paused outside the door and waited for a moment. The lamp shone more deeply into the faces, through the daytime veils, revealing the hollows fear had dug into them, the furrows and fissures round reddened eyes. Nathan had pulled his hat down over his forehead and turned up the collar of his coat. He stood motionless in the darkness, guarding the house.

Severin could remember Nathan Meyer from the day Dr. Konrad had been buried. In his mind he could see the tall, broad-boned figure with the irate mouth standing next to Karla among the mourners in the cold twilight of the winter afternoon. A sympathetic concern had stirred within him for the woman who had been his lover until a short while ago; beside the robust shoulders of the man her svelte elegance curled back in on itself in weary abandon. Since then he had not come across him one single time, not even later when Karla had moved in with him and the wine-bar in the dark alley was already in operation. Severin saw him again in a small coffee house near the Moldau which he used to visit before going to bed whenever he had spent the evening with Zdenka and his murderous and cowardly night thoughts kept him from going home. Recently he had felt the need to spend at least an hour alone with his thoughts after he had left Zdenka and her gentle caresses were no longer there to calm the restlessness which was beginning to draw its ever-tightening noose around him. His holidays were coming to an end. Autumn, sombre and narrow-chested, was waiting for him. His silent existence in the office would begin again, where the days were like walls, one beside the other, chafing his life in the narrow gaps between them. When Zdenka was with him and he could feel the warmth of her hand on his arm and hear her beautiful voice telling him of the great happiness of their love, then he would walk beside her with the expression of one who has been nursed back to health. His malaise returned to him together with mist that now descended on the early morning streets, prophesying the end of summer. As once at the beginning, he found himself again looking down with a twisted smile on Zdenka's blond hair as she snuggled up to him. When she had gone to bed and the light in her window went out, he dug his teeth into the flesh of his fingertips. He walked through the city and the street lamps traced his shadow on the paving stones behind him. In the coffee house he sat by the window and pushed the curtain aside. The gigantic rump of the Rudolfinum Museum stood out against a night sky in which the late summer stars were burning to embers like red Chinese lanterns.

It was on one such night that Severin got into conversation with Nathan Meyer. The latter had been watching him for some time from behind the newspapers he was reading and a thoughtful expression drew the corners of his lips down even farther as his long fingers tapped the ash from his cigarette into the brass ash-tray. At first Severin's response was morose and taciturn. He felt uncomfortable and it irritated him that the other was steadily scrutinising his face. But it was not long before he was sitting spellbound, listening to this man's spontaneous confession. They were alone in the low room of the coffee house, with only the heavy breathing of the sleeping waiter coming from one corner and, from the card-room, the thump of an ace being played. Strange revelations were made. Nathan's voice blazed with the blind, spiteful fury of the solitary, it was seething with the poison that ravages the hearts of cripples and lunatics: hatred of the world. His wet lips quivered from the depths of his soul as he spoke, preaching an angry refusal to believe in the goodness and glory of the earth with the unmitigated, arrogant scorn of a damned soul. He leant over to Severin with his dry, rasping whisper,

"There is a bit of the chemist in all of us who come from Russia. At home I have bombs and devices enough to demolish a whole street, if I wanted. But that is only something for the amateur. There are better, more subtle means, that are allowed by law, that the authorities license. Have you ever been to my wine-bar?"

An icy shiver ran down Severin's spine. He looked into Nathan's cunning, grey eyes and could suddenly understand him without further explanation. He was seized with terror of the man who went hunting souls without anyone noticing.

"A week ago a young man shot himself ", the Russian went on. "He stole money from the bank where he worked, to drink my champagne and sleep with Mylada. I went to see his corpse in the Institute of Pathology; a mere slip of a lad, scarcely over twenty. His mother had a stroke when she heard about it – and that is only the beginning. I know them all, those who go to the bar. I watch them when they think they are unobserved, from the darkness by the door."

Then after a pause, as Severin waited in silence,

"I have found a name for the place, a good name that will attract people: The Spider."

Severin stood up. There was a bitter taste at the back of his throat and he felt dizzy. Nathan's cropped head disappeared in the smoke of his cigarette and for a second Severin saw an image that made him catch his breath: it was the city with deep streets and a thousand windows; and in the middle was the wine-bar in the dark alley. The lamp over the entrance was like a staring eye and people were thronging round the door. They came one after the other, like midges round a light. Inside sat Mylada in her green dress. Invisible, huddled up beneath the curving legs of the piano, crouched an ungainly being that the people of the night called Pleasure ...

Severin shook himself and the picture disappeared.

"Wouldn't you like to see my laboratory some time?" he

heard Nathan Meyer ask.

"I don't know", he replied, and had to cling on to the back of
the chair to stop himself from falling.

V

The rainy days came, washing away the last traces of summer. There were great pools of water on the paths in the parks
and the leaves that the wind tore from the trees stuck to the
benches. The cabs drove round the city with soggy leather roofs
and boys splashed barefoot through the puddles and built dams
out of mud by the edge of the pavement. From the damp sky dusk
fell more quickly than usual at this time of the year.

Severin stood by his window. Slowly, by fits and starts, the
sparse life of the district where he lived wended its way through
the afternoon. A coal-cart rumbled over the cobbles and the
huge horses hung their heads morosely. A man scurried along
the houses, the cloth of his black umbrella gleaming in the wet.
Here and there a grubby paper kite flew up into the air, dragged
on its string through the rain by some child; then it would start
a clumsy, anxious fluttering and tumble to the ground. The bell
on the door of the corner shop jangled; a young woman with
frizzed locks over her forehead came out to look at the weather.
Then she lifted up her skirts so that her pretty legs could be seen
right up to the knees, and ran down the street.

Severin recalled the autumn rains of his childhood. It was all
just like today and his boyhood desires dredged a doleful yearning from his heart. The bell of the shop opposite his father's
house had had the same ring. Severin waited impatiently for the
door to be opened again. Once as a very small child, before he
went to school, he had been ill with pneumonia. Sometimes
during the illness a strange feeling had crept over him as he lay
at home in bed with the light from the street slanting across the
flowers painted on the ceiling. His mother was busy in the
kitchen and from somewhere came the drone of a barrel organ.
The fever had gnawed a round spot that felt soft and was covered
with a fine membrane. A comparison occurred to him: he

remembered the sweets that he used to buy at the market for a copper; as the sugar melted in his mouth the liquid centre felt soft to the tongue under a paper-thin skin. It was a sensation which seemed to have left him for good long ago. Now it returned, clear and distinct, and Severin recognised it again. At the same time a swarm of familiar images, that had faded with time, surfaced within him; he had forgotten them, and the rainy day swept them back into his memory: the sooty balcony with the iron railings where he invented childish games with his brother and shot at the cats in the garden with his catapult; old Julinka, whom his parents still provided for and who had to scrub the splintery wooden stairs in return; the summer evenings by the open door when the red clouds between the roofs had brought his first, uncomprehended tears and the maids in the neighbouring yards had sung the Czech folk-songs, whose banal sweetness still moved him even now.

Mylada knew those songs too.

Severin leant his head against the smooth pane. A wheedling pain twisted his lips into a sob.

Night had come, transforming the rain into a dripping fog which squeezed through the gaps in the windows and gave the sleepers uneasy dreams. Severin could not stand it in the house any longer. He had not been out since midday and stabbing cramps set the blood throbbing at his temples. He had made Zdenka wait in vain today and an irritating feeling of remorse had built up in his mind, like the mist veiling the gas-lamps outside. He threw his waterproof round his shoulders and pulled the hood over his hat.

On the market square of the district where he lived he surprised two figures who were embracing behind the empty fruit-stalls. Severin stood and watched them until the man noticed him and fled into the darkness with the girl. He was seized with an overpowering yearning for the simple happiness of these people. With dull and brooding concentration he tried for the hundredth time to discover what had led him off the beaten track of life into this desolate wilderness. And he was suddenly consumed with a painful, impotent lust, oppressed with fear and torn by doubt, for the kiss of the woman who had inflamed his desire at the very same moment when Lazarus had told him of the death of his child.

He stopped by the ramp leading up to the Museum. Below him stretched Wenceslas Square and the autumn mists hung in white clouds between the electric lights. Severin flung out his arms.

Mylada! he cried, and his voice fluttered through the mist like a trembling bird.

In the Spider the hands of the wall-clock had already reached the twelfth hour. The bar was packed and the provoking smell of spilt wine floated over the tables. Laughter climbed up the green smoke-rings from the cigars and fell back to the floor with a squawk. The noise of the conversations grew to an irrepressible roar that broke off with a gurgle whenever the music started up or one of the customers began to sing in a loud voice. Karla herself sat at the piano in a colourful and seductive outfit. As she played, she bent her beautiful head back until it touched the nape of her neck.

Severin sat behind her and ordered a bottle. He choked on the thick, reeking air of the room and sweat broke from every pore, making his shirt stick to his skin. Karla played any tune her guests requested. Her fingers sent the spurious drivel of operetta warbling round the room and the scent of her body fizzed in their throats with the wine and scorched through their veins. A senseless, reckless exuberance was rollicking inside their heads and swamping their hearts. Mylada detached herself from a group of very young men in tails with white cummerbunds. Her thin lips laughed with an infinite promise of pleasure as she leant over Severin.

"Give me a drink", she said, holding out her glass.

He watched her tongue as it darted out between her sharp teeth, and had to keep a hold on himself not to kiss her. He put his arm round her and pulled her down into his lap.

"I have already seen those eyes before. Have you a sister, Mylada?"

"I had a sister who looked very much like me, but she died."

Severin stroked the hair back from her face; she did not stop him and she clasped him with her legs. Her body was as small

as a child's and her breasts stiffened under her thin dress.
"Come to me tonight", he whispered, and she replied,
"She was called Regina; she was a nun."

VI

Severin had stopped counting time since Mylada had become
his mistress. The days coalesced into one single, richly coloured, blazing mirage, flooding everything with its dazzling
light. Everything that had had meaning for him, everything that
had depressed or excited him, disappeared out of his life as if it
had never existed. With the carefree assurance of a sleep-
walker, he carried out the activities which gave shape to his
existence. He did his work in the office without feeling the strain
which normally burdened these hours. He no longer felt the
furtive and malicious hatred in the things that used to offend
him, he only had room within himself for the boundless self-
indulgence of his love. Never would he have believed a woman
could make him feel the things he felt each day. Rapturous
depths opened up before him in which he submerged his wild
and bewildered senses and his paralysed soul.

Mylada understood his body. With the shrewd and experienced intuition of her depraved youth, she grasped his nature
and submitted to every whim she could discover there. She
uncovered the secret recesses of his desires and pursued them
to the roots of his nerves. She taught him her bizarre and unbridled love-games and intoxicated him with her caresses. Her
kisses were inventive and the joy they brought him was a sinful
and despairing lasciviousness. Often, when her arms were
round his neck and her eyes clouded with lust, he lost all sense
of the present. The room where they were seemed strange,
foreign, and the lamp by his bed gave a peculiar light. He saw
the sparks dancing beneath Mylada's eyelids and a golden wave
washed all the thoughts out of his mind.

Her weak and fragile body had an unsuspected power of love
within it. There was a passion in her which she squandered
without restraint, which clung to Severin and exhausted him.

Women had always been a disappointment to him. His experiences with them had always lacked that great, compelling force, that could overwhelm him and dictate to him, that was irresistible and deadly. For the first time a lightning-bolt struck his life, crushing it and bathing it in light. At times a memory approached him unasked, and Zdenka's image appeared and pleaded. At night, when he suddenly woke from sleep and stared at the darkness, it came to him and tried to save him. Then once more the sheen of her blond hair ensnared his heart and the sound of a voice came to him like a far-off bell. But the next day led him back to Mylada and on her lips he forgot the world.

When the afternoon came, and the fine spray of the October shadows hung on the walls, he sat at home and waited. The street noises sounded unclear and changed, and the passing carts made the floorboards tremble. Sometimes there was a roaring and a thudding in his head which frightened him and which he could not get rid of. He held his hands over his ears and realised that it came from within and that the noise was inside him. An anxious alarm burrowed its fingers into his intestines. Then the doorbell rang and Mylada came into his room and took off her coat.

He loved everything that belonged to her. Every dress that she wore on her fiery body became a fetish. He tried to reawaken her breath from the meshes of a veil she once left behind in his flat, and the odour of the gloves that he stole from her comforted him in the hours when he did not possess her. When, with cruelly lingering fingers, she undressed before him, the destiny which he could no longer escape and to which he bowed the knee, threw him at her feet. Sobbing, tormented by an rapture beyond this world, he brushed his lips against her petticoat.

He knew that when he left Zdenka for Mylada he had sacrificed her once and for all. It was too late to turn back, and the notion that there had been a time that was not full to overflowing with this love that was consuming him, was a pale wraith of a thought. Often, when he took her in his arms and she curled up in his lap like a naughty child, he saw, looking at him from beneath her eyelashes, the eyes of the nun he had knelt next to in the church in the summer. He told Mylada about the meeting and how she had smiled when he had spoken the Salve Regina beside her. Mylada laughed and began to talk about her sister, who had been dead for years, so that he must have been seeing a ghost. But Severin refused to accept it and stuck by his story. The white face of the young woman who had knelt by his side was clear and real in his mind, and the sultry fire of sinful desire she had set off still smouldered inside him.

Mylada allowed him his fantasies. With the delicate instinct, which she used to dominate men, she soon realised that they concealed a source of new and complex pleasures which she felt compelled to open up and taste. One day she arrived later than usual, when the room was already darkening in the autumn dusk. Feverish, exhausted by expectation, he opened the door. Before him, calm and wordless, her hands crossed piously over her breast, stood the young nun, just as he had seen her under the acacias on the embankment. Her limbs were enveloped in the wide flowing folds of her habit and under the black hood gleamed the same starry eyes.

"Regina!" he stammered.

She fell on him with a cry of delight and her lips sucked at his mouth. It was her kisses that told him it was Mylada. He ripped open the coarse cloth of her habit, under which her flesh shimmered like beautiful matt silk. He grabbed her by the belt and carried her to his bed.

"Regina! Regina!"

A miraculous joy beyond anything in the world ran through his veins like boiling metal and burnt a sweet, coral-red brand into his poor heart overwhelmed by love.

From now on Severin spent the nights that followed these afternoons in the Spider. Separated from the rest, he sat in his place and watched the customers courting Mylada. For each one she had a word, a bright note in her voice, a whispered promise that each thought was for him alone and that brought a surreptitious flush to his cheeks. But in between her glance flew back to Severin, and when she passed him her fingers stroked his hair. She looked at him when she sang the songs he loved, the songs that had an echo of the music of his childhood. She too had the swaying, soulful grace of Slav women which had attracted him to Zdenka. But she also had a dangerous nimbleness, a cunning sentimentality, which clung to the surface and did not demystify her being. Severin drank the dark red wine Karla poured for him and sat there, motionless. He took no share in the merriment which pressed itself upon him, and it did not rouse him from his absorption. In the middle of the mad exuberance of the rest he was alone with Mylada and his secret thoughts of the hour when she would next belong to him.

It was already light when he drained his glass and went out into the street. A man with a pole over his shoulder was in front of him, turning off the last street-lamps. A gaggle of gossiping women passed him carrying huge baskets on their backs. They were stallholders taking vegetables to the early market. Without getting undressed he stretched out on his bed to sleep.

One morning, as the door of the wine-bar was bolted behind him, he found Nathan Meyer standing beside him. His thin lips twisted in a mocking smile as he greeted him and walked some way down the alley with him. He cleared his throat uneasily and shook his head as he said goodbye.

"She's a bitch!" he said several times through his teeth, and Severin could not tell whether it expressed satisfaction, or a warning.

With a strange, almost fatherly expression, the Russian looked him in the eyes.

"She's a bitch, Severin! Believe me, she's a bitch!"

VII

His love for Mylada had appeared in Severin's life like a tongue of fire abruptly shooting up from the conflagration and casting its chilling light on the darkness around. Now, after a few weeks during which she had abandoned herself perversely to a caprice, she turned away from him, leaving him to the icy shades once more, and he was enveloped in a terrible and lonely horror. The fires of passion had burnt out his soul to an empty shell, and he could not understand how all that was left of them were the ashes and the pain of ugly, flickering, festering sores. With the frenzy of one who is completely lost, he rebelled against fate.

Every day he waited in his room for her to come. The hands on the grandfather clock creaked past each quarter and hours passed. Mylada did not come any more. He fell face down to the ground, and blood and spittle flowed from his distorted mouth, soaking the carpet.

At night in the wine-bar he grabbed her arm. He dug in his fingernails down to the bone so that she staggered and called for help and bit furiously into his wrist, tearing the skin to shreds. Finally, she managed to pull herself away.

"I don't want to! It's all over!"

Racked with disgust, he fled into the street. A gust of wind took his hat away, but he ignored it. Bare-headed, crushed by misery, he ran through the darkness, and the looming figure of terror pursued him, and there was no escape. A policeman's uniform glinted beside him and a voice barked a command. Severin swore in reply and ran on.

He stopped in the fields beyond the last suburb. His breath rattled in his throat and his veins throbbed, threatening to burst at his neck. He tore open his collar and gradually managed to collect himself. The clouds drifting across the sky parted for a while, exposing the moon. Severin recognised the place where he was. There was a ruined farm nearby where no one had lived for some time. In the summer tramps slept inside its fissured walls and by day the occasional rag-and-bone-man would search through the old garbage to see if there was anything left worth having.

A few paces farther on the footpath joined the road. The huge, newly built factories towered up along it and beyond them began the cemeteries. Severin had not been here since the death of Dr. Konrad. His thoughts went through the days that had passed since the funeral, picking their frightened and fragmented way round reality. The moon disappeared and darkness coagulated over the fields. Severin continued on his way, turning his back on the murky lights of the city and leaving them farther and farther behind. The night wind combed his hair and fingered his naked chest through his open shirt. His blood stopped its raging and calmed down. Behind the wrought-iron gate of the churchyard was the tree beside Konrad's grave which had once pursued him, even into his sleep. Severin laughed as he passed. He took a clump of earth and threw it over the wall.

Weariness clutched at his legs with a timorous arm. He thought of the farm by the road. He wanted to sleep, and if he could find a corner there to hide in until morning he would not have to go back to the city. He suddenly remembered that only recently the newspapers had been talking about the farm. There had been a suicide and the corpse of an army officer had been found amongst the rubble. Severin had known him, he had been a regular at the Spider. He recalled the evening when Karla had brought the news of his death to the wine-bar. At that time he had not concerned himself with it; love had churned up his soul and stopped up his eyes and ears. Now he could see the connection clearly. A wretched hatred, covered in boils, erupted within him; he raised his arm and shook his fist at the darkness.

The time following that night brought Severin's collapse. The tough vital force which he possessed, and which had withstood all his debauchery and crises, crumbled and broke under the pressure of a sadness beyond hope. He went sick and did not return to the office. He found it impossible to think or do anything that was not connected with the self-tormenting pleasure he took in his pain and which he kept on reliving from start to finish. After hours of self-absorbed apathy, he would be gripped by a merciless and uncouth anger. Then he would foam at the mouth and stifle his horrible cries in the pillows. He clenched his fists and shattered the glass of the mirror that showed him his forehead covered in peeling skin and his eyes reddened from lack of sleep. He avoided people who cautiously turned round and looked at him in the street and recognised the grey face with the swollen bags under the eyes.

That was how he was when Nathan Meyer found him one evening outside the Spider. He was staring into the circle of light thrown by the lamp over the door and his teeth were chattering when Meyer came up to him and put his hand on his shoulder.

"Don't go back in there", he said.

His voice was soft, with that tender and firm tone adults use when talking to children.

"Never go back in there, Severin!"

Then he took him by the arm and led him up the stairs to his room. Severin followed unresisting.

"What do you want from me, Nathan?" was all he asked, leaning his weakened body against the tall man.

Nathan Meyer turned up the lamp and pulled up a chair for his guest. In front of him he put a box of those long and slim cigarettes which he had sent from Russia and which he chain-smoked himself.

"Light a cigarette", he commanded.

Then he began to pace up and down the room. Severin sat and listened. It was the same tirade he had heard in the coffee house, all those weeks ago. His agitation chopped his sermon up into short sentences as he preached war against the world. But there was something else his words betrayed: friendly sympathy and unconcealed concern which Severin could not understand and which he found strangely touching, coming from those lips.

"What do you want from me?" he asked again.

Nathan Meyer stood in front of him.

"I like you, Severin."

He leant down with a smile.

"You are one of us! One of the brotherhood!"

"The brotherhood? What brotherhood?"

But there was no answer to his question. Meyer jangled his key-ring and opened his desk.

"You can be having a look at the things in there while I go downstairs for a bottle of wine. But watch your cigarette."

Curious, Severin stood up and pulled open the heavy drawer. Nathan Meyer had left him on his own, and he was visited by a strange feeling in this room with bookshelves covering the walls right up to the ceiling and the lamplight flickering on old furniture. In the drawer, carefully stacked one next to the other, were iron high-explosive bombs in all shapes and sizes, spherical hand-grenades, egg-shaped or square canisters with white fuses.

59

Severin bent over the open drawer. A bright-red thought shuffled its lascivious way through his brain and his hands trembled against his cuffs. He gave each bomb a discriminating scrutiny. There was one, a medium-sized, oddly shaped thing, which lay amongst the others like a black heart. Severin picked it up and stuffed it in his pocket.

"Well?" asked Meyer as he came back into the room with a full carafe and two glasses.

When Severin remained silent he murmured contemptuously, "Children's toys", and locked the drawer.

"Come on, let's drink a glass to the brotherhood."

VII

After weeks of cruelly abandoned solitude Severin could no longer control his desire to see Mylada again. The pale, anaemic visions which his imagination made appear before him and which he followed in the shadow of the night kept on leading him back to the place where the light from the wine-bar lamp fell on the street like a huge, dazzling wheel. The echo of Meyer's warning had long since died away in his soul. One evening, doubled up with shame and ravaged by longing, he was back in the Spider.

He could no longer bring himself to forgo the last and sharpest thorn in his suffering flesh. Mylada ignored him, as if he were some unknown customer. But he used the lascivious twist of her voice and the cunning glint of gold in her pupils to rekindle the memory of her passion and her pernicious and corrupting love. He called back the memory of the time when she had come to him dressed as a nun. He shuddered and sighed under her kisses and held in rapturous embrace a ghost that had once bewildered him in the summer, under the acacias.

Now he sat amongst the others with his elbows on the table. He held his hands over his face and through his fingers he watched Mylada laugh with the men and he rediscovered the lines of her body under her dress. Lazarus, the bookseller, was rocking her on his knees. His bald head was pressing against her breasts and Severin could see the furrows of his cranium under the taut skin. He recalled the evening when he had gone through the city armed with a rock in order to kill someone. Mylada was playing with his beard, which hung down from the old man's jaw, sparse and unkempt, and her bright eyes clouded over in a way that was so familiar. A feeling of disgust slithered up into his throat like a slimy fist. He drained his glass and left.

Outside, the winter had spread its deep and inexhaustible night sky over the city. Nowhere was there a star to be seen and the departing autumn was dragging a tacky, ice-cold trail of vapour behind it over the cobblestones. A tiny lamp was smoking by the mobile urn of a tea-vendor; two prostitutes in feather hats and bright-yellow summer coats having a quick bite to eat were talking and laughing. Severin went up and bought some cigarettes. One of the girls spoke to him and begged for a copper. He took a handful of silver out of his pocket and gave it to her.

He was in the grip of an apathetic and detached austerity. He did not know where to go, nor what to do. From the carpeted entrance to a bar came a warm blast with the smell of cheap spirits and the commissionaire raised his hand to his cap in salute. Severin thought of the years when he had spent his life in such places. He was overcome with a gnawing longing for those days. Then he had had a place of refuge. He had not been alone in his wretched, narrow existence; simple desires had kept him company, a lachrymose presentiment of the bewildering grandeur of the world. Now he knew better. Debilitated and filthy, ravaged and worn out, he was about to expire amidst the garbage, just because a nightclub hostess had sent him packing.

Now he could understand Nathan Meyer's talk. There were people, for whom the glory of life was nothing but marsh fire: cynics with an unlucky touch, pariahs hounded through the streets by abject fear, murderers, men with the mark of Cain. That was the brotherhood to which Severin now belonged.

He had always sensed it, even when as a boy he had read his book of wild adventures and longed for his own. The pale flames of his worm-eaten youth had always given off a reddish smoke that came from the foul recesses of his heart. The happiness

61

others enjoyed had always seemed like a children's picture-puzzle to him. He had played blindly with fate and had stumbled past its miserable mouse-traps without harming himself.

He looked up and saw that he had been walking in a circle. He could see the little lamp beside the urn glowing, and the man's white apron shone in the darkness. Severin suppressed a sob. That man had a home to go to and the candle-end behind the broken glass burnt with a peaceful light.

And himself, Severin?

He felt a pain deep within his innermost soul. The sweet image of a woman, buried beneath rubbish and debris, raised a sorrowful face towards him. But he threw back his head and refused to see it.

Or ...? Was it possible?

His limbs gave way under a mild and shaming weakness. By the steps of a house entrance he sank to his knees and cooled his brow on the stones. He folded his hands and shut his eyes, and just above him, in the narrow strip of sky between the houses, a shy star appeared, radiant.

A thin, pale-grey light was announcing the dawn when Severin pulled himself up and set off in the direction of the Old Town Square. The fleeting outlines of the colourful posters were already visible on the walls and the man with the urn was getting ready to go home. Outside the chemist's in the square a bleary-eyed young woman was leaning against the wall, tugging at the bell.

Sleepily, the concierge held out his sweaty hand to him and nodded in satisfaction when he recognised the late visitor. Severin gave him a coin and made his way up the stairs to Zdenka's apartment. For an endless moment his heart stopped beating before he knocked on the door.

A sound came from within.

"Is someone there?" asked a voice.

"It's me, Severin."

The door opened and a hot hand drew him into the room. The paraffin lamp with the green shade was smoking on the table. Zdenka was in her nightdress. Her hair fell in blond ringlets to her neck and she shivered with cold.

"Why have you come?" she asked in a calm voice. Severin took off his hat and held it in his hands. He glanced round, taking in the whole room in one long farewell look. The early morning light was trickling in through the curtains and making the glow of the lamp seem thin and shabby. Beside the bed was the cupboard where Zdenka kept her clothes and underwear. The purple china vase on the chest was cracked and the colour had faded from the handle. There was a bunch of withered flowers in it that they had gathered together in the woods, one day in the summer.

Zdenka looked at him and waited. Her nightdress was slipping down over her naked breasts and she hunched her shoulders with the cold. He stretched his arms out in a rehearsed, mechanical gesture. Then he dropped them again.

"Why have you come?"

He turned and went out of the door.

IX

The wind, which had spent the morning hours rattling the shopkeepers' signs, had gone to rest. A calm evening brought a clear sky, and a beautiful, pale sun began to shine. Severin sat up in his rumpled bed and looked at the clock. The long rest after a sleepless night had not strengthened him. He washed the hot daze from his eyes and dressed carefully.

Along the street he met groups of adolescent schoolboys who were making their way home and talking animatedly to each other. Severin turned to watch them with a vague feeling of envy. The change in the weather had lured people out of their houses and a throng was strolling along the pavements and gathering outside the shop windows. Girls with becoming velvet bonnets on hair done up in a pert style pushed their way through the crowd. A pair of lovers stood at the crossroads admiring the sunset. Streaks of poppy-red appeared along the edge of the roofs, setting the chimneys on fire. A fat cloud suddenly burst into flame and sailed across Charles Square like a huge lump of gold foil.

Severin made his way in leisurely fashion, with a cold and

determined curiosity. He was ambushed by the shadowy feeling which always came to haunt him when he had been exhausted and to which he abandoned himself without resistance. His consciousness split off and took on independent existence outside him. The past and the present rolled past him like pictures in a cyclorama and, bewildered and submissive, he was a spectator of his own life. The faces of the people walking beside him, the outlines of the houses that he knew, were invested with a new and special vividness which aroused his attention.

At the corners of the side-streets the chestnut vendors had set up their stoves. A warm radiance had settled over the city. A shrivelled old woman on crutches was hobbling laboriously across the road. Outside the doorways, long-haired students were chatting to maidservants and the blue twilight enticed cosy shadows from every corner. An early lamp glittered outside the Church of the Knights of St. Francis, filling the air with glassy colours.

Severin went onto the bridge. There was a cool breeze from the water which blew away the mood to which he had abandoned himself. Memory reappeared, sharp as a razor, tearing the delusive tissue woven by his senses to shreds. The evening fluttered over the river. A motor car with milky-white headlamps gave a melancholy toot and the bell of the little chapel at the foot of the Castle Steps was sounding the Angelus. Severin walked past the black stone statues on the parapet. He bit into his tongue and the blood flowed in his mouth, tasting like gall. This was not the city he knew. This was a peepshow with respectable citizens going about their business and St. John Nepomuk guarding the Moldau with hypocritical hands.

Twilight was thickening as Severin passed through the Bridge Tower leading into the Lesser Town near where the monument to Field Marshal Radetzky stood. Outside the gate of the main police station a soldier was marching up and down with a rifle over his shoulder, and the square with the leafy arcades was tinted like a yellowed copper engraving. Severin climbed the Spornergasse to Hradcany Castle. The city he knew was different. Its streets led one astray and ill fortune lurked on the thresholds. Damp, treacherous walls set one's heart beating, the night crept past blank windows, suffocating the soul in sleep. Satan had his traps set everywhere, in the churches and in the houses of the courtesans. His breath was in their murderous kisses and in nuns' habits he went on the prowl.

Outside the entry to the Castle courtyard Severin turned his head. Night had fallen and Prague was spread out at his feet with its brimming lights.

Somewhere a dog howled and its apprehensive barking sounded as if it came from the depths, from some long-forgotten shaft in the ground beneath the crooked alleys of the castle hill
...

In the Spider a large company had been gathered since the early evening. Lazarus was treating everyone to champagne. Mylada's birthday was being celebrated with obscene jokes.

Among them were many acquaintances from the group that used to meet in Dr. Konrad's apartment. Lazarus had invited them all, even Nicholas was there, sitting among them with a serious, bored expression, and the pock-marked painter who was living with the fair-haired Ruschena now. Mylada was sitting at the head of the table in all her capricious fascination. Her supple shamelessness delighted the men and exhilarated the younger folk. One after the other drank to her and she dipped her red tongue into each single glass. Lust danced like a flame across their faces and fumbled at her green dress. Somebody suggested a raffle, the proceeds from which should be drunk as soon as possible; amid cheers and laughter Mylada declared she would sleep with the winner. The price of the tickets was high, but in spite of that all but one had been sold when Severin entered to be greeted by loud hallos.

Mylada welcomed him.

"Do you want the last raffle ticket?"

She held the white scrap of paper between her fingertips.

"What can I win?" he asked.

"Me!"

Without a word he put all the money he had left into her hands and took the ticket.

The draw began. The numbers were put in an ice-bucket and

they all pressed shouting round the table; they were all in the grip of a furious excitement. Their foreheads were reddened with wine and intoxication gave a grotesque tautness to their features, turning them into the faces of beasts or gargoyles.

Mylada was blindfolded and took a ticket from the ice-bucket. There was silence in the room as she unfolded the paper.

"You're in luck, Severin", she said with a grin.

There was an envious pause.

Severin approached. The blood was pounding in his ears and he was pale. He held up the object he had stolen from Nathan Meyer's desk not long ago. Like a white worm, the fuse twisted round his arm.

"A bomb!" someone exclaimed and everyone shuddered at the shriek of terror.

"I have come to kill you ..."

His voice cracked. Red-eyed, he stared at the lamp.

Nicholas took the bomb out of his hand and stroked his cheeks, as if he were a child.

"Why?" he asked tenderly.

"Because I hate you!"

"And why didn't you do it?" whispered Mylada, looking up at him, her lips apart. She straightened up and her breasts brushed against him.

"I've won the raffle!"

A deathly shame threw him to the ground. He knelt down and put his head in her lap. He was overcome with sobbing and he cried. But the laughter of the drunken crowd flowed over him, transforming his tears into filthy, searing mud.

Night – Awake

From: **The Golem**

Gustav Meyrink

Night

It was the awareness of some disturbance in the tavern that roused me from my lethargy. Zwakh's last sentences were drifting away over the surface of my consciousness; I saw him moving his hands to demonstrate the piston of a large syringe going in and out, then the scenes that were unfolding all around us suddenly started to flick past my vision as quickly as if they were part of a clockwork peep-show, and yet with spectral clarity, so that for a while I completely forgot myself and felt like a cogwheel in a living mechanism.

The room had become one seething mass of people. On the raised platform were dozens of gentlemen in black tails; white cuffs, glittering rings; a dragoon's uniform with captain's epaulettes; at the rear, a lady's hat with salmon-pink ostrich feathers.

Loisa's distorted face was gazing up through the bars of the railing. I saw that he could hardly keep on his feet. Jaromir was there too, staring up fixedly and with his back tight, very tight, against the side wall, as if an invisible hand were pressing him against it.

The figures suddenly stopped dancing, the landlord must have shouted out something that had startled them. The music was still playing, but softly; it was unsure of itself, it was trembling, one could feel it distinctly. And yet the landlord's face had a wild, gloating expression.

A police inspector in uniform suddenly appeared in the doorway. He spread his arms out so that no one could leave. Behind him was a detective constable.

"So, we're dancing are we? In spite of the ban? I'm closing the place down. Mine host – you're coming along with me, and all the rest of you, off to the Station."

He barked out the words, like a military command.

The hulk of a landlord said nothing, but the gloating grin did not disappear from his face.

It merely froze.

The harmonica spluttered and died away in a whistle.

The harp changed its tune.

Suddenly all the faces were seen in profile, staring expectantly up at the platform.

Then an elegant figure in black made its nonchalant way down the few steps and walked slowly up to the Inspector.

The inspector's eyes were spellbound, fixed on the black patent-leather shoes strolling towards him.

The swell stopped one step in front of the policeman and his bored gaze travelled slowly from his helmet to his boots and back again.

The other young aristocrats up on the platform were bent over the railing, stifling their laughter with grey silk handkerchiefs.

The Captain of Dragoons stuck a gold coin in his eye like a monocle and spat his cigarette-end out into the hair of a girl leaning on a chair below him.

The Inspector went pale and in his embarrassment kept staring at the pearl in the aristocrat's shirt-front. The flat, indifferent gaze from the unmoving, clean-shaven face with the Roman nose was too much for him.

It made him uneasy. Crushed him.

He was stretched on the rack of the deathly hush in the tavern.

"Just like those effigies of knights lying with their hands crossed on stone coffins in Gothic cathedrals", whispered the painter, Vriesländer, as he looked at the aristocrat.

Finally the young swell broke the silence. "Errr ... Hmmm", he was imitating the landlord's voice, "Well, well, well, we have customers; isn't that nice." The pub exploded in a howling gale that made the glasses rattle. The toughs fell about laughing. A bottle hit the wall and smashed to pieces. The hulking landlord brayed obsequiously as he let us in on the joke, "His Highness Prince Ferry Athenstädt."

The Prince handed the Inspector his visiting-card. The poor policeman took it, saluted several times and clicked his heels.

Silence returned. The crowd listened breathlessly for what would come next.

Prince Athenstädt spoke again,

"The ladies and gentlemen whom you see gathered here are ... er ... are all guests of mine." With a nonchalant gesture His Highness indicated the down-and-outs. "Perhaps, Inspector, you would like me to ... er ... introduce you?"

The Inspector shook his head with a forced smile, muttered a few embarrassed words about "only doing his duty" and finally managed to come out with, "I see that this is an orderly establishment."

That put life back into the Captain of Dragoons: he rushed over to the lady's hat with the ostrich feathers at the rear of the raised platform and, to the cheers of the young aristocrats, dragged Rosina down onto the dance-floor.

She was so drunk she staggered round with her eyes shut. The large, expensive hat was all askew and she was wearing nothing over her naked body but long pink stockings and a pair of tails.

A signal, and the wild music started up again – "Trallala, trallala" – sweeping away the gurgling cry the deaf-and-dumb Jaromir emitted when he saw Rosina.

We decided to leave.

Zwakh called the waitress.

His words were swallowed up in the general noise.

The scenes I saw were as fantastic as an opium-induced hallucination:

The Captain has his arms round the half-naked Rosina as they slowly revolve to the music.

The deferential crowd has made room for them.

Then a murmur comes from the benches, "Loisitschek, Loisitschek", and people crane their necks as an even stranger couple joins the other on the dance-floor. An effeminate-looking young lad in pink leotard and tights, with long blond hair down to his shoulders, his cheeks and lips made up like a whore and his eyes cast down in provocative modesty, is clinging, lovesick, to the chest of Prince Athenstädt.

The harp was oozing a sickly waltz.

A sharp disgust with life rose in my throat.

I took a quick, fearful glance at the door: the Inspector was standing there with his back to the dance-floor, making sure he did not have to see anything, in hasty, whispered conversation with the detective constable, who was putting something back in his pocket. There was a clink of handcuffs.

Then the pair of them squinted over at the pock-marked face of Loisa, who at first tried to hide and then stood as if paralysed, his face chalky-white and twisted in terror.

A picture flashes before my mind's eye and immediately fades: the picture of Prokop, as I had seen him only an hour ago, leaning over the bars of the drain cover and listening, and a piercing cry of mortal anguish coming from below the ground.

I try to shout out, but can't.

Cold fingers have been thrust into my mouth, forcing my tongue up against my front teeth, filling my mouth like a lump that makes it impossible for me to bring out a single word.

I can't see the fingers, I know they are invisible, and yet I can feel them as if they were a physical presence.

It is perfectly clear to me that they belong to the spectral hands that brought the "Book of Ibbur" to me in my room in the Hahnpaßgasse.

"Water, water", shouts Zwakh, who is sitting beside me. They are holding my head and shining a candle into my eyes.

There is a whispered conference, "Take him to his flat – fetch the doctor – Hillel, the Synagogue Archivist, knows about this kind of thing – take him there."

Then I am lying on a stretcher, stiff as a corpse, and Prokop and Vriesländer are carrying me out.

Awake

Zwakh had run on ahead up the stairs, and I heard the anxious questions of Miriam, the daughter of the Archivist, and his attempts to reassure her.

I made no effort to follow what they were saying to each other, and I guessed more than heard that Zwakh was telling her that I had had an accident; they had come to ask for help to bring

70

me back to consciousness and give me first aid.

Still I could not move a muscle, still the invisible fingers held my tongue fast; but my mind was sure and firm and the feeling of terror had left me. I knew exactly where I was and what was happening to me and I did not even find it strange when they carried me, like a corpse, stretcher and all, up to Shemaiah Hillel's study, set me down and left me alone there.

I was filled with a calm and natural contentment, such as you feel when coming home after a long journey.

It was dark in the room and the blurred lines of the cross shapes in the window frames stood out against the dull, hazy gleam coming up from the street.

Everything seemed quite natural, and I was not in the least surprised when Hillel entered carrying a seven-flamed Menorah, nor that he calmly wished me 'Good evening' as if he was expecting me.

As he went about the room, adjusting a few objects here and there on the sideboard and then using the candelabra to light another seven-armed one, I was suddenly struck by something about him which until then I had not registered as special, in spite of the fact that we would meet on the stairs two or three times a week: the elegant proportions of his body and limbs, and the slim, delicate lines of his face with its high forehead. And, as I could now see in the light from the candles, he could not be any older than I was: forty-five at the most.

"You arrived a few minutes earlier than I had assumed", he began after a while, "otherwise I would have had the candles lit already." He pointed to the two candelabra and came up to the stretcher looking, as it seemed, with his dark, deep-set eyes at someone who was standing or kneeling by my head whom I, however, could not see. At the same time his lips moved, speaking soundless words.

Immediately the invisible fingers let my tongue go and the paralysis left me. I sat up and looked behind me: there was no one in the room apart from Shemaiah Hillel and myself.

The person who had come a few minutes earlier than he had been expecting must be me, then?

What I found much more bewildering than this in itself was

71

the fact that I was incapable of feeling the least surprise at it.

Hillel obviously guessed my thoughts, for he gave me a friendly smile and helped me up from the stretcher, pointed to a chair and said,

"There is nothing mysterious about it at all. It is only magic and sorcery – Kishuf – that frighten men; life itches and burns like a hairshirt, but the rays from the sun of the spiritual world are mild and warming."

I said nothing, since nothing occurred to me that I could say in reply. He did not seem to expect it, sat down opposite me and calmly continued, "A silver mirror, if it had feeling, would only suffer pain while it was being polished. Once it was smooth and shining, it would reflect all the images that struck it without suffering or emotion."

"Happy the man", he continued softly, "who can say of himself, 'I have been polished'." For a moment he was wrapped in thought and I heard him murmur a few words in Hebrew, "Lishu'oskho kivisi Adoshem." Then his voice was clearly to be heard again.

"Thou camest to me in a deep sleep and I have woken thee. In the Psalm of David it says, '*Then I spoke with myself, now shall I begin. It is the right hand of God that hath brought about this change.*'

When men arise from their beds, they think they have shaken off sleep and they know not that they have fallen victim to their senses and are in the grip of a much deeper sleep than the one they have just left. There is only one true state of wakefulness, and that is the one thou art now approaching. If thou shouldst speak to others of it, they will say thou art sick and they cannot understand thee. For that reason it is pointless and cruel to speak to them of it.

Thou carriest them away as with a flood;
They are as a sleep:
They are as grass which groweth up:
In the evening it is cut down and withereth."

*

72

I wanted to ask, "Who was the stranger who came to me in my room and gave me the "Book of Ibbur"? Was I awake or dreaming when I saw him?" but Hillel answered before even I could put the thought into words.

"Assume that the man who came to you and whom you call the Golem signifies the awakening of the dead through your innermost spiritual life. Each thing on earth is nothing but an eternal symbol clothed in dust.

How can you think with your eyes? Each shape that you see is a thought in your eye. Everything that takes on shape was a ghost before."

I felt ideas, which until then had been firmly anchored in my mind, tear themselves loose and drift like rudderless ships on a boundless ocean.

Placidly Hillel went on,

"Anyone who has been wakened can no longer die; sleep and death are the same."

"... can no longer die?" A dull ache gripped me.

"Two paths run beside each other: the Path of Life and the Path of Death. You have taken the "Book of Ibbur" and read in it. Your soul has been made pregnant by the Spirit of Life", I heard him say.

"Hillel, Hillel, let me take the path that all men take, the Path of Death!" everything within me screamed out loud.

"Men do not take any path, neither that of life nor that of death. They drift like chaff in the wind. In the Talmud it is written, 'Before God created the world he showed the souls a mirror, wherein they could see the spiritual sufferings of existence and the joys that followed. Some accepted the suffering. But the others refused and God struck them out of the Book of the Living.' But you are *taking* a path and you have set out on it of your own free will, even if you are no longer aware of it. Do not grieve; as knowledge comes gradually, so does memory. *Knowledge and memory are the same thing.*"

The friendly, almost kindly tone in which Hillel concluded this speech restored my calm, and I felt safe and sound, like a sick child that knows its father is close by.

I looked up and saw that the room was suddenly peopled with

figures standing in a circle round us. Some had white shrouds such as Rabbis used to wear of old, others had three-cornered hats and silver buckles on their shoes. But then Hillel passed his hand over my eyes and the room was empty once more.

Then he accompanied me out onto the stairs and gave me a burning candle for me to light my way up to my room.

*

I went to bed and tried to sleep, but sleep would not come and instead I found myself in a strange state that was neither dreaming, nor waking, nor sleeping.

I had snuffed the candle, but in spite of that everything in the room was so clear that I could distinguish each individual shape. At the same time I felt completely comfortable and free from that agonising restlessness which usually torments you when you are in such a mood.

Never before in my life had I been capable of such sharp and precise thought as now. The rhythm of health flowed through my every nerve, arranging my thoughts in orderly rows, like an army awaiting my orders.

I only needed to call them, and they stepped up and did what I wanted.

During the last few weeks I had been trying to carve a cameo out of sunstone without making any progress whatsoever; I never managed to make all the flecks in the stone fit in with the face I had in mind. Now I remembered the piece, and in a flash I could see the solution and knew precisely what line to take with the graver to do justice to the texture of the gem.

Formerly I had been the slave of a horde of fantastic impressions and visions and often I could not say whether they were feelings or ideas. Now I suddenly found I was lord and master in my own kingdom. Calculations, which previously I had only been able to do with much groaning on paper, now seemed to work themselves out in my head as if by magic.

All this was the result of my new-found ability to perceive and retain those things – and only those things – that I needed: numbers, shapes, objects or colours. And if it was a matter of

74

questions which could not be answered by means of such tools – philosophical problems and the like – then my inner vision was replaced by hearing, and the voice I heard was that of Shemaiah Hillel.

I was granted the strangest insights.

I suddenly saw things, which a thousand times previously I had allowed to slip past my ear as mere words, now clear before me, and soaked with significance in every pore; things I had learnt 'off by heart', I now 'grasped' at one stroke so that I 'owned' them. Mysteries hidden in the forms of words that I had never even suspected were now revealed to me.

The 'high' ideals of humanity, which until now, chests puffed out and besplattered with decorations, had looked down their respectable aldermanic noses at me, removed the masks from their features and apologised: they themselves were really only poor souls, but still, they were used to prop up an even more insolent fraud.

Might I perhaps not have been dreaming after all? Could it be that I had not talked to Hillel?

But no, there was the candle Shemaiah had given me. Happy as a little boy who has slipped out of bed on Christmas Eve to make sure the marvellous jumping-jack really is there, I snuggled back down into the pillows.

Like a tracker dog I penetrated further into the jungle of spiritual puzzles surrounding me.

First of all I tried to go to the point farthest back in my life that memory could reach. From there it must be possible, or so I believed, for me to see that part of my life which a quirk of fate had hidden in darkness.

But however hard I tried, I still could get no farther than seeing myself in the gloomy courtyard of this house with a view through the arched gateway of Aaron Wassertrum's junk-shop; it was as if I had spent a hundred years as an engraver of gems in this house without ever having been a child.

I had almost decided that any further groping around in the wells of the past was hopeless, when I suddenly realised with dazzling clarity that, although in my memory the broad highway of events ended at that arched gateway, that was not the case with a whole host of narrow footpaths which had presumably always accompanied the main road, but which I had ignored. 'Then where' – it was almost a shout in my ear – 'did you learn the skills by which you earn your living? Who taught you to engrave gems, and everything that goes with it? To read, to write, to speak, – to eat and walk, breathe, think and feel?'

Immediately I began to follow the advice that came from within me. Systematically I retraced my life.

I forced myself to follow an uninterrupted but inverted chain of thought: what had just happened, what led to it, what came before that and so on?

I was back at that arched gateway again. Now! Now! Only a little jump into empty space and surely I would have crossed the abyss separating me from my forgotten past? Then I saw something which I had missed on my way back through my thoughts. It was Shemaiah Hillel passing his hand over my eyes, just as he had done before in his study.

And everything was erased. Even my desire to delve into the past.

There was only one thing left that I had gained from it, the realisation that the sequence of events in one's life is a road leading to a dead end, however broad and easy it might appear. It is the narrow, hidden tracks that lead back to our lost homeland; what contains the solution to the last mysteries is not the ugly scar that life's rasp leaves on us, but the fine, almost invisible writing that is engraved in our body.

Just as I could find my way back to the days of my childhood, if I went through my alphabet book from back to front, from Z to A, to reach the point where I had started learning it at school, so too, I realised, I ought to be able to journey to that other distant home which is beyond all thought.

I carried a world of work on my shoulders. Hercules, I remembered, had also borne the weight of the vault of heaven on his head, and I saw the gleam of hidden significance in the old legend. And just as Hercules had managed to escape from it through his cunning in asking Atlas, 'Just let me tie a layer of rope round my head so that the awful burden does not crush my brain', so perhaps, I sensed, there was a dark path leading away from this precipice.

A deep distrust of blindly following my thoughts any farther in this direction suddenly crept over me. I stretched out straight in bed and covered my eyes and ears with my hands so as not to be distracted by my senses; so as to kill off every thought.

But my determination was smashed by an iron law: one thought could only be driven away by another thought, and if one should die there would already be the next, feasting on its flesh. I sought refuge in the roaring torrent of my blood, but my thoughts were ever at my heels; I hid in the pounding forge of my heart; a short while, and they had discovered me.

Once more Hillel's friendly voice came to my rescue, saying, "Keep to your path and do not falter. The key to the art of forgetting belongs to our brothers who follow the Path of Death; but you have been made pregnant by the Spirit of Life."

The "Book of Ibbur" appeared before me with two letters engraved in flame upon it: the one representing the bronze woman, throbbing, powerful as an earthquake; the other was infinitely far away: the hermaphrodite on the mother-of-pearl throne with the crown of red wood on its head.

Then Shemaiah Hillel passed his hand over my eyes for the third time and I fell asleep.

Folter's Gems

Paul Busson

With a violent jolt the cab stopped outside a large house in a fashionable part of town. The young doctor jumped down and rushed past the porter up the broad staircase. The servant who had just telephoned him from the coffee house was waiting by the half-open door on the first floor. On the small brass plate stood the name: Jerome Kerdac.

Once the doctor had entered, the servant immediately closed the door behind him, took his coat and hat and, with trembling hands, ushered him into a large room that was in semi-darkness; a flick of the switch and it was flooded with bright light from a chandelier of Venetian glass.

Dr. Klaar went up to the wide bed in which the sick man lay. A thin wisp of bluish gunsmoke was still twirling round in the light. There was a smell of scorched linen. The doctor's foot knocked against a hard object: it was the revolver with which Kerdac had shot himself.

The man in the bed had his eyes closed. His gaunt white face was motionless and his breathing weak. The doctor bent down over him and lifted the bedcover, which had been drawn up. He had placed the barrel of the gun below his left breast. There was a small, round hole with dark edges, a few spidery splashes of blood on his shirt next to the burnt patches round the bullet hole in his shirt, and that was all. Carefully, the doctor ran his hand over the man's back as he lay there unconscious. The bullet was still in the body. There seemed to be some damage to the heart; whether that was the case or not, there was not much that could be done for him.

Dr. Klaar got the servant to repeat his story, which he did with much sobbing and stammering, he had obviously not yet recovered from the shock. For some time now, he said, the Master had been melancholy and highly irritable; there had often been weeks when, without actually being ill, he had refused to leave his bed and he had eaten nothing for days on end. Sometimes he had seemed to be feverish, had rambled and seen horrible threatening visions. At night especially, he had often groaned and cried out loud, and several times he – the servant – had woken with a fright and hurried into the bedroom to stand by the Master. He, however, had always reprimanded him harshly for this and finally forbidden him once and for all from entering the bedroom at night unless he rang for him. Today the Master had had a particularly bad day, had moaned and groaned a great deal and had not had a bite to eat. At half past five in the evening he had rung for him and sent him out to do some shopping, which should have taken him about an hour. However, he had not quite finished his work and had still been in the house some twenty minutes later when the sound of a muffled report came from the bedroom. And when he had seen that the Master had shot himself he had immediately run to the telephone and had rung up the Café Central where, as he happened to know, the gentlemen from the hospital used to go to read the papers. That had been a quarter of an hour ago.

"Good", said the doctor. "Bring me paper and ink and then take what I write down to the police station at once. It is my duty to report this immediately."

At that moment the doctor noticed that Kerdac had opened his eyes wide and that his lips were moving. He hurried across to where his patient was breathing heavily.

"Send my servant back to his room", whispered Kerdac. "I would like to talk to you."

Dr. Klaar told him to stay calm, he was just going to write something to send to the chemist's.

"The chemist's, oh really?" groaned the injured man. "I heard everything that was said. Why the police? It will soon all be over. I have something important I would like to tell you."

He broke off and began to fidget with the blanket. His face was becoming visibly more emaciated and his nose stood out.

"The Hippocratic face", thought the doctor, and he realised that in that case it really did not matter if the police should receive his report ten minutes later.

He decided to allow the dying man to have his way, told the servant to stay at the ready in his own room and sat down close to his patient, who raised his top lip in a grateful smile. He felt unwilling to subject the poor man to the torture of a further examination. It was his opinion that the bullet was lodged in the lower part of the pericardium. It was a miracle that the organ could still function. It would continue to pump the blood laboriously round his body for a while, the heartbeat becoming more and more sluggish.

"Feel under my pillow", murmured Kerdac. The doctor did as he asked and pulled out a slim casket of reddish-brown Morocco leather. There was a coat of arms stamped on the lid, which gleamed dully with the patina of age. It showed a winged snake with a woman's head. Beneath it was written in gothic script: *A Folter*.

"Have a good look at it", said Kerdac. "I'm not going to die just yet. I feel fine." His eyelids slid down so that the doctor started forward. Kerdac was lying motionless and his breathing was regular, even if very weak.

Dr. Klaar opened the casket. It was lined with velvet that had once been white, but had long since yellowed. In twelve semi-circular compartments lay twelve thin, polished stones, smooth and transparent, with a crumbling black silk mask over them, like a protective covering. The mask had only one round opening, over the right eye, with a kind of raised lip, as if it were made for a small eye-glass to fit in. There was a narrow strip of parchment in the mask on which words in similar gothic lettering were printed, or written by a skilful hand.

The doctor gave his patient a questioning glance and then, when he kept his eyes tight shut, looked back at the strip. He found it completely incomprehensible, both the heading and the rest:

Folter's True Gems

Januarius	*Hyacinth*	*Eve*
Februarius	*Amethyst*	*Poppaea*
Martius	*Heliotrope*	*Salome*
Aprilis	*Sapphire*	*Selina*
Maius	*Emerald*	*Diana*

+Junius	Chalcedony	Nahema+
Julius	Cornelian	Astarte
Augustus	Onyx	Semiramis
September	Chrysolite	Lilith
October	Aquamarine	Undine
November	Topaz	Roxana
December	Chrysoprase	Helen

Call them all, except only Nahema.

Dr. Klaar had read it aloud. Like a fading echo, there came from the lips of the wounded man, "... except only Nahema."

And then Kerdac gave both the stranger by his bedside and the familiar objects in his room an astonished look, as if he had just woken from a deep sleep.

"I was unconscious?" he asked in a weak voice. "I could feel myself sinking ... deeper and deeper into the blackness ..."

A violent tremor ran through his body. His hand felt for the doctor's.

"Tell me ... doctor ... there is ... no hope, then? If you were to operate ...?"

Dr. Klaar instinctively looked away and tried to comfort the man with the usual meaningless phrases, to give him new heart. It was not the first time he had sat by a suicide's bed and witnessed the terrible awakening, the sudden recognition of a senseless, pathetic act which could not be undone. He thought of the poor seamstress who had died of phosphorus poisoning in his hospital three weeks ago; right until the very end all her thoughts, all her hopes had been concentrated on recovery, in spite of her wretched life, which she had tried to bring to a messy and excruciating end. Had she managed to recover, it would have meant nothing other than a continuation of her *via dolorosa*, doubly hard to bear because of the tiny, deformed and nameless creature that she, abandoned like a beast in the wild, had brought into the world in her icy attic. Happy were those who managed to kill themselves quickly, who slipped over into death during sleep, or whose end struck them like lightning in their prime, so quickly that they had no time for thought.

Kerdac had tears in his eyes when he saw the doctor's expression. But he was brave enough to come to terms with it.

"Then I will tell you everything", he said softly. "You will be the only one to know."

"You shouldn't talk too much", replied Dr. Klaar, with an uncertain glance at the clock. He was surprised to find himself still sitting here, instead of making the mandatory report.

"Please ... do stay ..."

A deep moan followed by a sobbing gasp indicated a painful convulsive fit. Kerdac clutched the doctor's hand as firmly as he could with his helplessly weak fingers, as if he was afraid he would be left to die alone and wanted to hold him there. When he had recovered somewhat, he began to gabble; gradually his voice calmed down and became clearer, although it was so soft that the doctor had to hold his ear close to the injured man's lips to keep him from overexerting himself. During the whole of his story, Dr. Klaar kept the strange casket in his hand.

"No one will mourn for me", said Kerdac, "there is no one who loves me. I have been alone since I was ten years old, completely alone. Do you know how sad that is? Do you know how a poor, timid lad like that can suffer in his cheerless existence? Huh! No one can know! ... It was a long time ago ... Later, when I left the institution where I spent the whole of my bleak childhood, they sent me to university. At the age of twenty-four I received a letter from the Chancery Court; my fortune, which until then had been administered by a grumpy old lawyer who otherwise did not concern himself at all with his ward, was paid out to me. I registered the fact with the dull indifference, the lethargy, which had become second nature to me. My circumstances were better than before, I had a large apartment decorated by a talented designer and buried myself in my books. Buying books, by the way, was the sole luxury I had allowed myself so far.

Presumably as a result of my lonely life, which had turned me in upon myself, I became interested in rare and occult works. With time I collected a great number of such books, from Agrippa of Nettesheim to modern, spiritualist works. I devoted my energies passionately to deciphering unknown oriental

82

manuscripts. At the same time I tried to practise magic. But apart from fleeting experiences and unusual dream-visions, which were probably the result of the obligatory incense burnt, some of which doubtless contained hallucinogenic substances, there was nothing that brought me closer to the mysteries I was seeking to fathom. Over the years I became acquainted with a few people who secretly concerned themselves with such matters and claimed to have seen more than I did. Perhaps they did really believe it. Once I came across a man who was said to be possessed of unheard-of magic powers and who pretended to be an Oriental. His disciples listened to his fantasies with imperturbable patience; in reality he was just a petty swindler who used his talent to pay for some of the minor comforts of life. His 'magnetic healing' was the thing that caused the authorities to have him deported back to his native Bavaria. So that led to nothing, either. Would you dry my forehead please, doctor?"

Kerdac's forehead was covered with large beads of sweat, and the other gently patted it with a towel. Perhaps it might be possible to lengthen this wretched life a little; the needle with the injection which he had kept at the ready easily penetrated the loose skin of his lower arm. The injection seemed to do Kerdac some good, he took a deep breath and continued in a somewhat more lively tone,

"I told you that as an example of the many disappointments I suffered. It was always the same. For ten rupees, a fakir in India, in Dharwangar, showed me the famous miracle of the mango tree. As he repeated his incantations, a young, light-green shoot appeared from the seed he had planted and grew higher and higher each time after he had covered it with a cloth. Finally I grabbed the pot with the seed from the fellow, in spite of his screams: the seed had been carefully split and a mango seedling very cleverly concealed within it. In the cloth were four other seedlings, each larger than the other.

Why am I telling you this? To show you that I am no novice in these matters and quite capable of distinguishing sham from reality; to make you understand that what drove me to fire that wretched bullet into my chest was more than the dreams of a fevered mind. It was real, of a reality that was so beautiful and yet so awful, that no living person can imagine the degree of horror I have lived through.

After the experiences I have described to you I banished my magic books to the depths of a huge, locked cupboard and set off to travel, unencumbered by mental luggage. It was no good. The rapid change of scene did not cheer up my melancholy temperament. If the Mediterranean sun shone more brightly on others, if the roses in Fiesole had a nasty odour which I found oppressive, if the blue sea smelled of fish and seaweed, then the fault lay within me. There must be something wrong with my eye, my hearing must have a string with an ugly note. How else could I explain why all I saw of a beautiful woman was the smut that the wind had blown onto her cheek and her veil had smudged? Why all I heard in a Beethoven concerto were the opening bars of a vulgar song repeated over and over again? Why, at a play that moved other people to the depths of their souls, could I only see the grubby scenery and the wrinkles of the actor who played the young lover? It was me! I was the cause of my own suffering!

Once I was in love, madly, unreasonably; I could not live without her. It may sound like an empty cliché, yet it still expressed the truth. This time I saw no physical defects. But I was tormented by a fiendish jealousy. I knew she was deceiving me and at the same time I knew that was not the case. Can you understand? I could not help it. There was something compelling me to think the worst of the woman I loved, and I tormented the only woman there was for me in the world with my insulting suspicions and my sarcastic words of renunciation until, hurt and deeply wounded in her most tender feelings, she left me, her face bathed in tears. And with that my life was really over, that is what has destroyed me. Of that I am sure."

Kerdac gave a deep sigh. A great weakness accompanied by a quivering of the muscles suddenly came over him, appearing to presage his rapid demise. But this time it passed, and he continued,

"I cannot remember anything that has given me real joy. I have tried everything and been disappointed by everything. It was my own shortcoming, I was incapable of joy. Eventually I gave up all attempt to enrich my life as pointless and fell back into my old state of complete indifference. I got up when I had had enough sleep, ate, drank and made my bored and futile way round the city.

One evening – I was living in Paris at the time – I was sitting in a boulevard café drinking a glass of beer. It was a warm, rainy day in spring. The lights were reflected in the wet cobblestones. The people streamed past; occasionally one would split off from the throng and come into the café; others who left it were immediately swallowed up by the living stream. I almost found it amusing to observe all these little scenes, which were like a symbol of life.

Suddenly I realised that a man had sat down at my table, something which made me very uneasy. I gave him a hostile look. It was a miserable, poorly dressed Jew with a reddish, unkempt beard and restless, anxious eyes. He drank his sweet liqueur with tiny sips and tried to take up as little space as possible. When he saw that I had noticed him he started and sketched a bow. After a while he addressed me in bad French, with the characteristic singing intonation of the Jews. He spoke very hesitantly, as if he was very embarrassed and I soon realised what he wanted. He had, he said, arrived in Paris only that day, with his wife and three small children, one of whom was very ill. He wanted to settle down here, but he had spent the whole day running round without success and he was starving and dog-tired. His wife was waiting for him, somewhere far out in the suburbs, and he hadn't a sou in his pocket to buy bread for his children. I gave him an irritated look, my first thought was that he was one of those countless importunate beggars who make a better living from some paltry speech they have got off by heart than many an honest working man. But his eyes looked at me with such passionate, desperate pleading in them and were fixed in such anxious expectation on my face that, contrary to my intention, I pushed a five-franc piece across the table to him. He erupted in such a flood of thanks and loud blessings that he was becoming a perfect pest. And when he went on to ask me whether I would not be willing to buy something from him I told him rather sharply it was time he disappeared. But he stayed calmly in his seat and took the casket that you have in your hand, doctor, out of his pocket and handed it to me. It had belonged, he said, to a fine gentleman in Vienna who had shot himself; he had bought it from the sale of his effects. It must be very rare and very old. He had asked his rabbi what it was, but he had commanded him to burn it and under no circumstances to sell it. But that would be a waste, and he was poor. Would I give him twenty francs for it?

Against my will, I opened the thing and bought it at once. It was a long time since anything had excited or surprised me; the effect on me of this casket, with the mask and strip of parchment, was like a glass of cool water to a man dying of thirst. I immediately put it in my pocket.

The Jew was still nodding to me gratefully and muttering blessings. He disappeared as he had come: I looked away for a moment, and when I turned back to the table, he was gone; in the end he had not dared to take the money; the gold coin lay beside my arm. I was sorry about that. I would have been happy to give the poor fellow the money. I never saw him again.

I made my way home as quickly as possible. I had a very pleasant apartment close to the Madeleine. I sent my servant out to bring some cold supper. After I had eaten I gave the casket and its contents a thorough examination. In vain I searched my books to see if anything was known of a magician called Folter, whose 'true gems' lay before me."

A further fit interrupted Kerdac. The doctor, constantly expecting the end, was in an inexplicable state of excitement, and the minutes seemed to drag before the pale lips opened to continue their story.

"I must hurry", he stammered. "I shall go downhill fairly rapidly from now. I was talking about that first evening? Well, it took me weeks of thinking and searching, weeks of torment, before I found the secret. It was one evening in September when I put the mask on once again and inserted the month's stone, the chrysolite, into the round hole. It was something I had tried a hundred times. And as I had done a hundred times before, I stared through the thin disc towards the light. In contrast to former attempts, this time I decided to wait until something –

anything at all – appeared, and I was prepared to wait the whole night if necessary. How long it took I cannot say. A very long time, certainly. Later on it happened more quickly. Well, there I sat for hours, spellbound, looking through the yellow stone. Then suddenly, involuntarily I would say, I started calling out the name Lilith countless times.

All at once it seemed as if something like a small cloud was forming in the centre of the transparent disc. But no ... now it seemed to be outside, in the corner of the room. My critical faculties began to fall asleep; all I could do was to stare fixedly at the yellow cloud, watching it grow and grow, watching the movement within it. It was as if I were paralysed. The figure of a woman became clearer and clearer ... a naked woman with long hair. Then I must have lost consciousness, for when I moved my hands again I felt as if I was waking from sleep, and the apparition had disappeared.

My first idea was that it was a vivid hallucination, which could only be explained by self-hypnosis, by the systematic overstimulation of the optic nerves. Then I went out. The whole evening, even in the theatre – a mindless vaudeville – the name Lilith kept appearing inside me. I remember that I had read various things about it: a she-devil – Adam's first wife – the succubus of the Middle Ages.

I was dreadfully tired, and went home early. Once I was in bed I fell asleep almost immediately. And I awoke almost as quickly, from contact with a body close to me. There was a woman in my room, beautiful as a vision, veiled in long, golden hair which crackled as it flowed over her shoulders. The web of gold gave off blue sparks.

And the strange thing was that I felt neither surprise nor terror. It seemed quite natural that she had come. I knew that this slim, supple body was that of my lover, the she-devil Lilith. Oh ... I had known her before. It was surely not the first time I saw her. I knew those sweet lips, those bright, blue eyes with the tiny pupils which were mere slits, like those of a cat. And I looked for the little drop of blood she bore like a ruby on her lower lip. I knew that it was always there, trembling, on her pale-red mouth. The yellowish, dusky light too, in which I saw my room, seemed something long familiar.

But those were not thoughts going through my mind ... there was only feeling ... I felt everything ... it was all inexpressibly clear and yet impossible to put into words. Just like the thoughts you might have of music ... or colours ... I don't know how to put it. In this and other nights, thoughts that took the form of words, ideas, were something alien, crudely physical, that would have torn me from her arms.

Imagine you could perceive sounds, harmonies with all your senses ... feel, smell, see them ... No! I can't tell you what it was like ... It was bliss. I dissolved into a dark, purple flame ... I fainted from joys that no one can even guess at. I swirled up in bewitching eddies of light ... bodiless and yet feeling with all my senses ... I was one with the woman, one single, godlike being ...

When I was woken by the gentle shaking of my servant it was past midday. I got out of bed and staggered across the floor; I was dazed, tired, drained. There was a livid mark on my neck, and on the crumpled pillow a shining spot. It was blood, Lilith's farewell kiss!

That day I avoided people. I did not want to see anyone. The light faded, evening came. I was in my bed once more, awaiting my lover, as my burning eyelids closed. But I slept the whole night through, a deep, dreamless sleep. She did not come, because I had not called her.

From that time on I lived for the night, and the day, with its noise and all its brightly lit ugliness, was a nightmare for me. At night I was a king, there was nothing on earth to compare with my glory, and I gave little heed to my wretched body, which paid for the flights of my spirit with fevers and anaemia. I regarded my body as a worthless machine, which was just to be kept going as long as possible. I could scarcely be bothered to have enough to eat.

But oh my friend, those nights! They all came when I called them in their months: Eve, the mother of mankind, in the beauty of her youth, with silky down on her arms and legs and a child's smile playing round her innocent lips; Astarte, the dark-brown goddess with the sultry eyes, dressed in gold, with cool, heavy jewellery; Selina, pale and sweet in her silver-blue tunic; Roxana with the scent of amber and yellow roses. With the blonde Poppaea I wandered through shimmering colonnades, her violet cloak rustling softly as I kissed her white face. Diana, supple and sunburnt, awaited me under the cork-oaks of the Pyrenees, and with Semiramis in her silver helmet I stood surrounded by the intoxicating glory of the blooms that filled her garden. Undine twined her thin girl's arms around me and, with a laugh, shook glittering drops from her green hair. To the dull thump of the hand drum, the piercing note of the whistle and the cascading harp Salome danced the dance that had once charmed Herod; her dark-green veils were spattered with the blood of John the Baptist. Oh, I can still hear Helen's soft, enchanting laughter and see the broad, bronze belt which jingled as it slipped from her slim waist ...

Ah, my lost bliss! Finally I did what was forbidden. The idea lodged within me and tormented me: Nahema! I struggled and suffered. And I was defeated. On the first day of June ...

I called her. She was the most beautiful of all and wore a wide cloak, grey and fine as the wings of a bat. Beside her everything seemed lifeless, pain and joy knew no bounds, every nerve seemed to respond individually, every sensation to grow to an extreme of intensity. I wept tears of joy and waited for the night, I only started to live when twilight fell, the twilight that was the colour of her cloak. And she came, night after night. The other stones had lost their power for me.

Then came the horror. It came wrapped in her cloak. Her divine body began to change ... every night she seemed older ... wrinkles appeared on her forehead ... ugly shadows ringed her eyes. Years seemed to separate one night from the next.

In the end she was a lemur with loose, parchment skin and a toothless mouth. She tortured me with disgusting caresses. She came every night ... and ... she told me I must die ... so that she might be rejuvenated. I must kill myself. She said it all the time, even by day she whispered it in my ear. The man in Vienna had been compelled to obey. In German 'Folter' means ... torture ..."

Kerdac suddenly let out a shrill cry and opened his eyes wide. His jaw fell to his chest.

Dr. Klaar started violently and bent down to him: Jerome Kerdac was dead. A little black blood trickled out of the bullet-wound. The doctor called the servant and went down the staircase with unsteady steps. He took the casket with him.

He had already been sitting for more than four hours looking through the mask. The thin, polished aquamarine glowed a greenish-blue before his throbbing eye. There was a deathly hush in the room. He had spoken the name and seen a little cloud form, but his reason kept watch and woke him from his trance again and again. My God! it was nonsense! Angrily he tore off the mask and rubbed his inflamed eye.

It was one of those evenings when the heart of the lonely is seized with a wild melancholy, a leaden sense of lost time; one of those days when withered hopes and desires we thought dead assert their power over us. Then we are visited by a dismal procession of thoughts and ideas, which we imagined we had long since overcome.

Dr. Klaar made his glum way home from the third-class inn where the young doctors used to take their meals. He almost burst into tears at the sight of his room with the smoking lamp, the furniture upholstered in cheap cotton rep and the ugly, cold stove. But then he managed to pull himself together and put his mood down to the nervous strain of the events of the afternoon. After that he calmed down a little.

It was the second time he had woken with a start. Something wet or cold had touched his face and he had the impression that a faint shadow had moved away from his bed and evaporated in the darkness of one of the corners of the room. He rubbed his eyes and blinked at the steady flame of the nightlight. Then he went back to sleep.

A few minutes later he gave such a violent start that he was out of bed before he was completely awake. Something was scurrying away from him ... the figure of a girl, almost transparent ... now it was gone. On the bedside rug were two elongated damp patches, on the floor the damp marks of tiny, slim feet ...

Dr. Klaar gave a scream like a startled animal. The dampness quickly evaporated and the floor took on its old appearance again. The doctor was still standing by his bed, babbling to himself.

And then he gave another scream. "Undine! That is madness! I'm going mad ..."

Quivering all over, he tore open the window. Icy autumnal air flowed over his face. He collapsed in a trembling fit and clasped his head in both hands as he crouched on the floor. Then he jumped up, grabbed the casket like one possessed and tipped the stones out; one after the other he flung them into the darkness, and down below the brittle discs splintered on the cobblestones. The parchment and mask he held over the flickering candle; he did not feel the flame as it blazed up round his fingers.

Shivering, he sat on a hard wooden chair in the middle of the room, waiting in mortal fear for the clear, grey light of dawn which was slowly, slowly creeping across the roofs.

Sergeant Anton Lerch

Hugo von Hofmannsthal

On the 22nd of July, 1848, before six o'clock in the morning, a reconnaissance party, the second squadron of Wallmoden's Cuirassiers, one hundred and seven cavalrymen under the command of their Captain, Baron Rofrano, set off from the mess in San Alessandro and rode towards Milan. The whole of the open, shining landscape was immersed in an indescribable calm; from the peaks of the distant mountains morning cloud rose into the gleaming sky like silent smoke-clouds; the maize stood motionless, and villas and churches shone out from among groves of trees that looked as if they had been washed. Scarcely had the troop advanced a mile beyond the last outposts of their own army than they saw the glint of arms among the maize fields and their advance party announced enemy infantry. The squadron formed up by the road for the attack; the bullets hissing over their heads with a strangely loud noise, almost a miaow, they charged across the fields, driving a company of men with a variety of weapons like quails in front of them. They were men from Manara's Legion with strange headgear. The prisoners were put in the charge of a corporal and eight men and sent to the rear. The advance party reported suspicious figures outside a beautiful villa with a drive flanked by ancient cypresses leading up to it. Sergeant Anton Lerch dismounted, took twelve men armed with rifles, surrounded the windows and captured eighteen students from the Pisa Legion, all handsome, well-mannered young men with white hands and long hair. Half an hour later the squadron captured a man in the dress of a peasant from Bergamo who aroused suspicion by his exaggeratedly harmless and inconspicuous behaviour. Sewn into his coat lining he was carrying extremely important and detailed plans regarding the setting-up of a volunteer corps in the Giudicaria and its cooperation with the Piedmontese army. Around ten o'clock in the morning a herd of cattle fell into their hands. Immediately afterwards they were opposed by a strong enemy detachment, from which they came under fire from behind a graveyard wall. The front line under their Lieutenant, Count Trautsohn, jumped the low wall and cut down the enemy as they rushed between the graves in confusion before the greater part of them escaped into the church and then out through the sacristy door into a dense thicket. The twenty-seven new prisoners stated that they were Neapolitan volunteers under Papal officers. The squadron had one dead. A detail, consisting of Corporal Wotrubek and Dragoons Holl and Haindl, rode round the thicket and came upon a light howitzer drawn by two horses which they took by slashing with their swords at the escort, grabbing the horses by the bridle and forcing them round. As he had sustained a slight wound, Corporal Wotrubek was sent back to headquarters to report the successful skirmishes and other pieces of good fortune, the prisoners were again sent back, but the howitzer was retained by the squadron which, after the escort had left, still numbered seventy-eight men.

Since, according to their statements, the various prisoners were unanimous that Milan had been completely abandoned by enemy troops, both regular and irregular, and had been denuded of guns and other military equipment, the Captain could not resist giving both himself and the dragoons the opportunity of riding into this large and beautiful city, lying there defenceless. Seventy-eight upraised naked blades moved forward amid the peal of the midday bells, the four trumpets sounding a thunderous advance to the steely glitter of the sky, jingling against a thousand window-panes and sparkling in reflection on seventy-eight cuirasses; the streets left and right like a disturbed ant-hill, filling with astonished faces; figures disappearing, blanching and cursing, in house doorways, drowsy windows thrust open by the bare arms of unknown beauties; past Santa Babila, San Felde, San Carlo, the famous marble cathedral, San Satiro, San Giorgio, San Lorenzo, San Eustorgio; their ancient bronze doors all opening and the hands of silver saints and bright-eyed women in brocade waving from the candlelight and clouds of incense; ever on the alert for shots from a thousand attics, dark entrances, low shops, seeing nothing but adolescent girls and boys with their white teeth and dark hair; looking out on all this from a trotting horse with gleaming eyes from behind a mask of blood-spattered dust; in by the Porta Venezia, out by the Porta Ticinese: thus the fine squadron rode through Milan.

Not far from the latter gate, where there was an esplanade planted with handsome plane trees, Sergeant Lerch thought he saw a female face that he recognised at the ground-floor window of a newly-built, bright yellow house. Curiosity made him turn round in the saddle and, since at the same time his horse started stepping rather awkwardly, so that he suspected it had picked up a stone in one of its front shoes, since also he was at the rear of the squadron and could fall out without fuss, all this made him decide to dismount, which he did after he had guided his horse half into the entrance of the house in question. Hardly had he lifted the second white-socked forefoot of his bay, to check the hoof, than the door of a room inside the house, which came out right by the front of the entrance, opened to reveal a buxom, almost young woman in somewhat dishevelled dishabille; behind her, however, a bright room with window-boxes, in which were a few pots of basil and some red geraniums, plus a mahogany cabinet and group of mythological figures in biscuit ware became visible to the Sergeant, whilst at the same time in a pier glass his sharp eye spotted the opposite wall, which was taken up by a large white bed and a concealed door, through which a corpulent, clean-shaven, oldish man was just retreating.

Meanwhile, however, the Sergeant had remembered the woman's name and many other things besides: that she was the widow or divorced wife of a Croatian Corporal in the Pay Corps, that nine or ten years ago in Vienna he had spent a number of evenings, often late into the night, with her, in company with another man, her actual lover at that time, and now his eyes sought her former slim but voluptuous form beneath her present plumpness. She, however, stood there and smiled at him in a slightly flattered Slav manner, which sent the blood pulsing through his strong neck and behind his eyes, whilst a certain affectation in the way she spoke to him, as well as her dishabille and the room furnishings, somewhat intimidated him. At that moment, however, as he watched a large fly crawling over the comb stuck in her hair with no other thought than how he would raise his hand to drive the fly away and then let it fall onto the back of her white, warm yet cool neck, he was filled from head to toe with the sense of the victorious skirmishes and other good fortune of the day, so that his heavy hand drew her head toward him, and said, "Vuic" – her surname had certainly not crossed his lips for ten years and her first name he had forgotten – "in a week we are going to move into the city and I am going to be quartered here", nodding in the direction of the half-opened door to the room. As he was speaking he heard several doors slam in the house, felt himself pulled away by his horse, first of all by mutely tugging at the bridle, then by neighing after the others, mounted and rode off after the squadron without any other answer from Frau Vuic than an embarrassed laugh as she threw her head back onto the nape of her neck. But the words he had spoken asserted his power. Slightly aside from the main column and no longer riding at such a smart trot under the heavy, metallic glow of the sky, his vision trapped in the cloud of dust accompanying them, the Sergeant became more and more immersed in the room with the mahogany furniture and pots of basil and at the same time in a civilian atmosphere, which still had a martial tinge, an atmosphere of comfort and agreeable violence with no officer to give him orders, a life in slippers, the hilt of his sabre sticking through the left-hand pocket of his dressing gown. The corpulent, clean-shaven man, who had disappeared through the concealed door, something half way between a priest and a retired valet, played an important role in his daydreams, almost more than the beautiful, wide bed and Frau Vuic's delicate white skin. At times the clean-shaven man played the role of a submissive friend who received his confidences, at others he was pushed into the background, forced to pay for Lerch's silence, was associated with all kinds of subversive activities, was in collusion with the Piedmontese, a papal cook, a procurer, the owner of suspicious properties with dark summer-houses for political meetings, and he grew into a huge, bloated figure in whose body you could drill twenty bungholes and draw off gold instead of blood.

There were no new incidents for the patrol during the afternoon, and no restraint on the Sergeant's daydreaming. But a thirst for unexpected rewards, for bounties, for ducats suddenly dropping into his pockets had been aroused within him. It was the thought of his first entry into the room with the mahogany furniture that was the splinter in his flesh around which his desires and lusts festered.

When, then, towards evening the squadron, with the horses fed and reasonably rested, was attempting to advance by a roundabout route towards Lodi and the bridge over the Adda, where they could expect to come into contact with the enemy, the Sergeant found a village with a partly ruined bell-tower that lay aside from the main road in a darkening hollow temptingly suspicious, so that, signalling Dragoons Holl and Scarmolin to accompany him, he left the main body of the squadron and rode off into the village, hoping to surprise a general with a modest escort and attack him or somehow or other earn a quite exceptional bonus, so heated was his imagination. When they reached the squalid place, which appeared deserted, he ordered Scarmolin and Holl to ride round outside the houses, the one on the left, the other on the right, whilst he, his pistol in his hand, prepared to gallop down the street; but soon, finding himself on hard stone flags, over which, moreover, some slippery, greasy substance had been poured, he was forced to rein in his horse and continue at a walk. There was a deathly hush in the village; not a child, not a bird, not a breath of air. To the right and left were small grubby houses from which the plaster had all flaked off; here and there something nasty had been drawn in charcoal on the bare bricks; looking in through doorposts that were devoid of paint, the Sergeant saw, here and there, a lazy, half-naked figure lounging on a pallet or dragging itself about the room, as if its hips were dislocated. His horse seemed heavy-legged and put down its back feet as if they were made of lead. As he was turning round to check the rear shoes, shuffling footsteps emerged from a house, and when he straightened up there was a female, whose face he could not see, crossing right in front of his horse. She was only half dressed; her torn and dirty skirt was dragging in the gutter and she wore dirty slippers on her bare feet; she crossed so close in front of the horse that the breath from its nostrils ruffled the shining, greasy chignon hanging down below an old straw hat over her bare neck, but she did not hurry at all or try to avoid the horseman. Two bleeding rats with their teeth sunk into each other rolled out from under a doorway on the left into the middle of the street and the one that was coming off worse gave such a pitiful squeal that the Sergeant's horse pulled up and stared at the ground, its head to one side and breathing audibly. Slight pressure from the Sergeant's knees set it moving again, but by that time the woman had disappeared into a house without him having been able to have a look at her face. From the next house a dog rushed out, head raised, dropped a bone in the middle of the street and tried to bury it in a gap between the flagstones. It was a grubby white bitch with droop-ing dugs; she scraped away with fiendish determination, then grabbed the bone in her teeth and carried it off a little way. By the time she began scraping again, three dogs had already joined her: two were very young, with soft bones and loose skin; without barking or being able bite, they pulled at each other's chaps with their blunt teeth. The dog that had come at the same time as them was a light yellow greyhound whose body was so swollen that its four thin legs could only carry it along very slowly. At the end of the fat body that was as taut as a drum, the head appeared much too small; its tiny, restless eyes held a horrible expression of pain and apprehension. Immediately two more dogs came running along: a skinny, white one of an exceptionally voracious ugliness, with black furrows running down from its inflamed eyes, and a half-bred dachshund with too long legs. The latter raised its head and looked at the Ser-geant. It must have been very old. Its eyes were infinitely tired and sad. But the bitch scurried mindlessly back and forth in front of the rider; the two puppies snapped silently with their soft muzzles at the horse's fetlocks, while the greyhound dragged its grotesque body close to its hooves. The bay was unable to move. The Sergeant drew his pistol to shoot one of the animals, but when it did not go off, he dug in both his spurs and clattered off over the flagstones. After a few steps, however, he had to rein in sharply: his way was barred by a cow that a boy was dragging by a taut rope to the slaughter. But the cow, shrinking back at the reek of blood and the sight of the fresh skin of a black calf nailed to the doorpost, braced its feet, sucked in the sun-kissed evening air though its flared nostrils and, before the boy had time to use the rope or his stick against it, grabbed with a pitiful look a mouthful of the straw the Sergeant had fixed to the front of his saddle. Then he had the last house of the village behind him and, riding between two low, tumbledown walls, could see the road continuing over an old, single-span stone bridge across an apparently dry ditch, but he sensed such an indescribable heaviness in his horse's gait, such a lack of progress, that each single foot-length of the walls to his right and left, even each centipede and woodlouse sitting on it, crept past laboriously out of his vision, and he felt as if he had spent an immeasurable time riding through this foul village. His horse now started to breathe with a heavy, rasping sound, but he did not immediately recognise the unaccustomed noise and, as he was looking for the cause of it, at first above or beside him and then in the distance, he noticed on the other side of the stone bridge and, as it happened, at the same distance from it as himself, a soldier from his own regiment approaching, a sergeant on a bay with white socks on its front legs. As he was well aware that there was no such horse in the squadron, apart from the one on which he was himself mounted at that moment, and as he still could not recognise the face of the other rider, he impatiently spurred on his horse to a lively trot, at which the other increased his speed by the same amount, so that now they were only a stone's throw away from each other; and then, as the two horses, each from its own side, each at the same moment, stepped onto the bridge with the same white-socked forefoot, and the Sergeant, with a fixed stare recognising himself in the rider, pulled up his horse and stretched out his right hand with the fingers spread against the apparition, at which the figure, similarly reining in and raising its right hand, was suddenly no longer there, Holl and Scarmolin, looking completely unconcerned, suddenly appeared from the right and the left out of the dry ditch and at the same time, from across the pasture-land, loud and not very far off, came the squadron's trumpets sounding the attack. Taking a rise in the ground at a full gallop, the Sergeant saw the squadron already galloping towards a copse, from which enemy cavalry armed with lances was rapidly pouring out; then, as he gathered the four loose reins in his left hand, he saw the fourth troop separate from the squadron and slow down, and now he was already galloping across the reverberating ground, already in the choking dust, already in the middle of the enemy, struck at a blue arm holding a lance, saw close beside him the Captain's face with eyes wide open and teeth bared fiercely, then suddenly he was hemmed in all round by hostile faces and foreign uniforms, plunged into a sea of brandished swords, stabbed the nearest in the neck and off his horse, saw next to him Scarmolin, with a laugh on his face, slash the fingers off a soldier's rein-hand and cut deep into the horse's neck, felt the melee slacken, and suddenly found himself alone, on the edge of a small stream, chasing an enemy officer on a grey stallion. The officer tried to take the stream, the grey refused. The officer pulled it round, turning his young, very pale face and the mouth of a revolver towards the Sergeant at the moment the point of his sabre entered his mouth, the whole force of a galloping horse concentrated in its tiny point. The Sergeant pulled out his sword and grabbed, in the place where the officer's fingers had released it as he fell, the snaffle of the grey, which lifted its hooves, lightly and delicately as a deer, over its dying master.

As Lerch rode back with his handsome prize the sun, setting in thick haze, cast an intense red glow over the meadow. Even places with no hoof-marks seemed covered in pools of blood. The glow was reflected back on the white uniforms and laughing faces, their cuirasses and saddle-cloths glistened and gleamed, and reddest of all were three small fig trees on which the laughing cavalrymen had wiped the grooves of their sabres clean. To the side of the red-spotted trees stood the Captain, and beside him the Squadron Trumpeter; his trumpet looked as if it had been dipped in red juice as he raised it to his lips and sounded the roll call. The Sergeant rode past each platoon and saw that the squadron had not lost one single man and captured nine extra mounts. He rode up to the Captain to report, the grey still by his side, its head raised, stepping lightly and sniffing the air like the handsome, vain young horse it was. The Captain had only half an ear for his report. He beckoned over Lieutenant Count

Trautsohn, who immediately dismounted and, with six dragoons who had similarly dismounted, went behind the line of the squadron to unhitch the light howitzer they had captured, and had the six men drag it to one side and drop it into a marshy place formed by the stream, after which he remounted and, first driving off the now superfluous two draught horses by hitting them with the flat of his sword, silently resumed his place at the front of the first platoon. Whilst this was being done, the squadron, which had formed up in two sections, was not actually restless, but there was a somewhat unusual atmosphere, that might be explained by four victorious skirmishes in one day, and that surfaced in soft outbreaks of repressed laughter as well as muttered calls to each other. The horses were not standing still either, especially those which had the captured mounts inserted between them. After such good fortune all felt the space to line up in was too restricted, such victorious cavalry should be charging in open formation against new opponents, slashing at them and seizing new prize horses. At that moment the Captain, Baron Rofrano, rode close up to the front of the squadron and, opening wide the large lids of his rather sleepy blue eyes, ordered clearly, though without raising his voice, "Release the extra mounts". There was a deathly hush throughout the squadron. Only the grey beside the Sergeant stretched its neck and almost touched the forehead of the horse on which the Captain was sitting with its nostrils. The Captain put away his sabre, drew one of his pistols from its holster and, wiping away a speck of dust from the shining barrel with the hand holding the reins, repeated his order in a slightly louder voice and immediately afterwards counted "One" and "Two". After he had counted "Two" he fastened his clouded gaze on the Sergeant, who was

sitting motionless in the saddle in front of him, staring fixedly at his face. Whilst Anton Lerch's fixed, unflinching gaze, in which there was just an occasional flicker of dog-like anguish which immediately died away, seemed to express a kind of fawning trust, which was the result of many years under the Captain's command, it was not the immense tension of this moment which filled his consciousness, but a diverse flood of images of an alien comfort, and from depths of his being of which he himself was completely unaware there rose a bestial rage directed at the man before him who was going to take away his horse, such a terrible rage at the face, voice, posture and whole being of the man, as can only be created in some mysterious way by years of living in close proximity. Whether something similar was going on inside the Captain, or whether he felt the whole silently infectious peril of critical situations was concentrated in this moment of mute insubordination is uncertain: with a casual, almost affected movement, he raised his arm and, curling his lip contemptuously, counted "Three"; the shot rang out and the Sergeant, hit through the forehead, slumped forward onto the neck of his horse and then fell to the ground between the bay and the grey stallion. But his body had not struck the ground before all the NCOs and men had got rid of their captured horses with a kick or a tug of the reins, and the Captain, calmly putting his pistol away, was once more able to lead the squadron, still quivering as if from a bolt of lightning, against the enemy, which appeared to be rallying in the blurred, twilit distance. But the enemy declined the renewed attack, and shortly afterwards the patrol reached the southern outpost of their own army without further incident.

DREAM AND NIGHTMARE

The Playground: *A Fantasy*

Franz Werfel

Heart longing alone hears aright.
(Wagner: Siegfried – The Woodbird.)

During the night before his thirtieth birthday Lucas had had a dream which he could not remember in the morning. What a strange awakening it had been! His body had lost all feeling. He felt just as your foot feels when you sleep with it in an awkward position; you can grab it and hit it, but it has become alien, it does not belong to you any more than a table or a book that you might hold. Only your own hand touching it can feel itself. That was what Lucas felt about his body when he woke up. It was as if his soul were hovering over the bed with a strange corpse in it, cool and without memory.

Slowly, he coalesced with himself again, but ever since that moment of awakening there had been a slight dislocation within him and in the way he saw the world.

Whenever he went to the window and looked out onto the central square of the little town, he would suddenly put his hands to his eyes as if his vision had to be corrected, for it was set at too great a distance and did not register the two ungainly carriages outside the 'Red Crab', nor the women with their baskets of fruit, the onion-shaped roof of the Town Hall or the young waiter dusting down the tables in the garden outside the beer hall.

Whenever he arrived home from the Ministry in the evening and sat down on the broad chair by his table, he had to jump up again straight away, for his heartbeat would suddenly start to race so that he felt dizzy and near to collapsing. Then he would lie down on the old, waxcloth-covered sofa, whose white, ena-melled pins shone with a patriarchal glow through the half-light of the paraffin lamp.

But there was no rest there, either.

He sprang back onto his feet, stretching his head forward into the darkness like a hunter. Massive silence was all around him. The high, muted violins of the sphere, which fills all space, shimmered. And in his ear the jets of ancient fountains began to sound as they splashed down into eroded stone basins in hidden courtyards. He listened with bated breath. But the word did not emerge from the rippling of the mysterious water.

He would go to bed exhausted.

A great and alien sorrow stopped him from falling asleep.

He felt as if he had been in an unknown world for an hour, where he had buried the being dearest to him, a woman, a friend, a child. Then he had woken up with the pain, but no memory of what the pain was about.

During the day he would sit in his office, staring at the clock above his desk. There was a scratching of pens. Malicious, dusty steps shuffled across the floor. Sometimes a silly remark was heard. A cackle of laughter came from one corner in reply.

But all he could hear was the seconds dripping into the bowl of time. On the hour it was full and would overflow, the superfluous drops ringing out. He could not hold himself back either, and had to repress a sob in his throat.

Once the office supervisor came up behind him.

"Mr. Lucas, how often must I repeat it? There is something wrong with the files again. Case Number 2080 is not closed. I keep on telling you! You can believe me with my experience!! People who are born with a silver spoon in their mouths and can pull strings are usually slipshod dreamers! If Daddy's one of the bigwigs, well then, of course ..."

"I am a dreamer, only I forget the dream."

Lucas said it quite clearly and was surprised to hear his voice.

The clerks, spiteful as schoolboys, creased up with laughter. The most spiteful of all kept a solemn face and was always the last to double up.

"You can't concentrate, can't concentrate", said the supervisor as he turned once more in the doorway, wiping his spectacles with a studied air.

One morning when Lucas woke up after a nasty, uneasy sleep, he heard himself say aloud, "Forgetting is a sin. Forgetting is the worst sin there is."

He propped himself up on his elbows, but he could not control his mouth, which was talking without him willing it.

"I must get up and search, search." He dressed slowly. There was a cloud round his neck, like a warm, misty lace ruff.

He took his rucksack out of the cupboard and stuffed some bread and spare clothing into it.

Then he took his walking stick and left.

"Where on earth am I going?" he asked himself, as if he was in a daze, when he stepped out into the empty square, blazing red in the sunrise.

"To search for the dream", answered the voice.

Lucas stepped out and had soon left the little town behind him. Some strange power drove his legs on so that his heart, exhausted from all the sleepless nights, could hardly keep pace. The many conical hills of the uplands faced him, strange and unfamiliar. The fog had long since dissipated. Only around the summit of Thundertop was one cloud gathered, as if it were the last breath of the extinct volcano.

A nuthatch with blue wings flitted past. High in the air hovered a bird of prey.

Lucas walked beneath a thin roof of birdsong. None was like another. The trees, both deciduous and coniferous, which surged in waves over the tops and tors, still had the somewhat ragged look of a belated April. But the fields and meadows were already full of dandelions.

Lucas left the road, left the footpath and turned off into a narrow green valley between two wooded hills. The grassy pasture was yielding to the foot, and that lightened his heart as he made his way. His desperate restlessness eased a little, and suddenly he threw himself to the ground and bit passionately into the earth. It was a lover's kiss. "O star that I kiss, you smell of woman."

He felt as if with this kiss he had come closer to the mystery he had been commanded to seek.

Without consciousness of a goal he continued on his way.

It must have been about midday when he left his airy valley for a narrower, rockier one. He had to clamber up the side of the mountain, for there was a stream roaring along the bottom. However, he soon found a cart-track. This path had many little wooden bridges with pointed roofs which it flung across the gorges. In the roof-vault over each bridge hung a Madonna with an oil-lamp.

Suddenly Lucas stopped.

He should proceed no farther, he felt.

Something within him was quivering, like the tiny deflection of the needle of a compass.

He closed his eyes and scrambled up the steep slope. At the top a calm, dense wood stretched out. The trunks stood rigid. Only the tops waved to and fro to a lumbering melody that came booming out of an immense distance, hovered massively for a moment and then boomed back into the immense distance.

Thus far Lucas had had no thought for food and drink. Nor had he needed it. Something was driving him ever onwards.

There was a memory that would not leave him. As a child he had gone with his father through a forest, his bearded father in front, he behind. Often his father would bend down for some herb or mushroom, often he would part the bushes when he suspected they might conceal a good find. They did not speak a word to each other. Suddenly his father was no longer there; he had disappeared amongst some saplings and left the boy alone. But he, mad with fear and sorrow, ran on down the path, looking for the other. He did not dare to shout. Some bashfulness, some qualm always stopped him from addressing his father as 'Father'. He was consumed with a double fear, for himself and for the man who had disappeared and who had perhaps collapsed somewhere off the path and was lying amongst the bracken.

Later his father had appeared from a thicket and the child showed no sign of what he had felt.

Lucas could not get this memory of his childhood fear out of his mind.

He kept hurrying onwards. A wordless message called, 'Keep going, keep going.'

Already the evening was draping its yellow and red flags across the branches.

The mountain leant down. He ran to the bottom. Now he was out of the trees.

He hurried through grass that grew higher and higher until it reached his hips. Like a new-created being, he sensed a different air and a swaying wind. Suddenly he was standing on the bank of a wide river. The current drew long, vigorous lines and wrinkles in the stream. The water bore off the dying evening like the still-smoking beams and debris of a conflagration.

The river banks were narrow. A strip of sand and grass on either side; but to the right and left the measureless forest rose up again.

Not a soul was to be seen.

Without wetting their wings, waterfowl shot in unerring arcs over the curvature of the water; above a marshy place near the water's edge a host of dragonflies trembled in glaring and delicate colours.

Dancing round in the eddies, peeled tree-trunks floated down on the current, and sometimes things of more mysterious form which disappeared in the twilight gloom. From the other bank now arose the great evening noise of the frogs and toads. Banks of mist gathered there too, billowing up and dispersing like dust clouds on the road. Wandering back and forth, they were like belated passengers on a rainy evening waiting for the bell of the approaching steamer somewhere along the Rhine, the Don or the bank of a great lake.

Lucas walked along the bank in the direction of the setting sun, where the last light was still floating on the surface of the water.

The twilight was almost gone now. From behind his back came the hum of darknesses edging forward like magic bees.

And now it was night.

Still he felt no hunger, nor a need to rest, was all soul following a scent, a track, like a ghost at the moment of apparition. His joints strewed his steps lightly on the ground before him, as if there were no resistance to overcome. He bounded along, carefree and secure, like a child led by the hand.

Suddenly he saw a light in the darkness, not far away and on this bank.

It came nearer.

Half still on the bank and half already in the water lay a mighty ferry, broad and flat. In it stood a huge man with a lamp buckled to his belt and thrusting a long oar into the sand, as if he were about to push off. His face was illuminated from below. On his head the man had an enormous straw hat, but it only covered half his hair, which was long and fell down onto his neck and over his ears. He had a snow-white walrus moustache and the ends were twisted and twirled and hung down well out from his face. Eyebrows, nose, cheekbones, they all resembled the portrait of the Hussite general, Zizka von Trocnow. Only the ferryman was no longer grey but yellowy white and seemed to be as old as the hills.

As Lucas approached the ferry he looked up. "What do you want?" he asked in an unfriendly tone and with the voice of a soldier from the days when you could still buy your way out of the army.

"I want to cross over."

"Why do you? Now? In the dark?"

"I must search."

The old boatsman began to laugh. "And where will you spend the night, my good sir?"

"Nowhere ... or in the wood ... what do I know?"

"In you get, quickly."

That was a lot friendlier already. With a mighty heave the old man pushed the boat off. A chain screeched in the water. Now the ferryman tucked his chin into his chest and the top of the oar against his shoulder. And thus he went, panting, snorting, pressing his whole life against the water, from the higher bows along the whole length of the boat, that was working its way forward at an angle to the current. Every time the old man had completed one length, one attack, he returned to the bows, dragging his oar behind him through the water.

The lamp at his breast twinkled and swayed. Lucas started. The old boatsman's eyes gave off a brighter light than the lamp! They stood above the blurred shapes of the water and the night like two unpredictable blue flames. After each thrust of the oar they seemed to grow wilder, to shine out farther. When they had reached the middle of the stream the old man paused from his work and spoke to his passenger.

"You might find what you are looking for at my house."

"What am I looking for, then?" said Lucas absently, trailing his fingers through the black water.

"You don't need to think I am stupid, young man! You are searching for a dream."

"Yes. I am searching for a dream I cannot remember. But how it is that you know that?"

"Don't let that worry you. It's nothing to do with the matter", said the ferryman in a deep, loud voice, turning his staring blue flames towards him..

Lucas closed his eyes.

"You could find your dream in my sloop, should the night be graciously inclined towards you. That's why I say you should spend the night with me."

Lucas was silent.

"Now then, there's no need to give yourself airs and make a fuss. Or do you find the idea of spending the night in my sloop so unpleasant, does it go against the grain? What? You silly boy! Other gentlemen have spent the night here and found their dream. Quite different gentlemen, fine gentlemen, the very finest! What do you say to my invitation?" The old man had thrown his straw hat away. His thick, long white locks bobbed up and down round his head. He held his oar high in the air. The reflection of the pale light behind the clouds lay on him and on the water.

Not at all apprehensive, with a feeling of reverence Lucas said, "Yes, I will spend the night in your house."

"House? That's neither here nor there! It's a sloop! You can see it now. Right by the water, my dear young man."

The ferry landed. The old man immediately tied it up then waited for Lucas to jump down from the side.

"The toll", he said seriously.

Lucas paid the ten pennies.

Then they both headed for the boat that served as a shack, the old man leading the way, this time carrying the lamp in his hand.

The ferryman led Lucas into a low room and hung the lamp on a nail. It was high enough for the room to be quite well lit and Lucas could see everything in it.

At first sight it did not look much different from the crib of an untidy and alcoholic worker. The inside window was open. On the shelf were empty and broken bottles, half a flowerpot, a bag of nails scattered everywhere and all sorts of other things. The things on the rough deal table in the middle of the room were in a mess as well: two beer glasses, greasy paper with left-over scraps of food, a small paraffin lamp and a few torn-up news-papers. But one wall was taken up with a wide bed with fresh, snow-white sheets. It was turned down, and seemed to be wait-ing for a guest, for a gentlemanly occupant. On a table of its own by the wall opposite was an ancient model of a galley such as came into use at the time of Columbus. But what most captured his eye were the countless pictures, large and small, which papered the wall, and of which some, like the last dwarf pines in the mountains, even crept up as far as the ceiling. Above the bed hung a very large oleograph. It represented God the Father, a huge figure seated in the clouds; at His feet, His hand outst-retched in a gesture of authority, Christ the Son, and flying down to earth in a halo of light, the dove of the Holy Ghost. That would not have been anything special, for it is a print that can be found in many peasant houses. But right next to it was a picture of a different trinity: Uranus at the top with his arms round Cronus, on whose knees a youthful Zeus was sitting. A third picture showed a mighty idol in the form of a phallus with two arms outstretched and each hand holding a further idol. A fourth picture seemed to represent an Egyptian trinity, a fifth the Tri-murti, a sixth the Nordic group of three gods, a seventh the Indian. And when Lucas looked closely he could see on all the pictures the same motif of the genealogy of the gods and the trinity.

His sight grew dim. Truly, a strange chapel, this boats-man's hut. While Lucas' soul was held in thrall by the countless gruesomely mysterious pictures, the ancient ferryman had sat down in a armchair, pulled off first one heavy boot then the other with a groan, and thrown them clattering to the floor. Now he stood up; barefoot and with swaying steps he came to Lucas' side. He seemed to be taller than before. His head touched the ceiling!

"Well may you stare, my lad", he said. "Comes to look for his dream and finds the most unusual collection!"

He pointed to the picture of God the Father, Christ and the Holy Ghost. "Father, son and holy ghost, and the same, again and again." His finger described a circle.

"Always the same. Father and son, father and son. Excellent. The third weak and watery, a hypocrite beside them, begets not and is the vindication of all kinds of wind-bags. Father and son. Everywhere father and son. Excellent!"

Suddenly his expression darkened.

"Always father and son. But who has heard of the *Grandfather?* Just as he is a father, so he must have a father. And as he begets, so he must have been begotten. Who has heard of the grandfather?"

The eyes of the old giant were clear, fiery and fearful. His whole body trembled. In the curve of his back there was something of the proud humility of one who has been dethroned. At that moment Lucas could understand the pain he felt. He gave him a deep look. The old man noticed it and suddenly changed the subject.

"My son, this bed is waiting for you. Lay yourself to rest. May you find here the dream you have lost."

Lucas obeyed. All his wakefulness and strength seemed suddenly to have left him.

The ferryman waited until he was finished. Then he took the lamp and turned to the door. Lucas sat up.

"What do they call you?"

The old man's voice suddenly took on a squeaky, toothless tone as he replied, "Well ... Grandfather, that's what people call me."

This was the dream vision that appeared to Lucas in that night.

He was lying, dead and rigid, on a massive catafalque swathed in black; however, he was not in a coffin, but in a

113

hollow in the catafalque which fitted the dimensions of a human body. His head alone was raised, resting on a pillow. To his right and left were two similarly sized depressions in the black trestle. He could not move, he was not breathing, and the unbeating inertia of his heart, the immense feeling of repose in his body, which was stretched out loosely, as if after terrible exertions, all said to him, 'It is over. You are dead'.

His eyes were open. He could see everything. And he saw that he was lying in the middle of a huge cathedral. The height of the vaulted roof was enormous, impossible to gauge. Immediately above his head, however, it had been pierced by a circular opening through which burnt a sky of deep gold, pouring its molten ore over his face without injuring or blinding him. His heart was not beating. His mind was not thinking. And yet: *he existed*. But this existence was a bliss which could be compared with nothing else. Whether hours, years or seconds passed, he knew not. The golden fire in the opening of the pantheon remained the same. Now and then gigantic storks flew over the cupola. Lucas could clearly see their legs hanging down gracefully like red threads below their wing-span.

All at once the three doors of the cathedral flew open: the massive middle door and the two somewhat smaller side-doors. At first there was nothing to be seen apart from the exuberance of a day such as the earth, such as no planet has ever known. A divine conflagration of all the colours streamed into the church, but all the dead man felt was, 'This is the true day'. And behold, in the middle door stood the old ferryman. With his height he reached to the point of the arch over the doorway. In his hand he held his oar, but now it was made of gold. From his shoulders to his feet a blue cloak hung round him.

Through the side-doors two processions entered, keeping pace with one another. In each, six masked figures bore a bier and placed it by the catafalque. Every step, every movement on the right and left was in time. From each bier they lifted a corpse and laid it in one of the hollows beside Lucas. It was all done very quickly. Hardly was the task finished than the cathedral doors closed; the ferryman and the masked figures had vanished and Lucas was alone with the two dead bodies.

Was it that his dream was interrupted, or was it that he became confused? Whichever it was, it seemed to Lucas that a long night had fallen and he kept his eyes shut.

And he woke once more in the cathedral, dead and stretched out on his catafalque. But the light in the dome had changed. It was hard, milky, dawning, and it did not stream but dripped. Before him, however, stood the old man. This time his oar was of ivory, his cloak black and embroidered with tiny silver magic stars. Each of the points at the end of his moustache had a bell hanging from it which jingled at every movement. And Lucas heard the old man's voice,

"Up you get, sleepy-head. Perhaps you will find what you are looking for here."

He touched him with his oar. Lucas felt life return to him and stood up on the top of the catafalque. He wanted to address the old man. But he had disappeared.

Lucas looked behind. The two other corpses, who had been laid out next to him, were also standing. The harsh light flowed softly round their apparition.

They were both men, the one in the prime of life, the other young, still almost a boy. Both were the same height and had the same figure as Lucas.

Although he had awoken from the dead, his vision was still veiled. He still could not recognise the faces of his companions. A breeze passed through the church.

The lights swayed.

And now Lucas recognised the older man. It was his father. How happy, beaming and red-cheeked was his face! The hair of his head and beard was thick and black, his posture defiant and swelled with the breath of health. That was not how his son remembered him. His memory was of a tired, sick man who dragged himself from one chair to another, a grey head at the table who groaned and fell asleep early. And yet perhaps, in the drawer of some forgotten desk, there was a photograph in which his father looked as he did now, so handsome, so manly, so *brotherly*.

Lucas felt himself crying. His bashfulness was gone, his bashfulness towards the man, the severe judge who sat in the bay window and demanded to see the maths test with red ink scrawled all over it. Without apprehension now, without fear or hatred, he went up to the man who had come through the trial of death at his side in this cathedral. He grasped his father's hand: the warm, soft, heartfelt clasp of a man who knew how to live. And his father drew his hand to him and pressed it fervently to his heart. For the first time in his life the son felt his father's heart, his living heart, beating, and his own heart beat with awe at this mystical experience.

The catafalque had disappeared and the men were standing under the open dome on the stone flags of the church, father and son close to each other, the youth a little way off.

Then his father said to Lucas, "Come", and led him by the hand to the youth.

Lucas looked at him and thought, 'My father has black hair, mine is brown and he is blond.'

Everything became brighter and brighter.

The young man gave the two a joyful laugh. His long hair waved, as if blowing in the wind. He was as sharp and strong as a blast from a trumpet, and the laugh of acceptance of the world never left his countenance.

His father leant over to Lucas and whispered, "We know each other, but he is our perfection." And Lucas saw that his father was crying, and tears of an unknown joy were running down his face, too. He could not stop them. He fell to his knees and kissed the feet of the handsome, laughing boy. But the kiss was a magic spell.

A great thunder arose, the cathedral broke like a delicate castle of glass and was gone.

But the three held each other by the hand; Lucas in the middle, his father on the left, the youth on the right. All around them raged vast festivities. The golden light and the unearthly conflagration of colours had returned. A thousand columns of people with fiery banners and huge, gleaming musical instruments were mingling in a dance of profound but incomprehensible design. The three, however, were taller than all the rest. Lucas could feel the waves of the throng breaking against his hips. He was aware that what he was feeling was the highest joy of creation. A thousand hymns sounded around him, but all had these words,

"See them marching, see them marching,
Generations without end."

Now he was floating up a hill of a tender green colour, his father holding his left hand, the youth his right. Women, whose dresses had slipped down from their breasts, threw themselves to their knees before them and begged them to touch them in blessing. But Lucas and his companions strode through the adoration of the thousand women. His gaze was fixed on the summit of the mountain. There stood the old ferryman. Now his cloak was of gold, his oar from some radiant, transparent metal. The little bells on his moustache were jingling wildly. In his free hand he held his lamp. The flame in it was invisible. Nearer and nearer Lucas came to the old man. Nearer and nearer! Then the flame in the lamp seemed to come to life, became brighter and brighter. But everything else grew pale.

And now the lamp was very bright and passing over his eyes.

He had woken up. The old man was leaning over his bed, shining the light on him.

"Up we get, young man, time you were out of the sheets. I have to go to my work."

Lucas sat up in bed. It was early dawn.

"Well, did you find your dream in my room?"

"There was a dream. It was a magnificent dream, but a different one from the one I lost."

"So you will have to continue your journey", said Grandfather with a furious expression.

"There, have your breakfast." He handed Lucas a large bowl of coffee and a slice of bread.

Lucas ate and drank.

Then they both went out into the open. Lucas had not cast one more glance at the pictures of the deities. He was afraid of them. In his soul rang out the words, 'Search, search.'

They came to the ferry. The old man untied it. On the other bank Lucas could see figures in the half-light. They looked like shades in Hades, waiting to be carried across the Styx.

"Where should I go now?" asked Lucas.

The old man pointed his hand straight in the general direction of the forest.

"Keep walking until it is evening. In different lodgings you will have more luck. Farewell."

The unrest in Lucas was reawakened. He did not look round again and walked into the forest.

Again he spent the whole day wandering through the vast forest. His eyes were turned inwards, but the dream of the night was unable to tie them down. They looked deeper and did not see what they were looking for. The youth was the first of the dream figures to fade. Lucas did not know who he was or what his significance was. His heart no longer recognised him. His father, too, soon changed back, in his consciousness, into the person he had been when he had sat at table, or in the bay window with the rug over his feet, making remarks about the passers-by.

A mysterious shyness stopped Lucas from thinking about the ferryman who called himself Grandfather. He never again wanted to think back to the horrible sorcery of the pictures of the gods in the boatsman's parlour.

The forest and the mountain meadows, the torrent and the mossy rocks, which had accompanied him on his way yesterday, had been the right answer to the flutterings of his imprisoned soul. For on that day it had been filled with longing, homesick for a far-distant childhood. The rustle of the leaves, the bustle of the water, how soothing had been their serenade. Whenever he had passed a pit in the woods, he had shivered and an awesome, long-forgotten word from boyhood rose within him: cavernous.

But today it was a different longing that would not let him rest. He was no longer homesick for the past. He was homesick for the future, he felt a yearning, incomprehensible and strange.

He left the forest and for hours walked through the countryside, across freshly sprouting fields and heaths, past many orchards.

Everything was in bloom. And he knew, as he went narrow-eyed through the scent and sweet, clear mist, that all this today was a descant of blessings above the dull vibrations of the puzzle within him.

But he was as restless as the day before. The most he could manage was to rest for a quarter of an hour on some bank or other. Then he was dragged straight back to his feet again: 'Keep going, keep going.'

Towards evening he reached some hills that were unknown to him. Misty blue conical hills that grew all of a jumble together. They looked like the hills in Chinese pictures. He came across people as well: an old man in a soldier's uniform carrying a mess tin, a beggar-woman squatting by the roadside, someone tottering down the mountain track with a pole carrying two tubs balanced across his shoulders. He had to go through a village. Tousled girls passed him driving geese. In the village square, beside the pond where ducks were quacking and boys splashing about in the shallow water, a beautiful tall lime tree already had its first leaves. Next to it was the shrine with a statue of the Madonna. From the knob at the top hung a bell on an iron ring. An idiot was pulling the rope and ringing down the evening. Lucas continued along the village street. When the village was a long way behind him he had to pass an inn. It was called "The Seven Devils". Whenever the door opened a brief wave of noise, music from an orchestrion, the stamping of dancers and the stench of beer poured out from the bar.

"Don't stop", he said aloud. The road kept climbing higher and higher towards the east. Above a mountain half the disc of the sun was still to be seen. Violet, pink and yellow glaciers surged above the wooded slopes and melted in the valleys. Lucas suddenly turned off the road and climbed up a hill. Then he went along the edge of the wood and came to a small farmhouse which, however, did not look quite like a farmhouse.

He stopped; his heart was beating wildly.

A woman appeared in the doorway. She was very tall. She wore no scarf on her head and her blond hair blazed in the evening light. But Lucas saw that at the side, at her temples, two thick grey strands were twisted into her massive crown of hair. She was not dressed as a peasant but was wearing a wide black dress of plain cloth, that, however, did not look particularly out of place in the doorway of the farmhouse. Her feet were bare and, in spite of the toil along stony tracks, the early rising and all the housework, white and without crooked toes. She was no longer young, but not old either.

"Welcome", she said in a deep voice. "I was expecting you."

"You knew that I would come?"

"You were announced." She raised her strong, right arm, letting the sleeve fall back.

"Do you know ..."

The woman interrupted Lucas.

"I do know. You will find a bed for the night here. Come."

She stepped back into the door. Lucas followed her. Her walk! It was calm, sublime. In spite of her beauty, Lucas felt no surge of desire. He sensed, 'That is no mortal woman!' They entered the parlour.

On the threshold Lucas could not restrain himself and asked, "Who are you?"

"The wife of the miner."

The room was low and filled with a colourful dusk. Lucas saw a mattress, furs and blankets, but no white linen. There was nothing white to be seen at all. In one corner was a gigantic globe. It was covered all over with sharp nails made from a wide variety of metals. Christ was standing on it on one foot, like a dancer piercing his old wounds with new nails at every step. Two huge cupboards stood close by each other, like neighbouring mountains. From one a very large amethyst druse with marvellous crystals shone down, from the other the bronze interlacings of a massive block of aragonite.

Lucas went over to the globe.

"What is that?" he asked.

"That is the Saviour ever pierced with nails."

"Did his sufferings not end on the cross?"

"No. Now he suffers more, since he dances over the sharp pins."

"Why are the nails made from different metals?"

"The hard heart of the earth takes many forms."

"But what is his sorrow?"

"The greatest."

"And what is the greatest sorrow?"

"Fulfilment destroyed", said the woman.

Lucas did not grasp the contradiction of these last two words; but he knew that only a woman could have spoken them.

The woman left him alone for a while.

Then she came back and set a meal before him, and put a glass of dark-red wine on the table as well and last of all a candle, for it was already quite dark.

Lucas thanked her. A feeling of great awe stopped him from eating in the presence of this dark, mysterious woman, to whom he had been announced and who knew about his seeking heart.

In the meantime she was going about some puzzling business.

There was a small, low table standing in a corner. On it were three little vases with dried flowers. In them the woman put fresh posies of spurge laurel. Then she dusted the table and laid a cloth over it. She placed the vases in a row and in front of each one a tiny, flat lamp with a little flame. In front of each of the lamps she placed one small bowl with milk and one with wheat grains. Lucas watched her, spellbound. She straightened up and stood there, tall in her black dress, tucking her arms into the wide sleeves as if she felt cold.

"It is for the children ..." And then, after a silence, "Good night. I hope that you find your dream." And with that the miner's wife had disappeared through the door.

This was the dream that Lucas dreamt in the second night.

He is walking through a marvellous, overgrown park full of blossom, keeping to the soft gravel path in the glittering sunshine. His heart is filled with a solemn strength. A brook is whispering at his side. Whole clouds of white butterflies lurch past overhead. Sometimes there is a bench, with no one sitting on it; wagtails bob up and down on willow branches which dip into the water; warmth and song is in the air. He walks quickly, tapping with his stick in rhythm on the gravel. Suddenly he notices that there is a figure far in front of him taking the same path. As he comes nearer he sees that it is a woman. She is wearing a flowing dress of gold brocade, but has thrown a shawl of grey crepe over it. He knows who this woman is whom he has never seen, and his body tenses with joy. He reaches her, goes trembling up to her side and says, "Beloved woman."

"My man", and his eyes and hers mingle.

"Why did you go on ahead?"

She, "Well, now you have caught me up."

He kisses her! Then he dreams of himself speaking.

"How is it possible! How is it possible! I know I had the heart of a dreamer, but it was fleeting and transient, as the hearts of dreamers are. From the gallery of the great opera houses I saw the beauties in their boxes. Tears poured from my eyes when an ethereal foot jumped down from the carriage-step. Once I spent many hours every day for a whole year standing at a tramway stop, because I once saw a woman board the brightly coloured carriage there. Two years later I found her. But my dream had become more powerful than the woman herself. Even the meekness of her hair could no longer help her. But now! Now you are here before I dreamt you and that is your great power. How was it possible?"

"Yes!" she said. "What all I had to go through! To be kissed in my sleep and not to know it! That sleep, all the time! And that after a childhood full of fear, after great ambition and girlhood radiance. I with the children in the last room. They are not allowed to scream, to cry. But he, the good master, ponders and ponders. And his high countenance reaches perfection. He is tired. In the night I have to stand outside chemists' shops. He becomes more and more tired. His thin lips will hardly close any more and his powerful teeth lie open in the effort of will. Then comes that day. I pass my hand over his forehead damp with the sweat of fear, and trembling he kisses this hand for the last time. But where was I then? Where was I? I must have everything around me. Everything! Everything!"

Lucas feels as if a wild, demented urge to destroy suddenly shoots out from her eyes. But then she says, gently and almost with a tiny fear,

"But you, my only one, you belong to me!"

And Lucas feels an almost malicious pride within him.

"Yes. I am enough for you."

"Oh my beloved! I have lived. The beasts both wild and

gentle gather round me. But you have woken me from the death that was that life."

They sit down on a bench. Somewhere an orchestra is playing. Above the orchestra floats the pure voice of a singer. She is singing an Italian cavatina.

Lucas feels himself speak.

"Is this melody not like a sweet mountain goat that a divine bearded huntsman chases from mountain to mountain? Now it is tumbling down the rocks of its cadenza and lies at our feet. Dead – Blest!"

"How you touch the heart of my heart."

"I spoke of music."

"We alone know what it is."

"It is our acceptance of God", he says.

"It is our acceptance of God's world", she says.

They stand up, they walk through endless meadows in silence.

Suddenly they find themselves by a huge Indian temple. Grotesque dancing idols stare down at them.

"We must enter." She strides on ahead. Lucas follows her.

Now they are in a large courtyard. In the middle a basin spreads its massive circle. But instead of mud and patches of water all that is to be seen is ashes, cinders with, here and there, a little flame still spurting up. In the middle of the basin rises a fountain-pipe, to which a long string is attached. "Your metal is full of dead stone, my love. You must step into the bath to purify yourself." Lucas jumps into the basin. She pulls the string. A wild rain of fire pours over him, without burning him. He steps out of his bath. "Am I pure now?" he asks. "Somewhat purer", she laughs. "But that was not fire, just fireworks, beautiful to look at." They leave the temple by the other side. Now it is summer. The corn stands high, ready for harvest, and the ears burst, just like a violin string breaking. Cornflowers and poppies everywhere, wayberries too, and the beautiful corncockle. The sun is burning hot.

"Oh, how warm is this ripening within me", says the woman. "I am nature. I."

The wind blows a lock over her forehead. She strokes it back with her hand.

'How beautiful that is', thinks Lucas.

And he says, "How beautiful you are. I love you."

She does not look at him. But a soft, blissful groan passes her lips. "This whole seething star is within me."

With a movement of her hand she swells the air, as if she were caressing the invisible pregnancy of a spirit.

Then she kisses him passionately.

"I never knew there was such a thing."

"I never knew it either."

"I thought there could be no such thing as happiness and that people lied because they did not dare to admit it to themselves."

"I thought it was the ugliest thing and brought nothing but disgust and exhaustion, which we men concealed in order not to be cruel."

"And now we have felt it." She takes his hand.

"Oh, hand, hand, hand", he says.

And she, "Now the evening is coming."

Lucas is standing with the woman by an open window. Outside it is dark and the garden is humming.

"Tonight I shall kiss you."

"I feel blissful", she says.

"Do you feel blissful because you have me?"

"Yes, but there is something else as well that makes me feel blissful, my love."

"Will I be permitted to kiss you tonight?"

"You will be forbidden to do anything else!"

Outside an angry bird begins its ugly, rasping call.

"Is that an evil sign?" he asks.

And she answers, "I do not know."

"Is what we are doing sinful?"

But she laughs.

And they embrace each other.

A terrace. How warm this night is. She is sitting, golden dark, in an armchair. Lucas, his hands behind his head, is lying on the ground staring into the stars.

"If we were crossing the equator those stars could be the Southern Cross."

A fixed star begins to sparkle coldly and in a hundred colours, like an evil splinter of ice. Lucas sees the secret star grow and grow. He senses, 'Now, in this very moment, the pitiless eye of the hunter has seen us."

'Don't speak', the voice within him calls out anxiously. But he is already saying it. "I feel an evil star above us."

He feels as if a whip should lash him across the back immediately: the punishment.

But she says, and fear is in her voice, "Don't look up and don't speak of those things."

The bird starts up again. Its croaking is powerful. It rasps as if it had a long, saw-tooth beak and were cutting down the trees in the garden, the trees of life, the forest of life. Lucas thinks, 'I will not mention it.' He looks at her and feels, 'She behaves as if she could hear nothing.'

Then, "Is there not a fatal trap laid for love?"

"Which one?"

"Desire."

There are tears in her eyes.

He goes on, "I feel now what the curse of dissipation is. It digresses. It distances itself from the loved one and that is how it kills." He throws himself down before her and whispers,

"We must become more and more like brother and sister to each other."

Now they are in a room. She is wearing a gown of white gauze and holding a candle in her hand.

The bird continues to saw through the night.

She shivers and says, "Close the window."

Lucas is sleeping. He is enveloped in a sweet smell of thyme. Suddenly he seems to hear a dreadful knocking at the door. He wakes up, jumps out of bed. And now he is on the staircase of a big house. Many people are running up and down in haste and terror. Women with their hair loose and in night attire. Some are carrying bowls and towels, some burning candles. They are all whimpering and moaning. He can hear words, "The woman!" "She is dying!" "Before it's too late!" "Send for help!" "The woman!"

Raving, he dashes out of the house, screaming, bellowing. He runs through the garden and clears the fence in one bound.

It is already morning. Cloud-giants float past. He races down a slope for many thousand yards; undergrowth throws itself in his path; he becomes entangled. And still he cries,

"God, God, God!"

Now he runs into a swamp, sinking in farther and farther. The mire reaches up to his chest. He is at the end of his tether. But he manages to work his way out. Now he is on the road. He cannot grasp anything any more.

On tiptoe he enters a room. She is dying in her bed. A cloth is across her forehead. She is so beautiful, her physical matter is floating. He curses the evil body in his clothes. He drags himself to her bed and falls to his knees.

"I am to blame!"

"There is no blame." She smiles, and in that second she is the triumph of the heathen world.

"I have killed you."

"We have killed", she comforts him softly.

He wails, "You must not die! You cannot die!"

But she says, and her features become glorious,

"If I die, then I am sacrificing myself for your destiny. Oh dreamer without pain! Harsh must be the reality that is to become reality for you. You must have reality, or you will never live or die.

Oh my lover, perhaps you are in hell."

She raises herself up a little, "Write your name on a piece of paper. They must put it under my tongue. That is how much I have loved you."

"Live ... live ... live", babbles Lucas.

She says, "What could have been the most sacred part, our perfection, has gone." She places her hand on Lucas' head as he

126

kneels before her. "Now go."

"Where?" he asks.

"Search, search", is the last he hears.

And then he awoke. Beside his bed stood the miner's wife. Now she wore a scarf over her head and a shawl round her shoulders.

"The hour has come, I must go to join my husband in the pit."

He looked round, confused. Outside dawn was just beginning to break.

"Did you find your lost dream?"

"No. It was not that one. It was another one. A sweet and terrible one."

The woman set milk and bread before him. He ate and drank. She watched him eating, and said,

"What was commanded us both has taken place. You found lodgings in my room."

"I have come closer to what I am searching for", he replied, "but I have not yet met it."

"You will certainly meet with it at the third time."

Now both were standing outside the door.

She bore two vessels in her hands. In one was milk, in the other red wine.

'That is the offering that is put for the dead at the entrance of the underworld', thought Lucas. And then he addressed himself, 'Where to now?'

In kindness, the woman took his hand.

"Keep on going straight through the forest. Let yourself be led. If you have not found your dream by midday, it is lost for ever. Climb Oak Hill when it appears before you. I have been there myself. There my dearest comes to meet me in the midday light. Women are not barred from reaching that place, but men always are, unless they are sent."

He felt that the miner's wife was no longer holding his hand. When he looked up, she was gone.

Once more Lucas entered the forest and walked for hour after hour. But this day there were no clearings, no valleys interrupting the forest and nothing jerked the wanderer out of his self-absorption. All the time his thoughts were with the woman in the dream, how she had lain there dying, and once more he felt himself sinking into the swamp, screaming for God; his fear had been reawakened, and all the dreamwords were like a cool air across the back of his neck.

His first day's journey had been homesickness, his second day's journey yearning, and that of the third day, love. It was midday, and every breath and odour was silent. And there was the hill covered with old oak trees that the miner's wife had spoken of. Did this hill live somewhere in his memory? Had he been at this place in his childhood? Lucas suppressed these notions. Then he followed a little footpath up the hill. On the top, in the middle of the oak wood was a clearing, and in this clearing was a large, low, round half-timbered building, old-fashioned, with gleaming windows. The whole was inexpressibly clean. The double doors stood wide open and a glistening gravel path ran through it.

Lucas went through the door into the yard. He was compelled to close his eyes, for he felt, 'I have dreamt all this.'

The sky above this yard was immeasurably blue. A lark was plunging up and down in the blue, beside itself with song. There was a raised pavement round the shrill white walls. And on this pavement a hundred strange things stood next to each other, blinding the eye.

They were all mechanical toys, a delight for children and simple minds. Lucas saw a puppet theatre. A conductor cut out of cardboard was raising his baton, but the curtain was down. Next to it was a little ebony Savoyard, holding the handle of his hurdy-gurdy. Here was a mechanical pierrot in white baggy trousers, over there a group of statues representing a scene from the life of Napoleon, and then a barrel organ and other mechanical instruments; all these and many others too.

For a moment Lucas forgot everything. A wild surge of childhood seized him again. He ran over to the mechanical toys and stared at them, engrossed.

Suddenly he felt that his right side was leaning down and that he was holding something warm and delicately small in his hand. It was a child's hand. A small child was looking at him.

Lucas felt a shock that spread to the last recesses of his being, a shock such as only people can know who have passed close to death, close to the abyss of extreme knowledge, or who have met themselves. It was his lost dream. Who was this beautiful, lively child with the soft blond hair and the most profound wisdom in his face, full of observant otherness? On his childish features lay the wisdom of those creatures who have never become estranged from themselves by birth or become one with themselves in the moment of death. But what was that? Were those not his features, right down to the last detail? Was that his childhood? Was that the design which he had been, to which he had inevitably failed to match up? Was it he himself? Was it his ...

He was overcome by an unknown, infinitely warm feeling, and yet the mysterious shock did not leave him.

Then the child said, "Go on, put a penny in."

They were standing in front of the puppet theatre. He put the coin in the slot. The curtain flew up. A thin, ragged, chirrupping polka started. On the stage a few little puppets in pink and sky-blue tutus revolved jerkily and without rhythm. One kept halting, another whirled round like mad on its axle. Then it was finished, and the curtain fell even more quickly than it had risen.

The boy gave Lucas' hand a squeeze.

"That was lovely, let's see some more."

They went over to the Savoyard. Again Lucas put a coin in the slot. The motor rattled. The brown hand on the crank moved in short jerks and, with much whistling and jingling, an ancient, almost mythical tune from an operetta rang out and then suddenly broke off.

"Good." The boy nodded his head.

"Let's go on."

Lucas made the clown dance and contort its limbs.

The child laughed wildly with joy.

Lucas lifted him up and looked him in the face. "Yes, it is you. Come with me. Come with me. Away from the beautiful playground. I will buy you other toys, much more beautiful ones."

The boy had an earnest expression.

"You can't take me with you."

"Why not?"

"Because only my mummy can take me."

"Where is your mummy?"

"Not here", said the child.

But Lucas kissed him passionately.

"I know where your mother is. She has not died. She is alive. I spoke to her last night. I'll carry you to her, my child. We'll find her, we shall find her."

The child shook his head.

"We must to talk to grandmother."

"Where is your grandmother?"

"In there."

"In the house?"

"Come, I'll show you her."

The child leads Lucas into the parlour of a farmhouse. There is a smell of decay. Spider's webs stick a thousandfold to the ceiling and to the arch over the low window. There is a wooden partition dividing the room in two. The old woman is sitting at the spinning wheel, right at the back in the half-light, in an ancient peasant costume, with a headdress from years gone by: no, it is a model, a doll. The grandmother is filled with straw and she does not move.

"Grandmother", calls the child.

The figure moves, creaks and stands up. It takes a few steps and becomes quite human. Now she comes to the barrier. She seems not to see Lucas properly at all. "There you are, sonny", says the grandmother in a strange dialect.

The child stammers, "Just think, grandmother, he wants to take me with him. He's seen mummy as well."

"First they send you to foster parents and then ..."

She lifts the child over the barrier and he holds up the palms of his hands.

Lucas sees the lines of his own hands. He feels, 'Never will I forget these little hands.'

Already without hope he says, "Grandmother, give me the child."

The grandmother does not listen to him. She takes the boy in her arms. He suddenly seems much smaller and is crying softly.

He too is like a wax doll.

"We're closing now", the grandmother barks at Lucas.

He leaves the room, he leaves the playground, he leaves the gate.

Only when he is back in the clearing does he turn round.

But by then the playground has disappeared and the *dream he had found again.*

He goes to the other side of the hill and sees before him the small town, which he had left three days ago.

How tired he is, infinitely tired.

"Now I have to go down there", he says out loud.

A Fragment of a Distant Event

Friedrich von Gagern

There was a mysterious experience connecting a Silesian lady – Polish to be precise – a certain Fräulein von R., with one of my relatives on my father's side who died – actually he was killed – long ago: Karl, usually called Carlos von Gagern.

This Carlos von Gagern was less well-known than my great-grandfather, the colleague of Goethe who came as near as one could to being his friend, the minister and favourite of Talleyrand who bustled to and fro at the Congress of Vienna; and he was less well-known than my great-uncle Friedrich, the general who was shot in the back by Hecker's Red Brigade at Kandern whilst carrying the white flag of truce, or than his brother Heinrich, the President of the National Assembly at Frankfurt in 1848, celebrated for his "boldness" in acting without consulting the princes; this Carlos von Gagern was even less well-known than my grandfather and is not to be found in any history book or encyclopaedia, yet he was by far the most interesting and adventurous of all our family.

He'd knocked around America quite a bit; had been Colonel of Engineers with Emperor Maximilian in Mexico; fought, or rather took part in secret missions, in the Carlist Wars; later – or in between – he had established and edited a soldiers' magazine in Vienna called *The Little Comrade*. Politics was the breath of life to such a wily old bird, who had been out in all wind and weather; not the politics of his cousins, in their grand ministries or at international congresses, but the ostensibly less important underground activity that in fact determined all the rest. This Carlos von Gagern must have belonged to secret societies. There was always a smell of conspiracy about him. His mysterious peregrinations were haunted by figures in masks or false beards: the *Camorra*, the *Vehmgericht*, secret lodges – no one knew for sure, neither while he was alive, nor after his death. And his relationship to the Polish lady remained unclear: was she his mistress? A confidential agent? What the events that follow do suggest is that there must have been a close spiritual bond between them.

At that time Fräulein von R. was living in Silesia. One night, after she had spent a long time writing letters, she was just tidying up her small sitting room prior to going to bed, arranging her correspondence, putting out the lamp and lighting the candle, when she heard a dull thud that seemed close behind her and yet to come from deep under the ground. She assumed the velvet curtain over the door to her bedroom had come loose and slumped to the floor, so she turned round, raised the candle and to her horror saw her friend, Carlos von Gagern, lying on his back in front of the curtain over the doorway to her bedroom, looking as if he were dead in spite of his staring eyes. Seeing him there she forgot that he was nowhere in the vicinity, never mind in the house, but travelling somewhere in the far north. With trembling hand she set the candlestick down and bent over the prostrate body; at the very moment she was about to touch it, the figure disappeared in a flash and the doorway was empty.

It was part of a clairvoyant vision, a fragment of a distant event, romantic, uncanny and hardly believable.

At the time Carlos was staying in Denmark – or was it Schleswig? – in an old castle, where he had a strange adventure, from the little he later revealed of it.

Presumably it was not without reason, or some suspicion, that he had gone to the castle. Whether on the night in question he had been woken by some noise, whether he had been prying round on his own account or whether from the very start he had been on the scent of a particular prey, whether he had been sent for or lured: whatever the reason, he had followed a masked figure through dark, twisting, secret passageways and all at once, too abruptly to have any chance of pulling back, had found himself stepping into empty space and falling. Some time later – how long, he had no idea – he woke in a murky, candlelit vaulted chamber surrounded by a whole band of figures masked like the judges of the *Vehmgericht* and holding darkly gleaming knives.

Under threat of the daggers, he had had to swear a solemn oath that he would remain silent for a limited, but unspecified period.

Then he was blindfolded and taken back to his room, or to some part of the castle where he knew where he was. It was an extract from this experience that the Polish lady had seen, a brief pictorial transmission. What is certainly true is that when she wrote to tell him about it Carlos charged her to maintain absolute silence and begged her not to go recounting such nonsense to anyone. Too late; the feminine urge to communicate had already been satisfied. It had, however, no serious consequences; she had not seen what had really happened and so could not reveal it.

The first sequel to these events took place years later in the Grand Opera in Paris. An elegant gentleman came to see Carlos in his box. It was, he said, his honour and pleasure, in the name of a company he was sure Monsieur le Baron would well remember, to release Monsieur le Baron from his oath and to reveal what details he could of an incident that had taken place all those years ago in the presence of Monsieur le Baron. The League, he went on, had achieved its goal, fulfilled its purpose, and, in discharge of its final obligation, had the honour of requesting Monsieur le Baron to be good enough to accept this token. With that a plump, red leather wallet wrapped in silk lay before Carlos, who was perhaps not as surprised as one might imagine. The messenger had disappeared. From that time onwards he used to tell the story of his Danish adventure and its conclusion, though with a certain discretion as to the *dramatis personae*.

One might have presumed it was a romantic fiction designed to conceal the murky political origin of some sudden increase in his financial assets. However, some years later, on December 19, 1885, Fräulein von R. had a second mysterious experience.

To the hum of the paraffin lamp she had half fallen asleep over a book. In this state of complete relaxation, of semi-consciousness which means heightened receptivity, she heard a racket outside in the hall, a noisy clatter, a heavy fall. She started, staggered to her feet and grabbed the lamp to see what the cats had been up to again; as she turned towards the door, there was Carlos standing right in front of her, pale and bloody ... standing was not actually the right word: his head and torso were hovering in the semi-dark, gradually disappearing until all that was left was the hollow-cheeked face, then only the greenish glow of the eyes, then nothing.

Fräulein von R. used to compare this inexorable shrinking of the image to slowly tightening the string at the top of a bag. She had never seen the aperture on a camera, and the obvious comparison, the pupil of the eye, never occurred to her.

She knew that Carlos was in Madrid. Realising, from the previous occasion, the significance of her vision, she spent a sleepless, agitated night thinking about it and trying to decide what to do; the next morning she wrote a letter warning, or at least preparing, his family. Carlos had long since married and had grown-up children, one son, a talented musician, and one daughter. It was better they should be prepared for the worst rather than have the blow fall unexpectedly. A carefully doctored version of her vision was a reasonable vehicle for this message, still leaving hope that the worst might not have happened.

Once again her vision was confirmed.

On the evening of December 19, 1885, Carlos von Gagern had been murdered by a masked man outside the Opera in Madrid. Some connection with the earlier mysterious events is likely, but has never been explained.

The dead man had company on his journey to the other world. Five days later, on Christmas Eve, his thirty-year-old daughter Margarete, usually known as Dona Gretina, committed suicide. She could not live on without her beloved father; there had always been something otherworldly about her. She had made careful preparations, transforming her bed into a catafalque with black crepe and flowers; lit by the solemn light of funeral candles, she had stabbed herself to the heart with a stiletto.

The Nightwalk

From: *The White Dominican*
or: From the Diary of an Invisible Man

Gustav Meyrink

That night I had a strange experience; others would call it a dream, for men have only that one, inadequate word to describe everything that happens to them when their body is asleep.

As always before I went to sleep, I had folded my hands so that, as the Baron put it, "the left lay on the right".

It was only through experience over several years that I came to realise what the purpose of this measure was. It could be that any other position of the hands would serve the same purpose as long as they result in the feeling that 'the body is bound'.

Every time since that first evening in the Baron's house I had lain down to sleep in this manner, and every morning I had woken feeling as if I had walked a long way in my sleep, and every time I was relieved to see that I was undressed and not wearing dusty shoes in bed and need not fear being beaten for it, as had happened in the orphanage. But in the light of day I had never been able to remember where I had walked in my dream. That night was the first time the blindfold was taken from my eyes.

The fact that earlier in the evening the carpenter had treated me in such a remarkable way, like a grown-up, was probably the hidden reason why a self – perhaps my 'Christopher' – which had until then slept within me, now awoke to full consciousness and began to see and to hear.

I began by dreaming I had been buried alive and could not move my hands or my feet; but then I filled my lungs with mighty breaths and thus burst open the lid of the coffin; and I was walking along a white, lonely country road, which was more terrible than the grave I had escaped from, for I knew it would never come to an end. I longed to be back in my coffin, and there it was, lying across the road.

It felt soft, like flesh, and had arms and legs, hands and feet, like a corpse. As I climbed in, I noticed that I did not cast a shadow, and when I looked down to check, I had no body; then I felt for my eyes, but I had no eyes; when I tried to look at the hands that were feeling for them, I could see no hands.

As the lid of the coffin slowly closed over me, I felt as if all my thoughts and feelings as I was wandering along the white road had been those of a very old, if still unbowed, man; then when the coffin lid closed, they disappeared, just as steam evaporates, leaving behind as a deposit the half blind, half unconscious thoughts which normally filled the head of the half-grown youth that I was, standing like a stranger in life.

As the lid snapped shut, I woke in my bed.

That is, I thought I had woken up.

It was still dark, but I could tell by the intoxicating scent of elderflowers that came streaming in through the open window, that the earth was giving off the first breath of the coming morning and that it was high time for me to put out the lamps in the town.

I picked up my pole and felt my way down the stairs. When I had completed my task I crossed the wooden bridge and climbed up a mountain; every stone on the path seemed familiar, and yet I could not remember ever having been there before.

In the high meadows, still dark green in the glowing half-light and heavy with dew, alpine flowers were growing, snowy cotton grass and pungent spikenard.

Then the farthest edge of the sky split open, and the invigorating blood of the dawn poured into the clouds.

Blue, shimmering beetles and huge flies with glassy wings suddenly rose from the earth with a buzzing sound, and hovered motionless in the air at about head height, all with their heads turned towards the awakening sun.

When I saw, felt and comprehended this grandiose act of prayer from mute creation, a shiver of deepest emotion ran through my every limb.

I turned round and went back towards the town. My shadow preceded me, gigantic, its feet inseparably attached to mine. Our shadow, the bond that ties us to the earth, the black ghost that emanates from us, revealing the death within us, when light strikes our bodies!

The streets were blindingly bright when I entered them.

The children were making their noisy way to school.

'Why aren't they chanting, 'Doo'cot, doo'cot, diddlediddle doo'cot' at me as usual?' was the thought that awoke in my mind. 'Can they not see me? Have I become such a stranger to them that they don't know me any more? I have always been a stranger to them', I suddenly realised with a startlingly new awareness. 'I have never been a child! Not even in the orphanage when I was small. I have never played games as they do. At least whenever I did, it was only a mechanical motion of my body without my desire ever being involved; there is an old, old man living inside me and only my body seems to be young. The carpenter probably felt that yesterday, when he spoke to me like a grown-up.'

It suddenly struck me, 'But yesterday was a winter evening, how can today be a summer morning? Am I asleep, am I walking in my sleep?' I looked at the street lamps: they were out, and who but I could have extinguished them? So I must have been physically present when I put them out. 'But perhaps I am dead now and being in a coffin was real and not just a dream?' I decided to carry out a test, and went up to one of the schoolboys and asked him, "Do you know me?" He did not reply, and walked through me as through empty air.

'I must be dead then', I concluded, unconcerned. 'Then I must take the pole back home quickly, before I start to decompose', came the voice of duty, and I went upstairs to my foster father.

In his room I dropped the pole, making a loud noise.

The Baron heard it – he was sitting in his armchair – turned round and said, "Ah, there you are at last."

I was glad that he could see me, and concluded that I could not have died.

The Baron looked as he always did, was wearing the same coat with the jabot of mulberry lace that he always wore on feast days, but there was something about him that made him seem indefinably different. Was it his goitre? No, that was no larger or smaller than usual.

138

My eyes wandered round the room – no, that was unchanged, too. There was nothing missing, nothing had been added. Leonardo da Vinci's "Last Supper", the only decoration in the room, was on the wall as usual; everything in its usual place. Just a moment! That green plaster bust of Dante with the severe, sharp, monkish features, was it not on the right-hand end of the shelf yesterday? Has someone moved it round? It's on the left now.

The Baron noticed me looking round and smiled.

"You have been on the mountain?" he said, pointing to the flowers in my pocket which I had picked on the way.

I mumbled some excuse but he waved it aside. "I know; it's beautiful up there. I often go myself. You have often been there before, but you always forgot it afterwards. Young minds can't retain anything, their blood is still too hot; it washes the memory away. Did the walk make you tired?"

"Not on the mountain, but on ... on the white country road", I said, unsure whether he knew it.

"Ah, yes, the white road", he mused, "there are not many who can stand that. Only someone who is born a wanderer. It was because I saw that in you, all those years ago in the orphanage, that I brought you to live with me. Most people fear the road more than they fear the grave. They get back into their coffins because they think that is death and that it will bring them peace; but in reality the coffin is life, is the flesh. Being born on earth is nothing other than being buried alive! It is better to learn to walk the white road. Only one must not think of the end of the road, for it has no end. It is infinite. The sun on the mountain is eternal. Eternity and infinity are two different things. The only person for whom infinity and eternity are the same is one who seeks eternity in infinity and not the 'end'. You must walk along the white road for the sake of the walk itself, for the pleasure of walking and not to exchange one transient resting place with another.

Rest – not a resting place – can only be found in the sun on the mountain. It stands still and everything revolves round it. Even its herald, the dawn, radiates eternity, and that is why the insects and flies worship it and stay still in the air until the sun comes. And that is why you did not feel tired when you climbed the mountain."

He suddenly gave me a close look. "Did you see the sun?" he asked.

"No, father, I turned back before it rose."

He gave a satisfied nod. "That is good. Otherwise we would have nothing more to do with each other", he added under his breath. "And your shadow went before you, down towards the valley?"

"Yes. Of course ..."

He ignored my surprise.

"Anyone who sees the sun", he continued, "seeks eternity alone. He is lost for the road. They are the saints of the church. When a saint crosses over, he is lost to this world, and to the next one too. But what is worse, the *world* has lost *him;* it is orphaned! You know what it means to be a foundling; do not consign others to the fate of having neither father nor mother. Walk the road. Light the lamps until the sun comes of its own accord."

"Yes", I stuttered, thinking with horror of the terrible white road.

"Do you know what it means that you got back into your coffin?"

"No, father."

"It means that for yet a little while you will share the fate of those who are buried alive."

"Do you mean Mutschelknaus, the carpenter?" I asked in my childish way.

"I know no carpenter of that name; he has not yet become visible."

"Nor his wife and ... and Ophelia?" I asked, feeling myself blush.

"No; nor Ophelia either."

'Strange', I thought, 'they live just across the road, and he must see them every day.'

For a while we were both silent, and then I suddenly burst out sobbing, "But that is horrible! To be buried alive!"

"Nothing is horrible, my child, that you do for the sake of your soul. I, too, have been buried alive at times. On earth I have often met people who are wretched and in great need and who rail bitterly at the injustice of fate. Many of them sought comfort in the doctrine that came to us from Asia, the doctrine of the Karma which maintains that no being suffers unless it has sown the seed within itself in a former existence. Others seek comfort in the dogma of the unfathomable nature of God's designs. They all seek comfort, but none have *found* it.

I have lit a lamp for such people by inserting a thought" – his smile as he said that was almost grim, and yet at the same time as friendly as ever – "in their minds, but so delicately that they believe it came of its own accord. I ask them this question: 'Would you accept the agony of dreaming tonight, as clearly as if it were reality, that you lived through a thousand years of unimaginable poverty, if I assured you now that as a reward you would find a sack of gold outside your door when you woke in the morning.?'

'Yes! Of course!' is the answer every time.

'Then do not bemoan your fate. Are you sure that you did not choose this tormenting dream called life on earth which, at the worst, lasts seventy years, of your own free will, in the hope of finding something much more glorious than a miserable bag of money when you woke? Of course, if you sow a 'God with unfathomable designs' you will one day reap him as a malevolent devil.

Take life less seriously and dreams more so, then things will improve, then the dream can become your leader instead of, as now, going round as a garish clown in the motley shreds of our daytime memories.'

Listen, my child. There is no such thing as a vacuum. That sentence conceals the secret that everyone must unveil who wants to be transformed from a perishable animal to an immortal consciousness. Only you must not apply the words merely to external nature; you must use them like a key to open up the spiritual realm; you must transform their meaning. Look at it like this: someone wants to walk, but his feet are held fast in the earth; what will happen if his will to walk does not weaken? His creative spirit, the primal force that was breathed into him at the beginning, will find other paths for him to tread, and that force within him that can walk without feet, will walk in spite of the earth, in spite of the obstacle.

The creative will, man's divine inheritance, is a force of suction; this suction – you must understand it in metaphorical sense! – would of necessity create a vacuum in the realm of first causes, if the expression of the will were not eventually followed by its fulfilment. See: a man is ill and wants to get better; as long as he resorts to medicines, the power of the spirit, which can heal better and more quickly than any medicine, will be paralysed. It is as if someone wanted to learn to write with the left hand: if he always uses the right, he will never learn to do it with the left. Every event that occurs in our life has its purpose; nothing is pointless; an illness says to a man, 'Drive me away with the power of the spirit so that the power of the spirit will be strengthened and once more be lord over the material world, as it was before the Fall.' Anyone who does not do that and relies on medicines alone has not grasped the meaning of life; he will remain a little boy playing truant. But anyone who can command with the field marshall's baton of the spirit, scorning the coarser weapons that only the common soldier uses, will rise again and again; however often death strikes him down, he will yet be a king in the end. That is why men should never weaken on the path to the goal they have set themselves; just as sleep is only a brief rest, so is death. You do not begin a task in order to abandon it, but to complete it. A task, however unimportant it appears, once begun and left half finished, corrodes the will with its poison, just as an unburied corpse pollutes the air of the whole house.

The purpose of our life is the perfection of the soul; if you keep that goal firmly in your sights, and in your mind and your heart every time you begin or decide something, then you will find yourself possessed by a strange, unknown calm, and your destiny will change in an incomprehensible way. Anyone who creates as if he were immortal – not for the sake of the object of his desires, that is a goal for the spiritually blind, but for the sake of the temple of his soul – will see the day come, even if it is after thousands of years, when he can say, 'I will it' and what he commands will be there, will happen, without needing time to ripen slowly.

Only then will the point be reached where the long road ends. Then you can look the sun in the face without it burning your eyes. Then you can say, 'I have found a goal because I sought none.' Then the saints will be poor in understanding compared with you, for they will not know what you know: that eternity and rest can be the same as the road and the infinite."

These last words were far beyond my comprehension; it was only much later, when my blood was cool and my body manly, that they reappeared, clear and alive. But that morning I heard them with a deaf ear; I just looked at Baron Jöcher and, in a sudden flash of recognition, I realised what it was that had struck me as different about him, an odd thing, his goitre was on the right side of his neck, instead of the left as usual.

Today it sounds ridiculous, but I was seized with a nameless horror: the room, the Baron, the bust of Dante on the shelf, myself, for one brief second everything was transformed for me into ghosts, so spectral and unreal that my heart froze in mortal fear.

That was the end of my experience that night.

Immediately afterwards I awoke in my bed, trembling with fear. The daylight was bright behind the curtains. I ran to the window: a clear winter's morning!

I went into the next room; the Baron was sitting there in his usual working clothes at his desk reading.

"You've slept in late this morning, my lad", he called to me with a laugh when he saw me by the door, still in my nightshirt, my teeth chattering with inner cold. "I had to go and put out the lamps in the town instead of you. The first time for many years. But what's the matter with you?"

A quick glance at his neck and the last drops of fear trickled out of my blood: his goitre was back on its usual left side and the bust of Dante was in the same place as ever.

Another second, and the earth had once more swallowed up the dreamworld; there was an echo fading in my ear, as if the lid of the coffin had fallen to, and then everything was forgotten.

Under the Spell

From: *The Other Side*

Alfred Kubin

My poor wife found it impossible to overcome these fits of anxiety. She grew visibly paler, her cheeks more and more sunken, and at every unexpected word I spoke to her she would give a nervous start. Things could not go on like this much longer, and it was only the fact that I had still not managed to see Patera that delayed our departure. Without his specific permission any thought of leaving the Dream Realm was futile. The Archive contained ten requests I had submitted, but the only replies they deigned to send were a few stilted excuses such as, "The time in question falls within a period of feriation for the Audience Bureau", or "The petitioner has repeatedly been advised that a respectable position in society is a *sine qua non* for the granting of an audience. He is recommended, therefore, to maintain an ordered way of life, the which he should ..." etc., etc. I was seething, and determined to open my friend's eyes to harm caused by this pernicious bureaucratic clique. "They'll be sorry for it!"

There was another thing that weighed against our journey home: *Our money was gone!* Yes, *simply gone!* Not one single penny was left from the hundred thousand.

"Well, there we have it, I knew it would happen", I said bitterly to my wife when I found out. It was not really her fault, poor thing, so I spared her any further weeping and gnashing of teeth. Theft or no theft, the money had disappeared and all we had to live on was what I could earn.

Thus ended our second year in the Dream Realm. Now my wife began to be tormented by fears during the daytime as well. The kitchen was at the back of our flat and looked out through a window onto the courtyard of the dairy; in the middle was a well-shaft, at the back a few stable doors.

"That well is haunted", she insisted. She claimed she had

heard strange hissing and knocking noises. I had noticed nothing, but to keep her happy I decided I should have a look, and so I went. Under the pretence that I wanted to look round the dairy I knocked until a half-deaf dairyman came to the door. A juicy tip quickly cured his dull-wittedness. I could look at whatever I liked, he shouted in my ear, before returning to his cubbyhole. Left to myself, I had no difficulty in setting about my investigation. I quickly passed through a whole series of dimly lit rooms. The building was set quite deep in the ground and the faint light had to squeeze in through small barred windows. There were many flat, round containers on long wooden trestles and wooden tubs standing in the corners. They were all filled to the brim with milk. There was one vault which was entirely given over to the storage of various implements. The walls were covered with tin pots, wooden boards and platters. I was in a hurry to find the courtyard, but instead of a way out into it, all I could find was more dark cellars with huge cauldrons hanging over cold fires. A pungent smell of cheese stung my nose. There they lay, dripping and stinking, regular rows of all sizes in an unsavoury closet, long and narrow, the mouldy walls covered with spiders' webs. It couldn't be there, so I retraced my steps, but in the sameness of cheese, milk and butter I found I had lost my bearings. I took a wrong turn and ended up in part of the subterranean labyrinth that was clearly not used at all. The arched ceiling was low, and rusty chains hung down from massive hooks. I could hardly see at all, but the slimy floor seemed to slope downwards slightly. All at once I stumbled down a few slippery steps and found myself in complete darkness. Blackest night and icy cellar air; somewhere above I heard a door slam to. Thank God I had a few matches with me. Then suddenly, from far away, I heard a noise. It sounded like distant hammering, but was becoming clearer with disturbing rapidity. In the light of a match I saw that I was in a passageway. I was seized with mortal fear. 'Away from here, I must get away from here', was my only thought. I ran, several times knocking my head against the dripping walls. Still the rumbling behind me grew louder, an awful, rhythmical thunder, like galloping. The light from my matches grew weaker, the damp air stifled the flame. The sound came nearer, obviously I was being pursued. Now I could clearly distinguish a puffing and groaning. It so chilled me to the marrow, I thought I would go mad. I plunged on as if a whip were cracking behind me, but then all my strength drained from me and I fell to my knees, almost fainting. Helplessly I held my hands up against the onrushing danger, my last matches flickering on the ground. Then the wild charge was upon me; a cold wind tore at me and I saw a white, emaciated horse; although I could not see it clearly, I saw what a terrible state it was in. The huge nag was almost starved and flung its enormous hooves around with the vigour of desperation. Its bony head stretched out in front, its ears laid flat, it dashed past me. Its dull, cloudy eye met mine: it was blind. I could hear it grinding its teeth and as, with a shudder, I watched it disappear, I saw its flayed, bloody crupper gleaming. There was no stopping the wild gallop of this living skeleton. I felt my way along the passage as the thundering died away, tormented by the vision of the dreadful bones. Soon I was rescued by the distant light of a gas lamp. In the state of shock I was in, it looked blurred to me. My tongue was rigid and my body like stone. When the fit had passed, I dragged myself towards the light. A staircase appeared, then another light; then I heard people talking and entered a familiar room: I was in the coffee house.

No one had noticed me enter. It was getting dark outside, the street lights were lit. I sat at a table by myself at the back, trying to collect my thoughts, make sense of the horrifying episode and get rid of the unpleasant dizziness I felt. I was not alone for long. A dignified old gentleman wearing a white cravat came into my corner and sat down at the table.

"It's a little quieter over here", he said.

I made no reply; my head was still awash with a maelstrom of thoughts and images. After a while he spoke to me again in a soft, sympathetic voice:

"That must have been the first time you have been through it; you found it a strain."

Now I looked at him, there was something gentle and friendly about the man.

"What do you mean?" I asked, exhausted.

"What do I mean? The Brainstorm, of course. Just take a look around." He gestured at the rest of the café.

It was only then that I realised something must have happened. It was surprisingly quiet for the number of customers that were there. On every face was an expression of exhaustion and distress.

"What on earth has happened?" I was beginning to feel afraid again.

"Just look at the people. It's all over now, by the way."

I felt I could trust him, he was harmless and engaging.

"I noticed straight away that it was the first time for you. It is a curse!" He sighed. The customers were all sitting silent, lost in thought, a few were whispering. Here and there the odd loud word reappeared. In the middle of the room broken glass was being swept up. The two chess players were like wooden dolls, each seemed to be spellbound by the other. I asked my companion to tell me something about the strange atmosphere, since I was completely ignorant. With his beautiful white locks, which went well with his sentimental, oddly fantastic eyes, he must have been well into his sixties.

"You can't have been in the Dream Realm long, at least not many years?" he began.

"It's nearly two now."

I gave a sign to the waiter and Anton, who was his old self again already, brought a brandy. The coffee house was gradually coming back to normal. The old man continued:

"Of course, it's difficult to find your feet if you've been used to something different. Here we are all under *the Spell*. Whether we like it or not, there is an inevitable destiny which works itself out through us. And we have to be grateful that it isn't something worse. As things are, at least we can sometimes have a good laugh at the nonsense that takes place on the large scale. But how many – how many! – there are who are not always willing to submit; new arrivals in particular try to kick against the pricks. Whenever that inner resistance against our immutable fate grows too strong, the Brainstorm comes; everyone suffers then; today was such a day."

He was silent; a dreary, resigned smile flitted across his face. I was speechless. Here I was on the track of a mystery, perhaps the great mystery that had been disturbing me for so long now. And now I told the old man what strange and unpleasant things had happened to me, even the dreadful secret of a few minutes ago which still had my heart in its grip. I left out nothing.

My companion heard me out thoughtfully and sympathetically. He shook his head a little and leant over to me,

"My dear young friend, do not rack your brains for nothing, never fight your inner voice. You are quite right, there are mysteries everywhere here, but they are inexplicable. It is people who are too inquisitive who tend to get their fingers burnt. Seek your consolation in work, Pearl is an excellent place to work. I used to feel the same as you. You are looking at a nature-lover, and I am sure you will believe me, when I tell you how much I suffered from the artificiality of this land. But with time one gets used to it; I have been living here for almost thirteen years, I have adapted to the conditions and have found much to interest me. One has to lower one's sights, that's all; even the smallest things can be a source of pleasure. I, for example, collect lice, dust-lice." His eyes lit up and he grew animated as he went on, with a mysterious smile on his face, "I am on the track of a new species. Yes, the Archives contain wonders that the *hoi polloi* have never even dreamt of. Room 69 is my hunting ground at the moment. His Excellency has graciously put it at my disposal, it contains all my hopes! But now I must be off."

With those words he took an old green case out of his pocket, extracted a pair of horn-rimmed spectacles and put them on. Before he left he gave me an old-fashioned bow and introduced himself, "Professor Korntheuer, zoologist."

I felt warmth towards him as I watched him leave. I liked everything about him: his eccentric attitude, his thick, snowy locks framing a likeable face still revealing a youthful enthusiasm, the fastidious cleanliness of his clothing, right down to his grey spats and galoshes.

But all the excitement of the day had taken its toll of me. My head thumped with a dull ache as I mounted the stairs to my apartment. It was just as I had expected: my wife was stretched out on the sofa, completely exhausted. She said nothing, and for my sake she tried to pull herself together; I maintained a tactful silence, for I was unwilling to tell a lie.

In bed, I tossed and turned restlessly. I kept imagining I could hear a rumbling noise and see a vacant, wide-open eye. My mind was almost completely taken up with what I had learnt from the Professor. So there was a spell; and the brainstorm? I pondered over the meaning of these words. I had certainly witnessed enough unusual things here. Only recently I had seen a few lads who were making a racket behind the house with rattles and drums. When I asked what they were doing I was told, "We are making background noise." Now I was beginning to find the nonsense irritating, I saw the madhouse behind it all. At the beginning it had been new, we had sat at our window just waiting for the grotesque cavalcade below. For the last few months, however, laughter had vanished from our home. My wife's health was slowly but steadily going downhill. At the same time the weird incidents increased. There were now things I had to keep from my wife if I did not want to put her life at risk. So I bottled up my worries inside me and felt moody and disgruntled all the time. Where was it all leading? I was going to rack and ruin myself.

A few days later I went out. New Year was just around the corner, but that did not mean much in this winterless land. I stole past the well-known façades; here in Pearl everyone adopted a particular gait: quiet, hesitant, uncertain, prepared for misfortune to strike at any moment. A few lonely street-lamps guided my path. Real dreamland lighting! Out of the general gloom, which blurred everything and enlarged it to gigantic proportions, there emerged unnatural physical details: a post, a shop sign, a gate.

I was coming out of the old, gothic convent, one wing of which contained a children's hospital, where I had collected two bottles of medicinal wine as a tonic for my wife. As I passed the church which was attached to it I noticed a black bundle in the shadow of the doorway. I heard a few indistinct words and the

149

bare stump of an arm was raised in pleading. Unthinking, I threw a few coins into the dark corner, but the next moment I stopped as if rooted to the spot. What a strange old woman's face it was in those filthy rags! I had to look at it more closely, there was some mysterious force compelling me. Reluctantly and with a feeling of disgust, I bent down to the old beggar-woman. It was not her stinking breath or toothless mouth that held me, but two horrible, bright eyes; like the fangs of a viper they lodged in my brain. I arrived home half dead with the shock. Was it real or the fearful product of an overstimulated imagination? I felt as if I had looked into a bottomless pit.

Such fits were too much for my nerves. I decided I would go to see Patera the very next day. If necessary, I was determined to scream, to *force* my way into his presence. He was my friend, he had invited me, it was up to him whether we went to rack and ruin or not. The mindless inhabitants of the dream town certainly had a wrong impression of him. Why were they so timorous, so shrinking and evasive whenever I mentioned the man? My friend did not deserve that.

That day was particularly ill-starred. My wife was groaning under her migraine; I made a few cold compresses for her and then collapsed on my bed, exhausted. Then – it must have been about one o'clock in the morning – there was a ringing and knocking at the door of our apartment. "It's that drunkard from next door", I thought angrily. Soon I heard him bawling my name as well, time after time. I was furious at his lack of consideration, leapt out of bed, slipped on my dressing-gown and took my walking stick from the corner of the room. I was going to teach the fellow a lesson he wouldn't forget! I opened the door onto the landing and there he stood, breathing beer fumes right into my face. Did I have a few cigars? – just as a loan – why didn't I pop across to his flat – my wife was invited too – he was going to make a hot toddy.

I could hardly control my fury. "This is outrageous! I think you might spare other people your scandalous behaviour! You'd better be off quickly before I throw you down the stairs, you bounder!" I yelled at him as loud as I could, I was boiling over with rage. With a vacant, drunken laugh, he stammered,

150

"Come on, just pop over." As he spoke, he grabbed me by the arm and tried to drag me. I lost my self-control. As quick as lightning I kicked him in the stomach so that he tumbled to the ground. The insolence of the fellow! An avalanche of thoughts poured through my mind.

'Now I really am going to complain, I won't put it off any more, I will get justice or else. I can't stand this confounded hole a moment longer!' You can understand my situation: for weeks I had been prey to the most horrible experiences, I was worried about my sick wife, our money had gone, and all around me I found nothing but hostility and scorn. A violent hatred of the whole of the Dream Realm made me lose my head: quivering with fury I jumped down the stairs and rushed straight off to the Palace, just as I was. I was going to demand satisfaction for the humiliations I felt I was being subjected to the whole time. I would do it, even if I had to drag Patera from his bed. I raced up Long Street towards the Great Square. Thick fog had descended and the flames of the gas-lamps appeared as glowing patches of yellow; I did not see a single passer-by, only the wet, filthy flagstones. I was almost raving, my mind had no room for anything other than how I was going to describe all these infamies to Patera. I just poured out my accusations aloud, eloquent phrases came to me without effort and I found touching words for my misfortune. Then I began to feel the cold. When I looked down, I had to admit that I was hardly correctly dressed to visit a gentleman. My whole costume consisted of an old dressing-gown with a floral pattern, a nightshirt under it and one slipper – the other must have fallen off while I was running. In the Great Square the fog was a little thinner: there was the Palace, towering up to the heavens like a gigantic cube. The bright disc on the clock-tower looked like a moon. The damp and cold brought me back to my senses; I recognised the foolishness of my plan. No, it was not the right moment, nor the right dress, to lodge a complaint. What did I look like, bare-headed, in my dressing-gown and with a walking stick at one o'clock in the morning? It brought me back to earth, and I turned round to make my way home. I took a short cut down a narrow side-street, the cold was becoming decidedly uncomfortable and my wife would worry until I returned. But tomorrow, tomorrow would be the day of revenge! To warm myself up, I fell into a gentle trot. A brightly lit window appeared and I ran towards it. Music, a tinkling piano, hoarse voices, singing! There was a strip of light across the street. My God! I mustn't let people see me like this! But I had already been spotted.

"Hey, you there! Step this way." Some suspicious figures approached. Now I knew that I had taken a wrong turning: I was in the French Quarter.

Things were still pretty lively there, and I was soon the centre of attraction. I was annoyed and embarrassed; they were laughing at my strange get-up. With an oath, I hurried on, more and more people following me. They were making coarse jokes, and I could work out how it was going to end. It was all very embarrassing; I would never find my way in these unsavoury alleys and culs-de-sac. Castringius would have known his way round. If only I had known where the police station was, but all I could see on either side were grubby dives and dens of vice; the gutters gave off reeking fumes. I strode out as fast as I could. A fellow with make-up on grabbed the tip of my dressing-gown and pulled it down. Smack! There was a slap round the face for his pains. But it would have been better if I hadn't bothered, for now the hubbub really started. With shouts and screams the hunt for me was really up. A gigantic, bloated woman stepped into my path and tried to trip me up. I easily jumped over her and lost my walking stick as I did so. She rolled around in the mud, clutching my nightshirt as a trophy. That gave me a slight lead, but now I knew it was a matter of life and death. I lengthened my stride like a demented greyhound. Never before had I been so sure in my strength. But behind me the wild uproar was increasing, half the French Quarter was on my heels; piercing whistles rang out, the ground became slimier and slimier, I had to be careful I didn't slip. 'I'll soon be exhausted, I can hardly escape', I thought, fear pounding at my temples. They threw bottles and knives at me as I ran to and fro through the alleys, crying as loud as I could at every corner, "Help! Police!" But no one came to help me, and from behind I could hear the scornful laughter of the wild mob. Mouth gaping, naked and despairing,

I literally flew along; no safety, no hope anywhere to be seen. Finally, I was already quite weary, I saw a tall narrow house. It blocked off the end of the alley, all the windows were lit and there was a red paper lantern over the entrance. The door was open; I rushed up the brightly lit stairs. The walls were painted in vivid colours and decorated with palms. On the first floor there was a woman coming towards me, a sublime vision, superb in a long, glistening silver chemise with her hair loose and magnificent arms. She was not particularly surprised to see me in the state I was in, and said with a smile, "Not to me! You must have made a mistake, sir, there is room five."

Delighted and embarrassed at her friendliness, I stammered breathless apologies, covering my nakedness with my hand. Then I opened the door she had indicated. Damn it all, there were two people in there already, also stark-naked! I slammed the door shut again. The rabble was now surging up the stairs. At the front was a policeman – *now* he came – roaring, "Where is the fellow? I'll report this. And the house will have to be closed down." Then the mob. My fair rescuer had disappeared and my bleeding feet seemed to weigh a ton. Taking a deep breath, I climbed up a few more steps and saw, written in large letters like a command, the words I had been waiting for, "Here". Once more providence had come to my aid! With my remaining strength I opened the door and pushed home the bolt behind me. For the moment I was safe, but the horde was already rattling the lock. "Open up! Open up!" came the piercing cry from a thousand throats.

I looked around like a hunted beast, then a sudden, desperate decision came to me like a flash of lightning. At the risk of falling to my death, I squeezed through a narrow window and felt round for something to hold on to. Yes! There was a wire, a lighting conductor. And with a miraculous confidence which I found incredible, I climbed down it. Silence and darkness all round. I collapsed to the ground, my legs could carry me no farther.

I was lying on a rubbish tip. The driver of a dung-cart on his nightly rounds lifted me up and took me home in his evil-smelling vehicle. My wife saw me arrive from the window. She had been through a terrible quarter of an hour, I had not been away for more than that.

A few days later I saw some dogs in the street playing with a bundle of coloured rags from which hung braid and tassels. I recognised my old dressing-gown, a piece of lost property floating round the streets of the dream town. My enthusiasm for Patera's creation was definitely a thing of the past.

The Wicked Nun

Karl Hans Strobl

One night I suddenly woke from a deep sleep. My first reaction was a certain surprise that I should wake up at all, since during the day I had been busy at the ruins of the Jesuit Barracks and was very tired. I turned over and tried to get back to sleep. But then I heard a cry which drove away all sleep. It was a cry of fear, and immediately I was sitting upright in bed. First of all I had to orientate myself. As often happens at night, I did not know where the door was and where the window. Finally I remembered that I have this strange characteristic of only being able to sleep along a north-south axis, so now I knew that the door was on my right and the window on my left; to my right, in her bed, my wife was as usual sleeping the calm, peaceful sleep of a child. After a while, during which I listened intently, I lay down again and told myself that I must have been dreaming after all, though it must have been a strangely intense and vivid dream for the cry to penetrate the murk of my consciousness so clearly. It took me two hours to get back to sleep.

During the day my work did not allow me to do what my mind wanted to, which was to concentrate undisturbed on my dream. Clambering around among the ruins of the Jesuit Barracks, I had to direct and supervise the demolition work. The sun shone down mercilessly and I was covered in dust from the crumbling masonry, which got into my lungs. Punctually at eleven o'clock, as every day, the Director of the State Archives, Dr. Holzbock, arrived to find out what progress we had been making. He was uncommonly interested in the demolition of the ancient building, the oldest parts of which went back almost to the time the town was established. As he had made the history of the region his speciality, he hoped that the dissection of this venerable corpse would provide much interesting information. We were standing in the great courtyard watching the workmen dismantle the first floor of the main wing.

"I am convinced", he was saying, "that we will make many

strange discoveries, when we finally get down to the foundations. The evidence of the past is subject to a force, which is similar to the physical force of gravity and which draws it downwards. I can't tell you how much old buildings like this fascinate me when they are so rich in history as this one. First of all a merchant's warehouse, then a convent, then a fortress for the Jesuits and finally a barracks. Built over a relatively large portion of the old town, which was encircled by walls, it seems to have been touched by all events, to have absorbed every manifestation of the life of the town, so that their traces remain. They leave deposits, layers in a sequence which reveals the succession of the ages; one could use them to establish a geology of history. I think we will find more odd things in the old masonry, not just pots of old coins and frescoes that have been whitewashed over, but petrified adventures and fossilised destinies."

Thus spoke the fanatical archivist as the picks worked at the solid masonry opposite us. An arcade had been exposed up there, and in my mind's eye I could see a procession of merchants, nuns and Jesuits who had spent part of their lives beneath the oppressive, grey vault of the passage. While Dr. Holzbock continued his rhapsody I decided – finding, as I do, anything romantic irresistible – to visit the ruins by night some time. I wanted to sense the thrill of the uncanny and to cultivate the ghosts of the ruin.

That night too, just as the previous night, I woke from my sleep and then shortly afterwards heard the terrible cry. I had prepared myself for it and made a great effort to pinpoint where it came from. But at the decisive moment I was seized by an inexplicable fear, so that I really could not say whether it came from inside the house or from the street. A short while later I thought I could hear the sound of people running in the street. I slept only fitfully for the rest of the night, my mind being occupied with the puzzling cry. When I told my wife about it over breakfast, her first reaction was to laugh. Then she said, with a worried look, "I think that working at the Jesuit Barracks has been rather a strain on your nerves. Why don't you take a holiday and let one of your colleagues take over from you for a while? You're overtired; you've a duty towards your own health as well, you know." But I refused to listen; digging in the rubble of the old building and looking for the things of which the Director of Archives expected so much had become a passion with me. My wife succeeded in one thing alone, and that was to get me to promise to waken her if I should wake up myself during the night.

That night again I started out of my sleep. Anxiously I hastened to shake my wife to wake her, and we sat up in bed beside each other. And there was the cry, piercing and quite distinct, from the street. "Can you hear it ... now, now ..." But my wife switched the lamp on and shone it in my face, "My God, what do you look like! There's nothing. I can't hear anything." I was so beside myself that I screamed at her, "Shut up ... and now ... now they're running along the street." "You're hurting me", cried my wife, for I was squeezing her arm, as if I could convince her by violence. "Didn't you hear anything?" "No! Nothing at all."

I sank back into the pillows, bathed in sweat, exhausted as if after strenuous physical labour, and incapable of giving my wife any kind of reassuring answer to her worried questions. Towards morning, when she was already sleeping again, I realised what I had to do to keep my reason. By remaining completely calm and collected throughout the day I managed to convince my wife that I had got over it. During dinner I joked about my nocturnal hallucinations and promised that I would sleep right through until the morning and forget all about the cry and the tumult in the street. I even promised I would apply for a long period of leave immediately this particularly responsible task was completed. As soon as I heard from my wife's regular breathing that she was asleep, however, I got out of bed and dressed again. As I was determined to counter any foolish thoughts I took Kant's *Critique of Pure Reason* and tried to immerse myself in its strictly logical sequence of ideas. But as midnight approached I fell prey to a restlessness which made me unable to continue reading. I found it impossible to follow the book's inexorable logic. There was something stronger pulling me away from it. Quietly I stood up and went outside. The trembling that was taking hold of me told me that the hour was approaching. Pressed against the side of the entrance, I waited; it took all my courage, but I was determined to put a swift end to the torture I had been going through each night by establishing its natural cause. Twenty yards away a gas-lamp was burning, giving sufficient light to the part of the street outside my house. A young man who had obviously had too much to drink came along the houses on the other side of the road, stopped at the house opposite and, after several unsuccessful attempts, finally managed to open the door. I could still hear the noise he was making in the hallway and up the stairs. Then all was quiet once more ... until suddenly the cry blazed up in the stillness. I stumbled back into the deep shadow and fumbled for the latch until I felt its cold metal in my hand. Beside myself with fear and desperation, I wanted to flee. But although I had not locked the house door, I found I could not open it. And already the sound of the hurrying steps of many people was coming from the street and something flew past me. I could not tell whether it was a person or just a shadow. At the moment I saw it, it did not seem to have the weight of a human body, but the impression it left on my mind was one of complete physicality, of a woman who was rushing down the street, a woman in a long, flowing dress which she had lifted up so that she could run more easily. And behind her, only a few steps behind her, came a whole throng of men in strange costumes, costumes that did not belong to the present. With them, too, I had the same experience: flitting past like shades, they yet left on my mind the impression of solid bodies. I still do not know what madness it was that compelled me to set off running behind them. It may have been similar to the madness which seizes men in battle, a frenzy which is stronger than the soldiers' fear and throws them into the enemy fire. I have never run as I did then; it was not so much running as gliding and floating, such as you usually only find in dreams. I could still see the chase before me, the woman in front and the throng of men in pursuit. I seemed to have been running like that for a long time, and yet I did not feel the least bit exhausted. Suddenly the woman disappeared; I saw the pursuing men flit wildly to and fro and then it seemed as if everything was sucked into the blackness of the night. To my astonishment, I found I was standing by the wooden fence around the ruins of the Jesuit Barracks, near the entrance, over which hung the sign saying 'No entry except on business'. I tore open the door and rushed in. There was the nightwatchman, leaning against a beam quite close to the entrance, who greeted me when he saw me suddenly appear. Pleased that my ambush had found him at his post, he straightened up to make his report. But I did not give him time to speak, "Didn't you see the woman? Just now ... she was wearing some long, grey garment that she had gathered up and she ran in here."

"I've seen nothing, sir, nothing at all."

"But, damn it all, they can't just have disappeared into thin air. Perhaps you were asleep after all? Asleep with your eyes open?"

The nightwatchman seemed hurt at this suggestion and assured me emphatically that he had not been sleeping but had not seen anything. So I started to search myself. I crawled round everywhere, checked all the corners of all the courtyards and did not miss out one of the many rooms and chambers with their jagged, half-demolished walls and the reflection of the lights of the town on the ceilings. In order to be able to see into inaccessible rooms I clambered over dangerous lumps of masonry, which threatened every moment to collapse.

Then I ran along half-open galleries where the lamps threw grotesque shadows onto the grubby wall-paintings. Originally the church had been completely enfolded by the old building, so that only the roof and tower had risen above the grey walls, but now it was almost completely exposed and contained masses of hiding places. But I found nothing there either, and went home with a heavy head and trembling legs; I kept trying to work out what I had seen, following different interpretations, but the only result was that I was more confused than ever.

"I hope you didn't hear anything last night?" asked my wife.

"No ... I slept soundly", I lied, and ducked my head into the wash-basin, so that my wife would not see the signs of my sleepless night in my face.

That day we made a discovery in the ruins which sent the

archivist into raptures. We were dismantling a beautiful old portal of particular artistic merit and had to proceed with great care as it was intended to erect it elsewhere. It consisted of two pilasters, each richly ornamented with flower and fruit motifs, bearing a beautiful arch over the entrance. On the ledges above the arch were statues of saints in the manner of the seventeenth century: saints holding their attributes in front of them, like cyphers of their fate. As we were lifting a Saint James from its base, its head fell from its neck and rolled a few yards before coming to a stop in the rubble. In the bottom on the head was a round, cylindrical hole, as if it had fitted onto an iron rod, and when we had lifted the body down we saw that it had a corresponding hole. At first I reproached the workers for their carelessness, but Dr. Holzbock, who had picked up the head and was scrutinising it intently, said, "It's not their fault at all. This isn't a new break, it's old. It was done deliberately, and I wouldn't be surprised ..."

At that moment one of the workmen came up to me and handed me a small roll of dirty paper, "That was in the hole", he said; "perhaps there's something written on it ..."

Holzbock gave me a look and took the roll from me. With extreme care, he tried to unroll it and eventually succeeded in spreading it out on the drawing board in my shed and fixing it with pins. It was a sheet of the strong parchment on which the most important documents of the past used to be drawn up. I found it impossible to make sense of the tangle of red and black lines. It appeared to be some kind of plan, but even with all my experience as an architect, I could make nothing of it. Dr. Holzbock, however, was determined to decipher the parchment, and asked to be allowed to take it away with him.

He was back even before we had finished work for the day, waving to me as soon as he saw me. He was quite solemn as he took me by the arm and led me through a small side door into the church, where we would be undisturbed. The isolated church was enriched by some of the colour from a wonderful evening sky, in which purple boats with white sails were floating across unfathomable depths of crimson and emerald. The tall, baroque silver candles around us stood in a kind of reddish haze, the Saint Agnes on the wall opposite had lost her melancholy expression as the dazzling reflections released a smouldering sensuality in her. The statues of the saints, the pulpit, the angels beneath the gallery were transformed, as if they had been liberated from the constraints of the day and were looking forward to the night, when they could be quite free and perhaps live a life of which we had no inkling.

Meanwhile Holzbock had taken the plan out of his briefcase and started to explain. "After thinking about it for a while, I came to the conclusion that the plan, in the form in which we saw it, was meaningless or, rather, that it concealed its meaning. When you look at the tangle of lines, the most you can make out is that it could be a plan, but it is impossible to say what it is meant to be a plan of. From the appearance of the paper and the style of the letters scattered about among the lines, I feel pretty certain in saying that it is from the first half of the seventeenth century, from a time, that is, when this building was still a convent. Now I have found a chronicle of the period which mentions the convent quite often and in quite hostile terms. As you probably know, in those days the strangest rumours went round about some convents, and my chronicle has plenty to say about this one, although not much to its credit. If we are right in our supposition that the parchment we found is a plan, then it probably indicated some secrets of the old building and was deliberately confused so that it would appear meaningless to anyone else. There is another consideration which strengthened my supposition. The portal that you began dismantling this morning is in one of the inner sections?"

"Yes. It was a decoration of the entrance to the section joining the northern and southern wings, in the façade that gives onto the so-called Trinity Courtyard."

"Good. And you will have noticed, then, that the top of the portal reaches the second floor, so that some of the figures, that is the heads of the statues, can be reached without difficulty from the second-floor windows."

"Certainly. We can go and check, if you like."

"No, stay here, I'm sure that is the case. So: from the second-floor windows the heads of some of the statues, including that of St. James, could easily be removed, if they are separate from their bodies. A dangerous document could easily be concealed in a cunningly devised cavity."

"So you think ..."

"Didn't I tell you right away the break wasn't recent? I was convinced there was some secret hidden in the tangle of lines scrawled on the plan. But how could I discover it? I had to be very careful before using any chemical reagents; the danger was that they might ruin everything. In my study of ancient documents I have often found reason to admire the manifold and artful secret devices of the Middle Ages. I know many of the formulae they used for secret documents; so-called sympathetic inks played an important part in them. The simplest kinds of sympathetic ink are those which turn invisible when they dry and only reappear when heat is applied to the paper, but that could not be what we are dealing with here, the scrawls on the plan are all too visible. But perhaps it could be the opposite: the extra, confusing lines might disappear when the paper was warmed, leaving only the important ones. That was one experiment I could try without worrying about damaging our find. Well, I tried it and it worked perfectly. Would you like to see it?"

Dr. Holzbock took out a small pocket lamp and lit it. Then he wrapped the plan round the casing. We waited in silence in the gathering dusk, which was only disturbed by the timid light from the small lamp. After a few minutes I thought I could see some of the lines grow paler; eventually they disappeared, leaving only a small number behind.

"A real ground plan", I said.

"And it's your job now to decipher it."

It only took me only a moment to sort it out. "Here we have the Trinity Courtyard and these are the cloisters, this here indicates the church, and from the sacristy there is a ... What's that? These lines don't correspond to any building, they must ... yes, there's no doubt about it, they indicate a subterranean passage leading out of the convent."

Dr. Holzbock was beside himself with joy to see his suspicions confirmed. I was excited too; it seemed to me that this discovery must in some way be connected with my nocturnal adventures. I was about to tell him about them, but was suddenly overcome with a strange reticence. I have never been happy to talk about events when they are just developing, I am afraid of the effect of the spoken word. Words are more powerful than we imagine and their influence on the future is as certain as it is powerful. But Dr. Holzbock must have noticed that something was going on inside me, for he looked almost concerned, and asked, "What's wrong, you look strange?"

But without answering I drew him into the sacristy. There I began to test the walls according to the measurements on the plan. At the point where the subterranean passage was supposed to begin, I found there was a huge cupboard against the wall. It was one of those gigantic wardrobes containing a wealth of vestments and precious objects, a well-made example of the old craftsman's art. It was also a monster, heavy as a rock, richly decorated with carving, a colossus, taking up the whole wall from floor to ceiling. Dr. Holzbock put its date of construction in the sixteenth century. We were both convinced that the entrance must be behind the cupboard, but we were both convinced that there must be some secret mechanism, without which we would find it impossible to move the leviathan.

"Enough for today", said Dr. Holzbock, and he persuaded me to go home, although my first intention had been to spend the whole night in the sacristy, as if I had to guard some precious object from thieves.

I was so preoccupied with our find and our conjectures regarding the plan, that my wife told me I looked quite distraught. She went on badgering me until I promised to ask for leave earlier than I had intended. Although I had determined not to spend another night out of my bed, a strange feeling compounded of fear and curiosity forced me to get up and go down to await the witching hour in the street.

Midnight struck, and immediately I heard the terrible cry. The noise of people running came nearer, and the chase passed me, exactly as it had the previous night. This time I could see clearly that the woman was wearing a long garment, similar to a nun's, that was partly open at the breast, as if she had thrown it on hastily. For a moment, she turned her face towards me, a beautiful, pale face with dark eyes that emitted a strange light. Again I was compelled to run after the throng, and again they all vanished at the boards round the ruin. But I was sure I had seen the pursued woman tear open the door and enter the demolition site.

"I suppose you saw nothing again tonight?" I screamed at the nightwatchman. The man drew back anxiously and assured me he had seen nothing. "But I know that she came in here. You must have seen a woman!" When the nightwatchman insisted that he had seen no woman, nor anyone else, I pushed him aside and started to search. Without stopping to ask myself why I was so determined to get to the bottom of the whole affair, I clambered over every pile of rubble, examined every section of half-demolished masonry and a hundred times I was sure I had seen a woman wearing a long, grey habit like a nun's in the deepest shadows. Once I suddenly whirled round because I had the feeling she was following me in the moonlight, stepping lightly and so close behind me that I could hear her breathing.

I opened the church with the key which some subconscious impulse had made me slip into my pocket earlier. It never occurred to me to consider that she could not possibly have entered the locked church. After I had convinced myself that there was no other living being in the church, I went into the sacristy and took out the plan. The moon was shining with a bright, green light on the old cupboard, so that the scrollwork looked as if it were made of brass. The beautiful carvings stood out against a golden brown background and in the light all the cherubs seemed to come to life with their high-spirited antics. I noticed a picture above the cupboard which I had not seen during the day. It was an old painting, so darkened by incense and the smoke from the candles that only the face of the saint it was presumably supposed to represent shone through the murk of the centuries. Or was that the face of a saint? Could it not be the portrait of a woman who had once lived within these walls? It seemed to me to have more life, more individuality, than a picture of a saint, and now, in the green moonlight I felt I had seen the face before. The dark, blazing eyes burnt into mine.

I trembled with inexplicable fear. An eerie thought crept into my mind. We often feel, when one of these thoughts suddenly appears in our mind, as if it were not born within us, as if it did not belong to us, as if it came from somewhere outside and were communicated to us, like a thought from another person. This feeling was so strong, that I had the impression it had been spoken beside me, as if someone had warned me ... as if a woman's voice had whispered a warning, yes, a warning ... the sense of this thought from outside was a warning. It was as if someone were whispering to me to beware of opening up the passageway that was marked on my plan. I tried to shake off the thought by ascribing it to this uncanny silence that seemed to be soaked in incense. The old walls of the sacristy had been disturbed by the vibration of the demolition of the neighbouring buildings, and there was a constant trickle of plaster down them. The moonlight seemed filled with the trickling dust, as if it consisted of grains of silver sand slipping through the hourglass of time. The more I tried to fill my mind with these observations of the physical surroundings, the more insistently the warning returned: I must give up the idea of carrying out my plan, otherwise I would bring down a great misfortune upon myself. I kept desperately trying to concentrate my attention on the marvellous play of the moonlight over the carved wood, but the outside thought just became more insistent, more piercing. For a brief moment I felt as if someone had put their hand on my shoulder and were whispering close to my ear. And then I could sense quite clearly an outside will trying to dominate my own. I looked up ... and into the dark, blazing eyes in the picture above the cupboard.

All at once it came to me with a clarity that was almost painful: I had seen those eyes earlier, when the chase rushed past me, they were the eyes of the woman who was being pursued. Although I am not by nature timorous, I was so startled that I lost my head. I did not scream and dash out, but I did something that was much worse: slowly, my eyes fixed on those of the portrait, I backed out step by step, as if I were trying to escape from some real, physical danger. In my hand I clutched the huge key to the church, just as when attacked by robbers one would grasp the first implement that came to hand as a weapon. At last I reached the church and slammed the sacristy door shut. It echoed through the darkness of the invisible vaults. The pictures and statues seemed to have changed their postures and were looking down at me with mocking grimaces.

I hurried out of the church.

Although I only managed to get back to sleep as the first light appeared, I still woke again soon afterwards, for I wanted to set the men to work on the saristy immediately. In spite of the nocturnal warning, I was determined to open up the passage-way. By day my fear had no power over me.

When I reached the site I found Dr. Holzbock already there, driven by the same impatience as myself. I chose some of the most skilful workers and instructed them how to go about moving the enormous cupboard. The portrait above it, that I looked at with some trepidation, turned out to be an ordinary, run-of-the-mill painting, so encrusted with dirt that one could not distinguish much more than a pale splodge which repre-sented the face of some saint. It was not in the least bit eerie, and I was about to ask Holzbock his opinion of it when he addressed me.

"You know", he said, "there must have been some pretty goings-on in this nunnery. Late yesterday evening I had another look at that old chronicle, and I believe this passage will have some interesting revelations for us. I think I gave you some idea of what the chronicle says about the convent. I read it right through again last night, in the hope of finding some clues to help us in our investigations. The nuns' usual fear of bringing their convent into disrepute had been replaced here by a wild shamelessness. They openly indulged in the worst kinds of licentiousness, and the chronicle records that frequently the neighbourhood was horrified by the sound of chinking glasses and riotous laughter that continued the whole night through. It must have been a kind of madness, a fury that had infected the whole convent and provoked the nuns to the wildest orgies. Often enough the citizens could see that even the church was lit up and by the noise they could tell that they had chosen the House of God as the setting for their feasting. The priests of the

166

town were invited to take part in the orgies and if, at the beginning, they would slip into the convent quietly at night, later they began to turn up openly in broad daylight. The men were often seen leaving the building with unsteady steps and flushed faces, drunken nuns were often seen stumbling round the convent courtyards and garden.

The good citizens observed all this with loathing, and it is hardly surprising that they reported the situation to the Bishop. The Bishop came to carry out the visitation himself, but all he found at the convent was a flock of pious nuns who led a contemplative life devoted to prayer, exactly as was to be expected of Brides of Christ, and his findings were only confirmed by his interviews with the clergy of the town. Their slanderous accusers were arraigned before a court, and the authority of the Bishop saw to it that their punishment was severe. Once the Bishop had left the town, the nuns' outrageous behaviour started again, but now there was no one who dared to complain, for fear of being punished himself.

Of all these debauched nuns, Sister Agatha was the worst and soon she was not content with the convent orgies. She must have been a most unusual woman, with a terrible, fiendish sexual appetite, that consumed and destroyed everything it came into contact with; she must have had the voracity of a beast of prey. In the chronicle it says that she often left the convent by a secret route and spent the night carousing in the town. She was frequently to be seen in the brothels and taverns of the slums in the company of all kinds of riffraff, gamblers and drunkards, as if she were one of them; she, who was of noble birth, from one of the leading families in the country. All the vices of her house, which had been carefully concealed for generations, became most horribly manifest in her. If any young man caught her eye, she would grasp him and not let him go but, like the wild and dissolute being she was, drag him down to her own level. She was soon notorious throughout the town, people spoke of her as of a nightmare, a ghost. Soon she was known as the 'wicked nun'. Then the French disease was brought into the town. Sister Agatha was infected, too, but she was incapable of changing her behaviour and continued her dissipated life. She continued to dance in the taverns, sat amongst the riffraff and fell like a vampire on the young men in the streets."

"What's the matter?" Dr. Holzbock broke off. "You look quite ill."

I waved the suggestion away and asked him to pause for a moment while I checked the workmen's progress. All round the massive cupboard the floor had been torn up and the plaster scraped from the wall, but they had not succeeded in moving it an inch. "I think", said the foreman, "the wardrobe must be fixed to the wall."

That was the only explanation, but in that case it must have been attached to the wall at the time when the sacristy was added on to the church. So either the plan was a hoax or ...

We looked at each other and Holzbock expressed the thought that was going through my mind, "The way to the passage goes through the cupboard." I was beside myself with impatience at the new delay and fuming at all these obstacles.

"But how can we find out where the passage goes? We would have to break the whole cupboard into pieces and we can't do that, it belongs to the Church. What can we do?" Dr. Holzbock was almost as impatient as I was.

Whilst he was thinking, I examined the whole of the cupboard, pressed any carving that jutted out, opened all the drawers that were not locked and measured it from all sides to see if there were any odd proportions that might suggest a concealed door.

"Don't bother", said Holzbock; "this cupboard has kept its secret from generations of inquisitive eyes and I'm sure it won't reveal it to us just like that. We'll have to search through the archives, perhaps ..."

I stopped listening. As I was trying to make a rough estimate of the height of the cupboard, my eye had caught the picture above it, and I suddenly sensed that it must provide the key. To Holzbock's amazement, I ordered the ladder to be placed against the wardrobe and climbed up. In such close proximity to the pale face, eye to eye with it, the terror of the previous night began to creep over me again. But I kept control of myself and began to examine the portrait. The layer of grime was so thick that even at this distance one could see little more than that it represented a woman wearing a habit like a nun's, whilst her head was without hood or ribbons, leaving her hair flowing free. Strangely enough, her locks were entwined and looked more like snakes, as one would paint the head of the Medusa. But the picture was in such poor condition that I could not say for sure. Around her neck she wore a piece of jewellery on a string. It was not the cross one usually finds on nuns, but a bangle, a mere ornament. It looked like a lily enclosed in a pentagon. I had the feeling I had seen this ornament somewhere else on the cupboard, a lily in a hexagon, a rhombus and a pentagon as here.

"Holzbock", I cried as I climbed back down the ladder, "I think I've found a clue to the mystery."

"You found a clue in that picture up there?"

"I think so. The key is a lily in a pentagon. Let's start looking."

Although I knew perfectly well that I had seen this motif, I was so confused that I could not find it again. Now, at the decisive moment, I was struck by an inexplicable tiredness, and all I could see of the cupboard was a hazy blur; it was a feeling such as a person who is freezing to death must have. Then I heard Holzbock call out, "Here is a lily in a pentagon. What now?"

All my concentration suddenly returned, as if I were faced with something ineluctable, where the outcome is in no doubt. I examined the lily, the workmen gathering round in curiosity. The wood seemed to be giving way under my touch, I pressed with all my strength, a groan came from the old cupboard, a groan from its innermost depths, and a narrow crack appeared, splitting it from top to bottom. We pushed at it with our shoulders, but the rusty hinges, which had not been used for centuries, only gave way reluctantly. The door opened little by little, giving us the opportunity to admire the cunning secret mechanism. To the external view, this part of the cupboard seemed to be the same as all the others, but pressing the lily made two apparently separate panels join to form a door; as it opened, so the compartments opened out to the right and left, until we found ourselves facing the rear wall. There it was not difficult to find the button we had to press to open that door as well.

Behind it was the dark opening of a passageway. I was about

to dash straight in, but my companion held me back. "Patience. First of all we must check that the air in there is breathable." A candle was fixed to a pole, lit and pushed into the passage. It flared up wildly, great pearls of the molten wax dripping into the darkness.

We entered the passage.

A few steps down, then straight ahead, a few more steps down and straight ahead. "I think we must be following the 'wicked nun's' secret route", whispered Holzbock. He merely thought so; I was sure. In spite of the fact that the air down there was relatively fresh, I was choking with apprehension.

"Jesusjosephandmary!" exclaimed the workman, who was carrying the candle ahead of us, and stopped. At this point the walls receded into the darkness as the passage opened out into a kind of crypt with four wooden coffins on wooden trestles in the middle. The coffins were quite simple and without ornamentation, though the style and shape suggested they were several hundred years old. Dr. Holzbock lifted one of the lids: in it lay a nun, her face shrivelled like a mummy's and her hands crossed on her breast; the clothes had disintegrated, so that in some places the flesh, that had not succumbed to decay, was visible through the holes.

We lifted the lids from the other coffins. In the fourth lay Sister Agatha, the 'wicked nun'. I recognised her at once, it was the woman who ran past my house at night, followed by a throng of furious men, it was the original of the painting in the sacristy.

I heard Holzbock's voice in my ear, "Did you know that one of these corpses is supposed to be Sister Agatha, the 'wicked nun'?"

"I do know; it's that one there. I recognise her. Just see how much better she looks than the others. You can tell the others are corpses, but that one ..."

Dr. Holzbock grasped my hand and said, "I think we should get out of this passage as quickly as possible, the air down here seems to be dangerous after all. Off we go."

It did not continue very far in front. Thirty paces further on we had to stop. Part of the roof had fallen in, blocking up the passage. According to my calculations we were beneath the road; I could tell the roof-fall could not have taken place very long ago, probably as a result of the vibration from the heavy lorries taking away the rubble from the old building. As there was a danger of further roof-falls, I ordered a shaft to be sunk from the road immediately so that everything could be checked and any necessary measures taken to prevent an accident. Then we made our way back through the crypt. As we passed the corpses I took another look to confirm my original impression. She really did look different from the three others, almost as if she were still alive. Her skin was still firm with a hint of colour and her smooth forehead shone. She was still beautiful and in the light of the candle she seemed to be peeping out from under her eyelids, as if she were observing us with furtive, surreptitious glances.

When we reached the sacristy, I had to sit down. I was breathless and my legs were trembling.

"I must tell you", said Dr. Holzbock, "how I came to the conclusion that one of the mummies in there is Sister Agatha. The explanation is in the chronicle, in the part that continues the history of the convent. The disease, of which Sister Agatha was the high priestess, spread, and eventually a terrible rage broke out among the citizens. They lay in wait for her and tried to kill her. But it seemed as if the danger merely heightened the thrill of her escapades. She became wilder than ever, and it was strange that she found a host of protectors, young men, who loved her despite the fact that they knew she had poisoned them. I said before that there must have been something fiendish about her. Her power over men's bodies was limitless.

One day, however, a crowd of armed men appeared outside the convent and demanded that Sister Agatha be handed over to them. The townsfolk's fury had reached its limit and they threatened to storm the convent and burn it down if they refused to deliver the 'wicked nun' up to them. At this, the Abbess felt compelled to negotiate with the leaders of the uprising. She promised to punish Sister Agatha, and asked for three days' grace. The cooler heads among the townsfolk managed to persuade the rest to accept this offer. After the three days had passed, the crowd appeared at the convent gates once more, where they heard the Abbess announce that Sister Agatha had suddenly fallen ill and died. The chronicle leaves it unclear whether it really was chance that came to the Abbess' aid or whether they committed murder to satisfy the citizens. In times such as those, the latter was just as likely as the former.

However, things did not quieten down, as the townsfolk had hoped. In spite of the funeral, in spite of the coffin in the grave, in spite of the headstone with the name of the 'wicked nun' for all to see, rumours arose that Sister Agatha was still alive. It was common at that time for people not to believe in the deaths of hated or well-loved persons, and that is what happened in this case. People claimed to have seen the nun in different places and talked about raids in the course of which she attacked young men, until they were convinced that the Abbess had merely put on a show to avert the threat to the convent. Some of the others, who believed Sister Agatha was dead, felt it was a desecration of the sacred burial ground to put her body beside those of honest and pious citizens.

So both the credulous and the suspicious combined to demand that the grave be opened to prove that the nun was in it. Their hatred of that woman must have been terrible. When the furious townsfolk's intentions became known in the convent, they secretly removed the body from the grave at night and took it back to the convent. As told by the chronicle it seems as if there was a serious uprising among the citizens when they found the empty grave. They marched to the convent, and when the corpse was shown them from a window, they threw stones and wood at it and one even fired his gun. And the chronicle comments that the most furious of them all were the young men who had loved her when she was alive. As they realised in the convent that even death would not protect Sister Agatha from the hatred of her pursuers, they kept the body there and entombed it in the crypt where they put nuns who, for some reason, had been executed. That is the crypt we found today. It is on the route she used for her excursions into the town."

"Exactly", I said.

"And now you must tell me what gave you the idea that we had found the 'wicked nun'. I hadn't told you the end of the story. And how was it that you could tell that one of the mummies was Sister Agatha? And what was it that made you examine the picture up there for a clue as to what to do next?"

What could I say to him? Could I tell him about the nocturnal apparitions. I tried to set him on the right track with a question of my own, "Did you not see any similarity between the picture and the dead woman in the crypt?"

"No", said Dr. Holzbock, scrutinising the picture, that was now clearly visible in the morning sunshine, "but you need to look at it from close to." He took the ladder, which was still leaning in the corner, but found it impossible to take the painting down from the wall. And I – I refused to help him. I told two of the workmen to assist him and then left, for I could not get out of my mind the superstitious thought that it would be better if the portrait stayed on the wall. Once more the nocturnal apparitions were threatening to take over, even in broad daylight. I found myself entangled in a bizarre series of events and shuddered at my inability to extricate myself. They had wrapped themselves round me like the tendrils of some creeper. When I was outside in the bright sunshine and the noise and dust of the demolition work I decided that I would not concern myself with it any more, but go sick the next day and start my leave. But before that I wanted to conclude my observations that night; I was convinced something decisive was about to happen.

Fifteen minutes later Holzbock came out with the two workmen to tell me that it was impossible to move the picture from the wall without breaking the frame or cutting out the canvas. "Don't shrug your shoulders like that", he said. "You're behaving as if you knew more about all these mysterious matters than the chronicle. You must tell me what your opinion is, I'm going to write an article on our find for the *Publications of the Historical Association.*

And with that he went, leaving behind the impression of a very decent and learned man, who was not too troubled by romantic tendencies.

I felt as if the day were never going to end. Each separate hour crept past, grey-faced, like a bored, lethargic shadow. When evening came, my wife noticed my excitement and I only calmed her down by promising that I was going to stop work the next day. Eleven o'clock came, and still the light was burning beside my wife's bed. Tonight of all nights she seemed unable to get to sleep, and I was almost beside myself at the thought that my plan might be frustrated. Finally, it was already approaching twelve, she bent over me once more and, as I was pretending to be asleep, put out the light with a sigh and, two minutes later, was too fast asleep to hear me quietly get up and leave the room. Just as I was going out of the front door the clock on the tower of the old convent church struck twelve. I heard the cry, the sound of people running, then the woman was rushing past me – it was Agatha, she looked at me with her fearful, glowing eyes – then came the crowd of her pursuers.

I dashed off after them.

Again it was the same dreamy gliding and floating; the houses to the right and left seemed to me like sheer rock faces guiding our course. There were only two things I could see clearly: the group of pursuers in front of me and the night sky above us which was covered with white scraps of cloud, like ice floes on a river during the thaw. In the cracks and rifts of the cloud blanket the sickle moon appeared from time to time, a boat on the dark, fathomless waters of the sky.

Now the chase had reached the planks surrounding the demolition site, and the figures all disappeared before my eyes. But this time the pursuers did not flit uncertainly to and fro, but seemed to be swallowed up by a funnel. It looked as if they swirled up like a column of smoke and then were sucked into the ground. Then I found myself standing by the shaft I had ordered the workmen to dig that day. It was surrounded by the soil they had dug out and there were a few planks of wood and two red lamps to warn passers-by. But the planks over the opening that led down into the crypt had been thrown to one side. I tore open the door in the fence and, without bothering to look for the nightwatchman, who was probably at some other part of the extensive site, ran between the piles of rubble to the great courtyard, which was still surrounded by remains of the surrounding buildings. I do not know who or what it was that told me to go there, it was a compulsion I could not resist. Hardly had

I found a hiding place behind the remains of the arcade than the courtyard filled up with figures.

It is almost impossible to describe what I saw. It was all like a dream and yet perfectly clear. The figures came from the church, which I could see before me in the moonlight. What I cannot say is whether they came out of the door, which was wide open, or whether they emerged from the walls. There seemed to be so many all at once, that they could not all have come out through the door. The strangest thing of all was that I could see their every animated movement, the whole confusion of gestures, could see them calling, shouting at each other, elbowing each other aside and pushing their way through the crowd, gesticulating wildly, but the only sound I could hear was the noise of many footsteps. I could see them talking, but none of the words became audible, none of the shouts reached me. It was as if I were watching what was happening on a stage which was separated from me by a wall of thick glass, which sound could not penetrate, so that I could see everything, but not hear it. This impression was heightened by the fact that the actors in this animated scene were all in costume. Most were clad in the comfortable dress of a burgher of the sixteenth century, a few more slovenly, like students, or more formal, like aldermen.

You can reach a certain point of horror where all concern for yourself disappears and you only live through your eyes, all the other senses appearing to have been switched off. That point I had reached, and I can vouch for the fact that everything I saw really happened. The whole courtyard was full of people and occasionally some of them came so close to my hiding place that I could clearly see their faces and their rather fixed expressions. After a while they stopped running to and fro and all attention was directed at the door of the church, from which a group of men came leading a woman in their midst. They jostled her, slapped her across the face and tugged at the rope they had tied round her neck. I saw her shoulders twitch, as if she were trying to rid herself of an irritating insect. One of the students pushed all the others back, rushed forward and appeared to hurl some insult at her face as he hit her twice over the head with the flat of his short sword. At that the woman raised her smooth, white forehead and looked at the man with dark, flaming eyes. It was Sister Agatha, the wicked nun. Constantly kicking and beating her, they dragged her into the middle of the courtyard, where a group of aldermen dressed in black was standing. I saw her upright figure in a pale, timorous moonbeam, facing a group of men in whom the furious hatred of the entire group seemed to be concentrated. The white scarf had slipped down from her head and she looked just as she did on the picture in the sacristy.

One of the aldermen stepped forward and, with the crowd pressing in on all sides, broke a white stick over the nun's head and cast the pieces at her feet with an expression of loathing. Then the people drew back and left the space free where the nun was standing beside a block; in front of the block rose the figure of a man in a red cloak. I could see the gruesome execution in all its details. I saw the man draw his broad sword and throw off the red cloak; I saw him undo the nun's habit, revealing her beautiful neck and shoulders, and I saw him force her to her knees by the block. I could have screamed out loud, and yet I was glad that those dark, menacing eyes, which, in the last few minutes, she had fixed on my hiding place, as if she had discovered me, were finally turned away from me. Now her head was on the block, the executioner's sword arced through the moonlight and a jet of blood spurted up. But it did not fall back to the earth in a cascade of drops, but stayed in the air, as if it had frozen on the spot, whilst the head, as if following the nun's last thought, fell from the block and rolled directly towards me. The crowd threw their hats into the air and broke into wild rejoicing, which I could tell from their expressions, although no sound reached me. As if on a sudden impulse, they all threw themselves on the corpse, hitting it, kicking it and dragging it around, as if their fury had not yet been completely assuaged. In the meantime, however, the head continued to roll undeviatingly towards me and came to a stop right by my hiding place. The dark, blazing eyes fixed themselves on me and, for the first time during the whole terrible scene, I heard some words, words from the mouth of the decapitated head, "You will remember the wicked nun". Then everything vanished, the seething throng, the head, the executioner and his block, leaving only the crescent of frozen blood hovering for a moment in the green moon-light.

There is nothing to add, apart from the fact that the next morning Sister Agatha's body was found in the crypt in a terrible state. Disfigured by buffets and blows, all its limbs had been broken and the head had been separated from the body with one clean cut. It was suspected it might be a case of sexual perversion; a thorough investigation was carried out, in the course of which I was interrogated myself. But the police inquiries led nowhere, for I was careful not to tell them what I had seen during the night.

On the morning of July 17, 19... the whole town was shocked by the news of a dreadful crime. The maid who worked for a well-known local architect and civil engineer, Hans Anders, had knocked on her employers' bedroom door several times with no result when she shook the door-knob in one final attempt at ten o'clock and discovered that the door was not locked. She entered to find Frau Anders lying in her bed in a pool of blood; of Herr Anders nothing was to be seen. The maid ran out onto the stairs, screaming and crying uncontrollably, and when the neighbours had eventually managed to get out of her what she had seen, the young student from the third floor, who seemed to have the coolest head of all the agitated and horrified inhabitants of the block of flats, immediately sent for an ambulance and informed the police. When the detectives appeared, they realised at once they were dealing with a case of murder. The young woman had been dead for several hours; her head had been separated clean from her body with one mighty blow. Otherwise, everything in the flat was as it had been, except for one picture from the bedroom which had been taken down and completely destroyed: the frame had been broken into tiny pieces and the canvas ripped to shreds. There was nothing to suggest the murderer had broken in from outside and in her statement the maid confirmed that Herr and Frau Anders had gone to bed at the usual time the previous evening. When asked whether over the past few weeks she had seen any evidence of a disagreement between them she thought for a while before

saying that she had noticed nothing except that they seemed to
talk to each other less and less and that the wife had begun to
suffer from an occasional nervous tic. In spite of this, the only
conclusion possible was that Herr Anders, for reasons unknown, had murdered his wife and then fled. The other inhabitants of the flats confirmed what the maid had said, but none
of the statements provided any evidence for a serious quarrel
which might have led to such a terrible deed. The police doctor
warned against assuming that the lack of any outward signs of
disagreement meant that the couple were living in harmony;
with a highly civilised couple like Herr and Frau Anders such
catastrophes often take place silently and under the surface. The
doctor's observations only served to confirm the inspector's
theory and he immediately organised an extensive search for the
missing husband.

Hans Anders was found that afternoon, sitting on a bench in
the town park, his hat and walking stick beside him, rolling a
cigarette. He showed no resistance when the sergeant asked him
to accompany him to the station, and said he had already thought
of going to the police himself to explain what had happened. It
was a smiling Herr Anders, obviously in the best of spirits, who
entered the inspector's office and asked if he could spare him
a few minutes, as he would like to tell him why he had cut the
woman's head off.

The inspector stared at him in horror, "You admit you murdered your wife, Sir?"

Anders smiled, "My wife? – No!" Then he proceeded to give
such a strange and fantastic explanation that neither the inspector, nor the examining magistrate, who took over the case that
evening, could make head or tail of it. The one clear fact to
emerge was that Hans Anders admitted to having chopped off
the woman's head with a Turkish scimitar from his own weapon
collection, but that he insisted the woman was not his wife.
When he saw their looks of incomprehension, he referred them
to his acquaintance, Dr. Holzbock, the Director of the State
Archives who, he said, would confirm everything. Before Dr.
Holzbock could be sent for, however, he appeared of his own

178

accord and made the following statement to the examining magistrate:

"I consider it my duty to make a statement to throw what light I can on Herr Anders' terrible story, as far as that is possible in such a mysterious and bizarre case. I have been acquainted with him for a long time and recently we saw each other every day on the site where Herr Anders was in charge of the demolition of the former Jesuit Barracks. You will be aware of my historical and archaeological writings; I hoped to make some more interesting discoveries during the dismantling of this building, which was several hundred years old. I came across certain clues which suggested an underground passageway, and Anders, whose competence in architectural matters is beyond question, followed them up with such astuteness – and luck – that we succeeded in locating an old crypt containing several mummified corpses.

You will remember that the day after the discovery one of those corpses was found in a condition which suggested some perverse crime had been committed, though the investigation was inconclusive. A few days after that, Hans Anders came to see me. Before I tell you what he said, I feel I must state that for some days previously he had struck me as a changed man: he was not his normal energetic and charming self, but restless, at times absent-minded and at others touchy, sometimes he would start trembling, as if he was wracked by terrible fear. I noticed this change particularly when he came to see me, and when I asked him what was wrong, he was evasive. Before long, however, his restlessness got the better of him and he burst out,

'Her picture was sent to my house today.'

'Which picture?'

'The portrait of Sister Agatha, the wicked nun.'

'What are you talking about, that's in the sacristy and fixed so firmly to the wall that it can't be taken down.'

'That's right', he said, 'you tried and couldn't take it down? But I swear that it's hanging in my flat now.'

'Who brought it to your house?'

'I don't know, I was out when it arrived. A stranger brought it, hung it on the wall and then went, without saying who had sent him.'

'But it must be possible to find out who employed him to take the picture to you!'

'That's just it, that's just what I cannot find out. Eventually I went to ask the parish priest, but he knew nothing about it either. When I asked him whether he laid claim to the picture, since it was part of the church effects, he said he was glad to be rid of it, he had long had the intention of removing it. The awful thing is, I could not put the portrait back, even if I wanted to.'

'Why?'

'Because it is now as firmly attached to my wall as it was to the sacristy wall before. It's incredible, but it's true, and I would like you to come and see for yourself.'

I must admit that I found Anders' story very strange. According to him, the picture was the portrait of Sister Agatha, one of the nuns whose mummies we had found in the crypt. In order to calm him down, I promised that I would visit him in the course of the next few days, and I remembered my promise towards the end of that week when I happened to be passing the block of flats where he lived. Anders was out but his wife was at home.

'I am so glad you have come', she said. 'I had already made up my mind to go and see you. You are the only person who has a fairly close acquaintance with my husband. He respects you, and I hope that means you will have some influence over him.'

When I explained that I was happy to do anything within my power to assist her, she immediately burst into tears and said her husband must be ill. He was looking so distraught, scarcely spoke a word all day and spent the whole night tossing and turning in his bed. Several days ago he had promised her he would ask for leave and go away for a holiday, as he was obviously tired and overworked, but now she could not persuade him to leave the town.

'I hardly dare suggest he see the doctor any more. At the merest mention he flies into a rage, as if I had suggested something humiliating.'

I agreed with her that the best thing to do would be to persuade him to take a holiday. Shortly after that, Anders arrived home.

He was visibly pleased to see me, and gave his wife a kiss, though I had the feeling nevertheless that there was something wrong between them. There was some invisible influence, a shadow, an insubstantial being, dividing them. On Frau Anders the effect of this influence was fear and on Herr Anders – I thought I must be wrong at first, but later my suspicion was confirmed – repugnance towards his wife, a repugnance mixed with fear. I found that most odd, since I knew that Anders had been very much in love with his wife. After a few minutes of polite conversation, Frau Anders withdrew, to allow me to keep my promise and try to persuade Anders to take a holiday. Scarcely had she left than he grabbed me by the arm and pulled me into the bedroom, 'Come with me', he said, 'and you shall see her.'

Above the ottoman – opposite the beds – was the picture from the sacristy. Beside it was a green curtain, which had been drawn back. It is a rather eerie picture, a face that seems to express the most violent depravity, and if it is indeed the portrait of Sister Agatha, then it fully confirms everything the old chronicle said about her scandalous behaviour. I went over to it with the intention of seeing if I could take it down; I wanted to show Anders that it was all his imagination and bring him back to reality. But he jumped up and pushed me away with such an angry gesture that I was quite taken aback.

'What do you think you are doing?' he said. 'It's impossible. It's there on the wall, and there is no power in the world that can move it.'

He had obviously forgotten that only a few days ago he himself had invited me to come to his flat to confirm his story.

'But why', I asked, 'did you have it put in your bedroom, of all rooms. That face could disturb even the most peaceful sleep.'

'I told you', replied Anders, 'that I was not at home when the man came. It was the man who brought it who hung it there without asking, and now I can't move it. I tried hanging a curtain over it but' – his voice became quite hoarse with excitement – 'she will not allow it. If I draw the curtain in the evening, it's been pulled back by midnight. She keeps on looking at me, all the time, with those terrible eyes. I can't bear it any longer. And

do you know why she is looking at me like that? I'll tell you.'
He drew me away from the picture and whispered, so quietly
that I could hardly understand him, 'She has sworn vengeance
on me, and she will keep her word. She is planning some dreadful deed, and I think I have an idea what it is.' Suddenly he broke
off with a question which, at the time, seemed completely
unconnected with his train of thought. 'Have you had a good
look at my wife?' But, before I could answer, he went on, 'Nonsense! I sometimes think ... but it's all nonsense', and then he
returned to the nun, 'She intends to destroy me because I opened
up the underground passage, because I was the one who ordered
the men to dig up the street, allowing her pursuers to enter the
crypt.' He waved away my objections, 'Believe me, my dear
Holzbock, that is the truth. I have thought the whole matter over
carefully, and if you had seen what I have seen, you would
agree.'

It was only later, of course, that I learnt what Anders meant
by these dark hints, but the words of the conversation etched
themselves indelibly on my memory, together with the expression on his face close to mine as he whispered to me. His behaviour suggested to me that he was seriously ill, but it was in vain
that I tried to persuade him to leave the town and spend a few
weeks in the mountains.

'I must stick it out', he said. 'There would be no point in trying
to flee. She would find me even if I were ten thousand feet up
in the mountains, just as easily as she found me here.'

The most frightening thing about him was that he was obviously wrestling with some ghostly delusion as if it were a real
power, and I pointed out to Frau Anders that this was where she
should try to influence him. 'Influence?' she said. 'I have not
even enough influence for him to let me call the doctor.'

To do something for the poor woman, I sent round my friend,
Doctor Engelhorn, to see Anders the next morning. But he flew
into a rage and the doctor had to beat a hasty retreat. It was just
then that I had to leave the town because I needed to search
through the archives at Pernstein Castle for an important historical document. It took me a few days to find it and in the
course of my search I made several other interesting finds, so

that I ended up staying on for several more days. On my return journey I left the train a few stations before the town to get some fresh air and walk the rest of the way through the woods. There is an inn on the way which is popular for outings, and as I passed I looked over the fence and saw Hans Anders sitting in the garden. I must admit that while working in the archives I had completely forgotten him, and seeing him there reminded me of the duty I owed to a friend. In order at least to find out how he was, I went into the inn garden and greeted him. I could tell he had had a lot to drink, and as he was normally extremely abstemious, I assumed it had something to do with his mysterious story.

'Ah, Holzbock, our Master of the Rolls', he called out to me, 'welcome in the name of scholarship.' He talked a great deal and so loudly that he aroused the attention of the ten or twelve other customers in the garden. To my half-pint of wine from the vineyards of southern Moravia, he downed three, and it was already beginning to get dark when I managed to persuade him to set off for home. We walked along the river and could already see the lights of the King's Mill ahead of us through the mist that was filling the valley when Anders finally began to talk of the matter, which I could tell had been occupying his mind all along.

'At last I know what she wants.'

'Don't keep talking about 'her', as if it were a real person', I snapped.

Anders stared at me. He was so at home in his fantasy world that he could not understand my protest. 'And do you know what is happening before my very eyes? It's terrible. She is taking over my wife.'

'What on earth do you mean by that?'

'She is taking over my wife, I can see the change taking place before my very eyes. It began with her eyes: an alien, watchful expression has appeared in them, she is observing me all the time, my every movement. Whenever I say something, a look of dreadful scorn flares up in them. Then her body began to change as well. My wife was smaller and plumper, the woman I now see at the table or sleeping beside me – or rather, pretending to sleep, for she is still watching me from beneath her closed eyelids – is taller and slimmer. She is hemming me in, spinning a web round me. She has murdered my wife and taken possession of her body, so as to be close to me, and on the day when the resemblance between her and the picture on the wall is complete, she will take possession of me, too. But I am determined that it will not come to that.'

With horror I realised that his nervous agitation had reached a point where one could talk of derangement. It was high time to take serious measures, and on the following morning I was discussing with my friend Engelhorn what to do next to help poor Frau Anders, when she was announced. She looked pale and distraught, with restless, hollow eyes; she had lost weight, which made her look slightly taller.

'Dear Frau Anders', I said, 'I know all about it.'

She burst into tears. 'How can you know. You can have no idea what I am suffering. My life has become a hell on earth, and that's not just an empty phrase, but the bitter truth. I can't bear it any more; my husband has changed completely, I can clearly see that he loathes me. He's watching me all the time, I can feel his terrible eyes on me, and he behaves as if he expected something evil from me. Sometimes he suddenly turns round with a furious gesture, as if he thinks I'm creeping up on him. And he hardly talks to me at all, and if I speak to him, he answers as if every word were a trap. And if I ask him why he is behaving in this odd way, he just gives a horrible laugh. Yesterday evening, for example, he had been out all afternoon and came home slightly drunk; I was just starting to get undressed when I suddenly found him behind me. He had been in his study; I had seen him through the glass door leafing through a notebook. And all of a sudden he was behind me. He had crept up on me silently, and when I turned round he grabbed me by the neck and said, 'A beautiful neck, and it's already been cut through once.' I was terrified and asked him what he meant by that. But he laughed his awful laugh again and pointed to the old picture on our bedroom wall, 'Ask her or, better still, ask yourself.' I could not get to sleep all night, I was thinking over those strange words. In the morning I got up and went to his room to find the note-book, for I thought it must in some way be connected with the change in him. It was still on the desk, it was almost filled with my husband's handwriting. I remembered then that I had often seen him writing in it during the last few weeks, in a strange, hurried manner, often as if he were distraught, and so irritable that any noise nearby would send him wild, and I would have given anything to know what it was that so absorbed and excited him. But as I was about to begin reading, I was overcome with a terrible fear which swamped my curiosity. I did not even dare to open it for fear ... for fear of learning something terrible. That is why I have brought it to you to ask you to read it and tell me what to do. You only need tell me as much as you think fit.'

With that she handed me this notebook, this notebook that I am now handing over to the authorities. You will find it contains a bizarre story, which just seemed to confuse matters to me; I leave it to you to fit all the pieces together.* Doctor Engelhorn and I tried to calm Frau Anders down and, although we were convinced that danger was near, we behaved as if she had nothing to fear. We managed to get her to go home in a reasonably composed state of mind after we had promised to read her husband's notebook and report on them to her the very next day. And that was our mistake, an unpardonable mistake; our lack of presence of mind and vigorous action cost the poor woman her life. That is the trouble with people: we see the danger quite clearly but do nothing to counter it in time. When we – Doctor Engelhorn and I – had read the notebook, we just stared at each other. 'He's insane', I said. But Doctor Engelhorn is a strange person; although trained in the exact sciences, he has retained a kind of superstitious belief in a kind of 'twilight zone' of the human soul. He takes every opportunity he can to quote Hamlet, 'There are more things in heaven and earth etc.', and whenever medical science is baffled, there is no one who is more pleased than Doctor Engelhorn. So I was not particularly surprised when he gave me a sceptical look.

'Insane? I'm not sure that I agree with you there. That is not the impression he makes on me. There are states of mind which are damned close to insanity and yet are not. To explain that,

* Hans Anders' story forms the first part of this report.

however, I would have ...'

I interrupted him, 'What else could it be?'

He merely shrugged his shoulders. 'I don't know.'

That conversation took place late in the evening. The next morning I heard that Frau Anders had been murdered. Hans Anders alone can tell us the events that led up to the terrible deed. We can only assume he was trying to free himself from a ghost, and the destruction of the picture fits in quite well with that. It will be up to the court to decide whether it is the psychiatrist who will have the last word in this strange story."

Thus Dr. Holzbock, the Director of the State Archives, concluded his statement.

Two days later the mysterious case of Hans Anders was brought to a kind of conclusion by the death of Anders himself. He was found in the police cell, sitting on his bed and leaning back against the wall, his left hand on his heart, his right arm hanging down loosely at his side in such a strangely twisted position that the police doctor shook his head as he began to examine it. It was broken in several places and dislocated, as if it had been crushed with tremendous force. But the cause of death, the doctor established, was heart failure due to a sudden shock.

The Kiss of the Stone Woman

Franz Theodor Csokor

It was about two o'clock in the morning and the disc of the moon was dissolving beneath a bank of mist in the western sky as the Lieutenant and his platoon reached the enemy town.

Often enough in the course of the dreary march they had been asleep on their feet, and now more than one of them blundered into the wrought-iron gates of the suburb they were passing through, and yet they stumbled doggedly on. Here they felt even more deserted and forlorn than outside the town on the track bordered by the wall of dark trees. In the semi-dark the bare trees of the avenue looked charred. Small villas squatted palely behind the sparse foliage of clumps of bushes which raised their twigs like hackles in front of them. They all seemed to have been abandoned, and the Lieutenant did not even bother to stop, since none of them seemed to offer a billet large enough for the whole unit for the rest of this autumn night, already quivering with the approach of morning. So the column wound its way through a gateway in a massive tower into the old town. There was a soft clinking as the ranks broke step. Here marching was much more difficult than on the broad highway. Alleys suddenly shot off, confusingly haphazard. The cobbles were a hindrance, too, buckling the feet: they were bumpy, as if they were being squeezed up by the ancient houses flanking the street which cowered there beside the road, low and chalk-white, in an attitude of senile malevolence. And not a sound nor light in any of them; only here and there, outside gaping doors dripping with blackness, stood abandoned household effects. Wailing from behind broken window-panes suggested abandoned infants; when torches slashed through the darkness, it was cats that scurried out of bare rooms. The men would have liked to clamp a rest onto such incidents; mercilessly the Lieutenant drove them on. The houses looked ready to pounce, their exits yawning black like tunnel openings, and, although there seemed no reason to fear an enemy attack, in view of the many reports of partisan activity, he felt it was not advisable to halt outside them, let alone camp out in one. The main contingent could do that when they arrived the next day; the advance guard needed open space around their quarters, in an emergency they would also have to serve as a fortress.

But such a place was not that easy to find, and so they marched on in growing irritation through this dead waste of stone, where the echo of their steps created an ambush at every corner. The skein of alleys became more and more warped and cramped, as if twisted by a gigantic pair of pliers, impossible to disentangle; then, after twenty minutes of weary tramping, around a tight bend the cathedral square abruptly opened out before the exhausted men, broad, sprinkled with nooks and crannies, paraffin lamps on its stone arcades glowing like bloody nails. And opposite them something needle-sharp steepled up from a huge dark mass, slitting the midnight-blue sky, whilst its unfinished twin tower peered at them dispiritedly over the high-pitched minster roof, as if it had made a similar attempt and then slumped back down.

The men straightened up, broke the silence; one sang. They were the first peaceful lights their eyes had seen in weeks of blazing forests and burning farmsteads. Soon the window of one of the dark houses round the square must surely pierce the night with its friendly yellow glow, full of the promise of rest! Their hope was not deceived. One building, detached from the others, had a red lamp burning over the lintel; as they approached they saw the bright spot of a lamp on the first floor and the glitter of light flashing through a gap in the shutters of a ground-floor window. The Lieutenant sent men to reconnoitre the house, and it turned out to be precisely what he was looking for, even though the exterior seemed so strangely derelict and eerie to him, as if it were the product of depravity and decay, that he made a cautious circuit of it himself. On all sides it was separated from its neighbours, with the additional protection against attack from the rear of a broad, dark canal; the façade was set against the cathedral, which returned its look defiantly. The single entrance was on this side too, high, well-preserved double doors. He ordered weapons at the ready as the bell was rung. After a while there was a shuffling of footsteps and the rasp of a key in the lock, then the doors creaked open.

An old woman appeared, wrapped up in a few clothes she had thrown on. What do you want?" she murmured. The girls have left." What do you think?" growled the sergeant. "Warm beds and no bugs." The man next to him switched on his torch. "What do we need girls for? We've got you!" In the bright beam the old woman screwed up her face to such ugliness that the raucous laughter came tumbling out of the platoon and she joined in with a toothless giggle. "Stop messing around, men", said the Lieutenant urgently, then, turning to the old woman, "Have you room for us?" "And how long for?" added the comedian with the torch. She grinned. "Until Judgment Day, sonny, if you like." "Sergeant", ordered the Lieutenant, "take three men, comb the building and report back here." "And you can be our guide, my pretty maiden", said the Sergeant, pulling the old woman along by the shoulder.

When they had gone, the rest unbuckled their knapsacks and squatted down, their knees drawn up with their rifles across them. It was drowsily warm in the hallway; added to that was a strange, overpowering smell, which struck every one of them the moment they entered, a sickly, rotten smell that might come from the mouldy walls. "Make-up on old apples", someone had said. The Sergeant and his men reappeared from the stairs, grinning and winking, and solved the puzzle. He had not noticed anything suspicious, but he had figured out the previous use of the building and revealed it to his superior officer, only with difficulty maintaining the seriousness appropriate to an official report. His announcement was greeted with stifled laughter until the Lieutenant's command to find somewhere to sleep put a stop to it.

The old woman lit a lamp and hobbled along in front of them. On the first floor she unlocked a door which had the extra protection of an iron grille and the soldiers, apart from one whom the Lieutenant left on the landing, stamped into a spacious room with the light they had seen from the market square outside hanging from the ceiling under a red vellum shade. It was overheated and the smell etched itself even more strongly on the stale air than in the corridor, but the soldiers paid that as little attention as the garish prints of Rubensesque deities on the walls and all the tawdry splendour of the room. All they had eyes for were the six-foot-long plush armchairs grouped around circular stone tables; hardly had the officer given permission than they were stretched out on them, almost dead to the world. The old woman seemed disappointed. "Why all the hurry? Each of the fine gentlemen could have had a room of his own. The little doves have all flown." But none of them felt like getting up again and the Lieutenant thought it better to keep them all together. "But it's no place for you here, Captain", she went on. He hesitated, "Only if there's a room nearby." "Along the corridor, Captain, it's just along a short corridor", she assured him. "Make up your mind. I'll get the bed ready anyway, just in case." With that she limped off without waiting for his answer. The Lieutenant still felt uneasy about the whole arrangement. "A second guard downstairs!" he ordered. "Outside the old woman's door. Any volunteers?" The young soldier who had teased her in the hall stood up. "Here, Sir! – I'm wide awake enough to catch any of you who fancies slipping into her bedroom", he joked, turning to his comrades, who grunted sleepy denials of any such intentions. The old woman appeared again, "Ready, Captain."

They went out into the corridor, followed by the young soldier. Through the window, that the Lieutenant ordered her to shut fast, they could see the mass of the cathedral looming over the roofs, dark and heavy, as if it were made of bronze. The Lieutenant indicated it to the old woman, "What do you call the church?" "It is the cathedral of Jehan the Warrior; he had it built seven hundred years ago in memory of his dead wife." "She was a martyr?" The old woman nodded. "They say her corpse had no head and in its place on the skeleton lay a swan's skull. The inhabitants believe she protects the town; they prayed at her tomb yesterday, before they fled." "And you, why did you stay?" She shrugged her shoulders. "I know your language; I've done nothing, you wouldn't harm me. This is the room, Captain." Turning round, she noticed the other soldier. "What does he want?" "He will be on watch in the corridor." "At your boudoir door", crooned the soldier. "God, such a young thing", said the old woman, touched with compassion, "wait, I'll put a glass of wine outside the door." The old woman held the lantern over the stairwell and let him go on ahead. Mechanically, the Lieutenant registered her shadow; curving round the snail-shell wall of the stairs, it seemed to pounce on the guard's shadow. "Such a young thing!" he heard her giggle through her cough; then, all at once, it was dark and still.

The Lieutenant opened the door to his room. A paralysing warmth clutched at him. A match replaced the weak light of his torch, but he almost jumped with fright when it flared up. It blazed back at him a hundredfold from all sides, and when the two candles on the oak tables cast their flickering light, he was astonished to see that the walls and ceiling of the room were covered with square mirrors. Looking up, he felt as if he were standing at the heart of a crystal, for above him were fantastically crinkled rooms ranged one over the other, with disjointed reflections of himself and the candles upside down inside them. In spite of this proliferation, the light from the candles did not bring brightness; it somehow seemed to contain darkness, as if seen through sooty window-panes. With a shake of the head, the Lieutenant began to inspect the room. Beside the door roared a well-stoked iron stove, its angled pipe eating a black hole in the wall. A wardrobe with a mirror front and a glass-topped wash-stand gave the room a touch of opulence, which was underlined by the blood-red velvet armchair by the window. The most bewildering item, however, was the massive four-poster bed, whose black drapes made it look as if some noble were lying in state there. In order to avoid the temptation to stretch out on it, the Lieutenant, overcoming his curiosity, did not touch the curtains, but first of all searched through the rest of the furniture to see if he could find a needle and thread, of which he was in urgent need. The wardrobe contained nothing but a pair of stiletto-heeled slippers and fragments of twigs; all the more numerous were the things the occupant had left behind on the wash-stand when she fled: make-up, soaps, bottles of perfume. But what he was looking for was not there, no more than in the drawer, which revealed a tube of lip-salve and the photograph of a jockey punctured with pins, documenting a wretched existence eked out among blows, exploitation and hysteria. These thoughts sent a rush of scorching blood to the Lieutenant's face as they awoke the picture of the little actress he had left behind, unprotected; he tore open his uniform and went to the window, where he had to break the glass with his bayonet because the bolt had jammed in the heat. He breathed in deeply as he leant out. Below him the canal rippled darkly; occasionally something even blacker glided across it, but that could have been a delusion from his overheated brain. The only thing left to be done before going to sleep was to take the map and make a quick sketch of tomorrow's march. He pulled the armchair up to the table and started by plotting in the route they had taken since leaving the regiment yesterday. But he could not find the name of the town. Or were his shimmering eyes already failing him entirely? He was dully aware of a swarm of memories, plans, desires buzzing round his head: was he hearing them, thinking them, seeing them ...? He could not distinguish between them any more; the one thing he did know was that he had to get up out of the soft upholstery of the armchair if he did not want his eyelids to fuse together, and he felt himself stand up ponderously and set off towards the swirl of fresh air at the window. But the way there led past the bed, surely a soft bed with fresh linen such as he had not slept in for months. His hands refused to obey; they parted the curtains ...

He started back. There was already someone lying on the pillows.

The Lieutenant rubbed his eyes and forehead, but the apparition remained: a woman, a sleeping woman. All his tiredness left him, such was the spell her face cast over him. And yet it was hardly what he would have called beautiful. It had an ageless expression, and only the dishevelled dark blond hair gave it a suggestion of youth, though there was also something virginally austere and capricious about its shape. The forehead was large for the rest of the features. The hard, thin nose that sprang from the slender, arched brows held a hint of crookedness, and deep furrows stretched down from the tight nostrils to clasp the lips. They, too, had something odd about the way they were set: compared with the full, rounded curve of the upper lip, the lower one looked as if it had been ground down and was pale, almost bloodless, giving the mouth a constant, almost frozen smile. The closed lids were bluish, as if stretched taut over brass spheres, suggesting deep sleep, but abruptly, as though they felt the brush of other eyes, a movement appeared in them which quivered through the whole body, dislodging the blanket for a round shoulder to take shape over the black silk of the night-dress. At the same time the eyes opened; neither fright nor surprise clouded the greenish-grey pupils. The girl simply said, as if he was expected, "I'm sorry, I've been waiting too long."

The Lieutenant looked at her in surprise then, remembering the recent history of the house, could not suppress a smile at the clever way the old dame had presented her last remaining protégée to him. So he sat down on the edge of the bed and fell in with her intimate tone. "A good job you woke up, otherwise I would have taken you for a ghost." "You would have regretted it", she said calmly, "the people they appear to here never talk about it afterwards." "Why ever not?" he joked. "Do they die from it?" "You said it", she smiled. This took him aback, but then he told himself he was a fool to be chatting to a whore about ghosts instead of making the most of the opportunity. "So what?" he cried, "I'll risk it and more, my pretty little ghost!" and he drew her to him as she reared up with a snake-like thrust. But then he felt himself pulled down, as if he were clasping a block of marble, and he yielded to her, overcome by the self-absorbed, icy sensuality of the way she took him. As he entered her, he sensed her lack of response; giving nothing herself, she received him coolly, eyes half-closed. Her coldness whipped him up to a furious compulsion to squeeze one groan, one sob of passion from her, but he spent himself in vain: she bestowed her favours with a sovereign disdain that made the slightest twitch of her high, taut shoulders an act of the utmost condescension. He sought her lips, but she withheld them with a sharp, "Not yet", and however much he twisted and turned, he could not manage to kiss them. He was about to plant his mouth on them when, with a shrill laugh, she slipped from under him and pushed him away. "Enough!" Her voice was so firm that he gave up any idea of a further assault. She lay back in the pillows and stretched, staring absently at the ceiling, as if she were alone. The Lieutenant felt he looked a fool; he racked his brains for a topic of conversation that would offer a bridge between them, for with this creature violence would just mean further humiliation. "Do you live here?" "No, across the market place." She pointed towards the corridor. "But that must be where the cathedral is?" "Perhaps", she said in a flat voice. "It varies. Once I did live here, and every evening I used to feed the black swans with the purple beaks. Did you see my swans?" He recalled the dark shadows gliding over the water below the window. "Yes. But why do you call them your swans?" "My husband gave them me as a present. Oh, he was a wild lord and his swans protected me when he put out to sea. One of his brothers once thought he would swim down the canal till he reached my house, but my favourite swan sailed out to meet him, and beat him with its wings and pecked him with its beak until he sank. When my husband heard of it on his return, he killed the swan and me – and –" The Lieutenant felt everything around him dissolving into confusion until he was no longer sure who he was and whether it was not his own fate he had just been listening to. "Stop!" he croaked and clenched his fists at her as she went on speaking in a monotone, as stony as her embrace had been, "– since then I have belonged to anyone whose fate it is to meet his end in my lord's town; but first of all –" He had been about to throw himself at her, but some inexplicable fear grabbed him by the throat and thrust him into the armchair, where he collapsed as if his spine had been broken. "Stop!" he panted once more, but she finished what she had to say in the same soft, level tones, "– but first of all I kiss them. Wait!" As if she were a viper, he dashed her from his lips as she suddenly struck upwards at them. "No!" Then she began to laugh; softly at first; but then it swelled, becoming loud, shrill, and the Lieutenant could not stop her, he stared at the woman from his knees, and she laughed and laughed, her mouth unmoving; or was it still the woman laughing? That was more like a stone statue, the head and overslender body with its small, imperious breasts held rigidly erect! A spasm of hatred jolted his body. She must be silenced! She must! He thrust himself up and grasped at her throat – something dark seemed to crash down on him; blindly he clawed about him as he plunged into a bottomless abyss.

Finally he found a hold and shovelled his way up through invisible, glutinous mud towards the half-light – reached it – was sitting – at the table in his room – with a guttering candle – opposite a huge cross – no, it was the wood of the window set off against a pale red sky; but the laughter still continued. He stumbled over to the bed and tore back the drape – it had not been slept in. A dream then, apart from the laughter, that horrible laughter, now it was coming in hoarse gusts, from below by the sound of it. From the earth? No, the old woman's bedroom was down there! An icy hand laid itself on his heart; he turned the door-handle: locked. He kicked it in. From the corridor he could see something dimly flitting to and fro across the market square, which was veiled in clouds of crimson smoke; at the same time there was the crackle of a distant rifle skirmish. "Partisans!" was the Lieutenant's immediate reaction; they had presumably lit damp wood and were waiting until the smoke would force the trapped soldiers out. He shouted for the Sergeant, tripping, as he did so, over something soft in the smoky corridor; when he touched it, it felt sticky and warm. The light of the match revealed the guard from the hall who, with his throat cut through, had dragged himself to his doorway to report the attack. Now clouds of smoke were billowing up the stairs, and still the laughing continued, although weak and ailing now. He threw himself into the fumes of the stairwell, heard voices pleading his name; shadows whisked down to the hall, hung in the air, sank to the ground; and there was the door to the old woman's room, wide open – but where was the young soldier? He raised his light. She had gone, and a whimpering bundle was writhing about on her bed like a worm on a pin; it was tied hand and foot to the bedstead, its clothes hanging in tatters, dripping blood down to the knees. A scream of horror rose to the Lieutenant's lips, but before he could help the mutilated soldier, he was torn away by cries from his men as the infernal uproar outside seethed ever closer. In the hall he met up with what was left of the platoon; they had managed to drive the insurgents out of the house, but only with difficulty, and they would be no match for them when they returned with reinforcements. Quickly, he glanced around to assess the situation. "Men!" he ordered, "we must get across the square. We can only hold out in the church tower. Save your ammunition! Fix bayonets!" A metallic click, and they set off.

In a few seconds they had stamped out the rampart of glimmering brushwood and were facing the enemy, who scattered in surprise, without waiting for the onset. Lips clenched, blackened with soot, fingers on the trigger, they set off for the cathedral, led by the Lieutenant. But now the partisans, after the initial shock of the platoon's sudden sally, had recovered their nerve. The one out in front was hurling screams from a mouth set like a foaming abscess in his face, and from around him black waves surged towards them. They approached in swaying clusters amid a cacophony of raucous shouts, jeers of abuse from the women and adolescent squeals; fists punched the air, here and there the gleam of firearms. The outnumbered unit seemed lost in the maelstrom of attackers, but finally the cathedral steps came down to meet them and they shoved their way up, hobbling, half naked, brushing the tangle of pursuers back with a few well-aimed shots. Then they were inside, hastily shutting the bronze doors, barricading them with pews and heaving a sigh of relief in the cool of this high nave which had probably not witnessed any fighting since the days of religious conflict. Now axes were smashing against the portal; it would surely hold until they were in the tower. Safe for a while, the soldiers swept their torches up and down the church. Along the side walls stone knights surveyed them from memorial slabs, hands on swords, small lions beneath their spurred feet. Impossibly emaciated saints gazed at them ecstatically from the niches in the massive clustered columns. Looking for the door to the tower, they came to the chancel and one of them lit the candelabra by the choir-screen. The high altar rose in terraces behind it, square grey blocks and faded gold, with a drop of blood floating in the air in front: the eternal flame of the sanctuary lamp. At the north side they turned back and found the confusion of figures on a baroque pulpit surging towards them: on the base Lucifer was being cast down into hell with a force that seemed to burst through the stone flags, whilst Saint Michael and all the

196

angels thrust with their spears from the canopy; in the quivering candlelight it almost came to life. They opened the door next to it, but it was not the stairs they were hoping to find. It gave onto the curving, filigree stonework of a courtyard surrounded by cloisters and two figures running across into the adjoining convent; quickly they barricaded this door as well.

But now the hammering on the west portal had stopped, a crescendo of noise surged in from the cloisters, the marble floor blazed in a swirl of colour from the flames shining in through the great rose window. Shots ripped through the side-door and clattered against the walls. Finally their assailants grouped together to batter the door down with brief thrusts, accompanied by the screech of metal and the groan of splitting wood. Then the Lieutenant found the stair and called to his men. But at that moment the barred door yielded under the impact of the cheering blow, cutting them off and sweeping them back against the pulpit, which they quickly climbed to pour shot after shot into the howling mob. At this the attackers divided into two groups: the cautious mass squeezed along the rear wall farthest from the soldiers towards the spiral stairs leading up to the pulpit, thus shutting the door to the tower, behind which the Lieutenant was hiding, whilst the rest furiously stormed the pulpit head on. That brought the unequal struggle to a rapid conclusion, and the Lieutenant could do nothing but watch from the organ, where he stood panting. Amongst the tangle of plaster figures, which seemed to join in like demons, the struggle foamed its way up to the platform of the pulpit, swallowing up the defenders one by one. They were all engulfed in the storm of triumph echoing back a hundredfold from the groined vaults. It pierced the Lieutenant to the heart, and without thinking he raised his revolver and emptied the whole magazine into the snarl of bodies. The shock of the attack stunned the mob for a second, then their howling fury erupted against the tower steps. The Lieutenant threw away his empty revolver and set off at a run. There was only one thought left in his mind: to stay alive until the reinforcements arrived! But then this hell-hole would explode in fire and blood! Now he was inside the first of the gigantic twins, the mutilated tower. He flew up the winding wooden steps, past the thudding from the housing of the huge clock; rats squeaked below, bats swept up past him, kestrels shot mewing out through the narrow slits in the masonry, whilst nearer and nearer came the raging thunder of the pursuit. That did not worry him, he knew they could only climb the narrow spiral in the tower one by one. Moreover, where he turned into the open gallery along the facade that led to the completed tower, he managed to use his bayonet to dislodge the ladder giving access, thus putting a temporary gap between himself and the enemy. He was bathed in warm air as he stepped out into the open. He was standing in the full, strong light of the morning sun, which glowed through the dissolving mist like a sharply incised disc, whilst in the town laid out below him only the spikes on the gables were caught in its rays and blazed up, as if in a presentiment of the revenge to come. For grains and threads of grey were trickling down the hillside opposite. The Lieutenant realised what it was and screamed with delight. Fifteen – no – ten minutes hidden in the stone forest of the pinnacles of the second tower, and then the battle-cry of his liberators would freeze his pursuers to the marrow and drive them back into their hiding holes; but this time they would find them, all of them! They only needed to ask him, him! He rushed on, panting. Gargoyles jutted out in his way; he crawled underneath them. The royal forebears of the stem of Jesse stuck their sandstone arms into his chest; he broke them off with a blow from the bayonet handle and threw the crumbling rock to the ground below. Nothing could stop him now, not even if the whole façade should come to life against him and swarm with men, as at the time when it was being built. Now he held the fate of this town in his hand, a remorseless, merciless fate! He had to steady himself for a moment. His lust for revenge was almost making him drunk, and his eye was already fixed on the square below, choosing the sites for the gallows.

But abruptly the enormous statue of a woman barred his path along the gallery, as if it had stepped out from the wall. Her profile seemed familiar, as did the imperious posture of her thin body, which pushed visibly against the thin folds of the drapery. He could only get past by climbing behind her, over the iron bar attaching her to the masonry. He quickly twisted himself into the gap; there was a crackling and crumbling of sandstone, but here was no place to pause for thought. For a mere heartbeat he had to step on the iron, but even that was too much. The bar bent and he was clinging to the woman in desperation. He swung round onto her front, the abyss below him: one more swing would take him onto the safety of the gallery on the farther side! To get a good push off, he pulled himself up until he was close to the stone face, that regarded him with a fixed smile. It was the face of the unknown woman he had spent the night with! He was about to scream out loud, but at that moment the overthin neck broke, and, as he plummeted in a breathstopping fall, his last sensation was of those lips, which she had withheld from him, now harshly sucking at his own.

DEATH

The Death of Christoph Detlev Brigge of Ulsgard

From: *The Papers of Malte Laurids Brigge*

Rainer Maria Rilke

Whenever I think of home, where there is no one any more, then I imagine it must have been different in former times. In those days people knew (or at least they sensed) that they had death *inside* them, like the seed in the fruit. Children had a small death inside them and grown-ups a large one. The women had it in their womb and the men in their chest. They *had* it there, and that gave them a peculiar dignity and quiet pride.

With my grandfather, the old Chamberlain, you could still tell just by looking at him that he bore his Death within him. And what a Death it was: it lasted for two months, and was so loud that it could be heard on the outlying parts of the estate.

The long, narrow manor house was too small for this Death, it looked as if we would have to add wings, for the Chamberlain's body grew bigger and bigger and he was constantly demanding to be carried from one room to another and would fall into a dreadful rage if the day was not yet over and there was no room left in which he had not already lain. Then off up the stairs went the whole procession – servants, maids and dogs, which he always had about him – led by the steward, into the room in which his mother had died, which had been kept exactly in the state in which she had left it, twenty-three years ago, and which no one else was allowed to enter. The curtains were opened, and the sturdy light of a summer afternoon examined all the shy, startled objects and pirouetted clumsily in the gaping mirrors. And the people were just the same. There were lady's maids whose curiosity was so aroused that they had no idea where their hands were, young servants who stared at everything, and old servants who went round trying to remember all the things they had been told about this locked room, where they now had the good fortune to find themselves.

But it was the dogs, above all, who seemed to be uncommonly

excited at being in a room in which all the things smelt. The tall, slender Russian greyhounds ran busily to and fro behind the armchairs, traversed the chamber with their long, rocking dance-steps, stood up like dogs on a coat of arms and, resting their slim paws on the white and gold window-ledge, looked with pointed, expectant faces and receding foreheads to the right and to the left down into the courtyard. Little dachshunds, the colour of new gloves, sat in the broad, silk-covered chair by the window, an expression on their faces as if everything was as usual, and a bristle-haired, grumpy looking pointer rubbed its back against the edge of a gold-legged table whilst on the painted top the Sèvres cups trembled.

It was a terrible time for those absent-minded, sleepy objects. It sometimes happened that books would be opened clumsily by some hasty hand and rose petals would tumble out, to be trampled underfoot; tiny, delicate things were grasped and, when they immediately broke, were quickly put back down again, some objects that had been bent were put behind curtains, or even thrown behind the golden trellis of the fire-guard. And from time to time, something fell, fell with a dull thud onto the carpet, with a ringing crack onto the parquet, but it broke on the spot, it shattered with a sharp crash or split almost noiselessly, for these things, pampered as they were, could not stand the least fall.

And had it occurred to anyone to ask what was the cause of all this, what had called down this wealth of destruction on that room, that had been so anxiously guarded, then there would have been one answer alone: Death.

The Death of the Chamberlain, Christoph Detlev Brigge of Ulsgard. For he, bulging hugely out of his dark blue uniform, was lying in the middle of the floor and not moving. The eyes in his large, alien, unrecognisable face were closed; he did not see what was happening. At first they had tried to lay him on the bed, but he had resisted, for he had come to hate beds since those first nights in which his illness had grown. Also, the bed up in that room had turned out to be too small, and there had been nothing left for it but to put him down on the carpet; he had refused to go downstairs again.

There he lay, and one might have thought he had died already. As it was slowly beginning to get dark, the dogs, one after the other, had left through the half-open door, only the wire-haired pointer with the grumpy expression was sitting beside his master, and one of his broad, shaggy paws lay on Christoph Detlev's large grey hand. Now, too, most of the servants were outside in the white corridor, where it was lighter than in the room; those, however, who had stayed in the room, darted occasional, covert glances at the huge, darkening heap in the middle, wishing that it were nothing more than a large suit of clothes over some broken thing.

But there was still something. There was a voice, the voice that no one had known seven weeks ago. It was not Christoph Detlev, to whom this voice belonged, it was Christoph Detlev's Death.

For many, many days now, Christoph Detlev's Death had been living at Ulsgard, and talking to everyone, and demanding. It demanded to be carried, demanded the Blue Room, demanded the small salon, demanded the dining hall. Demanded the dogs, demanded that they laugh, talk, play and be quiet and all at the same time. Demanded to see friends, women and men who had died, and demanded to die itself: demanded. Demanded and screamed.

For, when the night had come and those of the exhausted servants who were not sitting at his bedside were trying to get to sleep, Christoph Detlev's Death would scream, scream and groan and roar so long and so incessantly that the dogs, which at first joined in with their howls, fell silent and did not dare lie down and, standing on their long, slim, quivering legs, were afraid. And when, across the wide, silver, Danish summer night, those in the village heard his roaring, they got out of bed, as they did during a storm, dressed and stayed sitting round a lamp without saying a word until it was past. And pregnant women who were close to their time were put into the farthest rooms and into the cupboard beds behind the most solid doors; but they could hear it, they could hear it as if it were in their own bodies, and they begged to be allowed to get up, and came, white and wide-eyed, and sat down with the others with their blurred faces.

And the cows that were calving at that time were helpless and withdrawn, and one foetus that refused to come was torn, dead, with all the entrails from the cow's body. And all did their daily tasks badly and forgot to bring in the hay, because during the day they feared the night and because they were so weary from being startled into wakefulness and staying up so long that they could not concentrate on anything. And when they went to the white, peaceful church on Sunday they prayed there might be no more Lord of Ulsgard, for this Lord was a terrible Lord. And from the pulpit the minister proclaimed aloud what they were all thinking and praying, for he too had lost his nights and could not understand God. And it was proclaimed by the bell, which had found a fearful rival which sounded the whole night through and against which it was powerless, even if it set all its metal ringing. Everyone proclaimed it, and there was one of the young men who had dreamt he went to the castle and murdered the Master with his dungfork, and they were all so incensed, so overwrought, that they all listened as he told his dream, and, without at all realising it, looked at him to see if he were up to such a deed. That was what people felt and said in the whole area where a few weeks before everyone had loved the Chamberlain and felt sorry for him. But although that was what people said, nothing was changed. Christoph Detlev's Death, that was residing at Ulsgard, refused to be rushed. It had come for ten weeks, and ten weeks it stayed. And during those weeks it was more of a Lord than Christoph Detlev Brigge had ever been, it was like a king people call 'the Terrible', later on and for ever.

It was not the death of some ordinary man with the dropsy, this was the evil, princely Death that the Chamberlain had borne within him throughout his life and nourished with his own substance. All the excess of pride, will-power and lordly strength, which he had been unable to use up, even in his calm days, had entered into his Death, into the Death that now sat at Ulsgard squandering.

What a look would the Chamberlain have given any man who had demanded he should die a different death than this one. He died a hard Death.

The Prophecy

Arthur Schnitzler

I

Not far from Bolzano in the South Tyrol, on a small hill and
submerged in a sea of trees so that it is hardly visible from the
road, lies the small estate of Baron Schottenegg. A medical
friend of mine, who has been practising in Merano for the past
ten years and whom I met again last autumn, had introduced me
to the Baron. He was fifty years old and dabbled in the arts. He
composed a little, could play the violin and piano passably well,
and was not bad at drawing either. The one activity he had taken
most seriously in his earlier years was acting. The rumour went
that as a young man he had acted under an assumed name in
many small theatres up in Germany. Whatever the reason – his
father's continuing opposition, lack of talent or luck – the Baron
had given up his theatrical ambitions early enough to enter the
civil service without too great a delay, thus following a profession which was a family tradition and which for twenty years he
carried on faithfully, if without enthusiasm. But immediately
after the death of his father, when he himself was just over forty,
he resigned his post, and it became clear how deeply he was still
attached to the object of his youthful ambition. He had his
country house on the slopes of the Guntschnaberg restored and
gathered round him there, especially in the summer and autumn,
an ever-widening circle of men and women who performed
tableaux vivants as well as all kinds of plays that were easy to
put on. His wife, from an old Tyrolean middle-class family, not
really interested in the arts herself but intelligent and genuinely
fond of her husband, looked on his hobby with an air of gentle
mockery which was all the more tolerant as the Baron's interest
accorded with her own sociable instincts. For a critical observer,
the company gathered in the castle might not have seemed quite
sufficiently select, but even guests who normally tended to be
rather exclusive as regards birth and upbringing took no excep-

tion to the somewhat motley nature of the group which, anyway, the theatrical activity justified, whilst the name and reputation of the host and hostess quelled any suggestion of loose behaviour. At the castle I met, amongst many others whose names I no longer remember, a young count with a position in the Innsbruck administration, an infantry officer from Riva, a Captain on the General Staff with his wife and daughter, an operetta singer from Berlin, Baron Meudolt, who at that time had recently returned from his journey round the world, a retired actor from the court theatre in Bückeburg, a widowed Countess Saima, who had been an actress in her young days, with her daughter, and the Danish painter, Petersen.

Very few of the guests were actually staying in the castle. Some found rooms in Bolzano, others in a modest inn down on the road, where the narrow track to the estate branched off. But by the early afternoon most of the company were usually assembled at the house, and then rehearsals, sometimes directed by the former court actor, sometimes by the Baron, who never took a role himself, were held until late in the evening. Initially there was much laughing and joking, but gradually they were taken more and more seriously until finally the day of the performance approached; that took place, depending on the weather, their mood or preparation and, if possible, the setting of the play, either on the meadow bordering on the wood behind the castle garden or in the ground-level ballroom with its three high arched windows.

When I first visited the Baron, I had no other thought in mind than to spend an enjoyable day in a new place meeting new people. But, as things often turn out when one is wandering around aimlessly and in complete liberty and when, moreover, one is slowly growing older without any family ties to call one home, I let the Baron persuade me to extend my stay. One day became two, three and more, and so, to my own amazement, I found myself staying on until well into the autumn up there in the castle, where I had been given a very comfortably furnished room in a small tower with a view out over the valley. I will always remember that first stay in Guntschnaberg as pleasant and, in spite of all the noise and high jinks going on around, a time of quiet, since I had no more than a passing acquaintance with any of the other guests and, moreover, almost equally inspired to work and contemplation, spent a large part of my time in solitary walks in the woods. Even the fact that, out of politeness, the Baron had one of my short plays performed, did not disturb the calm of my stay, since nobody made any fuss of the fact that I was the author. In fact I found the evening of the performance a charming occasion as, on the green lawn in the open air, one of the minor dreams of my youth found such unexpected, belated fulfilment.

The lively activity in the castle gradually subsided; the holidays of the professional men among the guests had mostly finished, and the only occasional visitors were friends who lived in the vicinity. It was only now that I came to know the Baron more closely, and I found him a man of greater modesty that is usual in dilettantes. He was under no illusion that what went on in the castle was anything other than a superior party game. But since, in the course of his life, he had been unable to turn his unrequited love for acting into any kind of permanent relationship, he was content with the reflected glow that came to him, as if from a great distance, through the castle theatricals, happy, moreover, that there was no hint of many of the miseries that necessarily accompany professional activity.

On one of our walks he told me, without any suggestion of importunity, of the idea he had of putting on a play on his open-air stage that had been specially written with its unlimited space and natural surroundings in mind. This remark fitted in so well with a plan I had been mulling over for some time, that I promised the Baron I would provide what he had been looking for.

Soon afterwards I left the castle.

By the beginning of the next spring I had already completed a play that would satisfy the requirements, and I sent it to the Baron with a few friendly words recalling the pleasant days I had spent there the previous autumn. Soon after I received the Baron's reply and a warm invitation for the coming autumn. I spent the summer in the mountains and when the weather broke at the beginning of September I travelled down to Lake Garda, without thinking how close I was to Baron Schottenegg's castle. Yes, even now I feel that at that point I must have completely forgotten the little castle and all the goings-on there. Then on the eighth of September I received a letter from the Baron which had been forwarded from Vienna. This expressed, in mild terms, his surprise that they had not heard from me, and announced that on the ninth of September they would be performing the short play that I had sent him in the spring, which I really ought not to miss. I would, promised the Baron, particularly enjoy the children who were in the play and who even now insisted on going round in their charming costumes outside rehearsal and playing their roles on the lawn. After a series of coincidences, he went on, the main role had ended up with his nephew, Herr Franz von Umprecht, who, as he was sure I would remember, had taken part in two of the *tableaux vivants* the previous year, but who was now displaying a surprising talent as an actor.

I set off, reached Bolzano in the evening and arrived at the castle on the day of the performance, to be warmly received by the Baron and his wife. There were other well-known faces: the retired actor from the court theatre, Countess Saima and her daughter, Herr von Umprecht with his beautiful wife and the forester's fourteen-year-old daughter, who was to speak the prologue to my play. A large number of guests were expected that afternoon and at the performance in the evening there would be an audience of over a hundred, not only the Baron's guests, but also people from the surrounding area, who on this occasion, as so often, were free to come to the open-air theatre. As well as that, a small band had been engaged, consisting of professional musicians from a Bolzano orchestra plus a few amateurs, which was to play a Weber overture and an intermezzo, which the Baron himself had composed.

The mood at table was fairly exuberant, only Herr von Umprecht seemed somewhat quieter than the others. At first I had hardly been able to remember him, and I was struck by the fact that he kept on glancing at me, sometimes with a friendly look, at others rather shyly, without ever addressing me. Gradually his face became more familiar, and I suddenly remembered that the previous year in one of the *tableaux vivants* he had been in a monk's habit sitting at a chessboard with his arms on the table. I asked him if that was correct. He almost blushed when I spoke to him; the Baron answered for him and then, with a smile, remarked on his nephew's newly discovered talent for acting. At that Herr von Umprecht laughed to himself in a rather strange manner, then threw me a glance which seemed to express some kind of tacit understanding between us, and which I was at a loss to explain. But from that point onwards he avoided looking at me again.

II

Soon after the meal I retired to my room. Once more I was standing at the open window, as I had done so often the previous year, enjoying the pleasant view down into the sunlit valley which, narrow at my feet, gradually broadened until, in the distance, it opened out completely to embrace both town and fields.

After a short while there was a knock at the door. Herr von Umprecht entered and stood by the door as he said in a somewhat embarrassed tone, "Please forgive me if I'm disturbing you." Then he came a little further in, saying, "But if you can spare me a quarter of an hour, I am sure you will find what I have to say sufficient excuse for the disturbance."

I offered Herr von Umprecht a seat, but he ignored it and continued fervently, "You see, I find myself, in the most remarkable way possible, in your debt and feel obliged to thank you."

Naturally, the only possible explanation that occurred to me was that Herr von Umprecht was referring to his role, and as his thanks seemed rather excessive, I demurred. But Umprecht interrupted me immediately, "You cannot know what I am referring to. Would you be so kind as to let me tell you my story?" He sat on the window-ledge, crossed his legs and, rather obviously taking the utmost care to appear as calm as possible, began.

"As you perhaps know, I run my own estate now, but I used

to be in the army. And it was while I was in the army ten years ago – ten years to this very day – that an inexplicable event occurred which has, to a certain extent, overshadowed my life since then; today will see the end of it, and you are the unwitting cause. There must be some kind of psychical connection between us, and I expect you can explain it just as little as I, but at least you should learn of its existence. At that time my regiment was stationed in some wretched hole in Poland. Apart from our duties, which were never particularly demanding, the only distractions were drink and gambling. Added to that, we had to face the possibility that we might be stuck there for years, and not all of us could bear such a dreary prospect. One of my best friends shot himself after we had been there for three months. Another comrade, who used to be a most charming soldier, suddenly took to drink rather badly, became ill-mannered and liable to flare up at any time, almost unbalanced, and was involved in some kind of scene with a lawyer that cost him his commission. The captain in my company was married and – whether with good reason or not I have no idea – so jealous that one day he threw his wife out of the window. She was mysteriously unharmed and suffered no ill effects; her husband died in a lunatic asylum. One of our cadets, a nice lad but exceptionally stupid, suddenly got the idea he could understand philosophy; he studied Kant and Hegel and learnt whole sections of their works by heart, like children learning their school-books.

As for myself, I did nothing but get bored, so immensely bored that often, as I lay on my bed in the afternoon, I was afraid I might go mad. The barracks were outside the village, that consisted of at most thirty scattered shacks; the nearest town, a good hour's ride away, was grubby, smelly, disgusting and full of Jews. We had no choice but to deal with them from time to time – the hotel-owner was a Jew, likewise the cobbler. That we behaved in the most offensive manner possible towards them, you can imagine. We were particularly hostile towards them because a prince, who had been assigned to our regiment with the rank of major, used to return the greetings of the Jews with extreme politeness – whether as a joke or because he liked them,

I do not know – and, moreover, made a protégé of the regimental doctor, who was quite clearly of Jewish extraction.

I wouldn't, of course, be telling you all this if it hadn't been precisely this idiosyncrasy of the prince that brought me into contact with the person who was to initiate the mysterious connection between you and me. He was a conjurer, the son of a Jew who ran a liquor shop in the neighbouring Polish town. As a young lad he had gone to work in a business in Lvov, then to Vienna, and somewhere along the way he was taught a few card tricks. He taught himself more and mastered all sorts of conjuring tricks until eventually he had reached the stage where he could travel around performing in public, in music halls or clubs. In the summer he always returned to his home town to visit his parents. He never appeared on stage there, and so the first time I saw him was in the street, and I was immediately struck by his appearance. He was short, skinny and unshaven, probably about thirty years old, and dressed in an outfit of a grotesque elegance that was completely unsuitable for the time of year: he used to stroll around town in a black frock coat and a shiny top hat and wore the most magnificent brocade waistcoats; when the sun was bright he clipped a dark pince-nez to his nose.

One evening there were fifteen or sixteen of us sitting after supper at our long table in the officers' mess as usual. It was a sultry night, and the windows were wide open. Some of the chaps started a card school, others went to the window to chat, the rest sat in silence, drinking and smoking. Then the duty corporal came in and announced the conjurer. We were somewhat amazed, but the man just walked straight in, full of confidence, and, with just a touch of the Jewish *argot*, said a few words in which he thanked us for our invitation. As he did so, he turned to the Prince, who went over and – simply to annoy us, of course – shook him by the hand. The magician took it as a matter of course, and said that he would show us some card tricks first and then give us a demonstration of his talents at mesmerism and chiromancy. He had hardly finished when some of the officers, who were playing cards in one corner, noticed that the court cards were missing: the magician gave a wave of the hand and they came flying in through the open window. The tricks that followed were also very entertaining and superior to anything of that kind that I had seen. I found the experiments in mesmerism, which he performed next, even stranger. It was not without a shudder that we watched the philosophical cadet, after he had been put into a trance, carry out the magician's commands and jump through the open window, climb up the smooth wall onto the roof, dash round the four sides of the building close to the edge and then slide back down into the square. After he had come down, but was still in a trance, the Colonel said to the magician, "Sir, if he had broken his neck, you would not have left the barracks alive, I assure you." I will never forget the look of contempt which was the Jew's silent answer to this remark.

Then he said slowly, "Would you like me to read your hand, Colonel, and tell you when *you* will leave these barracks, dead or alive?" I don't know what the Colonel or any of the rest of us would normally have replied to this rather brazen question, but the general mood was already so chaotic that no-one was surprised when the Colonel held out his hand and even imitated the Jew's *argot* as he told him to read it. This all took place out in the barracks square and the cadet was still standing against the wall in a trance with his arms stretched out as if he were being crucified. The conjurer took the Colonel's hand and studied the lines carefully. "Seen enough, Yid?" asked a lieutenant who was fairly drunk. The conjurer glanced up and said, solemnly, "My stage name is Marco Polo." The Prince put his hand on the Jew's shoulder and said, "My friend Marco Polo has sharp eyes." "Well, what can you see?" asked the Colonel, somewhat more politely. "Do I have to say?" asked Marco Polo. "We can't compel you", said the Prince. "Tell me!" cried the Colonel. "I would prefer not to", replied Marco Polo. The Colonel laughed out loud. "Out with it, it can't be that bad. And if it is bad, it doesn't have to be true." "It is very bad", said the magician, "and true as well." Everyone was silent. "Well?" asked the Colonel. "The cold won't trouble you any more", replied Marco Polo. "What?" exclaimed the colonel, "Is the regiment finally going to be posted to Riva?" "About the regiment I can't see anything, Colonel. All I can see is that by the autumn you'll be a dead man." The Colonel laughed, but everyone else was silent; I assure you, we all felt as if from that moment on the Colonel was a marked man. Suddenly someone deliberately gave a very loud laugh, others followed suit and we traipsed noisily back into the mess.

"Well then", cried the Colonel, "that's me sorted out. None of you other gentlemen curious?" One said jokingly, "No, we prefer to preserve our ignorance." Another suddenly came to the opinion that there were religious grounds for rejecting this way of foretelling one's destiny, and a young lieutenant declared vehemently that people like Marco Polo ought to be locked away for good. I saw the Prince in a corner talking to one of the older officers and heard him say, "Where do miracles start?" I went over to Marco Polo, who was getting ready to leave, and said to him, without anyone else hearing, "Foretell my future." Mechanically he took my hand. Then he said, "The light isn't very good in here." I noticed that the oil-lamps had started to flicker and the lines on my hand seemed to quiver. "Come outside, Lieutenant, into the barracks square. I prefer the moon-light." He held me by the hand and I followed him out through the open door.

I was suddenly struck by an odd thought. "Listen, Marco Polo", I said, "if all you can manage is what you've just shown the Colonel, then I think we shouldn't bother." Immediately he let go of my hand and smiled. "You are afraid, Lieutenant?" I quickly turned round to see if anyone had heard, but we had already passed through the barracks gate and were on the road leading to the town. "The thing is, I would like to learn something specific", I said. "Words can always be interpreted in different ways." Marco Polo looked at me. "And what would that be, Lieutenant? ... To see your future wife, perhaps?" "Could you do that?" Marco Polo shrugged his shoulders. "It might be ... it would be possible ..." "But that's not what I want", I interrupted. "I would like to know what my life will be like at some point in the future, in ten years' time, say." Marco Polo shook his head. "I could not tell you that ... but I might be able to do something else." "What?" "Some moment, any moment from your future I could show you like a picture." I did not understand straight away. "In what way do you mean?" "The way I mean it is this: I can conjure up a moment from your future life, right here where we are standing." "What?" "All you have to do, Lieutenant, is to tell me which moment." I still didn't quite understand, but I was very curious to see what happened. "Good", I said, "if you can do that, I would like to see what I will be doing ten years from today, ten years to the very second ... Do you understand, Marco Polo?" "Certainly, Lieutenant", said Marco Polo, gazing at me fixedly. And with that he vanished ... but the barracks had vanished too, which a moment before I had seen gleaming in the moonlight, and the wretched hovels had vanished which lay scattered around the moonlit plain, and I could see myself, as you sometimes see yourself in a dream ... I saw myself aged by ten years, with a brown beard, a scar on my forehead, lying on a stretcher in a meadow and kneeling at my side a beautiful woman with red hair, her hand over her face, a boy and a girl next to her, dark woods in the background and two foresters holding burning torches nearby ... *You* are amazed, are you not?"

Indeed I was amazed, for what he had just described was precisely the scene with which my play was to end at ten o'clock that evening, the play in which he had the part of the dying hero.

"You still have your doubts", said Herr von Umprecht, "and I don't blame you at all for it. But I will soon get rid of those doubts."

Herr von Umprecht put his hand in his pocket and took out a sealed envelope. "Please examine what is written on the back." I read it aloud, "Sealed under legal scrutiny on January 4, 1859; to be opened on September 9, 1868." Underneath was the signature of Doctor Artiner, a Viennese lawyer I knew very well.

"That is today", said Herr von Umprecht. "Today it is ten years since I had the mysterious encounter with Marco Polo, a mystery that will be resolved by the play without really being solved. You see, it has been as if destiny were playing a cruel game with me: various possible ways in which the prophecy might be fulfilled would alternate most strangely, sometimes appearing with a menace of probability, then melting away, reappearing with inexorable finality, vanishing into thin air, returning ... But let me get back to my story. I'm certain the apparition itself did not last for more than a moment; I could still hear the same loud laugh from the lieutenant in the mess that I had heard before the apparition. And then Marco Polo returned, with the hint of a smile around his lips – whether of mockery or sorrow, I am still not sure – doffed his top hat, said, "Goodnight, Lieutenant, I hope you are satisfied", turned and walked slowly along the road in the direction of the town. He left the next morning, by the way.

My first thought, as I made my way back to the barracks, was that it must have been some kind of illusion that Marco Polo, perhaps with the help of an invisible assistant, had managed to create with some kind of reflections. As I crossed the parade ground, I saw to my horror the cadet still standing against the wall in the attitude of crucifixion. He had obviously been completely forgotten. I could hear the excited voices of the others, talking and arguing inside. I grabbed the cadet by the arm; he woke up immediately and showed not the least trace of surprise, he just could not understand the excitement that had gripped all the other members of the regiment. With a kind of fury, I immediately joined in the impassioned but empty discussion that had arisen on the strange events we had witnessed, and my contribution probably made no more sense than the others'.

Suddenly the Colonel shouted, "Well, gentleman, I bet I'll still be here next spring! Forty-five to one?" And he turned to one of the officers, a lieutenant, who had a certain reputation for betting and gambling. "No takers?" Although it was clear that the lieutenant was tempted, he seemed to feel it was improper to make a bet with his commanding officer on the latter's death, and so he just smiled. He probably regretted it: two weeks later, on the second day of the grand manoeuvres the Colonel fell off his horse and was killed on the spot. And afterwards we all realised that it was precisely what we had expected.

It was after this event that I began to reflect on my nocturnal prophecy with a certain unease; a strange diffidence had inhibited me from telling anyone else about it. It was only at Christmas, when I was on leave in Vienna, that I shared the secret with one of my fellow-officers, a certain Friedrich von Gulant – you may have heard of him, he wrote some charming poems and died very young ... Well, he it was who helped me draw up the diagram you will find in this sealed envelope. He felt that such incidents should not be lost to science, whether in the end their premises turned out to be true or false. I went with him to Doctor Artiner, who witnessed the sealing of the diagram in this envelope. Until now it has been kept in his chambers and only yesterday sent to me, at my request.

I must admit that at first the seriousness with which Gulant treated the matter depressed me a little; but after I stopped seeing him, and especially when, shortly afterwards, he died, I began to find the whole affair quite ridiculous. Above all, I was convinced that I controlled my own fate. There was no force in the world that could compel me to wear a bushy brown beard and be lying down on a stretcher at ten o'clock in the evening on the 9th September, 1868; I could keep away from woods and meadows, and I didn't need to marry a woman with red hair, nor to have children. The only thing that I could perhaps not avoid would be an accident, a duel say, which would leave a scar on my forehead. For the moment, then, I was reassured.

One year after the prophecy I married my wife, Fräulein von Heimsal; soon afterwards I left the army and devoted myself to farming. I looked at several small estates and, however odd it might sound, I checked whether they contained an area that might be similar to the lawn in my dream (as I liked to call the apparition). I was close to buying one, when my wife inherited an estate in Carinthia, with some fine hunting. On the first tour of inspection round our new property I came to a meadow which, on a slight slope and surrounded by woodland, seemed in some odd way to resemble the locality that I might perhaps have every reason to beware of. It gave me a slight shock. I had not told my wife about the prophecy. She is so superstitious that, had I done so, it would have preyed on her mind right up to" – he gave a relieved smile – "the present day. So of course I could not tell her of my concern. Myself, however, I reassured with the thought that I did not have to spend September 1868 on my estate.

In 1860 I had a son. Even when he was a baby I thought I could see a similarity between his features and those of the boy in my dream; at times it would fade, at others it became clearer than ever, and today I can openly admit to myself that the boy who will be standing next to my stretcher this evening at ten o'clock will be the very image of the boy in the apparition. I have no daughter of my own, but three years ago it happened that my wife's widowed sister, who had lived in America, died, leaving a little girl. At my wife's request I crossed the Atlantic and brought the girl back to live with us. The first time I saw her I thought she resembled the girl from my dream completely. It did cross my mind to leave the girl with strangers in the foreign country, but of course it was a shabby impulse which I immediately rejected, and the child came to live with us. In spite of the increasingly close resemblance of the children to those in the prophetic apparition, I found reassurance in the thought that my memory of their faces in the dream might well be wrong. Indeed, I had almost stopped thinking of that evening in the backwoods of Poland, when, two years ago, I received a further portent, which naturally shocked me.

I had been away from home on business for some months; when I came back, my wife appeared with red hair, and her similarity to the woman in my dream, whose face I hadn't seen of course, seemed to me complete. I had the bright idea of concealing my horror by pretending to be angry; I even deliberately worked myself up into a fury, for I was suddenly struck by an almost insane idea: if I could separate from my wife and children, then all the danger would be gone and I would have fooled destiny. My wife burst into tears, sank as if heartbroken to the floor, begged forgiveness and told me the reason for the change. When we were in Munich the year before, I had been particularly taken by the portrait of a red-haired woman, and my wife had formed the plan of having her hair dyed to make her more like the portrait whenever the opportunity should present itself. I of course implored her to return her hair to its natural colour as soon as possible, and when she had done that, everything seemed all right again. Did that not prove that it was still I who was in control of my destiny? ... Did not everything that had happened so far have a perfectly natural explanation? ... Were there not thousands of others who had estates with meadows and woods and wives and children? ...

And the one thing that might have frightened a superstitious man was still missing, or had been until last winter: the scar, which you can now see in all its glory on my forehead. Excuse me for saying so, but I am not a coward; I twice fought a duel when I was in the army, on quite dangerous terms even, and another one eight years ago, shortly after I had got married and had already resigned my commission. But when last year for some trifling reason – my greeting was too casual – a gentleman challenged me, I decided" – Herr von Umprecht blushed – "to apologise. The whole affair was dealt with according to the rules, but I know for certain that I would have fought the duel if I had not been gripped by a mad fear that my opponent might wound me on the forehead, thus dealing destiny another ace ... But, as you can see, it was to no avail, there is the scar. And the moment when I received the wound was probably the one moment in the whole of the ten years which made me most conscious of how defenceless I really am.

It was one evening last winter; I was travelling by train between Klagenfurt and Villach, and there were two or three people in the compartment, all completely unknown to me. Suddenly the window shattered and I felt a pain in my forehead; at the same time I heard a hard object strike the floor; my first reaction was to touch the spot: it was bleeding; then I quickly bent down and picked up a sharp stone from the floor. The other passengers in the compartment were startled. "Is something wrong?" one called out. They realised I was bleeding and did what they could for me. But one man, I could see him quite clearly, seemed to be cowering back into the corner. At the next station they brought water and the railway doctor put on an emergency dressing, but I, of course, was not afraid I might die from the wound, I knew that it was to leave a scar. A discussion started in the compartment, we wondered whether it was attempted murder or a schoolboy prank; the man in the corner said nothing, he just stared straight ahead. I got out at Villach. Suddenly the man appeared at my elbow and said, "It was meant for me." Before I could answer, before I had time even to think, he had disappeared; I never managed to find out who he was. Someone with a persecution mania, perhaps ... but perhaps it was someone who had good reason to believe he was being pursued, by the husband or brother of a woman he had seduced, and whom I might well have saved, because I was destined to have this scar ... who can tell? ... After a few weeks it was blazing on my forehead in precisely the same place where I had seen it in the dream. It was becoming increasingly obvious that I was involved in an unequal struggle with some unknown, mocking power, and I began to feel more and more uneasy about the day when the dream was to reach its final fulfilment.

In the spring we received my uncle's invitation. I was determined not to accept it. I had no clear memory of the estate, but it did seem possible to me that the dreaded scene could be there. However, as my wife would not have understood a rejection of the invitation, I decided that I would come here with her and the children at the beginning of July, with the intention of leaving the castle as soon as possible and travelling further south, to Venice or the Lido. On one of our first days here the conversation came round to your play; my uncle told us about the small roles for children it contained and asked me to allow the little ones to join in. I had nothing against it. It had been decided that the hero should be played by a professional actor. After a few days I was overcome with fear that I might fall seriously ill and not be able to leave. So one evening I announced that I intended to leave the castle the next day to visit some seaside resorts for a change of air. I had to promise to be back at the beginning of September. The same evening a letter came from the actor sending back his role for some reason or other. My uncle was extremely irritated. He asked me to read the play, perhaps I would find someone among our acquaintances who would be suitable for the part. So I took your play up to my room and read it. Try to imagine my feelings when I came to the end and found it contained the very situation that had been prophesied for the 9th of September of this year, right down to the very last detail.

I could hardly wait for the morning to tell my uncle that I was willing to play the part. I was afraid he might have objections, for, since I had read the play, I felt as if I were safe once more, and if I missed the opportunity of acting in your play, I would be at the mercy of the unknown power once again. My uncle agreed immediately and from then on everything was straight-forward. We have been rehearsing every day for several weeks, I have already been through the situation I face this evening fifteen or twenty times: I am lying on the stretcher, young Countess Saima with the beautiful red hair is kneeling before me, her hands over her face, and the children are standing at my side.

As Herr von Umprecht was finishing, my eyes were caught once more by the envelope that lay on the table, still sealed. Herr von Umprecht smiled. "Quite right, I haven't shown you the proof yet", he said, and broke the seal. A folded sheet of paper appeared. Herr von Umprecht unfolded it and spread it out on the table. What I saw was a complete plan of the situation in the last scene of my play, as if I had drawn it up myself: the background and sides were sketched in and labelled "woods"; roughly in the middle was a line with a male figure on it, and above it was written, "stretcher". Above the other stick-figures was written, in tiny letters and red ink, "woman with red hair", "boy", "girl", "torch-bearer", "man with hands raised". I turned to Herr von Umprecht, "What is this: 'man with hands raised'?"

"Ah", said Herr von Umprecht hesitantly, "that I almost forgot. It was like this: in the dream there was also an old man brightly lit by the torches; he was completely bald, clean-shaven, wore glasses and a dark green scarf round his neck and he was standing there with his hands raised and his eyes staring wide."

This time I was the one who was surprised.

We said nothing for a while; I felt an strange unease and asked him, "What do you think? Who might that be?"

"I assume", said Umprecht calmly, "that one of the audience, perhaps one of Uncle's servants or one of the peasants, gets overexcited at the end of the play and rushes onto the stage ... or perhaps destiny is arranging one of those little coincidences that don't surprise me any more, and some escaped inmate of a lunatic asylum will come dashing across the stage at the very moment when I am lying on the stretcher."

I shook my head.

"What did you say? ...Bald – glasses – green scarf ...? Now the matter seems even stranger than before. The man that you saw in the apparition was in fact one of the characters I originally intended to include in the play, but then cut out. It was the woman's mad father, who is mentioned in the first act and whom I thought of having dash onto the stage at the end."

"But the spectacles and scarf?"

"The actor would have contributed those himself, don't you think?"

"Possibly."

We were interrupted. Frau von Umprecht had sent to tell her husband she would like a word with him before the performance, so he left. I stayed in my room for a while, carefully studying the diagram Herr von Umprecht had left on my table.

III

Soon I felt an urge to go and see the spot where the performance was to take place. It was behind the castle and separated from it by a delightful flower-garden, which ended in a hedge. There some simple wooden benches had been set up in about ten rows, the front ones of which were covered with dark-red carpeting. Beyond them were some music-stands and chairs; there was no curtain. The separation of the stage from the audience was suggested by two tall, spreading pine-trees; to the right there was a thicket of tangled shrubs, behind which, invisible to the audience, was a comfortable armchair for the prompter. The left-hand side was open, affording a view down into the valley. The background to the stage was formed by tall trees; it was only in the middle that they were closely crowded together, on the left narrow paths approached out of the shadows. Farther back among the trees a small clearing had been made with chairs and tables where the actors could sit while waiting for their cues. For the lighting they had set up a row of tall old church candelabras with huge candles on either side of the stage and auditorium. Behind the shrubs on the right was a kind of open-air storage-room for props; amongst other small items that were needed for the play, I could see the stretcher on which Herr von Umprecht was to die at the end. As I walked across the meadow, it glowed in the soft light of the evening sun. I had naturally been thinking about Herr von Umprecht's story. Initially I had not ruled out the possibility that Herr von Umprecht was one of those fabricators of fantastic stories who will go to endless trouble to prepare a hoax, just in order to attract attention. I even imagined it was possible that the lawyer's signature had been forged and that Herr von Umprecht had brought in others to be able to carry out his plan properly. I was particularly sceptical about the unknown man with his hands in the air who could well be an accomplice of Umprecht. But my doubts were contradicted by the role that man played in my first version, which no one could know about, and to the favourable impression I had formed of Herr von Umprecht. However improbable, fantastic even, his whole story seemed to be, something inside me wanted to believe it; it might have been the rather foolish vanity of seeing myself as an instrument of fate.

In the meantime things had started moving around me; servants came out of the castle, candles were lit, locals, some of them in peasant costume, were slowly coming up the hill and standing shyly beside the benches. Soon the lady of the house appeared with some of the guests, who spread themselves over the front benches. I joined them, chatting to acquaintances from the previous year. The members of the orchestra had appeared and taken their places; the composition was unusual enough: two violins, a cello, a viola, a double bass, a flute and an oboe. Immediately, and clearly too soon, they began the Weber overture. Right at the front, not far from the band, stood an old peasant who was bald and had some kind of dark cloth wrapped round his neck. Perhaps, I thought, fate has marked him out to put on a pair of spectacles, go mad and run onto the stage. The daylight had faded completely, the tall candles were flickering a little in the gentle breeze that had arisen. There were signs of life behind the bushes, the company had followed hidden paths to approach the stage. It was only now that I thought of the others who were to appear, and I realised I had seen none of them apart from Herr von Umprecht, his children and the forester's daughter. Now I heard the loud voice of the producer and the laughter of young Countess Saima. The benches were all taken, the Baron was sitting in one of the front ones, talking to Countess Saima. The orchestra struck up and the forester's girl came forward to speak the prologue that introduced the play. Its plot was the fate of a man who, gripped with a sudden desire for unusual adventures and far away places, leaves his family without saying goodbye and, in the course of one day, suffers so many trials and tribulations that he decides to return before his wife and children notice his absence; but one final adventure on his way home, close to the gate of his house, results in his murder, and he greets his family with his dying words, leaving them with the inexplicable mystery of his departure and death.

The play had begun, and the actors spoke their parts very pleasingly; I enjoyed the simple presentation of what was a simple plot and initially forgot Herr von Umprecht's story. After the first act the orchestra played again, but no one listened, so lively was the chatter on the benches. I was not sitting down myself but standing, unseen by the others, close to the stage on the left side where the there was a clear view down into the valley. The second act started; the breeze had become slightly stronger and the flickering light contributed not a little to the effectiveness of the play. Then the actors disappeared into the woods once more and the orchestra started up again. Quite by chance, my eye fell upon the flautist, who was clean shaven and wearing glasses; but he had long white hair and there was no sign of a scarf. The intermezzo finished and the actors returned to the stage. Then I noticed the flautist lay his instrument on the stand in front of him, take a long green scarf out of his pocket and wrap it round his neck. I found it extremely disconcerting. The next moment Herr von Umprecht made his entrance; I saw how his eye was caught by the flautist, how he noticed the green scarf and hesitated for a moment; but the next he had himself back under control and was speaking his lines fluently. I asked a young lad in simple clothes sitting next to me if he knew the flautist, and he told me it was a schoolmaster from Caldaro. The play continued, the end was approaching. The children, following the stage directions, wandered across the set, noises in the woods came nearer and nearer, there was screaming and shouting; it fitted in quite nicely that the wind increased, making the branches sway; finally Herr von Umprecht, the dying adventurer, was carried in on the stretcher. The two children rushed up to him, the torch-bearers stood motionless at either side. The wife came on after the others and sank down beside the murdered man, her features distorted with anxiety; he tried to open his mouth one last time, tried to sit up, but – as it was written in the script – did not manage to. Then there was a sudden gust of wind that threatened to blow out the torches; I saw one of the members of the orchestra leap up: it was the flautist and, to my astonishment, he was bald, his wig had been blown off his head; hands in the air, the green scarf fluttering round his neck, he rushed towards the stage. Automatically I turned to look at Herr von Umprecht. He was gazing fixedly at the man, as if in a trance; he tried to speak – was clearly unable to – sank back onto the stretcher ... Many of the audience thought it was still part of the play, even I was not sure what it meant.

In the meantime the flautist had run past the stretcher, still pursuing his wig, and disappeared into the woods. Umprecht did not move; another gust of wind blew out one of the torches; some of the people at the front became restless; I heard the Baron's voice calling for quiet; they calmed down, and the wind fell, too ... but Umprecht still lay there motionless, not even moving his lips. Countess Saima screamed; of course the audience thought it was all part of the play, but I pushed my way through the crowd onto the stage and I could hear the people getting up behind and following me, surrounding the stretcher ... "What is it, what's happened?" ... I grabbed a torch from one of the torch-bearers and shone the light on Umprecht's face ... I shook him, tore open his doublet; by that time the doctor had come up and was feeling his heart, his pulse; he asked everyone to give him room and whispered a few words to the Baron ... Frau von Umprecht pushed her way to the front, gave a scream and threw herself over her husband, the children stood there thunderstruck, unable to comprehend ... Nobody could believe what had happened and yet everyone was telling someone else; and a minute later the whole assembly knew that Herr von Umprecht had suddenly died on the stretcher on which he had been carried in.

Gripped by the horror of it all, I left that very same evening and hastened down into the valley. A strange fear has stopped me from ever visiting the castle again. I saw the Baron in Bolzano the next day; I told him Umprecht's story, just as he himself had told it to me. The Baron refused to believe it, so I took the paper with the mysterious diagram out of my wallet; he gave me a bewildered, almost frightened look and handed the paper back to me: it was blank, no writing, no drawing ...

I made attempts to locate Marco Polo, but the only fact I was able to establish was that he last appeared three years before in a low Hamburg music hall.

But what remains the most puzzling of all these puzzles is that the schoolmaster who chased his wig with his hands in the air and disappeared into the woods has never been seen again; not even his corpse was found.

Editor's Postscript

I was not personally acquainted with the author of the above report. In his day he had been a fairly well-known writer but by the time he died ten years ago, at the age of sixty, he had been more or less forgotten. His literary remains went, without any particular instructions, to the friend from Merano who is mentioned in these pages. I became acquainted with this friend, a doctor, during a stay in Merano last winter. We used to discuss all kinds of mysterious topics, in particular ghostly apparitions, telekinesis and prophecies, and he gave me the attached manuscript to publish. I would have taken it for a work of fiction had not the doctor, as mentioned in the report, been present at the theatrical performance described at the end, and been personally acquainted with the schoolmaster who disappeared in such a mysterious manner. As for the magician, Marco Polo, I can well remember as a child on holiday by the Wörthersee having seen his name on a poster; it stuck in my memory because just at that time I was reading the book of the journeys of the great traveller of the same name.

"Pour avoir bien servi"

Leo Perutz

I heard this strange story some time ago in the saloon of a French steamer, which was taking me from Marseilles to Alexandria. We were not able to go up on deck very much; we had constant bad weather and had to find some way or other of passing the time. Of all the discussions and conversations I heard during those days, what particularly stuck in my mind was the story from a Mr. J. Schwemmer, an engineer from Kiev, who told it after a long and heated debate in order to dispute the claim that the modern doctor has the right, nay, even the duty, forcibly to terminate the sufferings of a patient who has no hope of recovery.

I cannot say why this story in particular made such a deep impression on me; in fact, as soon became apparent, it was only marginally connected with the topic under discussion. Perhaps it was the sudden appearance, in the midst of all our banal and superficial discussions, of the dreadful reality of two pale, suffering human beings, their lips twisted and quivering with pain. Even today I sometimes see the young woman in my mind's eye, see her leaning back wearily in her wheelchair, her fearful, longing glance resting almost tenderly on the green vase on the mantelpiece. And in my dreams I still sometimes hear her husband's cry, it rings in my ears with a terrible sound that freezes me to the marrow, even though in reality I never heard the cry from the lips of the husband himself, but from a weak, croaking, old man's voice that belonged to the aforementioned Mr. Schwemmer from Kiev.

This is the story told by the old engineer, and I will recount it as he told it to us on board the *Héron*, a little more briefly, perhaps, but I am sure I have not omitted any essential details.

"Years ago I lived in Paris. I shared an apartment in a small, one-storey building in a side-street in an out-of-the-way suburb with a former student friend whom I had not seen for several years and then, to my delight, come across in Paris. In the years in between he had completed a doctorate at a German university, published two books on art and obtained, shortly before his marriage, a position as librarian to some Count. He was still young, thirty at the most, and it was only his wife's misfortune that could have made him so tired and prematurely aged.

His wife was ill. She was paralysed; she had been attacked by one of those nervous disorders whose victims, or so I believe, come mostly from people who overexert themselves intellectually: as a girl she had studied medicine in Zurich. By day she sat in her wheelchair, usually silent and without complaining much, but the nights! Those nights! One night her screams were so dreadful that the concierge's two children dashed out into the street in sheer terror and refused to come back for the rest of the night. During such nights the doctor and her husband did everything they could to comfort her, promised that the pain was bound to lessen soon and that in a short time she would be well again; but she, as a former medical student, knew better than any of us that there was no cure for her suffering, that the resistance her young body put up to the disease was in vain, that one day the end would come but, and that was the worst thing about it, not all that soon.

And her husband loved her. His work only occupied him for a few hours each day, but he soon came to hate it, to feel it irksome. As a young student, he had found his subject fulfilling, satisfying, almost intoxicating even – to the rest of us his passion for old books and rare manuscripts had seemed almost morbid – now he had lost all interest in it. In his study, in the street, in the omnibus, wherever he was there was but one thought in his mind: to return home as quickly as possible! Basically, his whole day was a detour on the way to his wife. Several times he told me what the reason for his unease was: his wife possessed a revolver. She had had it since she was a girl and it was concealed somewhere in the flat, of that he was quite certain. But he had never been able to discover the hiding-place, however often he had searched through the rooms. Of course, she was paralysed and could not reach the revolver herself. "But once, just imagine, she tried to bribe the maid!"

Every time he told me about this he went quite pale with fear at the thought that she might have managed to get the gun while he was out. I responded to his story with the feeling, faint and tentative at first, then stronger and stronger, that that would almost be the best thing for the couple, and that fate had chosen me to help these two wretched people. Now, of course, I know that it was a crime not to stifle that thought at birth. How can a foolish young man presume to take into his own clumsy hands the destiny of two people whose past he was not part of and whose secret thoughts and hidden desires he cannot know.

But in those days I was young and inexperienced and full of misunderstood catchwords and immature ideas, and I felt so sorry for my poor friend, scarcely thirty years old and already grey-haired.

These are the two people in my story. Russians, both of them, I think I said that already, didn't I? They had very little contact with Parisian society, nor did I ever meet any of our countrymen in their house. Sometimes I had the feeling people were avoiding them. Once someone told me the husband had betrayed a Russian student, who was wanted by the police, and was, anyway, a Russian government agent. But I gave little weight to that kind of claim; such stories are told about many of my countrymen who, for whatever reason, live abroad, and it's always more or less the same story.

And now I will tell you of the day when I committed a crime – for it was a crime – and of the green vase with the Chinese dragons covered in red scales which was the constant focus, day and night, of the invalid wife's tender, longing glances. And if I recount the events of that day, in which my part, as I am well aware, was not one to be proud of, then I do it without shame and without regret, for it all happened a long time ago and I know now that it was not I who was to blame, but that unfortunate delusion, the silly idea that I had been chosen by fate to put an end, with a surgeon's steady hand, to the wife's torment and the husband's misery. It was on that very day that the feeling within me was stronger than ever before, for the young woman had had a very bad night and none of the three of us had had a wink of sleep. It was only as morning came that things improved slightly, the man had left the house, dog-tired, to go to his work and she was in her wheelchair; I was sitting opposite her, but I have forgotten how the conversation came round to her younger days and the time she spent in Zurich. "Would you like to see an old picture of me?" she asked, and when I said yes, she thought for a while and then said, in a voice which sounded perfectly calm and nonchalant, "Bring me the green vase, there on the mantelpiece." She said it quite calmly, but I could feel the blood rushing to my head, my knees trembled and I suddenly knew that this was the long-sought hiding-place of the gun. I just managed to stand up, brought the vase and began to empty it out onto the table; I was acting as if in a dream. On top was a letter and one pink and one light green ribbon, then a fan and a withered posy and finally the photographs: two pictures of herself, then the portrait of a young man with intelligent, handsome features. "That is my friend Sascha", she said, and I knew that he was dead without her saying so. And I found a photo of her husband too, it was from his university days and showed him surrounded by his fellow students, and I was on the picture as well, looking rather comical because I had a long wooden student's pipe in my mouth. And then, right at the bottom, was the case with the revolver.

My hand was trembling as I took the case out of the vase, for this was the moment of action, that I knew, and I was in no doubt as to what I should do. I wanted, I had to hand the gun over to the sick woman, even though others in their stupidity might call it 'murder' and call me to account for it. If no one had the courage, then I did, and I was doing what was best for this man and this woman. And I remembered a few words that I had once read on an old French medal, 'pour avoir bien servi'. I went all soft inside at the thought of the service I was doing my friend, and then I heard her voice, a cool, calm voice, saying, "Please, let me have the case", and I pulled myself together and managed to say, "I will open it myself."

When I felt the revolver in my hands, I was suddenly struck with cowardice, all my decisions and plans collapsed and I was seized with horror at the service the invalid woman was demanding of me. The thought of the responsibility I was taking

232

weighed down on me, what I really wanted to do was to throw the gun as far away from me as possible, instead of giving it to her, and the woman must have read all that in my eyes. "See", she said, "the thought of this revolver was my one comfort during those terrible nights, the only thing I had to cling on to. My whole life over the last three years has been a constant movement towards and away from that green vase. Sometimes my wheelchair was so close that I could almost have touched it with my hand. Once my husband almost discovered the hiding place. He was within a hair's-breadth of my secret. I felt my heart stand still with fear." And then, abruptly and quite simply and without any drama in her voice, she said, "Please give me the gun."

I wouldn't have done it; I wouldn't have given her the gun, I would have thrown it away from me into a corner of the room; but at that moment I saw her husband coming through the garden. And the way he dragged his feet, slowly and wearily, over the gravel, back bowed, a broken man, and the way he nodded to me with such an old, earnest face, all gave me back my assurance, I was the surgeon once more who would make the healing incision with a cool eye and steady hand. I was no longer in any doubt as to what I should do and as I looked out the window and returned the husband's greeting, I handed the revolver over the table to the woman.

What happened next is quickly told. I was suddenly filled with a terrible fear of what was bound to happen in the next few seconds. 'Don't watch!' a voice screamed within me. 'I can't bear to see her raise the gun, put it to her forehead, press the trigger. I can't bear to see that.' I turned my back on her and faced the door. I heard him coming up the stairs. Then he opened the door, said "Hello", was stretching out his hand, coming towards me. Two steps and he stopped, turned as white as the walls and screamed, "Jonas, Jonas, what have you done!" And, "For God's sake, Jonas, take the gun away from her, quick!"

I still had time to do it. With one step I could have been beside her, torn the gun from her grasp. But I stayed with my back to her and clenched my teeth. Stand firm! Just for this one moment! The healing incision. I am his doctor. He'll thank me for it later.

'Pour avoir bien servi!'

He behaved in an odd way. Instead of rushing up and taking the gun away from her, he had fallen to his knees. For a few seconds there was complete silence in the room, I could hear his teeth grinding. Then he suddenly screamed, a terrible, loud scream, "Don't do it, Maria! Don't do it! I swear I didn't write the letter, Sascha wrote it himself." He gave one more scream, which went right through me, suddenly turned to me and said, "Jonas, what have I ever done to *you*?" and gave me a look which I could not understand. Then he buried his face in his hands. And that was when the shot rang out.

When the smoke had dispersed I must have given a scream like a madman. The woman was still sitting in her wheelchair, still unharmed, the smoking revolver in her hand. On the floor lay her husband, motionless, spattered with blood, a bullet through his forehead.

I just stood there, I didn't know what to do. I tried to work out exactly what had happened, but the whole room was spinning. I bent over the dead man, his face was twisted in fear, I tried to recall where I was and what it all meant, but my mind was empty apart from a few ridiculous words going round and round inside it, 'pour avoir bien servi'; and then I heard the invalid woman's voice, cold and cutting and dripping with hatred as she said:

"He was the one who betrayed Sascha to the police, the swine. Thank you for helping me, I have waited three years for this moment."

The story was over. The old man leant back in his chair and stared with his dull, weary eyes at the ceiling. The rest of us sat there in horrified silence, only the two lively girls from Vienna, who were playing with the Captain's bulldog in the corner, began to giggle and laugh, because at the end of the story it suddenly turned out that the old gentleman, who so far had been known as Mr. J. Schwemmer, was called Jonas – Jonas!

The Gypsy's Prophecy

Friedrich von Gagern

A gypsy had foretold that young Count C., an Austrian officer, would die in a graveyard. There was a story connected with
the gypsy and her prophecy. One hot summer long this beautiful, blooming, nut-brown maid had been the Count's lover; his
passion for hunting made frequent solitary excursions plausible, and they met and made love in the woods. A whispered
rumour appeared from somewhere or other, forcing C. to break
off the relationship, which was not compatible with his honour
as a nobleman – and an officer – and to pay a hefty sum to buy
the silence of the blackmailing leader of the gypsy band. In spite
of all this, it is said that he could never forget his gypsy lover.
Of the prophecy itself he would often speak quite openly,
although he would only talk in general terms about who had
made it, merely mentioning that she was a gypsy. He took the
prediction more lightly than the separation. At most one could
be buried in a graveyard, he would say, hardly die, unless one
committed suicide there; it must have been a slip of the tongue.
Count C. showed little enthusiasm for the pursuit of love, or
rather, it appeared in sporadic outbursts: fits of debauchery
would be followed by weeks or months of depression and cold
contempt. In his whole life, he would say, there had only ever
been one woman with whom he had found true fulfilment, all
the rest had been worth nothing ... One knew some of the facts,
suspected others, and said nothing.

At the beginning of the unfortunate – for Austria – campaign
of 1859 C. became a very close friend of Count Auersperg, a
cousin of my grandfather's. It was in the idle days of May, which
the hideously incompetent and lethargic General Gyulai spent
sitting with sufficient forces in excellent morale, between the
Ticino and the Siesa, watching the deployment of the French
and their Piedmont allies with Olympian detachment, instead of
disrupting it with a rapid counter-offensive or mounting a div-
ersionary attack on Turin. On the evening of 18th May C. was

sitting together with Auersperg and several others; their mood was not quite dejected, but somewhat oppressed; what wouldn't old Radetzky, the hero of 1848, have made of the situation! Well, thank God at least that Stadion, in whose division C. and Auersperg were serving, was going to push across the Po and try to provoke some response from the enemy. Then, suddenly, in the middle of all the talk of strategy, the regiment, their families, hunting, horses and women, little C.'s gaze became fixed, he paused, went pale then flushed, leapt up and stretched out his arms towards some vision. "Szárika! Jesus, where have you come from?" His comrades looked at him in astonishment. "What is it, what's wrong?" C. went on staring out into the night, his eyes wide open. "Szárika! ... Have you ... was it ... but that was ..." Eventually they managed to bring him back to reality, but he just sat there, staring gloomily into space. Perhaps a touch of marsh fever? ... Szárika? ... That night C. buttonholed Auersperg and unburdened his heart to him.

Szárika, the gypsy: her real name was Sara, a name that was particularly frequent among her people and particularly sacred to them. Yes, the story was true. He had found leaving her hard, very hard; a few times he'd seriously considered deserting and running off with her, to America. Hadn't been able to forget her with any woman since, couldn't love another, couldn't make love to another; torment and shame. She, Szárika, had seemed to find the parting quite easy, had gone on just as one went from one day to the next, uncaring, with the mindless natural apathy of an animal almost, whilst he, together or apart, was in thrall to her, an unquenchable longing burning inside him. Only she had foretold, with a grin of satisfaction, that he would never "love" another and that she would "visit" him once more; the prophecy concerning his death she had not read in the cards or his hand, but in a particular mark on his body ... And a moment ago she had appeared to him, not an illusion, not a ghost, just like the unfaded image in his memory, so real, so alive that he imagined he could hear the purr of her husky voice, feel the warmth of her presence, smell the pungent tang of her skin. She had seemed to grow out of the darkness that was gaudy with the bivouac fires all round, and he had felt her gaze physically: all his bodily fluids had drained to his bowels, taking his strength with them, and his neck and brain had been seized with an eerie shivering. Then she had inexplicably disappeared.

On a threadbare ribbon over his breast C. wore an amulet that Szárika had once given him, a heart shape, cut and stitched from scraps of woollen material which had long since lost all their bright colours, and through which something like grains of sand could be felt. This amulet C. now gave to Auersperg, despite his protestations, together with a note charging him, once the campaign was over, to look for Szárika in such and such places and give her a considerable sum of money, some three thousand crowns, from the C. estate. "Buck up, old chap, you can't know you're going to die; perhaps it'll be me, and you'll go home safe and sound." In reply C. gave him a melancholy look. "No, Auersperg. Listen: you will be wounded, but you will return home; I will fall, that's certain, and soon, you'll see; that's what Szárika came to tell me." "But I thought you were to die in a graveyard?" "It must have been a mistake, perhaps I got hold of the wrong end of the stick; you'll see." Auersperg tried to laugh, "Well, as you're in your prophetic vein, how will the war turn out?" "The war? Badly." "Just because you're in the dumps? Impossible; us with our new long-range rifles." "You'll see; it'll end badly." "Well, what about my brother in Hess' Division?" "Your brother? Franzl? Franzl's going to fall." That put an end to Auersperg's questions. He felt a shiver come over him. "How do you know all that?" "I don't know; I just feel it. You'll see." The next day Stadion's advance across the Po was agreed and preparations set in train.

Twelve thousand men and twenty cannon descended upon the enemy. They were not ready either; they lay behind the hills along the river banks, where they were getting into formation. The first contact was with the Piedmontese army under Sonnaz, Sonnaz hurriedly sent to the nearest allied commander, Baraguay, for support. The afternoon skirmish was concentrated round the village of Montebello. After initial, easy successes, the Austrians were forced to withdraw; the village graveyard, situated on high ground, was the position they held onto longest, in the face of fierce attacks. C. died of dreadful wounds, his destiny was fulfilled, his longing quenched for good.

Auersperg came out of it uninjured, as he did out of the bloody and desperate battle on the Brida and even out of Magenta, where the starved and exhausted Austrians, thanks to the military genius of the moronic, pop-eyed, wire-pulling General Gyulai, lost the battle, their foothold, their reputation, twelve thousand men and three hundred officers. He made contact with his brother after the two armies had eventually been united. At Solferino, the midsummer's day Battle of the Two Emperors with thunder rumbling all round, both of them were under fire at different points. A bad shoulder wound put Anton out of action; chance took him to his brother, both of whose legs had been torn off by a French cannonball. The dying Franz still had enough strength to recognise his brother; he knew nothing of his own condition, he merely felt cold and empty, already sailing on waves of music into eternity. "Jesus, Tonerl, been wounded? Bad? Get it dressed right away ... I'm fine, you know, fine, don't worry ... Cheerio, see you again in Bohemia." Then it was all over. Two weeks later the Emperors of France and Austria signed the truce.

Auersperg, back home, his wound healed, faithfully carried out the commission. He put out a search for Szárika and one of her name was actually traced in the official records; however, he could not give her C.'s legacy, she had died during an epidemic almost a year previously. At that point he opened the amulet his friend had given him. All it contained was a powder, not unlike pumice stone, mixed with small granules of something like bone and a tuft of curly black hair.

Auersperg fell into a brooding melancholy. So far everything had come true: C.'s death in the graveyard, his own wound, his brother's death, the humiliating end to the war. His comrade had seen through the darkness of the present, as if he were possessed by another soul, or as if he were looking from a brighter world beyond, perhaps in his tremor of premonition he had already been half way there. And then his brother's "See you again in Bohemia." It might have been spoken in the delirium of death, it might have been a misunderstanding, but it was like a warning that he could not get out of his mind. There were Bohemian branches of the Auersperg family, but there was hardly any contact with them, no connection apart from the name. Several times he discussed it with a cousin with whom he was very friendly; the cousin – my grandfather – thought up all kinds of explanations to reassure him: the death throes, visions, failing speech ...

But the visions of the dying are not delusions. The year 1866 arrived, the stab in the back, the infamous fratricidal war. Anton, now sure of what fate had in store for him, marched with Benedek and fell at Sadowa.

Later, a comrade who came back told them how Auersperg, mostly in a gloomy mood, had always foretold the outcome of the campaign to his close friends; he had also said he had seen his dead brother on the morning of the battle, gently trotting on his horse through the dawn mists rising from the Bistritz ...

Gracchus the Huntsman

Franz Kafka

Two boys were sitting on the harbour wall playing dice. A
man was reading a newspaper on the steps of a monument in the
shadow of its sabre-wielding hero. A girl at the fountain was
filling a tub with water. A fruit-vendor was lying down beside
his wares and looking out to sea. Through the empty openings
of the window and door one could see two men at the back of
the inn drinking wine. The innkeeper was sitting by a table at the
front, dozing. Gently, as if it was being carried over the waves,
a boat floated into the little harbour. A man in a blue smock came
on land and pulled the ropes through the rings. Two other men
in dark coats with silver buttons followed the seaman, carrying
a bier on which there was obviously someone lying underneath
the large silk cloth with a floral pattern and fringes.

No one on the quay took any notice of the new arrivals. Even
when they put down the bier to wait for the boatman, who was
still occupied with the ropes, no one came up to them, no one
asked any questions, no one had a good look at them.

The boatman was held up a little longer by a woman who, a
child at her breast and her hair all tousled, now appeared on
deck. Then he came and pointed to the straight lines of a two-
storeyed, yellowish house that stood on the left, close to the sea;
the bearers picked up their load and carried it through the door
that was low, but flanked with slim pillars. A small boy opened
a window, just caught sight of the group disappearing into the
house, and hastily shut the window again. Then the door was
closed as well, it was made of neatly mitred planks of black oak.
A flock of pigeons, that until that point had been flying round
the bell-tower, landed in front of the house. As if their food was
kept in the house, the pigeons gathered outside the door. One
flew up to the first floor and pecked at the windowpane. They
were brightly coloured, well-fed, lively birds. The woman on
the boat threw them some seeds in a great arc; they picked them
up and flew across to the woman.

A man in a top hat with a black ribbon round it came down one of the steep, narrow alleyways leading to the harbour. He looked round attentively, everything worried him, the sight of rubbish in a corner made him frown. There was some peel on the steps of the monument, he flicked it off with his stick as he passed. When he reached the door, he knocked, at the same time taking his top hat in his black-gloved right hand. It was opened immediately; the long hallway was lined with at least fifty small boys, who bowed.

The boatman came down the stairs, greeted the man, led him upstairs; on the first floor he walked with him round the delicate, flimsily built loggia encircling the courtyard and then both of them, the boys crowding along behind at a respectful distance, entered a large, cool room at the rear of the house which looked out not onto another house but a bare, grey-black rock-face. The bearers were setting up some long candles on either side of the bier and lighting them, but that did not create any light, the only effect was literally to rouse the sleeping shadows and send them flickering round the walls. The cloth was drawn back from the bier. On it lay a man with a tangle of hair and beard and a bronzed skin, more or less resembling a huntsman. He lay there motionless, apparently not breathing and with his eyes closed, yet it was only the surroundings that suggested he might be dead.

The new arrival went to the bier, laid his hand on the forehead of the man stretched out on it, then knelt down and prayed. The boatman signed to the bearers to leave the room; they went out, clearing away the boys who had gathered outside, and closed the door. Even then the silence did not seem sufficient for the man at prayer, he glanced at the boatman, who understood and went out by a side door into the adjoining room. Immediately the man on the bier opened his eyes, turned, with a smile of pain, to face the man in black and said, "Who are you?" He, not showing any surprise at all, stood up from the floor and replied, "The Mayor of Riva."

The man on the bier nodded, indicated a chair with a weak gesture of his outstretched arm and said, after the Mayor had accepted his invitation to sit down, "I knew, of course, but in the first few moments I always find I have forgotten everything,

everything goes round and round, and it is better that I should ask, even if I know. And you probably also know that I am Gracchus, the huntsman?"

"Certainly", said the Mayor. "The announcement came during the night. We had been asleep for some time. It was towards midnight that my wife called out, 'Salvatore', – that is my name – 'look at the pigeon at the window.' It really was a pigeon, but the size of a cock. It flew over and said into my ear, 'Gracchus, the dead huntsman, will come tomorrow, welcome him in the name of the town.'"

The huntsman nodded and passed the tip of his tongue through his lips, "Yes, the pigeons fly on ahead. But, Mayor, do you think I should stay in Riva?"

"I cannot say yet", replied the Mayor. "Are you dead?"

"Yes", said the huntsman, "as you can see. Many years ago – many, many years it must have been – I fell from a rock whilst I was chasing a chamois in the Black Forest, in Germany. Since then I have been dead."

"But you are alive, as well", said the Mayor.

"In a way", said the huntsman, "In a way I am still alive. My funeral barge went the wrong way: a false movement of the tiller, a momentary lack of attention on the part of the boatman, the distraction of the beauty of the Black Forest, I don't know what it was, all I know is that I remained on earth, and that since then my barge has been travelling the waters of this earth. During my life I wanted no other home than my mountains and now, after my death, I am travelling through all the countries of the world."

"And you have no part in the world beyond?" asked the Mayor, wrinkling his brow.

"I am still", replied the huntsman, "on the great staircase leading up. I roam the infinite space of this flight of steps, sometimes at the top, sometimes down below, sometimes to the right, sometimes to the left, always in motion. The huntsman has become a butterfly. Don't laugh."

"I'm not laughing", protested the Mayor.

"Very understanding of you", said the huntsman. "I am forever in motion. But if I pull myself up as far as possible until I can see the gate shining at the top, I always wake up in my old barge to find it drearily stuck in some earthly waterway. The basic mistake in my erstwhile death is grinning down at me from the walls of my cabin. Julia, the boatman's wife, knocks and brings to my bier the morning drink of the country we happen to be travelling along. I lie on a bare wooden bed, wearing – I am not a particularly pleasant sight – a grubby shroud, my hair and beard, grey and black, are inseparably entangled, my legs are covered by a large, silk cloth with a floral pattern and long fringes, intended for a woman. At my head is a church candle which gives me light. On the wall opposite is a small painting, obviously representing a bushman, who is pointing his spear at me and concealing as much of himself as possible behind a magnificently decorated shield. You see all kinds of silly pictures on ships, but this is one of the silliest. Otherwise my wooden cage is quite empty. The warm air of the southern night comes in through a porthole in the side, and I can hear the water slapping against the old barge.

I have been lying here ever since the time when I was still alive, was still Gracchus the huntsman, and I fell from a rock while I was chasing a chamois in the Black Forest where I lived. Everything took its proper course. I chased, fell, bled to death in a ravine, and this barge was supposed to bear me to the afterlife. I can still remember how happy I was the first time I stretched out on these planks. The mountains never heard me sing as these four walls did, murky as they were even then.

I had lived happily, and I was happy to die; gladly I threw down, before I came on board, all the junk – shotgun, game bag, hunting rifle – that I had always been so proud to carry, and put on my shroud like a girl her wedding dress. I lay here and waited. Then the misfortune occurred."

"A dreadful fate", said the Mayor, raising his hand as if to ward off a like evil. "And you are not at all to blame for it?"

"Not at all", said the huntsman. "I was a huntsman – what is the blame in that? I was employed as a huntsman in the Black Forest where there were still wolves. I would lie in wait, shoot, kill, skin – what is the blame in that? My work was blessed with success. 'The great huntsman of the Black Forest', I was called.

Where is the blame in that?"

"It is not my place to decide on that", said the Mayor, "but I don't find anything to blame in it, either. But who is to blame, then?"

"The boatman", said the huntsman. "Nobody will read what I am writing here, nobody will come to help me. If helping me were a set task, all the doors of all the houses would stay shut, all the windows would stay shut, everyone would lie in bed, the blankets pulled over their heads, the whole earth would be an inn at night. There is some point to that, for no one knows of me, and if they knew of me, they would not know where I was, and if they knew where I was, they would not know how to keep me there, they would not know how to help me. The idea of helping me is an illness and the cure is to stay in bed.

I know that, so I don't shout out for help, even if there are moments – uncontrolled as just now – when I think about it intently. But all I need to do to drive away such thoughts is to look around me and recall where I am and where – as I think I am justified in saying – I have been living for centuries."

"Extraordinary", said the Mayor, "extraordinary. And now you propose to stay with us in Riva?"

"I do not propose", said the huntsman, laying his hand, to excuse his irony, on the Mayor's knee. "I am here, that is all I know, that is all I can do. My barge has no tiller, it sails with the wind that blows in the lowest regions of death."

Outside the Law

Franz Kafka

Outside the Law stood a doorkeeper. A man from the country
came to this doorkeeper and asked to go into the Law. But the
doorkeeper said he could not let him go in just then. The man
thought this over and then asked whether that meant he might
be allowed to enter the Law later. "It is possible", said the
doorkeeper, "but now now." As the door of the Law was open
as always and the doorkeeper stepped to one side, the man bent
down to see into the interior. When the doorkeeper noticed that,
he laughed and said, "If it tempts you so much, why don't you
try to go in, even though I have forbidden it? But remember, I
am powerful. And I am only the lowest doorkeeper. But outside
each room you pass through there is a doorkeeper, each one
more powerful than the last. The sight of just the third is too
much even for me." The man from the country had not expected
such difficulty; the Law is supposed to be available to everyone
and at all times, he thought, but as he took a closer look at the
doorkeeper in his fur coat, his large, pointed nose, his long, thin,
black Tartar moustache, he decided it would be better to wait
until he was given permission to enter. The doorkeeper gave
him a stool and let him sit down at the side of the door. There
he sat for days and years. He made many attempts to be allowed
in and tired the doorkeeper with his requests. Quite often the
doorkeeper would briefly interrogate him, asking him questions
about the place he came from and many other things, but they
were uninterested questions, such as important people ask, and
at the end he always said he could not let him in yet. The man,
who had equipped himself well for the journey, used everything, no matter how valuable, to bribe the doorkeeper. The
latter accepted everything, but said, as he did so, "I am only
accepting this so that you will not think there was something you
omitted to do." Over the many years the man observed the
doorkeeper almost uninterruptedly. He came to forget the other
doorkeepers and this first one seemed to him to be the only

obstacle to his entry into the Law. He cursed the unfortunate chance, loud and recklessly in the first years, later, as he grew old, he just muttered to himself. He grew childish and, since as a result of his years of studying the doorkeeper he had come to recognise even the fleas on his fur collar, he asked the fleas to help him and persuade the doorkeeper to change his mind. Finally his vision grew weak and he did not know whether it was really becoming dark round him, or whether his eyes were deceiving him. But now, in the dark, he could distinguish a radiance, which streams, inextinguishable, from the door of the Law. Now he had not much longer to live. Before his death all the things he had experienced during the whole time merged in his mind into a question he had not yet put to the doorkeeper. He gestured to him, since he could no longer raise his stiffening body. The doorkeeper had to bend down low to him, for the difference in height had changed considerably, to the man's disadvantage. "What is it you want to know now?" asked the doorkeeper, "you are insatiable." "Everyone seeks the Law", said the man, "so how is it that in all these years no one but I has asked to be let in?" The doorkeeper realised that the man was near the end and so, in order to be audible to his fading hearing, he bellowed at him, "No one else could be granted entry here, since this entrance was intended for you alone. I am going to go and shut it now."

Shadowtown

Franz Theodor Csokor

Sixty-five!

Set your face firm! Steel your muscles till the skin stretches tight, fit to burst!

Seventy-five!

The red car is turning into a raging animal trying to buck sky-high, but we stay in the saddle, clamping it between iron-hard thighs, furiously spurring it on!

Ninety!

"Faster!" hisses the woman. It's folly, intoxication, drunken madness – and we feel like whooping with exhilaration. The road pours into us; the air whishes past our ears with the sound of scythes through corn-stalks; behind us the dust is swept up, heaves and billows, swirls and tussles with the storm we raise; fields flit past; bushes bristle at us with a menace of twigs, gnarled willows grin. Something scurries across in our path. Animal? – Human? – Over it we go!!

I noticed how grey and wretched we looked, all of us. The director at the wheel, his thin lips frozen in his courteous smile; his wife beside me, just as when I found her with gaping lips: the dose of veronal was not quite enough. And me, reflected in the rear-view mirror, hollow-cheeked, bedaubed with dust, a poor harlequin.

A hundred and ten!

The horn squeals as if the car were in unbearable pain.

Was that not the bulge of a town on the horizon? It disappears in a smudge of dust; another glimpse, and it's gone again. Barns resembling monstrous coffins spin past with the ploughed fields, gliding like silent ships through the swell of the earth all around. Spires scribble all over the blue of the sky. Poplars bubble up along the road, standing on parade: straight as arrows, atten-tion! As if we were driving into a churchyard, I think; I can see the town gate glooming up ahead, distant but growing, blocking our path; masonry, lath and plaster is piled up around it, pushes up against it as if the stones felt the cold.

A jolt: the director at the wheel is roused from his inertia to give a genuine laugh such as I have never heard from him before – it disconcerts me; then a red net wraps itself round my skull and my pulse starts to ripple and slither, but that doesn't frighten me any longer: praecordial trauma my doctor calls it. A lasso tightens round my heart, dragging it through all my arteries, then slackens off, again and again.

As it does now! I come up for air, up from the depths of my body, my blood is released, its thunder drowns the engine. Hurrah! In front: the town we shall take by storm, the gate girt with walls, a slim belfry, crumpled gables; it rushes towards us, expands, devours us. And inside we ease up, we glide along softly, as if everything were submerged beneath water. We are tamed by the narrow street; it runs on ahead of us, silent and empty of people, although the air is warm and inviting, redolent with the rich, balmy sun of a spring twilight. It is May.

May. The actress beside me cannot see my caressing glance, she is watching her husband. They have been tormenting each other for nine years now, nine years to equal a thousand. They inhabit adjoining territories, the words between them are weary and silent; she has lovers, he always has a new mistress, the only thing that attracts him is the act of seduction. But at heart she loves only him, he only her, with a clear, merciless, inescapable love, as if it were predetermined from the beginning of time. Occasionally they come together, and then they do not know whether to kill each other or to die for each other.

The director looks up from the steering wheel and turns to his wife, he turns to me as well, but at the same time his gaze, dispassionate as ever, is toying with the distance beyond us. "Shadowtown", he says, but I do not know whether that is the name of the place or whether it is something he has just thought up. And why does he throw a challenging look at his wife as he says it? She must be the loser, I suddenly realise, he is a hundred times more of a woman than she, and with a man's mind and will-power into the bargain!

These alleys squeeze us, lead us round in a circle or shrink to a stump. A wall keeps returning; over it we can see a lake shimmering. An old woman comes out of one of the very low houses – there is nothing but low houses here, with their roofs pulled down tight over their ears! She hardly gives us a glance. "Which is the way out?" I ask. She shakes her head, as if it were impossible and disappears into one of the cellars.

We can't get lost in a little town like this? Or are we never going to get back out into the open again? A ridiculous idea! The tall, red church I saw as we entered is our marker now. We were heading straight for it. It stood like a huge animal, guarding the tangle of alleyways at its feet; round curves and corners it drew us towards it. But then the road forked, mocked us whenever we thought we were almost there. A close of canon's houses, ancient masonry, presumably the presbytery, all of them devoid of life, blocked our path; finally the square embraced us. There the cathedral towered up, gothic brick, twin-towered, an adamant monk with his arms stretched up to heaven. On the sills a profusion of grass and saplings: structure returning home, to nature.

We were turned away by the locked door. A strange relief on the tympanum puzzled us; we went up close to look at it: with his bare hands a Saint George was strangling a snake, which had wrapped itself round his armoured legs and was trying to pull itself up him. His charger, a unicorn, stood by, its halter round the tree from the Garden of Eden. This symbol of chastity was his only companion; unlike every other portrayal, this one lacked the lady he set free. His triumph was overlaid with sorrow; his features radiated the aching purity of those who have suffered long torture.

I was overcome with a leaden sadness, which clearly oppressed the others as well. The actress abruptly bent over her husband's hand and kissed it; she was sitting beside him now, her shoulders sagged forlornly against him, seeming to bear the sorrow of the whole world. His hands did not leave the wheel; only his smile was clouded, a calm severity made his features almost like those of the knight above the cathedral door. 'Let's go!' was the vehement desire within me, for my heart was already rushing to my head as well; it needed the rhythm of the machine imposed on it, that would put everything to rights. And it happened; my silent wish was fulfilled.

In front of us cowered a row of almshouses; their monastic structure resembled the church and they were probably from the same period. And there was someone standing there, the old woman again: she must have made incredible speed, or did all the old people in his strange town look the same? Had they come to be akin over the long years, just as earth, when trodden down, is indistinguishable, earth, which they would soon become themselves? 'Force her to speak', I commanded myself, but for that I would need some banal question that belonged to the coarse material world – the whereabouts of an inn, for example – which would break the spell cast by the old woman, who seemed to come straight from the brush of a Rembrandt. I received my answer even before I had spoken; "The Traveller's Rest", it came like a voice from the crypt, and the old woman waved her hands around at the same time: was she making the sign of the cross over us, or was she indicating the direction? My friend seemed to assume the latter; he drove on.

From the cathedral square six echoing blows thudded to the ground; it was the Angelus, the hour when the mind opens to receive divine thoughts, but also the soft hour of seduction, of betrayal. There was a strange brightness revealing everything; in spite of the fading sun, we and all the things around us appeared with precise and painful clarity; we could almost see into each other's minds. I wanted to point this out to the woman, but her eyes were embracing her husband. 'That is the way people look at little children when they haven't any of their own!' I thought.

The car floated through an arched gateway – yes, 'floated' was the word, we moved so smoothly we could hardly feel the ground. In a niche an ecstatic saint was stretched upon the rack; his stone arms, broken off, were excruciating to see. Above him was a sundial with a strange motto curving round the circle of the hours, "Quaelibet vulnerat, ultima necat": "Each one wounds, the last one kills". But that was, I assumed, the end of all the strangeness, for beyond the gate was a welcoming inn, a broad, grey, ancient farmhouse; on the threshold stood the innkeeper, a tall man with a quiet face that seemed not unfamiliar to me.

There was nothing that might be called special about it when we went in. The room, its ceiling festooned with withered wreaths, was obviously used for local dances and country celebrations, and here we came across signs of life. That is, there were many people sitting there in the half-light; they were drinking or smoking, only no one was talking. They looked as if they had long since said everything there was to say, and were afraid of irritating each other with the mere sound of their voices.

Without a word, the innkeeper moved softly behind the bar. 'Like a dead man', I thought to myself, for his features revealed a weary sagacity, such as befits only God's ripe harvest, the dead who have truly rounded off their lives. I did not attempt to pass this thought on to my friends: since we had entered the town I had the feeling, which was becoming stronger all the time, that we suddenly knew so much about each other that speech was unnecessary between us.

A twitching melody came from another room. It was a Javanese dance tune; it consisted of a despairing repetition of the same sequence of notes which sounded as if it was derived from one of their dirges; the playing was clumsy, with the same mistakes being repeated.

"We must go through your role", the director reminded the actress, as we sat down at a table where another man was sitting, his face turned towards the shadows. I was surprised. She had no engagements for the near future, and yet my friend was behaving as if there were nothing more urgent. Besides, they were the very first words he had addressed to her since we had driven through the town gate.

The gentle innkeeper brings some wine. He doesn't talk to us, just looks at us as if he wanted to express something, but he definitely says very little, only "Welcome" – or "Amen"; yes, "Amen", that was probably it. And the man at the table turns to face me, and it is my brother. "Julian", I murmur, without surprise. He nods.

Behind me the director starts muttering something to the

actress; it is presumably her role. I feel I know the work it is from, but can't remember the name of the writer. One single sentence keeps being repeated, "Our Father, who art in Heaven ..."

And then I suddenly realise my brother Julian fell in the War, on the Stry; he is buried somewhere in Russia. And yet he is sitting here. And now a lithe woman, a puma in clothes, is waving to me from the door; it's Evelyne, Evelyne who died last year, who laughed as she toyed with all kinds of male beasts until she fell into love and drowned; and there is Heinrich, the theatre manager, with his sardonic grin; it was at the same time that I heard he had chosen death; and there are lots of others here from the other side, I gradually recognise them. And the Java-naise trickles on. And a couple stand up and dance to it, slowly. And the innkeeper's soft, sad glance embraces them all. And the red wine has a bittersweet taste. And the actress behind me keeps repeating after her husband, "Our Father, who art in Heaven ..."

No, I must be dreaming, so I try to close my eyes in my dream – that makes you wake up. It's an old remedy that our nursemaid taught us to drive away a nightmare. But the vision I have behind my closed lids, surely that must be the dream? There is a crashed car and blood running over the ground, a lot of blood, and bodies screaming with gaping flesh. And as I look on, my neck and arms are racked by terrible pain. I must open my eyes! I want to wake up, damn it! "Our Father, who art in Heaven ...", I can hear it beside me, so they must all still be here, they are all round me, why won't they help me, then? Poor advice, Nanny! I am crying, I can't hear myself, but I know that I am crying. All I can see is a lot of stupid faces staring at me in horror; what can they want? I'm asleep, of course, dreaming ...

Then at last a human countenance appears above me; my old nursemaid is looking down at me. "Nanny", I feel myself say, "take me home." And she is stroking me, and now it's the old woman from the town, of course, that's who it is, and now I can open my eyes, carefully, and everything reappears out of a mist, the inn and the people around me, but now there is colour in their cheeks, as if the blood had come back in their veins; they are alive like me. And the Javanaise plays on, and a couple are dancing ... And the actress is repeating, louder and louder, "Our Father, who art in Heaven ..." And my brother is smiling, and I want to embrace him, but someone is holding my hands down. Or have I no hands any more?

What does it matter? I am awake again. Back in life once more, in the life of this little town, which isn't so odd as it at first seemed to us. In fact, everything seems perfectly straightforward here, it is what must have come before that now seems like a pointless diversion. And my brother must be of the same opinion, he's nodding to me warmly, and the actress is smiling a smile of relief at her husband, who for the first time is giving her a clear-eyed look, full of love, and the words she is saying speak to me of home, and my old nanny is bending over me again, and all around me she is like a safe, dark cave which will protect me as I fall asleep ... like a dead man ...

No ... like a child ...

The Destruction of Amsterdam

From: *The Green Face*

Gustav Meyrink

The hours crept by unbearably slowly, the night seemed unending.

Finally the sun rose; the sky remained inky black, but around the horizon there was a vivid, sulphurous gleam, as if a dark bowl with glowing edges had descended over the earth.

There was an all-pervading, matt half-light; the poplar outside the window, the distant bushes and the towers of Amsterdam were faintly illuminated, as if by dim floodlights. Beneath them lay the plain like a huge, blind mirror.

Hauberrisser scanned the city with his binoculars; in the wan light it stood out from the shadowy background as if frozen in fear and expecting the death-blow at any moment.

A ringing of bells washed over the countryside in tremulous, breathless waves and then came to an abrupt halt; a dull roar filled the air and the poplar was bent groaning to the ground. Gusts of wind swept over the meadows like the crack of a whip, flattening the withered grass and tearing the sparse, low bushes up by the roots.

A few minutes later the whole landscape vanished in an immense dust-cloud, and when it reappeared it was scarcely recognisable: the ditches had been whipped into white foam, the windmills were transformed into blunt stumps squatting on the brown earth as their torn-off sails whirled through the air high in the sky. The pauses between blasts became shorter and shorter, until eventually nothing could be heard but the constant roaring of the wind. Its fury redoubled by the second; the wiry poplar was bent at right angles a few feet above the ground, branches gone, it was little more than a smooth stem, fixed motionless in that position by the immense force of the mass of air rushing over it.

Only the apple tree stood still, as if protected by some unseen hand in a haven of stillness, not one single leaf moving.

A never-ending shower of missiles flew past the window: beams and stones, clods of earth and tangles of brushwood, lumps of brickwork, even complete walls.

Then suddenly the sky turned light grey, and the darkness dissolved into a cold, silvery glitter.

Hauberrisser assumed the fury of the tornado was subsiding, then noticed to his horror that the bark of the poplar was being stripped off in fibrous scraps, which disappeared instantly. The next moment, before he could really grasp what was happening, the tall factory chimneys towering over the south-west part of the docks were snapped off at the roots and transformed into thin spears of white dust which the hurricane carried off at lightning speed. They were followed by one church tower after another: for a second they would appear as black shapes, whirled up in a vortex, the next they were lines on the horizon, then dots, then nothing.

The vegetation torn up by the storm flew past the window at such a speed that soon all that could be seen through it was a pattern of horizontal lines. Even the graveyard must have been ripped open, for now tombstones, coffins, crosses and grave-lamps flew past the house, never deviating, never rising, never falling, always horizontal, as if they were weightless.

Hauberrisser could hear the cross beams in the roof groaning, every moment he expected it to be torn apart; he was about to run downstairs to bolt the front door so that it would not be blown off its hinges but, with his hand on the knob of the bed-room door, he stopped, warned by an inner voice that if he opened it the draught would smash the window-panes, allowing the storm that was sweeping past the front of the house to rush in and transform it into a maelstrom of rubble. It could only avoid destruction as long as the hill behind protected it from the full blast of the hurricane and the rooms remained shut off from each other, like cells in a honeycomb.

The air in the room had turned icy cold and thin, as if in a vacuum; a sheet of paper fluttered round the room, then pressed against the keyhole and stuck there, held fast by the suction.

Hauberrisser went back to look out of the window. The gale

was blowing the water out of the ditches so that it spattered through the air like fine rain; the meadows gleamed like smooth grey velvet and where the poplar had stood there was now a stump crowned by a flapping shock of splinters.

The roar of the wind was so constant, so deafening, that Hauberrisser began to think that all around was shrouded in a deathly hush. It was only when he went to nail back the trembling shutters, so that they would not be blown against the glass, and found he could not hear the hammering, that he realised how great the din outside must be.

For a long time he did not dare look out again, for fear that he might see that St. Nicholas' had been blown away, and with it the nearby house on the Zeedijk harbouring Swammerdam and Pfeill; when he did risk a tentative glance, he saw it still towering up undamaged, but it was an island in a sea of rubble: the rest of the frieze of spires, roofs and gables had been almost completely flattened.

'How many cities are there left standing in Europe?' he wondered with a shudder. 'The whole of Amsterdam has been ground to dust like crumbling rock; nothing left of a rotten civilisation but a scatter of rubbish.' He was gripped with awe as he suddenly comprehended the magnitude of the cataclysm. His experiences the previous day, his exhaustion and the sudden eruption of the storm had kept him in a state of constant numbness, from which he only now awoke to clear consciousness.

He clutched his forehead. 'Have I been sleeping?'

His glance fell on the apple tree: as if by a miracle, the splendour of its blossom was completely untouched. He remembered that yesterday he had buried the roll of papers by its roots; it seemed as if an eternity had passed since then. Had he not written in them that he had the ability to leave his body? Then why had he not done so, yesterday, through the night or this morning, when the storm had broken?

Why did he not do it now?

For a brief second, he managed it. He saw his body as a foreign, shadowy creature leaning at the window, but in spite of the devastation, the world outside was no longer the dead, ghostly landscape of his previous experiences: a new earth was spread out before him, quivering with life, spring hovered on the air, full of glory, like a visible manifestation of the future, his breast trembled with the presentiment of nameless raptures; the world around seemed to be a vision that was gradually taking on lasting clarity; and the apple tree in blossom, was that not Chidher, the 'ever green tree'?

The next moment Hauberrisser was back in his body gazing out on the howling storm, but hc knew now that the picture of destruction concealed within it the promise of the new land that he had just seen with the eyes of his soul.

His heart beat in wild, joyous anticipation; he felt that he was on the threshold of the last, highest awakening, that the phoenix within him was stretching its wings for its flight into the ether. His sense of the approach of an event far beyond any earthly experience was so strong, that he almost choked with the intensity of emotion; it was almost the same as when he had kissed Eva in the park in Hilversum, the same gust of icy air from the wings of the Angel of Death, but now it was permeated with the fragrance of flowers, like a presentiment of the approach of life imperishable. He heard the words of Chidher, "For Eva's sake I will give you never-ending love", as if it was the blossoming apple tree that was calling them to him.

He thought of the countless dead who lay beneath the ruins of the destroyed city on the horizon, but he could not feel sorrow. 'They will rise again, if in a different form, until they find the last, the highest form, that of the 'awakened man' who will die no more. Nature, too, is ever renewed, like the phoenix.'

He was suddenly gripped by an emotion so powerful, that he felt he must choke; was that not Eva standing close beside him? He had felt a breath on his cheek, and whose heart was beating so close to his, if not hers?

He felt new senses ripening within him to reveal the invisible realm that permeates our earthly world. Any second the last veil that kept it from his eyes might fall.

"Give me a sign that you are near, Eva", he quietly implored. "Let my faith that you will come to me not be disappointed."

"It would be a poor love that could not overcome time and space", he heard her voice whisper, and his scalp tingled at the intensity of his emotion. "Here in this room I recovered from the torments of the earth and here I am waiting with you until the hour of your awakening has come."

A quiet, peaceful calm settled over him. He looked around; the whole room was filled with the same joyful, patient expectancy, like the half-stifled call of spring; each object seemed about to undergo the miracle of a transformation beyond comprehension.

His heart beat audibly.

The room, the walls, the objects around him were, he sensed, only delusory, external forms for his earthly eyes, projecting into the world of bodies like shadows from an invisible realm; any minute the door might open behind which lay the land of the immortals.

He tried to imagine what it would be like when his spiritual senses were awakened. 'Will Eva be with me? Will I go to her and see her and talk to her? Will it be just as beings of this earth meet each other? Or will we become formless, colours or sounds that blend together? Will we be surrounded by objects, as we are here, will we be rays of light, soaring through the infinite cosmos, or will the material world be transformed and ourselves transformed along with it?' He surmised that, although it would be completely new and something he could not at the moment grasp, it would also be a quite natural process, perhaps not unlike the formation of the whirlwinds which he had seen yesterday arise from nothing, from thin air, and take on shapes perceptible to all the senses of the body; yet he still had no clear idea of what it involved.

He was quivering with the presentiment of such indescribable rapture that he knew that the reality of the miraculous experience awaiting him would far surpass anything he could imagine.

The hours slipped by.

It seemed to be midday: high in the sky a gleaming disc hung in the haze.

Was the storm still raging?

Hauberrisser listened.

258

There was nothing by which he might tell: the ditches were empty, blown away; there was no water, no hint of any movement in them; no bushes as far as the eye could see; the grass flattened; not a single cloud crossing the sky, nothing but empty space.

He took the hammer and dropped it, heard it hit the floor with a crash and concluded that it was quiet outside.

Through his binoculars he could see that the city was still suffering the fury of the cyclone; huge blocks of stone were thrown up into the air, waterspouts appeared from the harbour, collapsed, towered up again and danced out towards the open sea.

And there! Was it a delusion? Were not the twin towers of St. Nicholas' swaying?

One collapsed suddenly; the other whirled up into the air and exploded like a rocket; for a moment the huge bell hovered free between heaven and earth. Then it plunged silently to the ground. Hauberrisser's heart stopped still. Swammerdam! Pfeill!

No, no, no, nothing could have happened to them. 'Chidher, the eternal tree of mankind, will shield them with his branches.' Had Swammerdam not prophesied he would outlive the church?

And were there not islands, like the blossoming apple tree there in its patch of green grass, where life was kept safe from destruction and preserved for the coming age?

Only now did the thunder from the crash of the bell reach the house. The walls vibrated under the impact of the airwaves on one single, terrifying note, a note so piercing that Hauberrisser felt as if the bones in his body had shattered like glass; for a brief moment he felt consciousness fade.

"The walls of Jericho have fallen", he heard the quivering voice of Chidher Green say aloud in the room. **"He has awakened from the dead."**

A breathless hush ...

Then the cry of a baby ...

Hauberrisser looked around, disorientated.

Finally he found his bearings

He clearly recognised the plain, bare walls of his room, and yet at the same time they were the walls of a temple decorated with a fresco of Egyptian deities. He was standing in the middle, and both were reality: he saw the wooden floorboards and at the same time they were the stone flags of the temple, two worlds that interpenetrated before his very eyes, fused together and yet separate. It was as if he were awake and dreaming in one and the same moment. He touched the whitewashed wall with his hand, could feel its rough surface and yet at the same time knew without mistake that his fingers were stroking a tall, gold statue, which he believed he recognised as the Goddess Isis sitting on a throne.

In addition to his previous, familiar human consciousness, he had acquired a new consciousness, which had enriched him with the perception of a new world, which touched the old world, enveloped and transformed it, and yet in some miraculous way let it continue the same.

Each sense awoke, doubled within him, like blooms bursting from their buds.

Scales fell from his eyes. Like someone who for his whole life has only known two dimensions and suddenly finds he is seeing rounded forms, he could for a long time not grasp what had happened.

Gradually he realised that he had reached his goal, the end of the path that is the hidden purpose of every human being. His goal was to be an inhabitant of two worlds.

Once more a baby cried.

Had Eva not said she wanted to be a mother when she came to him again? The thought was a sudden shock to him.

Did not the Goddess Isis have a naked, living child in her arm?

He lifted his eyes to her and saw that she was smiling.

She moved.

The frescos were becoming sharper, clearer, more colourful, and all around were sacred vessels. Everything was so distinct that Hauberrisser forgot the sight of his room and only had eyes for the temple and the red and gold paintings round the walls.

Lost in thought, he gazed at the face of the goddess and slowly, slowly a dull memory rose to the surface: Eva! That was

Eva and not a statue of the Egyptian goddess, the Mother of the World!

He pressed his hands against the sides of his head, he could not believe it.

"Eva! Eva!" he cried out loud.

Again the bare walls of his bedroom appeared through the temple walls; the goddess was still there on her throne, still smiling, but close in front of him was her earthly likeness, a young woman, the picture of living beauty.

"Eva! Eva!" with an ecstatic cry of boundless rapture, he clasped her to him and covered her face with kisses: "Eva!"

For a long time they stood entwined at the window, looking out at the dead city.

He felt a thought speak within him, as if it were the voice of Chidher, "You are united to help the generations to come, as I do, to build a new realm from the ruins of the old, so that the time may come when I, too, may smile."

The room and the temple were equally distinct.

As if he had the double head of Janus, Hauberrisser could see both the earthly world and the world beyond at the same time, and clearly distinguish all details, all objects:

> He was a living man
> Both here and beyond.

THE MACABRE

Dr. Cinderella's Plants

Gustav Meyrink

Do you see the little blackened bronze statue over there between the two lamps? That has been the cause of all the weird experiences I have had in recent years.

These phantom perturbations which have so drained my energy are all links in a chain which, if I pursue it back into the past, comes back every time to the same starting point: the bronze.

If I pretend to myself that there may be other causes of my anxieties, the image nevertheless recurs to me, like another milestone along the road.

But where this road is leading me – to ultimate illumination or to ever-increasing horror – I have no desire to know, wishing only to cling on to those occasions when for a few days I feel relief from my doom and can sense freedom until I am overcome by the next shock.

I unearthed the thing in the desert sands of Thebes one day as I was prodding about with my stick, and from the very first moment, as I was examining it more closely, I was struck with a morbid curiosity to know what the image might signify – I have never wanted to know anything quite so urgently.

In the beginning I would ask every explorer I met, but without success. Only one old Arabian collector seemed to have some idea about what it meant.

"A representation of an Egyptian hieroglyph," he proposed; the unusual position of the arms of the figure must indicate some kind of mysterious ecstatic state.

I took the bronze with me back to Europe, and hardly an evening went by without my falling into the most remarkable reveries about its mystery.

An uncanny feeling would come over me on these occasions as I brooded on some poisonous and malevolent presence which was threatening, with malicious relish, to break out of its lifeless cocoon in order to fasten itself leechlike upon me, and to remain, like some incurable disease, as the dark tyrant of my life. Then one day, as I was concerned with quite a different matter, the thought which made sense of the whole riddle struck me with such force, and so unexpectedly, that I staggered under its impact.

Such shafts of illumination strike into our souls like meteors. We know not whence they come: we witness only their white-hot gleam as they fall.

It is almost like a feeling of fear — then — a slight — as — as if some alien — What am I trying to say?! I'm sorry, some-times I get so forgetful, especially since I've had to drag this lame leg along. Yes, well, the answer to my brooding thoughts appeared suddenly stark in front of my eyes: *imitation*!

And as if the one word had demolished a wall, I was overcome by the flood-waves of a realisation that that alone must be the key to all the mysteries of our existence.

An uncanny, automatic act of imitation, unconscious, perpe-tual, the hidden guide of every creature!

An omnipotent, mysterious guide – a masked pilot, silently stepping on board the ship of life in the grey of the dawn. Rising up out of those measureless chasms into which our soul delights to descend when sleep has closed the gates of day! And perhaps down there in those abysses of disembodied existence there stands the brazen image of a demon willing us to be like him, to shape ourselves in his likeness —

And this word: "imitate", this brief call from the ether became a road for me, and I set out on it at that same moment. I took up the pose, raised both arms above my head in imitation of the statue, and lowered my fingers until the nails just brushed my scalp.

Nothing happened.

No change, either within me or round about me.

So as to make no mistake in my pose I looked more closely at the figure, and saw that the eyes were closed, as if in sleep.

I decided that I had had enough, broke off the exercise, and put further action off until nightfall. When that came I stilled the ticking of the clocks and lay down, reassuming the position of my arms and hands.

A few minutes passed in this state, but I cannot believe that I could have fallen asleep.

Suddenly there seemed to come echoing out from somewhere inside me a sound, as of a huge stone rumbling down into the depths.

And as if my consciousness were tumbling after it down a monstrous staircase, bouncing two, four, then eight and ever more steps at a time, my memory leaped back through my life, and the spectre of apparent death cloaked itself about me.

What then happened I will not say: none can say it.

People laugh at the idea that the Egyptians and Chaldaeans are supposed to have possessed a magic secret, guarded by uraeus snakes, and never betrayed by any one of the thousands of initiates.

There are no oaths which can possibly bind so securely, we think.

And I, too, thought this once; but in that instant I understood.

It is an event in no way connected with human experience, where perceptions lie as it were one *behind* another, and there is no oath that binds the tongue – the merest thought of a hint at these things, here on this side, and it is enough to alert the vipers of life into taking aim to strike at your very heart.

So the great secret stays hidden, for it conceals itself and will remain a secret for as long as the world lasts.

But all that is merely incidental to the searing blow which has struck me down for ever. Even someone's superficial fate may be shifted on to a new track if his consciousness can break through the barriers of earthly perception for just one moment.

A fact, of which I am a living example.

Since that night, when I had that out-of-body experience (I can describe it in no other way), the course of my life has changed, and my existence, previously so unhurried, now reels from one inexplicable, horrific experience to another, towards some dark, unfathomable goal.

It is as if a devil's hand is measuring out my periods of lucidity in ever-diminishing quantities, thrusting into my path images of terror which grow in awfulness from one occasion to the next, as if slowly and stealthily to create a new and unheard-of form of madness in me, a form imperceptible to an outsider, unsuspected, known only through the nameless torment of its victim.

In the course of the next few days after the experiment with the hieroglyph I began to experience sensations which I took at first to be hallucinations. In the midst of all the sights and sounds of everyday I would become suddenly aware of strange roaring noises or jarring undertones in my ears, or catch sight of shimmering colours which I had never seen before.

Bizarre figures would appear, unheard and unseen by anyone else, acting out incomprehensible and unfathomable plots in shadowy gloom. They would shift their shapes, lie suddenly still as death, then slither down along the gutters in viscous elongation, or squat stupid and exhausted in dark doorways, as if drained of existence.

This condition of hypersensitive awareness does not persist – it waxes and wanes like the moon.

The steady decline of my interest in others, whose desires and hopes impinge on me only as if from a distance, suggests to me that my soul is engaged upon some dark journey, far far away from the rest of humanity.

At first I allowed these whispering voices filling the edges of my consciousness to lead me along. Now, I am like a beast of burden, strapped firmly into its harness and obliged to follow exactly the path along which I am being driven.

And so one night I was again dragged awake and forced to wander aimlessly through the silent alleyways of the Kleinseite, just for the sake of the impression that the antiquated houses make upon me.

This part of Prague is uncanny, like nowhere else in the world.

The bright light of day never reaches down here, nor yet is it ever quite as dark as night.

A dim, gloomy illumination emanates from somewhere or other, seeping down from the Hradschin on to the roofs of the city below, like a phosphorescent haze. You turn into a narrow lane, and see nothing: only a deathly darkness, until suddenly a spectral ray of light stabs into your eyes from a chink in a shutter, like a long, malevolent needle.

Then a house looms out of the fog – with decayed, drooping shoulders it stares vacantly up into the night sky out of blank lights set into the receding forehead of its sloping roof, like some animal wounded unto death.

Next door, another building leans inquisitively forward, glimmering windows searching eagerly in the depths of the well down below for a trace of the goldsmith's daughter who drowned there a century ago. And if you go further on across the uneven cobbles and then suddenly turn to look back, you'll very likely catch sight of a pale and bloated visage staring after you from the corner – not at shoulder height, no, but quite low down, at about the level where you might expect to meet the gaze of a large dog.

There was nobody out in the streets.

Deathly still.

The ancient entries held their lips firmly clamped shut. I turned into Thungasse, where Countess Morzin has her great house.

There in the mist crouched a narrow building, no more than two windows broad, a disagreeable wall with a hectic pallor; and here I was gripped spellbound as I felt my mood of hyper-sensitivity rising within me.

Under such conditions I act spontaneously, as if driven by another will, and I scarcely know what the next moment will make me do.

So, in this state, I pushed open the door which had been merely standing ajar, and, passing down a passage, descended a stair to the cellar, all as if I really belonged in this house.

At the bottom, the invisible rein holding me in check was relaxed and I was left standing in the darkness, painfully aware that I had done something entirely without purpose.

Why had I gone down there? Why hadn't I even thought of putting a stop to such pointless ideas? I was ill, patently ill, and I took comfort in the fact that it could be nothing else: the mysterious, uncanny force had nothing to do with it.

But in the next moment I realised that I had opened the door, entered the house and gone down the stairs without once bumping into anything, like someone who knew every step of the way: my hope evaporated on the instant.

My eyes slowly became accustomed to the darkness, and I looked about me.

There on one of the steps of the cellar stair someone was sitting. – How could I have got past without touching him?

I could only see the crouched figure rather indistinctly in the darkness.

A black beard covered a bare chest; the arms were bare too. Only the legs seemed to be encased in trousers or perhaps a loincloth. There was something fearful about the position of his hands – they were so extraordinarily bent back, almost at right angles to the joint.

I stared at the man for a long time.

He sat there with such corpse-like rigidity that I had the sense that his outline had somehow become etched into the dark background, and that this image would remain until the house itself fell into ruin.

A cold shiver overcame me, and I went on down the twisting passage.

At one point I reached out to touch the wall. My fingers closed upon a splintered wooden trellis, such as creepers are trained on. They seemed indeed to be growing there in great profusion, for I almost got caught up in a maze of stalky tendrils.

The odd thing was that these plants (or whatever they were) felt warm to the touch and full of life – altogether they seemed to have a certain animal quality.

I put my hand out once more, but immediately snatched it back again: this time I had touched a round ball about the size of a walnut, which felt cold and which shrank away on the instant. Was it a beetle?

Just then a light flickered on somewhere, and for a second the wall in front of me was lit up.

Everything I had known of fear and horror up until then was as nothing to this moment.

Every fibre of my being shrieked out in indescribable terror. My paralysed vocal chords gave vent to a silent scream, which struck through me like a shaft of ice.

The entire wall, right up to the ceiling, was festooned with a network of twisted veins, from which hundreds of bulbous berry-eyes gazed out.

The one I had just fingered was still snapping back and forth, giving me a glance full of suspicion.

I felt faint, and staggered on for two or three more steps into the darkness. A cloud of different smells engulfed me, heavy, earthy, reeking of fungus and ailanthus.

My knees gave way and I beat the air about me. A little glowing ring appeared in front of me – the last dying gleam of an oil-lamp which flickered fitfully for a moment.

I leaped towards it and with trembling fingers turned the wick up, just in time to save the tiny sooty flame.

Then I swung round, holding the lamp protectively in front of me.

The room was empty.

On the table, where the lamp had been, there lay a longish object, glittering in the light.

My hand reached out to it, as for a weapon.

But it was no more than a light, crudely-made thing that I picked up.

Nothing moved, and I breathed a sigh of relief. Carefully, so as not to extinguish the flame I ran the light along the wall. Everywhere the same wooden trellis-work and, as I could now clearly see, overgrown with veins, evidently all patched together, in which blood was coursing.

In amongst them countless eyeballs glistened horribly, sprouting alternately with hideous warty nodules like black-berries, and following me slowly with their gaze as I passed. Eyes of all sizes and colours, from brightly shining irises to the light blue tone of the eye of a dead horse, fixed immovably upwards. Some, shrunken and black, looked like rotten nightshade berries. The main stems twisted their way out of jars filled with blood, drawing up their juice by means of some unfathomable process.

I stumbled on shallow dishes filled with whitish fatty lumps in which toadstools were growing covered in a glossy sheen;

toadstools of red flesh, that shrank away at a touch.

And all seemed to be parts of living bodies, fitted together with indescribable art, robbed of any human soul, and reduced merely to vegetative organisms.

I could see clearly that they were alive in the way that the pupils in the eyes narrowed when I brought the lamp closer. Who could be the devilish gardener who had planted this horrible orchard?

I remembered the man on the cellar steps.

I reached instinctively into my pocket for a weapon – any weapon – and felt the sharp object I had previously found. It glittered, bleak and scaly: a pine cone assembled out of a multitude of pink human fingernails.

With a shudder I dropped it and clenched my teeth: I must get out, out – even if the thing on the stairs should wake up and set about me!

And I was already on my way past him, ready to thrust him aside, when I realised he was dead, yellow as wax.

From his contorted hands the nails had been wrenched, and incisions in his chest and temples indicated that he had been a subject of dissection. In pushing past him I must have brushed him with my hand – he seemed to slip down a couple of steps towards me and then stood upright, his arms bent upwards, hands touching his forehead.

Just like the Egyptian figure: the same pose, the very same pose!

The lamp smashed to the floor and I knew only that I had flung the door open to the street as the brazen demon of spasmodic cramp closed his fingers round my twitching heart.

Then, half-awake, I realised that the man must have been suspended by cords attached to his elbows: only by that means could he have been brought upright by slipping down the steps; and then, then I felt someone shaking me. "Come on, the Inspector wants to see you."

I was taken to a poorly-lit room, tobacco pipes ranged along the wall, a uniform coat hanging on a stand. It was a police station.

An officer was holding me upright.

The Inspector at the table stared past me. "Have you taken his details?" he murmured.

"He had some visiting cards on him. We've taken those." I heard the policeman reply.

"What were you up to in Thungasse in front of an open street door?"

Long pause.

"Hey, you!" warned the policeman, giving me a nudge.

I stammered something about a murder in the cellar of the house in Thungasse.

The policeman left the room.

The Inspector, still not bothering to give me a glance, embarked on a long speech, of which I heard very little.

"What are you talking about? Dr. Cinderella is a great scientist – Egyptologist – he is cultivating all sorts of new carnivorous plants – Nepenthes, Droseras and suchlike, I think, I don't know. — You should stay indoors at night."

A door opened behind me; I turned to face a tall figure with a long heron's bill – an Egyptian Anubis.

The world went black in front of me as Anubis bowed to the Inspector and went up to him, whispering to me as he passed: "Dr. Cinderella." –

Doctor Cinderella!

At that moment something important from the past came back into my mind – and then immediately vanished again.

When I looked at Anubis once again he had become nothing more than an ordinary clerk with something birdlike about his features. He gave me my own visiting cards back. On them was printed:

Dr. Cinderella

The Inspector suddenly looked straight at me, and I could hear him saying: "You're the Doctor himself. You should stay at home at night."

And the clerk led me out. As I went I brushed against the coat hanging on the stand.

It subsided to the floor, leaving the arms hanging.

On the whitewashed wall behind, its shadow raised its arms aloft, as it attempted awkwardly to take up the pose of the Egyptian statuette.

You know, that was my last experience, three weeks ago. I've had a stroke since then: I have two separate sides to my face, and I have to drag my left leg along.

I have looked in vain for that narrow, fevered little house, and down at the station nobody admits to knowing anything about that night.

The Preparation

Gustav Meyrink

The two friends were sitting in a corner of the Radetzky Cafe by the window, deep in conversation.

"He's gone – he went off with his man to Berlin this afternoon. The house is completely empty: I've just been round there to check. Those two Persians were the only inhabitants."

"So he really did fall for that telegram?"

"I never doubted he would for a moment. The name of Fabio Marini will make him do anything."

"That surprises me a bit, since he lived with him for so long – until he died, in fact. What else could he expect to find out about him in Berlin?"

"Aha! Professor Marini is supposed to have kept quite a lot secret from him – he said so himself once, in passing, about six months ago, when dear old Axel was still with us."

"Is there really something in this mysterious preparation method that Fabio Marini invented, then? Do you honestly believe in it, Sinclair?"

"It's not at all a matter of 'believing'. When I was in Florence I saw with my own eyes a child's corpse that had been prepared by Marini. I tell you, anyone would have sworn the child was just asleep – not a trace of rigor, no wrinkles or creases – it even had the pink skin of a living being."

"Hm.. You think the Persian may actually have murdered Axel and..."

"That's not something I'd swear to, Ottokar, but it is the moral duty of us both to get to the bottom of what happened to Axel. What if some kind of poison had merely produced an analogue of rigor mortis in him? My God, when I think how I pleaded with the doctors at the Institute of Anatomy – begged them even to make some attempt at resuscitation. What on earth are you getting at, they said, the man is dead, that's obvious, and any interference with the body without Dr Daryashkoh's permission is quite improper. And they showed me the contract which explicitly said that after Axel's death his body was to become the property of whoever owned the document, and in respect of which he had already received, on such and such a date the sum, duly receipted, of 500 Crowns."

"No, really? That's horrible! And to think that something like that is legal in this day and age. The more I think of it the more incensed I get. Poor old Axel! If he had only known that this Persian, his worst enemy, might come to own the contract. He always thought the Institute of Anatomy itself..."

"And the lawyer couldn't do anything?"

"It was pointless. They wouldn't even take any notice of the old milkwoman's evidence, who had once seen Daryashkoh in his garden at sunrise cursing Axel's name for so long that he started foaming at the mouth. Of course, if Daryashkoh hadn't qualified as a doctor in Europe... But what's the point of talking – are you coming or not, Ottokar? Make up your mind."

"Sure, I'll come – but take care we don't get caught as burglars! The Persian's got a spotless reputation as a scholar. Mere reliance on suspicion, for Heaven's sake, is hardly a plausible reason. Don't get me wrong, but are you absolutely sure you weren't mistaken in thinking you heard Axel's voice? Don't get angry, Sinclair, please, but tell me again *exactly* what happened that time: weren't you just a little bit worked up somehow beforehand?"

"But not in the least! Half an hour before that I had been up on the Hradschin, looking at Wenceslas' Chapel and St. Vitus' Cathedral again; you know what old buildings they are, with those sculptures that look as though they're made of congealed blood and which always make such a deep and unaccountable impression on the soul whenever you see them. And then I went to the Hunger Tower and along Alchemists' Lane to the steps down from the Castle, and was brought up short at the little door in the Castle wall that leads to Daryashkoh's house, because it was standing open. And at the very same moment I heard a voice – it must have come from the window, and I'll swear it was Axel's voice – calling out: 'one – two – three – four'.

God, if only I had gone in straight away; but before I could pull myself together from the surprise that Turkish servant of his had slammed the door shut. I tell you, we've got to get into that house! We must! What if Axel were really still alive? Look, nobody will find us; who ever uses those steps at night-time anyway? And you've no idea how good at picking locks I am these days!"

The two friends passed the time wandering idly up and down the streets before embarking on their plan. Then at dusk they scaled the wall and at last found themselves standing before the Persian's old-fashioned house.

This isolated building stands on the slopes of Fürstenberg Park, leaning like an inanimate watchman against the wall that encloses the grass-grown steps up to the Castle.

"There really is something horribly sinister about this garden and those old elms down there," whispered Ottokar Dohnal. "Look how the Hradschin stands out so threateningly against the skyline. And those windows, all lit up in the embrasures of the wall! Even the air is different, here on the Kleinseite, as if all the life in it has drained off deep underground for fear of the Death that stalks above.

Don't you ever get the feeling that this whole shadowy scene will one day just vanish like a mirage, a fata morgana, and that all the pent-up life that's waiting here somewhere in suspended animation will suddenly revive, wraithlike, and turn into something totally and horribly unexpected? I know I do. And just look at those gravel paths down there, glimmering white, like veins."

"Oh, do come on!" urged Sinclair. "My knees are knocking with all the tension. Here, hold the plan for me."

The door was soon opened and the two of them felt their way up an ancient staircase, which was barely illuminated by the light of an overcast sky striking fitfully through the round windows.

"We'll have no lights, Ottokar – they might be seen from down below, or from the summer-house outside: follow me closely... watch out, there's a broken tread here. The door to the corridor is open... here, here on the left."

They suddenly found themselves in a room.

"For Heaven's sake don't make such a noise!"

"I couldn't help it – the door slammed of its own accord."

"We shall have to strike a light. I'm afraid of knocking something over all the time, there are so many chairs in the way."

At that moment a blue spark blazed on the wall, and they heard a sound like a sighing intake of breath. A faint grating noise became apparent, seeming to come from floor and walls, and out of all the joints in the woodwork at once. There was a moment of total silence again, and then a croaking voice started, loud and slow: *One... two... three.*

Ottokar Dohnal cried out, scraping madly at his matchbox, his hands quivering with fear. At last there came a light – light! And the two friends were revealed staring at each other, chalk-white. "Axel!" — *fo-our... ffffive... sssix... ssseven...*

The counting was coming from an alcove in the corner.

"Light the candle – quick, quick!"

eight... nine... te-en... ele...

Suspended on a copper rod hanging down inside the recess was a blond-haired human head. The lower end of the rod had been driven straight through the top of the skull, and the neck below the chin was concealed under a silk scarf. Beneath it projected trachea, bronchi and two pink lungs. Between them, beating steadily, was the heart, surrounded by a number of gold-coloured wires which led away to some kind of electrifying machine on the floor. Fat veins, gorged with blood, carried the circulation up from two narrow-necked reservoir bottles. Ottokar Dohnal had put the candle down on a little stand, and was now clutching his friend's arm in a faint.

It was Axel's head, with carmine lips and a blooming complexion – alive. The eyes, widely staring and with a wild expression were focused on a burning-glass hanging on the wall opposite and which seemed to be draped with Asiatic weapons and hangings.

Everywhere they could make out the bizarre designs of oriental fabrics.

The room was otherwise filled with preserved animal specimens – snakes and apes in various contorted poses amidst a jumble of books lying about on the floor.

In a large glass bowl on a bench at the side a human abdomen was floating in a bluish liquid. Gazing gravely down upon the whole scene from a pedestal above was the plaster bust of Fabio Marini.

The onlookers stood, struck dumb, staring hypnotised by the heart of this monstrous human clock, beating and quivering with life.

"God help us, let's get away. I'm going to pass out. Damn that Persian monster!"

They made for the door. As they did so there came again that queer grating noise, seeming to come this time directly from the preparation's mouth itself. Two blue sparks flashed, and were reflected by the burning-glass precisely into the pupils of the dead eyes opposite. The lips parted, the tongue poked out and curled behind the front teeth as the voice rasped: *a quarr – ter passst.*

The mouth closed and the face stared blankly out again.

"Horrible, horrible – the *brain* is still functioning – it's still alive. — Out, get out, — into the open! The candle, get the candle, Sinclair!"

"Open the door, for God's sake! Why can't you open it?"

"I can't – there, look there!"

The handle on the inside of the door had been replaced by a hand, a human hand, with rings on its fingers – the dead man's hand, in fact. The fingers curled in the air.

"Come on, use a cloth! What are you afraid of? It's only old Axel's hand!"

Outside in the corridor they watched as the door swung slowly shut behind them. A black glass plate on the outside was inscribed:

Dr Mohammed Daryash-Koh
Anatomist

The candle-flame flickered in the draught wafting up the tiled stairwell.

Ottokar staggered to the wall and fell to his knees with a

groan: "Look, look at that!" – He was pointing to the bell-pull.

Sinclair held the candle closer, then with a loud exclamation dropped it, and the tin candlestick clattered away down the stone steps. In the darkness they followed it in a mad rush to the bottom, hair standing on end, lungs bursting with the effort.

"Persian Fiend – The Persian Fiend!"

The Head

Karl Hans Strobl

It was completely dark in the room ... all the curtains closed
... not a glimmer of light from the street and quite still. My friend,
myself and the stranger were holding each other by the hand in
a quivering, convulsive clasp. A dreadful fear was about us,
within us ...

And then ... a gaunt, gleaming white hand came through the
darkness towards us and began to write with the pencil that was
lying ready on the table where we were seated. We could not see
what the hand was writing, but we could feel it inside ... as it was
being written ... as if it were there before our eyes in letters of
fire ...

It was the story of the hand, and of the man it once belonged
to, that the gleaming white hand was writing on the paper in the
deepest midnight darkness:

"I am walking up the steps covered in red cloth ... and ... I do
after all have a strange feeling in my heart. Inside my breast
something is swinging back and forth ... a huge pendulum. But
the rim of the pendulum disc is as sharp as a razor-blade and each
time the swing of the pendulum grazes my chest I feel a keen
pain ... and it takes my breath away, and I want to groan out loud.
But I bite my teeth together, so that no sound can pass, and
clench my fists, tied behind my back, so that the blood spurts out
from under the nails.

Now I am at the top. Everything is prepared, all they are
waiting for is me. I am calm as they shave my neck, and when
it is done I ask for permission to speak to the people for one last
time. It is granted ... I turn round and see the endless mob, a sea
of heads thronging round the guillotine, all those dull, stupid,
animal faces, some with expressions of vulgar curiosity, others
of obscene lust, human beings *en masse*, making a mockery of
all that the word human stands for, and I find the whole business
so ridiculous that I am forced to laugh out loud.

Disapproving lines appear in the officious expression of my executioners ... how damned insolent of me not to take the matter seriously, tragically even ... but I had better stop teasing these good souls and begin my speech:

"Citizens", I say, "citizens, it is for you that I die, for you and for Liberty. You have misunderstood me, you have condemned me ... but I love you. And as proof of my love, hear my testament. Everything that I possess, shall be yours. For example ..."

And I turn my back on them and make an unmistakable gesture ...

From all around comes a roar of outrage ... with a sigh of relief I quickly lay my head in the opening ... a rushing, hissing noise ... all I feel is an icy burning in my neck ... my head falls into the basket.

Then I feel as if I have put my head under water and it has filled my ears. The noises from the outside world that reach me are dark and muddled, at my temples is a droning, buzzing sound. All across the area where my neck has been sliced through I feel as if large quantities of ether were vaporising.

I know that my head is in the wicker basket, my body up on the scaffold, but I have not yet the sense of complete separation; I feel my body fall onto its left side, the feet kicking feebly, my clenched fists, tied behind my back, twitch slightly, my fingers stretch out convulsively and then retract. I can also feel the blood flowing out of the stump of my neck, and as it empties I can sense my movements becoming weaker and weaker, and also my awareness of my body weakening, darkening, until below the cut in my neck all gradually becomes blackness.

I have lost my body.

In the complete darkness below my cut-off neck I suddenly sense red spots. The red spots are like fires on a dark, stormy night. They dissolve and spread like oil on still waters ... when the edges of two of the red spots touch I can feel a light electric shock in my eyelids and the hair stands up on my head. And now the red spots are beginning to rotate, faster, ever faster ... a multitude of wheels of fire, blazing, molten sun-discs ... they twist and swirl, drawing long tongues of fire behind them, and I have to close my eyes ... but I can still feel the red wheels of fire within me ... between my teeth I feel as if every gap is packed with dry, glassy grains of sand. Slowly the flaming wheels pale, the whirling slows down, one after the other is extinguished, and everything below the cut through my neck goes black for a second time. This time it is for ever.

I am filled with a pleasant lethargy, an easy-going lack of responsibility, my eyes are heavy. I cannot open them any more and yet I can see everything around me. It is as if my eyelids were made of glass, transparent. I see everything as through a milky-white veil with a delicate tracery of pale pink veins over it, but everything I see is larger, clearer than when I still had my body. My tongue is paralysed; it lies in my mouth, heavy and sluggish as a lump of clay.

My sense of smell, on the other hand, is a thousand times sharper, I not only see things, I smell them, each one different, with its own characteristic odour.

In the wicker basket beneath the blade of the guillotine there are three other heads apart from my own, two male and one female. The woman's head has rouged cheeks with two beauty spots, powdered, coiffeured hair with a golden arrow stuck through it, and two dainty diamond earrings in its tiny ears. The heads of the two men are lying face down in a pool of half-dried blood; across one runs the poorly healed scar of an old wound, the hair on the other is already sparse and grey.

The woman's head has its eyes screwed tight and is motionless. I know that it is watching me through its closed lids ...

We lie like that for hours. I watch the sun edge its way up the scaffold of the guillotine. Evening comes and I begin to feel chilly. My nose is stiff and cold and the chill of evaporation I feel on my neck is becoming unpleasant.

Suddenly raucous shouting; it comes nearer, quite near, and all at once I feel a powerful hand grab me by the hair and lift me out of the basket. Then I feel some pointed object pushed into my neck – a spearhead. A mob of drunken sansculottes and harpies has fallen upon our heads. A giant of a fellow with a puffy red face is brandishing the spear with my head on it high above the frenzied, jeering, screaming throng.

A tangle of men and women is fighting over the jewels from

the woman's head. They writhe and roll, kicking and punching, biting and scratching.

Now the fight is over. Shouting and cursing, they separate, each one who has secured a part of the spoils surrounded by a jealous crowd ...

The head is lying on the ground, begrimed and mutilated, showing the marks of the grasping hands, its ears torn by the violence with which the rings were ripped off, its exquisite coiffure dishevelled, the powdered strands of deep blond hair trailing in the dust. One nostril has been slit open by a sharp blade, its forehead shows the mark of the heel of someone's shoe. Its eyelids are half open, the blank, glassy eyes staring straight ahead.

Finally the crowd sets off. There are four heads stuck on long poles. The fury of the crowd is directed mainly at the man with grey hair. That man must have been particularly unpopular. I do not know him. They spit and throw lumps of filth at him. There, a handful of mud from the street thumps into his ear ... What is that? Did he not twitch? Slightly, imperceptibly, with one muscle only, visible to me alone?

Night comes. They have arranged us heads on the iron bars of a palace gate. I do not recognise the palace, either. Paris is big. In the courtyard armed citizens are camped round a huge fire ... Scabrous songs, jokes, roars of laughter. The smell of roast mutton reaches me. The fire gives off a costly fragrance of rosewood. The wild mob has dragged all the furniture from the palace out into the courtyard and is now burning it, piece by piece. The next to go is an elegant sofa with delicate scrollwork ... but they hesitate and do not throw the sofa on the fire yet. A young woman with coarse features and wearing a loose bodice which reveals her full, firm breasts, is insisting on something with the help of vigorous gestures.

Is she trying to persuade them to let her have the elegant sofa, has she suddenly felt the desire to see what it is like to be a duchess?

The men are still hesitating.

The woman points at the bars with our heads on the spikes and then back at the sofa.

The men hesitate, finally she pushes them aside, draws one of the armed men's sabres, kneels down and uses the blade to lever out the little enamelled nails with which the heavy silk covering is attached to the wooden frame. Now the men are helping her.

Again she points to our heads.

One of the men walks over rather hesitantly. He looks for the one she wants. Then he climbs up the iron bars and takes down the maltreated, violated woman's head.

The man shudders with horror, but he seems to be acting under some kind of compulsion. It is as if that young woman by the fire, the young woman in the red skirt and open bodice, has hypnotised all the men around with her savage, sensual stare, like some beast of prey. His arm held out stiffly, he carries the head by the hair back to the fire.

With a wild screech of delight the woman grabs the head. Twirling it round, she swings it three times over the blazing fire.

Then she squats down and takes the head in her lap. She strokes it caressingly over the cheeks a few times ... all the men have gathered in a circle around her ... now she is taking one of the little enamelled nails in one hand and hammer in the other, and with a light blow she drives the nail right into the skull.

Another tap of the hammer, and another nail disappears into the luxuriant hair.

As she hammers, she hums a song. One of those terrible, strange, sensual folk songs, full of ancient magic.

The bloody monsters around her are silent and pale with horror, their eyes staring aghast at her out of dark sockets. And she hammers and hammers, driving nail after nail into the head, all the while humming her strange, old charm to the rhythm of the hammer-blows.

Suddenly one of the men gives a piercing cry and jumps up. His eyes are bulging, his mouth is covered in foam ... he throws his arms backwards, twisting his body to the right and left as if in painful convulsions, and from his mouth come piercing, animal cries.

The young woman hammers on, singing her song.

Then another jumps up, howling and swinging his arms

around. He grabs a brand from the fire and jabs it into his chest, again and again, until his clothes begin to glow and thick, stinking smoke spreads all round him.

The others sit there, pale and motionless, and do nothing to stop him.

A third jumps up, and now the same frenzy grips the rest. A deafening noise, a screaming and a wailing, a screeching and a howling and a roaring, a tangle of flailing limbs. Any that fall do not get up ... the others continue their stamping over their bodies ...

In the middle of this orgy of madness sits the young woman, hammering and singing ...

Now she has finished; she sticks the head covered with tiny enamelled nails on the end of a bayonet and holds it high above the howling, leaping mass. Then someone scatters the fire, the burning wood is pulled out and thrown in a shower of sparks into the blackest corners of the courtyard ... it grows dark ... grunts of lust and a wild scuffling, as if from some furious struggle: I know that all these crazed men, these wild beasts, have thrown themselves on the one woman, biting and clawing at her ...

Everything goes dark before my eyes.

Did consciousness remain just long enough for me to witness all these horrors? Dawn comes, dark and indistinct, like the fading light on a dull winter's afternoon. Rain falls on my head. Cold winds tousle my hair. My flesh becomes loose and weak. Is it the beginning of decomposition?

Then there is a change. My head is taken to a different place, to a dark pit; there it is warm and quiet. Light and clarity return to me. There are many other heads with me in the dark pit. Heads and bodies. And I notice that the heads and bodies are joining up again, as well – or as badly – as they can manage. And with the contact they rediscover their language, a soft, inaudible language in which they think to each other.

I long for a body, I long to be finally rid of the unbearable coldness where my neck is cut, such a coldness that it almost seems to burn hot. But I look round in vain. All the heads and bodies are joined together. There is no body left for me. But eventually, after a long, laborious search, I find one ... right at the bottom, hiding in a corner ... a body that is still without a head, a woman's body.

Something inside me rebels against uniting with this body, but my desire, my longing overcomes it and, impelled by will-power alone, I approach the headless body and see that it too is striving to reach my head; and now the two cuts touch with a mild shock and a feeling of gentle heat. One thing stands out above all: I have a body once more.

But strange ... after the initial feeling of comfort is over, I sense the enormous difference between my two components ... I feel as if completely different fluids are meeting and mingling, fluids that have no similarities with each other. The woman's body, which my head now crowns, is slim and white, and its skin has the marble coolness of an aristocrat who bathes in wine and milk and uses costly oils and lotions. But on its right-hand side, covering the hip and part of the stomach, is a strange drawing, a tattoo. Composed of fine, extremely fine, blue dots is a pattern of hearts, anchors and arabesques with the elaborate initials I and B intertwined and repeated. Who can the woman have been?

I know I will learn that some time, and soon! The vague corporeal darkness below my neck is developing an outline. I already have a picture of my body, though an unclear, blurred one, and this picture is becoming more definite, more precise, by the minute. At the same time there is the painful mingling of the fluids from my two component parts. And suddenly I feel as if I had two heads ... and this second head – a woman's head, bloody, disfigured, distorted – I can see before me, completely covered with small enamelled nails. That is the head that belongs to this body, and at the same time it is my head, for in my skull and my brain I can clearly feel the hundreds of little points, I want to roar with pain. Everything around me merges into a red veil, which ripples as if it were torn back and forth by violent gusts of wind.

I can feel now that I am a woman, only my mind is masculine. And now an image is emerging from the red veil ... before me I can see myself in a room decorated with sumptuous extrava-gance. I am lying down, buried in soft white furs and ... naked. Before me, bending over me, is a man with the harsh, coarse

287

features of one from the common mass of the people, with the work-calloused hands and weather-beaten skin of a sailor. He is kneeling over me, pricking my soft flesh with a sharp needle to make his strange design. It hurts and yet causes me a strange, sensual pleasure at the same time ... I know that the man is my lover.

Then a short, needle-sharp pain makes my whole body contract in a quiver of delight. I wreathe my white arms round the man's neck and pull him down to me ... I kiss him and place his hard, calloused hands on my shoulders, on my breasts, and kiss him again in a wild frenzy and wrap myself round him and clutch him tight so that he gasps and groans.

Now I have my teeth round his brown throat, round the throat I love, the sight of which has often sent me into raptures, my tongue is licking his throat in a moist caress ... and now – now I must press my teeth into the hard brown flesh – I cannot help it – I must bite into his throat ... I bite and I bite ... his groans become a death rattle ... I feel the man twist and turn convulsively in my arms ... but I do not let go ... his body becomes heavy, heavy ... a warm stream flows down my body. His head falls back – I let him slip from my arms – with a muffled thud he lands on his back on the soft carpet, a thick stream of blood pouring from the bite in his neck. Blood, blood everywhere, on the soft white polar-bear skins, on me, everywhere.

I start to scream, hoarse rough sounds come from my throat. The chambermaid rushes in, she cannot have been far away, perhaps by the door in the next room ... was she eavesdropping? For a moment she stands rigid, as if unconscious, then, without a word, she throws herself over the body of the dead man ... without saying a word, without shedding a tear, she buries her face in the blood streaming down his chest. But I see her clench her fist; now I know everything ...

And then I see another scene ...

Again I can see myself, and yet at the same time it is I myself who am sitting in the wooden tumbril which is taking me to the guillotine. Then I am standing up there on the scaffold, looking at the sun for the last time, and as I turn round I catch sight of a young woman who has pushed her way right to the front of the crowd ... that woman ... the lover of the man who was the instrument of my pleasure ... in a red skirt, her bodice loose, her face pale and twitching, hair streaming ... her eyes have a savage gleam, like a beast of prey, moist, as if from stifled grief, and with a lustful sparkle, as if in expectation of pleasure. She raises her clenched fists to her face, her lips move ... she wants to speak, to mock me and curse me, but all that comes is a strangled, incomprehensible cry ... I lay my head below the blade.

Now I know everything.

I know whose head it was that, in the night, by the blazing light of the bonfire, suffered a gruesome vengeance that reached beyond the grave; I know, too, who the young woman was, who, in the same night, in the darkened courtyard, was crushed and torn limb from limb by wild beasts ... my head aches from the hundreds of sharp nails ... I am tied to this body ... to this body wracked with horrible memories and terrible pains, to this beautiful body steeped in sin that has tasted all the delights of hell.

I am being torn apart by my two conflicting halves ... oh, but not for long ... I feel a slackening in all my limbs, my flesh softens, falls away, my internal organs are becoming spongy, dissolving ... decomposition is beginning ...

Soon night will embrace me and my two conflicting selves ... the night of decay ... the bodies will disintegrate and the spirit will be free."

The hand stopped writing and vanished.

A Country Doctor

Franz Kafka

I was in a very awkward predicament: an urgent journey lay ahead of me; a seriously ill boy was expecting me in a village ten miles distant; heavy snowstorms covered the wide open spaces between myself and him; I had a carriage, a light one with large wheels, just the type of thing for our country roads; wrapped up in my fur, the bag with my instruments in my hand, I was in the courtyard, all ready to go; but there was no horse – no horse. My own horse had died the previous evening as a result of overexertion during this icy winter; the maid was running round the village to find a horse to borrow; but it was pointless, I knew, and I stood there, useless, more and more covered in snow, becoming more and more immobile. The girl appeared at the gate, alone, waving the lantern; of course, who is going to lend out their horse now, and for such a journey? I strode across the yard once more; I could see no way of getting there; distracted, tormented, I kicked out at the broken door of the pigsty, which had not been used for years. It opened, flapping back and forward on its hinges. Warmth, and a smell like that of horses came out. There was a dim stable lamp swinging from a cord inside. A man, crouching down in the low shed, turned his open, blue-eyed face to me. "Shall I harness the horses?" he asked, crawling out on all fours. I did not know what to say, and just bent down to see what else there was in the sty. The maid was standing beside me. "You never know what there is in your own house", she said, and we both laughed. "Gee-up, brother! Gee-up sister!" shouted the groom, and two horses, powerful, strong-flanked beasts, appeared one after the other in the doorway, which they filled completely, and pushed their way out, their legs tucked into their bodies, lowering their well-formed heads like camels, emerging solely through the force of twists of their rumps. But immediately they stood up straight, long-legged, the steam rising thickly from their bodies. "Help him", I said, and the willing girl hurried to get the groom the harness for the carriage. But scarcely was she beside him, than the groom puts his arms round her and hits his face against hers. She gives a scream and flees back to me; the marks of two rows of teeth are stamped in red on the girl's cheek. "You animal!" I scream in fury, "do you want the whip?"; but immediately I remember that he is a stranger; that I do not know where he came from, and that he is helping me of his own free will when everyone else has failed me. As if he guesses my thoughts, he does not take my threat amiss, just turns round once to look at me, harnessing the horses all the while. "Get in", he says then, and indeed, everything is ready. I realise that I have never ridden behind such a fine pair of horses and climb in with a sense of pleasure. "But I will drive", I say, "You don't know the way." "Certainly", he says, "I'm not going, anyway, I'm staying with Rosa." "No", Rosa shouts, and runs into the house with an accurate presentiment of her fate; I hear the clatter of the chain as she fastens it; I hear the lock engage; I also see her put out all the lights, first in the hall and then rushing right through the house, so that she cannot be found. "You are coming with me", I say to the groom, "or the drive is off, however urgent it is. I wouldn't dream of giving you the girl as the price for the use of the horses." "Off we go!" he says, clapping his hands; the carriage is swept away, like logs in the current; the last thing I hear is the door of the house breaking and splintering under the groom's attack, then my eyes and ears are filled with a booming which penetrates all my senses equally. But only for a moment for, as if the patient's courtyard opened directly onto my gate, I am there already; the horses are standing quietly; the snowstorm has stopped; moonlight all around; the parents of the sick lad rush out of the house; his sister behind them; they almost lift me out of the carriage; I can understand nothing of their confused chatter; in the sick-room the air is scarcely breathable; the stove has not been tended and is smoking; I am going to open the window; but first I want to see the sick boy. Skinny, not feverish, not cold, not hot, with empty eyes and no nightshirt, the boy pushes himself up under the eiderdown, winds his arms around my neck, whispers in my ear, "Doctor, let me die." I look round; no one has heard; his parents are standing silent, bent forward, awaiting my verdict; his sister has brought a chair to put my bag on. I open the bag and rummage around among my instruments; the boy keeps on reaching out towards me from the bed to remind me of his request; I pick up a pair of tweezers, examine them in the candlelight and put them back. 'Well', comes the blasphemous thought, 'the gods do really help in cases like this, send the missing horse, add a second to speed things up and, to cap it all, throw in a groom ...' Only now do I remember Rosa; what can I do, how can I save her, how can I pull her away from under that groom, ten miles distant, uncontrollable horses hitched to my carriage? Those horses which have somehow managed to loosen their harnesses; and now, I don't know how, push open the windows from outside; each one puts its head in through one window and, unruffled by the screams of the family, look at the sick boy. 'I'm going to drive back right away', I think, as if the horses were asking me to leave, but I let the boy's sister, who thinks I am overcome by the heat, take my fur coat. A glass of rum is put out for me, the old man pats me on the shoulder, the sacrifice of his treasure justifies the familiarity. I shake my head; trapped in the old man's narrow circle of thoughts, I would feel sick; that is the only reason I refuse the drink. The mother is standing by the bed, luring me over there; I follow and, as my horse neighs out loud to the ceiling, place my head on the boy's chest, my wet beard making him quiver. It confirms what I already know: the boy is well, his circulation could be better, his doting mother could give him less coffee, but he's well, the best thing would be to kick him out of bed. But it's not my place to set the world to rights, so I leave him be. I am appointed by the district and do my duty to the utmost, to the point where it is almost too much. Badly paid, I'm still generous and obliging to the poor. On top of all that I have to provide for Rosa; the lad may well be right and I want to die as well. What am I doing here, in this endless winter! My horse has died and there's no one in the village who will lend me his. I have to get my horses from the pigsty; if they didn't just happen to be horses I would have to drive a pair of sows. That's the way things are. And I nod to the family. They have no idea about all this, and if they did, they wouldn't believe it. Writing prescriptions is easy, but to communicate with people beyond that is difficult. Well, that's my visit here over, I've been called out unnecessarily once again, I'm used to that, the whole district uses the night bell to torment me, but that I had to sacrifice Rosa this time into the bargain, that beautiful girl who's been living in my house for years without my hardly ever noticing her – the sacrifice is too great, and I have to think up all kinds of far-fetched explanations for myself, to stop me laying into this family which, with the best will in the world, cannot give Rosa back to me. But then, as I'm closing my bag and waving to them to bring my fur, and the family are all standing together, the father sniffing at the glass of rum in his hand, the mother, probably disappointed with me – what on earth do these people expect? – biting her lips with tears in her eyes, the sister waving a blood-soaked handkerchief, I somehow find that I am, all things considered, prepared to admit that the lad is perhaps ill. I go over to him, he smiles at me, as if I were bringing him the most strengthening of soups – aha, now both horses are neighing, I presume the noise is prescribed by higher authority, to facilitate the examination – and I discover that, yes, the lad is ill. A wound the size of the palm of the hand has opened up in his right side, in the hip region. Pink, in many shades, dark at the centre, getting lighter towards the edges, delicately grained, the blood seeping through unevenly, spread out like an open-cast mine. That was from a distance. From close to a further complication appears. Who could see it without giving a soft whistle? Worms, as thick and as long as my little finger, pink from their own blood and bespattered with the boy's, are twisting up, with tiny heads and lots of legs, towards the light, anchored to the inside of the wound. Poor lad, there's nothing I can do for you. I have found your great wound; this flower in your side will destroy you. His family is happy to see me busy; his sister's telling his mother, his mother his father, his father a few visitors who are coming in through the moonlight of the open door, on tiptoe, balancing with arms outstretched. "Will you save me?" whispers the boy with a sob, dazzled by the life in his wound. That's just typical of people round here. Always demanding the impossible of their doctor. They've lost their old faith; the priest is sitting at home, plucking the vestments to pieces, one after another; but the doctor is expected to be able to do everything with his delicate, surgeon's hands. Well, it's up to you: it wasn't my idea; if you insist on making a holy man of me, I'm happy to let you have your way; what else could I expect, an old country doctor who has been robbed of his servant girl! And they come, the family and the village elders, and undress me; the school choir led by the teacher is outside the house and sings, to an extremely simple melody:

Undress him so that he can heal.
If he can't heal, then strike him dead!
It's only a doctor, only a doctor.

Undressed, my fingers in my beard, my head bowed, I calmly look at the people. I am quite composed and superior to all of them, and I remain so, despite the fact that it is of no help to me, for now they have taken me by the head and by the feet and are carrying me to the bed. They lay me down along the wall, against the side with the wound. Then they all go out of the room; the door is closed; the singing falls silent; clouds cover the moon; the bedding is warm around me; the shadowy horses' heads sway in the windows. "Do you know", I hear a voice in my ear, "I have very little faith in you. You didn't come on your own two feet, someone just got rid of you. Instead of helping, you are taking up space on my deathbed. Most of all, I'd like to scratch your eyes out." "Quite right", I say, "It's a disgrace. But I am a doctor. What should I do? Believe me, it's not easy for me either." "You think I should content myself with that excuse? I suppose I'll have to. I have to be content with everything. I came into the world with a handsome wound; that was all I was endowed with." "My dear young friend", I say, "your fault is that you don't see things from a wider perspective. I tell you – and I have visited every sickroom, far and wide – your wound is not that bad at all. Created with two blows of the axe at a sharp angle. There are many who offer their sides, but they hardly even hear the axe in the forest, let alone it coming nearer." "Is that really so, or are you deceiving me in my fever?" "It is really so, take the word of honour of a medical officer of health with you to the other side." And he took it and fell silent. But now it was time to think of my escape. The horses were still faithfully at their posts. My fur and bag were quickly gathered up; I didn't want to waste time dressing; if the horses made as good speed as on the way here I would jump straight from this bed into my own, so to speak. Obediently, one horse stepped back from the window; I threw the load into the carriage; the fur flew too far, just one sleeve caught on a hook. That would do. I jumped onto the horse: the reins trailing loose, one horse hardly hitched to the other, the carriage swaying to and fro, the fur coat at the rear dragging through the snow. "Gee up!" I said, but they did not gee up; as slowly as old men we went through the snowy wastes; for a long time we could hear behind us the children's new, but erroneous, song:

Rejoice, all ye patients,
The doctor is laid in your bed!

I'll never get home like this; my flourishing practice is lost; a successor will steal everything, but to no avail, for he can never replace me; my house is tyrannised by the loathsome groom; Rosa is his victim; I refuse to visualise it. Here I am, an old man driving round and round, naked, exposed to the frost of this miserable epoch, with an earthly carriage, unearthly horses. My fur is hanging over the back of the carriage, but I cannot reach it and none of my mobile patients will lift a finger, the scum. Cheated! Cheated! Respond to a faulty night-bell just once – it can never be remedied.

Lucifer's Drum

From: *Walpurgisnacht*

Gustav Meyrink

Polyxena found herself in the sacristy of the Chapel of All Saints in the Cathedral. Silent and lost in memories, she did not resist as Bozena and another serving woman, whom she did not know, pulled a mouldy, threadbare, musty gown decorated with tarnished gold, pearls and jewels, stolen from the treasure-chamber, over the white spring dress she was wearing. In the light of the tall candles, thick as a man's arm, they secured it with pins and clasps.

The last few days lay behind her like a dream.

She saw them float past: images that are determined to wake for one last time before they fall asleep for ever, shadowy, insubstantial and divorced from any response, as if they belonged to some time that had never existed. Slowly they passed, bathed in a dull, sombre light. As each one disappeared there was a pause before the next, during which the dark-brown grain of the old, worm-eaten sacristy cupboards appeared before her eyes, as if a breath of the present were returning to whisper to her that she was still alive.

In her memory Polyxena could find her way back as far as the moment when she had fled from the Dalibor Tower and wandered through the streets of Prague until her sudden decision to return to the custodian's cottage in the Courtyard of Limes, where she had spent the whole night sitting by Ottokar's bed as he lay unconscious with a palpitating heart, and resolved never to leave her lover again. Everything before that moment – her childhood, the time at the convent, and those years spent among old men and old women, dusty books and all sorts of ash-grey things – seemed lost without trace, as if they had happened to an unfeeling portrait, instead of to her.

From this blackness words began to emerge which were joined by images from the past few days:

She can hear Zrcadlo, the actor, talking, as he had in the Dalibor Tower, but more urgently and only to a small group, to the revolutionaries of the 'Taborites', Ottokar and herself. They are in the filthy parlour of an old woman people call Lizzie the Czech. A lamp is smoking. A few men are lounging around, listening to the madman. Again, as in the Dalibor Tower, they believe he has been transformed into the Hussite leader, Jan Zizka.

Ottokar believes it, too.

She alone knows that it is only memories of an old, forgotten legend that come from her mind, acquire shape and enter the mind of the old actor to take on a spectral reality. Without her actively willing it, the magic 'aweysha' pours out of her, she can neither stop it nor guide it; it seems to act of its own volition, seems to obey other orders than hers; it is born within her breast, that is where it springs from, but another hand holds the reins. She feels that it may be the invisible hand of her ghostly ancestor, Polyxena Lambua.

Then her doubts return; it could be the voice in the Courtyard of Limes praying for the fulfilment of Ottokar's longing that is setting the magic force of the 'aweysha' in motion. Her own desires have died away. "Ottokar should be crowned, as his love desires it for my sake, even if only for a brief hour. What do I care whether I find my happiness through it or not?" It is the last wish that has the strength to raise its whispering voice within her, and even that is probably spoken by her painted likeness rather than by Polyxena herself. Concealed within it like a vampire is the undying seed of the old, bloodthirsty clan of fire-raisers, which has been passed on to her over the generations and which is now using her as a tool in order to partake of the life and fecundity of the impending events. In the gestures and speech of the actor before her she sees how the legend of Zizka, the Hussite general, is gradually being transformed and adapted to the present; a shudder runs through her.

She foresees the end: the ghost of Jan Zizka will lead these crazed men to their deaths.

And in a flurry of images the magic force of the 'aweysha' gives her premonitions physical form, so that Ottokar's longing will be transformed from dream to reality: in Zizka's voice Zrcadlo orders that Ottokar is to be crowned, then he seals his prophecy by giving the tanner, Stanislav Havlik, the task of skinning him and using the skin to make a drum; that done, he thrusts a dagger into his own heart.

Obedient to the command, Havlik bends over the body. Seized with horror, the men flee. She alone cannot; something holds her fast by the door. The likeness within her wants to look on.

At last, at long last, the tanner has finished his bloody task.

Another day appears before her: hours of ecstasy and all-consuming love come and then vanish.

Ottokar is holding her in his arms and telling her of the time that is approaching, a time of happiness, of splendour and glory. He will surround her with all the majesty of the earth; there will be no wish that he will not be able to fulfil for her. Under the ardour of his kisses, her imagination breaks the shackles of impossibility. The hut in the Courtyard of Limes turns into a palace. In his arms she can see the castle that he is building for her rise in the air. He presses her to him, and she feels his blood enter her, feels she will bear his child. And she knows that by that he has made her immortal, that a spiritual ardour will sprout from the heat of coupling, that the body imperishable will rise from her perishable flesh: life eternal that the one gives birth to from the other.

A new image from her memory: she is surrounded once more by the monstrous figures of rebellion, men with fists of steel, blue jackets and scarlet armbands.

They have formed a bodyguard. After their model, the old Taborites, they call themselves the 'Brothers of Mount Horeb'.

They are carrying her and Ottokar through streets decked with red flags that flutter from the houses like swathes of blood.

Beside them and behind them is a howling, raging mob carrying torches and screaming, "Long live Ottokar Borivoj, Emperor of the World, and his Empress, Polyxena!"

The name Polyxena sounds foreign, as if it does not belong to her; within her she can feel the portrait of her ancestress

298

exulting in the homage she takes as her due.

In the brief moments when the howling subsides the harsh laughter of Havlik's drum can be heard; the tanner has become a human tiger, his teeth bared in ecstatic savagery as he leads the procession.

From side-streets comes the sound of fighting and death; isolated groups, who are still resisting, are being butchered.

She has a vague feeling that all this is happening at the silent command of the painted figure in her breast, and is filled with joy that Ottokar's hands remain unsullied by murder.

He is holding on to the heads of the men who are carrying him, and his face is white. His eyes are closed.

Thus they climb the steps of the Hradschin to the Cathedral.

A cavalcade of madness.

Polyxena woke to full consciousness; instead of the images from her memory, it was the bare sacristy walls that she saw round her once more, and the grain of the old cupboards.

She saw Bozena throw herself to her knees and kiss the hem of her gown. She tried to read the expression on her face: there was no trace of jealousy or sorrow, only joy and pride.

With a sound like thunder, the bells sounded out and made the flames of the candles tremble.

Polyxena stepped out into the nave.

At first she was blind in the darkness, only gradually did the forms of the silver candelabra under the red and yellow lights resolve themselves. Then she could see dark shapes struggling with a figure in white between the pillars and trying to force him to go to the altar – the priest who is to marry them.

She could see him refuse, resist, brandish a crucifix.

Then: a cry, a fall – struck down dead.

Scuffling.

A pause – muttering – a deathly hush.

Then the great door is flung open. The glare of torches fills the Cathedral from outside. The organ flickers in the red glow.

They drag in a man in a brown monk's habit.

His hair is snow-white.

Polyxena recognises him. It is the monk who stands in the Crypt of St. George every day to explain the black stone sculpture, "The dead woman, who bore a snake instead of a child under her heart."

He, too, is refusing to go to the altar.

Threatening arms reach out towards him.

He screams and pleads and points to the silver statue of St. John Nepomuk. The arms sink. They listen to him, bargain with him.

Muttering.

Polyxena guesses what it is: he is prepared to marry Ottokar and herself, but not at the altar. She realises he has saved his life; but only for a short space, they will kill him once he has pronounced the blessing. In her mind's eye she saw once more Zizka's terrible fist smashing down on a skull and she could hear his words, "Kde más svou ples? Monk, where is thy tonsure?"

This time, she knows, it will be his spectre that guides the fists of the mob.

A pew is dragged in front of the statue and a carpet thrown over the stone slabs. A boy struts down the aisle, bearing an ivory rod on a purple cushion.

A whisper goes through the crowd, "The sceptre of Duke Borivoj the First!"

It is handed to Ottokar.

He takes it as if in a dream and kneels down in his king's robe. Polyxena kneels beside him.

The priest appears before the statue.

Then a loud voice cries, "Where is the crown?"

The throng becomes restless and only calms down when the priest raises his hand.

Polyxena hears his trembling voice speak words of devotion and intercession, such as the Anointed One spoke, and an icy shiver runs down her spine as she remembers that the lips that speak them will be silenced forever within that very hour.

The marriage ceremony is over. Jubilation echoes round the cathedral, drowning a faint whimpering. Polyxena does not dare turn round to see; she knows what is happening.

"The crown!" The voice rings out again.

"The crown! The crown!" the cry is taken up from pew to pew.

"It's hidden at Countess Zahradka's", someone shouts. They all throng to the door, a wild surge.

"To Countess Zahradka's! Countess Zahradka's! The crown! Fetch the royal crown!"

"It's made of gold, with a ruby at the front!" comes a screech from the gallery – Bozena, who always knows everything.

"Ruby at the front", runs the description from mouth to mouth, and they are all as certain as if they had seen the crown with their own eyes.

A man climbs onto a plinth. Polyxena recognises the lackey with the vacant stare. He throws his arms about and screams in such a rapacious frenzy that his voice cracks, "The crown is in the Wallenstein Palace!"

No one is in doubt any more. "The crown is in the Wallenstein Palace!"

Behind the howling mob march the grim, silent figures of the 'Brothers of Mount Horeb', with Polyxena and Ottokar on their shoulders again, as on the way to the Cathedral. Ottokar is wearing the purple robe of Duke Borivoj and carrying his ivory sceptre.

The drum is silent.

Polyxena's gorge rises in a surge of hatred for this screaming rabble that can be roused to a frenzy of rape and plunder in a few seconds. 'Lower than wild beasts they are, and more cowardly than the worst cringing cur', and with a deeply cruel sense of satisfaction, she imagines the end of it all, the inevitable end: the rattle of machine-gun fire and the mountain of corpses.

She glances at Ottokar and gives a sigh of relief. 'He sees and hears nothing. It is like a dream to him. God grant him a quick death, before he wakes.'

She is completely indifferent to her own fate.

The gate of the Wallenstein Palace is firmly blockaded. The

mob attempts to climb the walls, and falls back down with bloody hands: the top is all covered with broken glass and iron spikes.

One of the men brings a huge beam.

Hands grasp it.

Back and forward. Back and forward: the monster charges the obstacle again and again, splintering the oak doors with a dull thud until they are wrenched off the iron hinges and disintegrate.

In the middle of the garden is a horse with a red bridle, glassy eyes, a scarlet blanket on its back and its hooves nailed to a board on wheels.

It is waiting for its master.

Polyxena saw Ottokar bend forward, staring at it, and put his hand to his forehead, as if he were suddenly coming to. One of the Brothers of Mount Horeb went up to the stuffed horse, took the bridle and rolled it out into the street. They lifted Ottokar up onto it, whilst the rest of the horde stormed into the house with blazing torches.

Windows crashed to the pavement, the glass shattering into a thousand fragments; silverware, gilded armour, swords encrusted with precious stones and bronze grandfather clocks were thrown out and clattered onto the cobbles, piling up into mounds. Not one of the Taborites even looked at them. From inside could be heard a loud tearing noise as they set about the tapestries on the walls with their knives.

"Where is the crown?" Havlik shouts to those in the palace.

"Not here" – roars of laughter – "Countess Zahradka will have it", comes the reply amid all the bellowing and braying.

The men lift the board with the horse onto their shoulders, break into one of their wild Hussite songs, and set off at a march towards Thungasse, preceded by the bark of the drum.

High above them, his purple robe fluttering in the breeze, sits Ottokar on Wallenstein's charger, as if he were riding over them.

The entrance to Thungasse was blocked by a barricade; a band of ancient servants, led by Molla Osman, welcomed them with a hail of bullets and stones. Polyxena recognised the Tartar's red fez.

To ward away any danger from Ottokar, she involuntarily directed a current of will-power at the defenders; she can feel the 'aweysha' strike among them like a lightning bolt, so that they are seized with panic and flee.

Only Molla Osman is unaffected. He calmly stands his ground, raises his arm, aims and fires. Struck in the heart, the tanner throws his arms in the air and collapses.

The yapping of the drum is suddenly silenced.

But immediately – Polyxena's blood freezes in her veins – it starts up again, more muffled than before, but more bloodcurdling, more inflaming; in the air, echoing back from the walls, rising from the ground, it is all around. 'It can't be. It's just the echo. My ears much be playing tricks on me', she tells herself and looks for it. The tanner is on his face, his fingers clutching the barricade; the drum has disappeared, but the drum-roll, suddenly turning high and shrill, flies on the wind.

The Taborites swiftly removed the stones and cleared the way. The Tartar kept on shooting, then he threw his revolver away and ran back up the alley into the house of Polyxena's aunt, Countess Zahradka, where all the windows were brightly lit.

With the terrible drum constantly sounding in her ears, Polyxena found herself carried triumphantly forward beside the towering, swaying, dead horse that gave off an overpowering smell of camphor.

High above her sits Ottokar.

In the bewildering glare of the criss-crossing lamps and torches Polyxena is sure she caught sight of a shadowy figure flitting through the crowd, now appearing, now disappearing, now here, now there. It seems to be naked and wearing a mitre on its head, but she cannot make it out clearly. Its arms are moving up and down in front of its chest, as if it were beating an invisible drum. When the procession stops outside the house, it suddenly appears at the top end of the street, a shadowy drummer formed from the smoke, and the rattle of the drum seems to come from a great distance.

'He is naked; his skin has been stretched over the drum. He is the snake that lives within men and sloughs its skin when they die ... I ... ' her thoughts become confused. Then she sees the white face of her Aunt Zahradka, distorted with hate, appear over the iron bars of the first-floor balcony, hears her shrill and mocking laugh and her howl of fury, "Off you go, you dogs, off you go!"

The bawling crowd, forcing its way along the street behind them, comes nearer and nearer. "The crown! You must give him the crown! You must give your son the crown!" screams the bedlam of furious voices.

"Her son?!" Polyxena exults, and she is almost torn apart by a wild, unbridled joy. "Ottokar is of the same blood as I!"

"What? What do they want?" asked the Countess, turning to those behind her in the room. From below Polyxena can see the head of the Tartar, as he nods and gives some answer, and hears the biting scorn in the old woman's voice, "To be crowned, that's what he wants, is it? Ottokar Vondrejc wants to be crowned? I'll put the crown on his head myself, I will!"

The old woman disappears into the room. Her shadow appears on the curtains, bends, as if she were picking something up, and straightens up again.

Angry hands are hammering on the door below. "Open up! – Fetch that iron bar! – The crown!"

Then Countess Zahradka reappears on the balcony, with her hands behind her back. Ottokar, in the saddle of the stuffed horse carried on the men's shoulders, is almost on the same level as she is, his face is only a short distance away from hers.

"Mother! Mother!" Polyxena hears him cry. Then a stream of fire blazes out of the old woman's hand.

"There you have your crown, bastard!"

Shot through the forehead, Ottokar tumbles from the horse.

Still deafened from the dreadful report, Polyxena knelt beside her dead love; she kept on calling his name, and all that she could see was a drop of blood like a ruby on his forehead. She could not comprehend what had happened.

Finally she understood, and knew where she was. But all she saw around her appeared as a tumult of phantasmal images: a raging mob storming the house; a horse on its side with a green board attached to its hooves: a toy blown up to gigantic proportions. And beside it Ottokar's sleeping face! 'He looks like a child dreaming of Christmas', was the thought that occurred to her. 'His face is so calm. – That cannot be death? – And the sceptre! – How happy he will be when he wakes up and finds that he still has it.'

'Why has the drum been silent for so long?' she looks up. 'Of course, the tanner was shot dead.' It all seems so natural to her: that the red flames are pouring out of the window; that she is sitting on a kind of island, surrounded by a stormy sea of howling people; that the sound of a shot comes from inside the house, with just the same strange and earpiercing echo as the previous one; that the mob, gripped with terror, suddenly ebbs, leaving her alone with the dead Ottokar; that the air around her seems to cry, "The army is coming!"

'There is nothing strange about that, I always knew that was how it had to end.' The only thing that strikes her as new and remarkable is that the Tartar can suddenly appear in the middle of the blaze on the balcony and jump down to the ground; that he calls to her to follow him, an order that she obeys without knowing why; that he runs up the alley with his hands in the air to where a line of soldiers wearing the red Bosnian fez is standing, their rifles against their cheeks; that they let him through. Then she hears a sergeant scream to her to throw herself to the ground.

'Throw myself to the ground? Why? Because they are going to shoot? Does the man think I'm afraid they might hit me? I am with child, Ottokar's child. It is innocent, how could they kill it! I am entrusted with the seed of Borivoj's line, which cannot die, only sleep until it reawakens. I am immune.'

The crack of a salvo sounds close in front of her, so that for a second she loses consciousness, but she continues calmly on her way. Behind her the shouting of the crowd stops abruptly. The soldiers, standing close beside each other, are like teeth in

305

the jaws of some monster. They still have their rifles pressed against their cheeks. Just one of them moves aside with a jangle of equipment and lets her pass through the gap.

She wanders into the empty jaws of the city; she seems to hear the drumming of the man with the mitre again, soft and muffled, as if from a great distance; it leads her, and she follows past the Elsenwanger Palace: the wrought-iron gate has been torn off its hinges, the garden is a scene of devastation: smouldering furniture, the trees black, the leaves scorched.

She turns her head a fraction. 'Why should I look? Oh, I know why, there is the portrait of ... Polyxena. Now it is dead and can rest in peace.' She looks down at herself and is astonished to see the brocade gown covering her white dress.

Then she remembers. 'Oh yes, we played at 'kings and queens'! I must take it off quickly, before the drum stops and the pain comes.'

Later she is standing by the wall of Sacré Coeur, pulling the bell. 'That is where I want my picture to hang.'

The Silver Shoe of Bartlett Greene

From: *The Angel of the West Window*

Gustav Meyrink

I have been rummaging around in my cousin's papers again. On the desk in front of me is a slim volume bound in bilious green morocco. The binding dates from the late seventeenth century at the earliest and the manuscript text must be by John Dee himself – the flow and shape of the letters corresponds to the diary. The tome shows signs of having been burnt, parts of the text have been destroyed.

There is an inscription in tiny letters on the fly-leaf, and in a strange hand! It reads:

"To be burned if ever the eye of Black Isaïs should appear in the waning moon. If ever thou hope to be saved: burn it!"

Some later, unknown (!) owner of the book must have taken the warning to heart. Perhaps he sensed "Black Isaïs" was observing him from the waning moon and threw the book into the fire to be rid of it. That would explain the burnt pages. But who was he who felt it come alive in his hands? And who can have recovered it from the fire before it dissolved into ashes?

There is nothing to tell me that.

What is certain is that the warning is not in John Dee's own hand. One of his descendants must have inserted it after some terrifying experience.

I append such portions of the morocco-bound volume as are still legible:

Notebook of John Dee, dated 1553, that is, 4 years after the 'Diary'.

The Silver Shoe of Bartlett Greene

These notes have been written down by me, Master John Dee

– vain, bungling fool that I was – after many days of torment, to be a memorial and a glass wherein I may look at my soul. And may it serve as a warning to those of my blood who may come after me. They shall wear the promised crown, of that I am more certain today than ever before. But the crown will grind them into the dust – just as I have been cast down to the ground – if they let their folly and their pride blind them to the enemy that every hour lurks in wait, that he might encompass our destruction.

The higher the Crown,
The farther the Devil can pull us down.

The following is an account of what God allowed to happen to me on the day after Easter Monday in the year 1549:

On the evening of the day when my uncertainty and torment about my future fate had reached its peak, Captain Perkins and the armed guards of the Bloody Bishop – as people justly call that monster in human form that sits in his lair in London under the name of Bishop Bonner – forced their way into my house and arrested me in the name of the King: in the name of that consumptive child, Edward! My mocking laughter only served further to enrage the guards and it was with difficulty that I escaped physical violence.

I had managed to gather up the papers to which I had just committed all my doubts before the soldiers came crashing through the door, and I concealed them in a safe place in the wall where, fortunately, anything that might betray me was already hidden. It was fortunate, too, that I had long ago thrown Mascee's ivory spheres out of the window, for I deduced from Captain Perkins' clumsy questions that they were particularly interested in those spheres. There must be something about those 'wondrous objects from Asia'; the lesson to be drawn from that is not to trust the Muscovite at all.

The escort of brutish soldiers rode hard through the damp night and the early morning saw us in Warwick already. But there is no point in describing the nights spent in the saddle and the days in guard-rooms and towers until we finally reached London and Captain Perkins thrust me into a cell below the ground. From all these and other measures that were taken I could tell that secrecy was paramount and that they went constantly in fear of an attempt to free me by force – though I cannot think who would have undertaken it.

It was the Captain himself who did me the honour of pushing me down the steps of my cell. When the last bolt had thundered shut I found myself in silent, pitch-black darkness. The pounding of blood in my ears had previously gone unnoticed; now it overwhelmed me like the crashing of breakers on a deserted shore.

All at once I was startled to hear a fearless mocking voice reverberating round the cell; like a greeting from the depths of darkness, it seemed to come from an invisible wall opposite me:

"Welcome, Master Dee, welcome to the dark realm of the lower gods. That was a pretty trip you took down those steps, my Lord of Gladhill."

The scoffing welcome was followed by a peal of laughter; at the same time there was the rumble of an approaching storm outside, and straightway the eerie laughter was drowned by a deafening clap of thunder. Immediately the darkness of the cell was lit by a flash of lightning; the brief glimpse afforded by the sulphurous glare sent icy needles round my scalp and down my spine: I was not alone in the dungeon; a man was fastened to the massive blocks of the wall opposite the door through which I had been pushed; heavy shackles kept his arms and legs spread wide apart, like some human St. Andrew's cross.

Was he really there? I had seen him in the glare of the lightning, the length of a heartbeat and then he was swallowed up by the blackness again. Had I imagined it? Behind my eyelids, burnt onto the retina, I could see the fearful image, as if it had been produced from within my brain, as if it emanated from the depths of my soul and had no corporeal reality. How could a sentient being be stretched out in the awful torture of that cross and still talk calmly, mockingly, and still let his scornful laughter ring out?

Again the lightning flickered; the flashes followed in such

quick succession that the dungeon was lit by quivering waves of pallid light. By Our Saviour! there was a man hanging there, there was no doubt of it: a giant of a man, with flowing locks of ginger hair almost concealing his face; above the tangled beard the thin-lipped mouth hung half open, as if he were about to let out another roar of laughter. His features showed no sign of suffering in spite of the excruciating pain the heavy iron rings, into which his wrists and ankles had been forced, must have caused. At the sight of him I had only managed to stammer a few words – "Who are you, hanging on the wall?" – when a thunderclap drowned the rest. "You should have recognised me in the dark, my dear Doctor!" came the mocking reply. "It is said that one who has lent money can recognise his debtor by the smell alone." A dart of icy terror constricted my heart. "Does that mean you are ...?"

"Yes: Bartlett Greene, chief raven of the Ravenheads, Protector of the Faithless at Bangor, victor over St. Deniol's empty boast and now mine host here at the Sign of the Iron Ring, ready to receive a benighted traveller such as your Honour, O mighty Patron of the Reformers."

The mocking speech ended with a wild burst of laughter which, miraculous though it seemed, made his whole, crucified body shake without appearing to feel the slightest pain.

"Then I am lost", I muttered, and collapsed onto the worm-eaten wooden stool that I now noticed.

The storm reached its thunderous peak. Even if I had wanted to converse with him, the raging elements would have made question and answer inaudible; as it was, I did not feel much like speaking. My death seemed inevitable and in my imagination I saw that it would not be an easy death. Clearly it was public knowledge that I was the wire-puller behind the Ravenheads. I was only too aware of the nature of the measures the Bloody Bishop thought essential "to bring the fallen sinner to a state of penitence, that he might glimpse paradise from afar."

Fear clawed at my throat. It was not fear of death, of a clean death befitting a gentleman; the fear that unmanned me and left my senses in turmoil was the fear of the slow approach of the inevitable torture, the fear of the fumbling fingers of the executioner as he drew out my lingering death. It is the fear of the pain that precedes death that traps us in the net of earthly life; were it not for that pain, man would live free of fear.

The storm raged, but I heard it not. From time to time a shout or a rumble of laughter would reach me from the blackness of the wall opposite; I heeded neither. Terror and reckless plans for my impossible escape were all my mind had room for.

Not for one moment did it occur to me to pray.

After the storm had abated – when, I do not know, it may have been hours later – my thoughts, too, became calmer, more collected, more cunning. The first thing I recognised as certain, was that I was in Bartlett Greene's power, assuming he had not already confessed and betrayed me. My fate depended on his silence alone.

I had just come to the decision that I should cautiously try to work on Bartlett Greene to get him to see that he was doomed and therefore had nothing more to lose in keeping silent about my part in the affair, when I was startled by something so unbelievable and terrifying that I forgot all my plans and artifices, even all my hopes: Bartlett Greene had set his huge body swaying on the iron chains, as if he were dancing. As the first light of a May morning filtered into the cell, the crucified outlaw swung higher and higher, and with a lithe gracefulness, as if he were enjoying the motion of a hammock slung between two silver birches. And all the while his joints and sinews crunched and cracked as if he were stretched on the rack.

And then Bartlett Greene began to sing! At first his voice was almost melodious, but it soon took on the screech of the bagpipes as he ground out a hoarse hymn to earthly pleasures:

"Heave ho! Heave ho!
The blossom hangs on the bough
After the moult of May.
Heave ho!
Miaow, Tom Kitten, miaow
Sing your roundelay.
Heave ho!

Heave ho! Heave ho!
Tom shall go seeking his Kitty
After the moult of May.
Heave ho!
Come follow me, my pretty,
On the green grass we will play.
Heave ho!

Heave ho! Heave ho!
All night Tom plays on his fiddle
After the moult of May
Heave ho!
While Kitty sings hey diddle diddle
To the moon and Black Isaye.
Heave ho!"

I cannot describe the fit of horror that shook me as I listened to the wild chanting of the leader of the Ravenheads; I thought the torture had suddenly driven him mad. Even today, as I write it down, my blood runs cold.

There was a rattle of the bolts of the iron-clad door and a warder came in with two underlings. They released the crucified Greene from the wall and let him tumble to the ground like a toad caught by a harvester's scythe. "That's another six hours over, Mister Greene", one of the turnkeys mocked. "I reckon you'll have soon outswung any other prisoner on that wall. If you're lucky you might be allowed another go at it; and if Satan turns the pain to pleasure, then there'll be a fiery chariot calling for you like Elijah; but it won't take you up to heaven, oh no, I reckon it'll head straight for St. Patrick's Purgatory and that'll be the last we'll see of you."

Bartlett Greene gave a satisfied grunt and dragged his stretched limbs to a heap of straw. Then he turned his blasphemous fury on the turnkey:

"Verily I say unto thee, David, thou holy turd of a goaler, today thou wouldst be with me in paradise – if I had a mind to go there. But I would not raise thy hopes, thou'll end up in a different place than thou thinkst, papistical scum. Or shall I spit on thy forehead and baptise thee in the name of the Lord, my son?"

I saw the two soldiers cross themselves in fear. The goaler drew back in superstitious awe and made with his hand the sign the Irish use to ward off the evil eye. He screamed at Greene:

"Look not at me with thy wall-eye, thou first-born of hell! St. David of Wales, that has watched over me ever since I sucked at my mother's breast, will shield me against thy curses."

Then he and his henchmen stamped out of the cell, followed by the mocking echo of Bartlett Greene's laughter. They left a loaf and a pitcher of water. For a while all was quiet.

As the light grew stronger I could see the features of my fellow prisoner more clearly. His right eye was a pale, milky-white disc which seemed to follow you with a fixed glare of infinite spite. It was the eye of a dead man who had seen some horrible sight as he died. The white eye was blind.

This is the first of a number of pages that have been damaged by fire. The text becomes more and more deficient, but the general sense is clear.

"Water? That's malmsey, that is", roared Greene as he clamped the pitcher between his wrists – his hands hung down useless – and took such a great swig that I feared my portion, too, would run down his throat, for I was parched. "To my twisted body it is like wine – glug – I never feel any pain – glug – nor fear! Fear and pain are twin weaknesses. I will tell you something, Master Dee, that none of your scholars know, for all their book-learning – glug – I will be truly free when I have cast off this mortal flesh – glug – I am proof against what they call death until I have completed my thirty-third year. – Glug – On the first of May, when the witches dedicate their cats to the Black Mother, my time will be over. O that my mother had kept me one month longer in her belly, my stench would be none the worse for it and I would have time to show the Bloody Bishop, that novice, that bungler, how a real master carries out torture. You will find the Bishop —" (scorch marks)

— Greene tapped me with his finger below the neck. My

jerkin had been torn by the guards and my chest was naked; he touched my collar bone and said, "That is the mystical bone I am talking about. It is called the *corvine appendix* – the Raven's tail. It contains the mystical salt of life that does not decay in the earth. From this comes the Jews' talk of the resurrection of the body at the last judgment — but they misunderstand; we who are initiated into the secret of the new moon – glug – rose again long ago. And what is the sign by which I know this, Doctor Dee? In spite of your Latin and all your learning, you seem not to have made much progress in the Art. I will tell you, then: because the bone shines with a light that the others cannot see — (scorch marks)

— understand." These words from the outlaw made my scalp crawl with fear and I had great difficulty in keeping my voice steady as I asked, "So for my whole life I have borne a sign which has not been revealed to me?" To which Bartlett Greene replied with great earnestness, "Yes, Master, you are marked with the sign of the Living Lord, the High One, the Invisible One, the Keeper of the Chain, which none shall ever enter because none ever leave it who are born to it; one from the outside would never find the entrance before the end of the days of the blood. Be of good cheer, Master Dee, even though you may be of the other stone and part of the contrary circle, yet I will never betray you to the vermin that is beneath us both. We are raised above the common herd, that sees but the outer show and will be lukewarm for ever and ever! — " (scorch marks)

— confess that I heard these words with an inner sigh of relief, even if secretly I began to feel ashamed of my fear of this simple giant, who bore his torture with such a light heart; a most fearful martyrdom awaited him as a reward for the silence he had promised me.

"— was a priest", continued Bartlett Greene, "and my mother a lady of rank. Lady Tenderloin she was called. I still do not know where she came from, nor where she went. A fine figure of a woman she must have been; she was called Mary until my father made a whore of her." At this Greene let out his strange, unfeeling laugh, paused and then went on, "My father was the most fanatical, cruel and at the same time most cowardly priest

314

I ever met. He told me he had taken me in out of pity, so that I might do penance for the sins of my unknown father – he was unaware that I had secretly discovered that he was my father — ordered me to do penance and forced me to stand on the stone flags in the church in my nightshirt for hours on end, praying all the while that the sins of my "father" might be forgiven. And when I fainted with exhaustion and lack of sleep he took his whip and beat me till the blood ran. My heart was filled with black hatred of Him who hung there on the cross above the altar. And then, I know not how it came about, I found that the litany I was forced to repeat had turned itself about in my brain and came out of my mouth the wrong way round: I was saying the prayers backwards and it was balm to my soul. It was a long time before my father noticed, since I murmured the words to myself, but when he did he roared out in fury and terror, cursed my mother's name, crossed himself and ran to fetch the axe to strike me down. But I was quicker and I split his skull from scalp to chin; one eye fell out and stared up at me from the stone slabs. And I knew that my widdershins prayers had gone down to the centre of Mother Earth, instead of rising to heaven, as the Jews claim the singsong whinings of their holy men do.

I have forgotten to tell you, Brother Dee, that one night my right eye was blinded by a great light that suddenly appeared to me – it could also be that it was struck from behind by a whiplash from my father. I cannot tell. Perhaps when I split his skull it was the fulfilment of the law that says, "An eye for an eye and a tooth for a tooth." Yes, my friend, I can truly say that this wall-eye, that fills the rabble with fear, is the fruit of long nights of prayer.

— fourteenth year of my life when I left my father lying on the altar with a double head and fled by devious routes to Scotland. There I was bound apprentice to a butcher, for I thought I would find it easy to strike the bulls and calves with the cleaver, I who had hit my father clean through his tonsure; but it was not to be, for, whenever I raised the cleaver, the scene in the darkened church rose before my inner eye and I was loth to desecrate the fair memory with the murder of an innocent animal. So I left and for many months wandered round the Highlands where I played my wailing pibrochs to the crofters and villagers on a set of pipes I had stolen. Whenever they heard my music, it made their blood run cold, though they could not say why. But I knew full well that the tunes followed the text of the litany which I had been compelled to repeat before the altar; they still sounded within me, still the wrong way round, still back to front. And I played the goatskin pipes at night when I strode over the darkened moors alone. Especially when the moon was full I felt a longing to hear the music of the backwards prayers, and it was as if each note ran down my spine to my feet as they walked, and from there into the womb of the earth. And once, at midnight – the first of May, the night of the druids' feast, and the moon was on the wane – an invisible hand rose from the ground and held me fast by the foot, that I could not move, neither forward nor back. Straightway I stopped my piping and stood as if rooted to the spot. An icy blast – from a chasm in the earth before me, so it seemed – blew over me and froze me from head to toe; and as I also felt it on my neck, I turned round and saw standing behind me One in the garb of a shepherd, with a crook in his hand that was forked at the top like the letter Y. He was followed by a herd of black sheep. But on my way there I had seen neither sheep nor shepherd, so that I thought I must have walked past him with my eyes closed and half asleep, for he was not like an apparition, as one might think, but of flesh and blood; so too were his sheep, as I could tell from the smell of damp wool they gave off — (scorch marks) — He pointed to my wall-eye and said, 'Because thou art called— '" (scorch marks)

This must be a description of some deep esoteric mystery, for written in red ink by another hand at the top of the half-burnt page was:

If Thy heart be faint, read not on! If Thou trust not in Thy Soul's strength, choose now: ignorance and peace, or Lust for Knowledge and damnation!

There follow pages that are utterly ruined. The fragments of script that are still legible suggest that the shepherd revealed to Greene mysteries that seem to be connected with the cult of a dark goddess of antiquity and the magical influences of the moon; there appears to be reference to that terrible rite that is still known in Scotland today as the *Taghairm*. It further appears that at the time of his imprisonment in the Tower Bartlett Greene was still a virgin, which is all the more remarkable as chastity is not a quality one normally associates with brigands. The text is too fragmentary to tell whether this was from deliberate choice or from an inborn aversion to women. From then on the text is relatively undamaged:

"— only understood the half – but at that time I was only a 'halfling' in such matters – of what the shepherd told me of the gift that Black Isaïs would give me, for how could it be that a tangible object should come from the incorporeal realm. When I asked him how I should recognise that the time had come, he said, 'Thou shalt hear the cock crow'. That made no sense to me, the cocks crow every morning in the village. Nor could I see that it should be a special boon not to know fear or pain on earth; it seemed of little account to me, that thought myself bold and fearless enough. But the fruit ripens on the bough, and when its season came I heard the cockcrow the shepherd had talked of, but within me. Until that time I had not known that everything must first come to pass in the blood before it can take on corporeal shape. Then I received the gift from Isaïs – the 'Silver Shoe'. In the long years of waiting I was subject to strange visions and visitations: damp, invisible fingers touched me; I felt a bitter taste on my tongue, a burning sensation in my head, as if a hot iron were branding me with a tonsure, shooting pains in the palms of my hands and soles of my feet; I could hear a sound as of a cat crying in my ear. Strange characters, which I could not read, but which looked like those in Jewish manuscripts, appeared like a rash on my skin, but vanished as soon as the sun shone on them. Sometimes I was hot with desire for a woman, which then did seem strange to me, since I have ever felt disgust at the daughters of Eve and their lewd dealings with men.

Then, when I felt the cock-crow rise up my spine and, as had been foretold, a cool shower sprinkled my head in baptism, although there was no cloud to be seen in the sky, I went on the first of May, the night of the druids' ceremonies, to and fro across the moor. I sought not, but I found, of a sudden, a chasm opened up in the ground before me — (scorch mark) — drawing the cart with fifty cats, as the shepherd had ordained. I made a fire and carried out the rite of the cursing of the full moon – the horror of it sat deep in my heart and my blood was like icy needles coursing through my veins. Then I took out the first cat, impaled it on the spit and began the 'Taghairm' by slowly roasting it over the fire. Its dreadful screaming pierced my ears for many minutes; they seemed like days to me and time itself seemed to stretch until it was nigh unbearable. How could I bear the same horror repeated fifty-fold? For I knew I must not stop until the last cat was roasted and I knew that I must not let the screaming be interrupted. Soon those still in the cage lent their voices to the chorus, and I felt the spirits of madness, that slumber in every man, begin to stir and tear my soul to shreds. However, they did not stay inside me, but poured out of my mouth like breath in the cold air and flew up to the moon and wreathed it in swirling mist. The shepherd had told me that the goal of the 'Taghairm' was to transfer, by the torment of the ceremony, the deep roots of fear and pain that were within me to the black cats that had been dedicated to the Goddess; of such roots of fear and pain there were fifty. And when the 'Taghairm' had drawn all fear and pain out of my blood and they had been absorbed into the moon-world whence they came, then would my true being appear and death and his minions would be overcome for ever. And when this came to pass, I would forget who I had been and lose all consciousness of myself. 'When its time is come', he had also said, 'then shall your body be devoured by flames, as the cats were, for the law of the earth must be satisfied, but what is that to you!' — Two nights and one day the 'Taghairm' lasted, and I lost all feeling for time and all around, as far as my eye could see, the heather was black with the dreadful suffering. But during the first night my inner senses were made manifest. The first thing I noticed was that I could distinguish each individual voice in the cats' screeching chorus of terror. The voices plucked at my heart-strings till each one snapped.

Then my ear awoke to the music of the abyss and since then I know the real meaning of 'hearing' – you can take your fists out of your ears, Brother Dee, I have finished with the cats. They are beyond pain now, perhaps they're in heaven playing cat and mouse with the souls of fat priests.

The full moon was high in the sky and the fire was extinguished. My legs trembled so that I swayed like a reed in the wind. For a while it seemed as if the earth itself were staggering through the sky, for I saw the moon flutter hither and thither until it was drowned in blackness. Then I knew that I was blind in my other eye, since I could no longer see the woods or hills around me, only darkness and silence. I know not how, but of a sudden I could see with the wall-eye that had been blind before; and I saw a strange world where blue birds with bearded faces like men hovered in the air, stars with long spiders' legs ran across the sky, stone walls walked about and fishes signalled to each other with their hands in dumb show. There were many other curious things, and all seemed strange to me and yet familiar, as if I had been there from the very start of memory but had just forgotten it. And did not 'before' and 'after' have a different sense for me, as if time had slipped sideways? — (scorch marks) — the distance a black pall of smoke rose from the earth and spread out as flat as a board, widening at one end until it stretched like a dark triangle ponting down out of the sky; then it burst and a fiery red gap split it from top to bottom and within was an enormous spindle whirling round — (scorch marks) — saw the dreadful figure of the Black Mother, Isaïs, plucking human flesh from the distaff to spin it with her thousand hands — blood dribbling down from the gap — some drops splashed up from the ground, sprinkling my body, like one that has the red plague, which must have been the mysterious baptism of the blood — (scorch mark) — the Great Mother called and woke her daughter, that had slept within me like a seed-grain, by which I came to Life Eternal, ever conjoined with her in dual being. – Even before that time I had never been subject to the lusts of the flesh, but since then I was proof against them for all time, for how could a man be gripped by the Curse who had found his own womanly nature within himself? – Then, when I could once more see with my human eye, a hand appeared from the chasm in the moor bearing something that gleamed dully like silver. I could not grasp it with my mortal fingers, but Isaïs' daughter within me stretched out a cat's paw and gave me the shoe – the 'Silver Shoe' which takes away all fear from him that wears — (scorch marks) — joined a troupe of strolling players as a tight-rope-walker and animal tamer; the tigers, leopards and panthers hissed and spat and drew back from me in terror when I turned my wall-eye on them, and I found I could walk on the high wire, although I had never been taught to. Since I had been wearing the Silver Shoe, all fear had left me and my 'bride' within me drew all the heaviness from my body so that giddiness and falling were impossible.

I see by your face, Brother Dee, that you are asking yourself, 'With all these gifts, why did Bartlett Greene remain an outlaw and a mountebank?' I will tell you: the baptism of fire and the 'Taghairm' released my strength that I might become Captain of the Ravenheads that go unseen and that I might pipe a pibroch at the Papists from over the water that their ears would ring with it for centuries to come. Let them draw up their cannon and fire – boom! – they will not harm me. Do you doubt that I wear the Silver Shoe, learned Master Dee? See here, o you of little faith", and Bartlett Greene placed his right foot against the heel of his left shoe, in order to push it off, then suddenly paused, sniffed the air and bared his sharp teeth. I heard his mocking voice say, "Can you smell it, Brother Dee? The panther comes!" I held my breath and it seemed that there was indeed a stench of panther in the air. Straightway I heard a footstep outside the cell door and a moment later the heavy iron bolts creaked open.

[..]

The first weak rays of the early morning sun had just penet-rated to our cell when a man, scarcely of middle height and all in black, entered alone. In spite of his corpulence his gait, indeed, his whole body, betrayed a supple agility. I was im-mediately struck by the pungent smell given off by his cassock as it fluttered out behind him in a gust of air: the cell was filled

320

with the stench of a beast of prey. This chubby-faced, red-cheeked man of the cloth – one would have taken him for a jovial wine-soak of a monk had it not been for the strangely fixed, half imperious, half furtive look in his yellow eyes – this man in the garb of a simple priest and without any bodyguards – if there were any, they kept well out of sight – was, I knew straightway, none other than Bishop Bonner, the Bloody Bishop of London, in person. Bartlett Greene remained squatting on the ground in silence opposite me; only his eyeballs swivelled slowly back and forth, attentively following our visitor's every move. Strange to relate, at the sight of my abused fellow-prisoner all my fear left me and I followed the example of the Captain of the Ravenheads and sat quietly on my stool, as if completely indifferent to the presence of our visitor pacing up and down between us.

Without warning he whirled round on Bartlett Greene, gave him a light tap with his toe and, like a panther pouncing, suddenly bellowed at him in a parade-ground voice:

"Up!"

Greene scarce raised an eyebrow. With a smile in his eyes he squinted up at the man who had ordered his body to be broken, drew a deep breath into his broad chest and roared back his mocking reply:

"Too soon, O trumpeter of Judgment! the hour of the resurrection of the dead has not yet come. For lo! I am still alive!"

"That I can see, thou abomination of Hell", replied the Bishop in a remarkably gentle voice, full of priestly concern and contrasting both with the sense of his words and with his previous bellowing assault. And my Lord Bishop continued in the same mild tones:

"Hear me, Greene: the Lord in His wisdom and His unfathomable compassion has provided that should you repent – and confess – your descent to the burning pitch of Hell may be postponed, perhaps even for all eternity. We will not cut short the time you have for repentance here on earth."

The only answer from Greene was a half-repressed, rumbling kind of laugh. I saw a spasm of fury cross Bonner's face, but he had himself well under control. He stepped up to the miserable lump of maltreated flesh that was still twitching with silent laughter on the rotten straw in front of him and went on:

"I can see you have the constitution of an ox, Greene. The search for truth with the instruments of torture has merely twisted your body a little, when others would already have rendered up their stinking souls to Satan. I hope to God that our barber, or even the physician if need be, can patch you up again. You can trust in my mercy as you have come to know my severity. This very hour you can leave this sty together with" – the Bishop's voice throbbed with a most cordial, persuasive purr – "your fellow sufferer here, the good Doctor Dee, your intimate companion."

That was the first time the Bishop had taken the least notice of me. Now that he suddenly spoke my name I felt a shock run through me, as one who is rudely woken from some dream. For until that point it had seemed to me as if I was observing from a distance some flight of fancy, some play performed by the comedians that had nothing at all to do with my own fate. Now that was all over as the Bishop gently but ruthlessly dragged me from my daydreaming onto the stage of this most cruel tragedy. If Greene confessed he knew me, I was lost!

But scarce had the sudden horror of my precarious position set my heart pounding and the blood throbbing in my veins than the imperturbable Greene turned his face towards me with incredible composure and growled:

"A doctor? Here with me on this straw? I thank thee for the honour, Brother Bishop. I thought thou hadst given me a tailor for company, one that wouldst teach how fear makes the soul fly out at the breeches."

Greene's insults were so unexpected that they wounded me in my old pride and I leapt up in real anger, none of which escaped the cold, observant eye of Bishop Bonner. But straightway I perceived honest Greene's intent and was filled with a great calm, so that I played my part in the comedy with great aplomb and responded to my cues from Greene or the Bishop with an apt response.

Although inwardly fuming that his panther's leap had once more missed its prey, my Lord Bishop concealed his disappointment behind a snarling yawn that, indeed, recalled the baffled fury of a great cat.

"You are sure, then, you do not know this man, neither in person nor by reputation, my dear Bartlett?" the Bishop went on in cajoling tones. But Greene merely replied in a surly mumble:

"Would that I knew the chicken-livered poltroon, the milksop thou hast brought to my door, good Master Cuckoo. I would give much for my eyes to behold this whining cur precede me through thy flaming gate to Heaven – but that does not mean I will clutch any turd of a quacksalver to my bosom like thee, Cousin Bonner."

"Still thy blasphemous tongue, thou son of Belial!" The Bishop finally lost control of his temper and screamed at Greene as a threatening clash of weapons came from outside the cell door. "Pitch and wood are too good for thee, thou first-born of Beelzebub! Thou shalt burn at the stake on lumps of sulphur so thou shalt have a foretaste of the pleasures that await thee in thy father's house!" the Bishop shouted, livid with fury and grinding his teeth so that the words could scarce come out. But Bartlett Greene gave a peal of laughter and started to swing wildly back and forth on his broken limbs; the mere sight of it made me flinch with horror. "Thou'rt mistaken, Brother Bonner", he brayed. "Sulphur is nothing to me. The French have a use for sulphur baths such as would not come amiss for thee neither, coz. But listen, my son: in the place where thou shalt come when thy time is up, mere sulphur is counted as musk oil, or as balm of Arabia!"

"Confess, thou swine, thou demon", Bishop Bonner flung back at him with a roar as of a lion; "confess that this John Dee is confederate in thy outlawry and murder or — "

"– or?" echoed the mocking voice of Bartlett Greene.

"The thumbscrews!" panted the Bishop, and warders and men-at-arms swarmed in. But Greene raised his racked body with a wild yell of laughter, proffered his right hand to the Bishop, then quickly stuck the outstretched thumb between his teeth and bit it off at the root with one crunching snap of his mighty jaws and with a jeering cackle spat it into the horrified Bonner's face, so that blood and spittle ran down from his cheeks onto his cassock. "There!" with a fearful shriek of laughter he roared, "there, screw that up your — " and a host of the most obscene imprecations cascaded over the Bishop, such that, even if my memory could retain the smallest part, yet my hand would refuse to write them down. In the main Greene was assuring the Lord Bishop, with the most loathsome promises, of the care and attention he would lavish on him from the "other side", when he, Greene, had flown from the flames of the bonfire to the land beyond, that he called the "Green Land". He would not tease or torment the Bishop with pitch or sulphur, oh no, he would repay evil with good and send his "dearly beloved son" most sweet-smelling and irresistible she-devils, such as would make a Frenchman of any pope. And his every hour on earth should be spiced with the honey and gall of hell, for on the "other side" —

"On the other side, my lad", – thus Greene finished his monstrous sermon – "thou shalt wail and gnash thy teeth in thy hell, and thy stench shall rise up from the mire, to us, the Princes of the Black Stone who are untouched by pain."

It would be impossible to describe the succession of dreadful thoughts, the stream of furious passions, or even the shadow of horror that crossed Bishop Bonner's broad face during this flood of curses. The powerful figure stood there as if rooted to the ground; behind him the rabble of mercenaries and turnkeys shrank into the darkest corners, for each and every one had a superstitious fear of the wall-eye, as if it were an evil eye that might put a curse on them for life.

Finally Bishop Bonner roused himself and slowly wiped the sweat from his face with his silken sleeve. Then calmly, softly, but with a hot, hoarse voice, he said:

"Think not thou can teach me any new tune of the Arch-Deceiver, thou witch's spawn. But thou remindst me to hasten, for such an evil demon should enjoy the light of heaven's sun no longer than is needful."

"Go thou", was Greene's scornful reply. "Take thy stench from my nose, carrion crow, the very air thou hast breathed needs purifying!"

The Bishop gave an imperious wave and his henchmen

rushed to grasp Greene. He, however, curled himself up into a ball, rolled over onto his broad back and stretched his bare foot towards them, at which they stumbled back. "See", he shouted, "see the Silver Shoe that the great Mother Isaïs gave me. As long as I wear it I shall know neither fear nor pain. I have outgrown such childish frailty!" I winced to see the foot had no toes; the naked stump looked like a crude metal shoe: the silver leprosy with its glittering crust had eaten them away. Greene was like the leper in the Bible of whom it is written: he was white as shimmering snow.

"Plague! Leprosy!" shrieked the men-at-arms, throwing down their spears and rushing out of the doorway of the cell in mindless flight. The Lord Bishop stood there, his face yellowish-green with horror and repugnance, wavering between pride and fear, for even those learned in the art do count the silver leprosy the most contagious evil. Slowly the Bishop, who had thought to slake his lust for violence on his miserable prisoners, retreated step by step before the approaching Greene who, thrusting his leprous foot forward, continued to spit out his scorn and blasphemy at the prince of the church. Bishop Bonner put a stop to it, though in no way that testified to his bravery; as he hurried to the door he gasped:

"Even today this canker shall be consumed in seven-fold flames. And thou, thou accomplice of the lowest depths of Hell" – the reference was to me – "thou shalt taste of the flames that free us from this beast, that thou mayest examine thy soul, perchance it can still be purified. It will be a merciful favour then if we hand thee over to the fire that burns for heretics."

That was the last blessing I received from the lips of the Bloody Bishop. I must admit that is gave rise to the most horrible fancies which sent me tumbling through chasms of fear and torment. It is said of the Lord Bishop that he has mastered the art of killing his victims three times: the first with his smile, the second by his words and the third by the executioner; and truly, he subjected me to the most agonising martyrdom before the unbelievable miracle of my salvation delivered me from the third death at the hand of that man.

Scarce was I alone with Bartlett Greene again than he broke

the silence with a rumble of laughter and turned to me with an almost benevolent air:

"Brother Dee, I can see your scalp crawling with fear, like a thousand ticks and fleas in your hair. But, as truly as I have done my utmost to free you from suspicion of association with me – good, I see that you do recognise it – just as truly can I say that you will escape from this trap alive; at most they will singe your beard a little when I am dispatched to heaven. You must suffer it like a man."

Incredulous, I raised my weary head that was throbbing painfully with all the fear and anxiety I had been through. As so often happens when the soul is exhausted with an excess of excitement and calamity, I was suddenly indifferent to all around me, as if I were free of all care; I even laughed indulgently at the cowardly fear that had filled the Bishop and his henchmen at the sight of my cell-mate's "Silver Shoe" and, my defiant spirit aroused, I moved closer to the doomed giant.

Greene remarked my intent and gave a strange grunt by which – with the sharpened ear shared suffering gives – I understood that the savage was moved by something that was, considering his utterly different nature, akin to human emotion.

He cautiously felt inside his leather jerkin, which was all he had to cover his naked chest, and called to me:

"Fear not to approach, Brother Dee; the gift of my gentle mistress is such that each man must earn it himself. I could not bequeath it to you, even if I would."

Once more his half-muffled laughter sent a chill down my spine. Then he went on:

"So I have played my part in denying the Romish priests the pleasure of discovering we make common cause. But I did it not for love of thee, my noble companion, but because that which I know and cannot change compelled me. For thou, Doctor Dee, art the royal youth of this age and to thee is promised the crown in the Green Land and the Mistress of the Three kingdoms awaits thee."

These words from the mouth of a common outlaw struck me like a lightning bolt and I was hard put to it to keep my composure.

Quickly my mind coupled the possible with the probable and at once it seemed to me that I perceived a connection between the vagabond and necromancer, Greene, the witch of Uxbridge Moor, and Mascee.

As if he could read my thoughts, Greene went on:

"The weird sister of Uxbridge I know well, and the Tutor to the Czar of Muscovy too. Beware him! He is a gambler; but thou, my Brother, shouldst rule of thine own design! The red and the white globes, which thou threw out of the window — "

I laughed defiantly:

"You are well informed, Greene. Is Mascee, then, one of the Ravenheads?"

"If I say 'thou'rt wrong' or if I say 'it may be' thou art none the wiser for it. But what I will tell thee is — " and the brigand detailed, by hour and minute, everything I had done in the night when the Bishop's men had taken me and he described the very place where I had all my writings hidden, the place I dare not even confide to this diary. With a laugh, he told me things I had done which no man could know, as if he were me myself, or a spirit that had ever been about me.

I could no longer keep back my astonishment and my secret horror of the mutilated leader of the brigands, the condemned man who laughingly commanded the most mysterious arts and powers. I stared at him and stammered, "You know no pain; you – so you say – enjoy the powerful aid of your mistress and goddess, that is named Black Isaïs, who can see the most secret doings of man, – how comes it then that you lie here in chains, your limbs all torn, and soon to be consumed by flames, and do not walk out through these walls by your magical power?"

Whilst I spoke Greene had taken from within his jerkin a small leathern purse which he held loosely in his hand so that it swung to and fro like a pendulum. He said with a laugh:

"Did I not tell thee, Brother Dee, that my time is up according to our Law? As I consecrated the cats to the fire, so must I now consecrate myself to the fire, since today my years number three and thirty. Today I am still that Bartlett Greene whom they may torture, tear apart and burn, and it is that son of a priest and a whore that speaks to thee; but on the morrow I shall put that off and the Son of Man shall be the groom in the House of the Great Mother. Then shall the time of my reign be come, and all of you, Brother Dee shall feel my rod as I rule in eternal life! — That thou shalt alway be mindful of these words and shalt follow my road, take this, my earthly wealth for thine inheritance — "

The text of the diary has once more been deliberately damaged. It looks as if it was deliberately destroyed by John Dee's own hand. But the nature of Bartlett Greene's gift to him is clear from the first lines of the next passage preserved in the diary.

(Scorch mark) — so that towards the fourth hour after noon all the torments that the Bloody Bishop could think up for his revenge had been made ready.

When they had taken Bartlett Greene away and I, John Dee, had been alone for a half hour, I took out the gift yet again; it was nothing remarkable, a piece of black coal, about the size of my fist and polished in the form of a regular octahedron. I looked closely to see if there were not, according to the instructions of its former owner, images of present events in distant places to be seen on its gleaming faces, or even whether future happenings from my own life might appear, as in a mirror. There was nothing of the like to be seen because, as I suppose, my soul was troubled, which Greene himself had said was detrimental to any such operation.

Finally I caught the sound of bolts being drawn back and quickly hid the mysterious coal in the innermost lining of my jerkin.

Hardly had I done so than a troop of the Bishop's heavily armed guards entered, and my first thought was that they had come to execute me on the spot and without trial. But their purpose was otherwise; in order to break my obdurate spirit, I was to be taken to the fire to see Greene burn at the stake and be brought so close that it would singe my beard. Perhaps Satan himself had whispered in Bonner's ear that Greene, in his mortal anguish, or I myself, confused by the terrible sight, might yet be brought to confess our complicity or some other deception. But he deceived only himself. I will not waste many words describing something that has been branded on my soul for life; I will briefly tell how the roasting of Bartlett Greene made a very different dish for the Bishop to swallow than the one he had pictured to himself in his desire to savour his victim's torment.

At the fifth hour Greene mounted the pyre with such a spring in his step as if it were his bridal couch. And as the words appear under my quill, I am reminded of what he said to me, namely that he hoped that day to be the bridegroom of his Great Mother, by which blasphemous speech he doubtless meant his return to the bosom of his black mother, Isaïs.

As they tried to take him to the stake he laughed aloud and called out to the Bishop, "Take care, priest, when I sing the Hymn of the Journey Home, that thou mind thy bald pate, for I am minded to sprinkle it with drops of pitch and fiery sulphur, that thy brain shall burn until thou make thy own journey to Hell!"

The bonfire had been constructed with cruel and devilish cunning, such as had never been seen before, nor, God willing, will ever be again in this vale of sorrow. It was a pile of damp, ill-burning elm logs with above it a stake to which they fastened Greene with iron clamps. Around this martyr's pole hempen threads full of sulphur were twined from top to bottom and above the head of the victim hung a broad crown of pitch and sulphur.

When the executioner pushed his torch into the pyre the first things to flare up, as if they were torchwood, were the sulphured threads which took the oily flames to the garland over the malefactor's head so that drops of sulphur and pitch slowly began to rain down upon him.

However, although it was horrible to behold, for the singular man at the stake it seemed as if it were but a refreshing spring shower or manna from above. And all the while he kept up a stream of insolent remarks at Bonner so that it seemed more as if the Bishop on his velvet cushions were the accused, rather than his victim on the bonfire. His sins were trumpeted abroad in public; Greene knew of his most secret transgressions and did not withhold them, so that had he been able to with good grace, my Lord Bishop would gladly have sacrificed the pleasure of watching the execution. He seemed bound by some spell and must needs sit there silent, trembling with shame and fury; then, foaming at the mouth, he screamed an order at his henchmen that they should hasten to put an end to the spectacle that he had thought before to draw out to the very last second. It was miraculous to see how none of the arrows that rained upon Greene could silence him; it was as if his whole body were invulnerable. Finally dry wood, with much kindling and tow mixed in, set the pyre blazing, and Greene disappeared in smoke and flames. But then he began to bellow out his song, more joyfully than in the cell, where he had swung from the wall, and the crackling of the wood was drowned in the spine-chilling rapture of his wild singing:

"Heave ho! All night Tom plays on his fiddle
After the moult of May.
Heave ho!
While Kitty sings hey diddle diddle
To the moon and Black Isaye.
Heave ho!"

It was deathly still around the place of execution; all the executioners and guards, the judges, priests and nobles felt their skin crawl with fear and loathing until every limb seemed paralysed; and the sight made me want to laugh out loud. Before all the rest, however, sat my Lord Bishop, Edward Bonner, like a grey ghost on his throne, his hands clamped on the arms, gazing fixedly into the flames. As the last note of the song died away on the lips of the blazing Greene I saw the Bishop stagger forward with a cry like a condemned man. Was it a gust of wind blowing through the fire, or were there truly satanical powers at work there – from the top of the pyre a wreath of flames, like yellow tongues of fire, suddenly flew, fluttered, plunged and whirled upwards into the sky over the episcopal throne and the head of Bishop Bonner. Whether it really was singed by a drop of sulphur as Greene had prophesied only minutes before, I cannot say; from the grimace of terror on the face of the Bloody Bishop it would almost seem so, but it was impossible to tell in the general tumult of men and weapons that filled the reeking courtyard.

One final detail I must record for accuracy's sake: When I regained my senses a lock of hair, singed off my own head, floated down to my feet as I brushed the confusion of the last hours from my forehead.

SATIRE

From: **The Great Bestiary of Modern Literature**

Franz Blei

THE KAFKA: The Kafka is a magnificent and very rarely seen moon-blue mouse, which eats no flesh, but feeds on bitter herbs. It is a bewitching sight, for it has human eyes.

THE MEYRINK: The Meyrink is the only mooncalf which dropped to earth and which is now in captivity. It is occasionally put on show by its captor. For a while pregnant women were banned from viewing it, because of the occurrence of a few premature births caused by shock, but the ban has been lifted, since women with child are by now so accustomed to the sight that it raises no more than a gentle smile. Officers of the Imperial Austro-Hungarian Army and German Deputies wanted to ban the public exhibition of the Meyrink because, so they said, it gave a distorted reflection of them in its one big eye. The owner succeeded in proving, however, that the reflection was not distorted, but that it was the object which distorted the eye of the Meyrink. The numbers visiting the Meyrink have declined considerably since the appearance of so many other mooncalves running around free; whether they all dropped from the moon is impossible to say, but they have certainly been dropped on the head.

THE SCHNITZLER: Schnitzler is the name of a racehorse which runs at Freudenau out of the Fischer stable and which, in his day, was a favourite with all the ladies and girls-about-town of Vienna because of the melancholy mettle he used to show. People would bet on Schnitzler because they liked him, even though they knew he would not even be placed. Because Schnitzler was such a favourite, and to encourage the granddaughters of the girls-about-town to come to Freudenau, the Jockey Club has agreed to let Schnitzler, whenever and as long as he runs, always come third, even if he pulls up after the first lap. Long may he run.

Wetherglobin

Gustav Meyrink

I

Motto: Dulce et decorum est
pro patria mori.

The rumour ran from mouth to mouth, from newspaper to newspaper: Professor Domitian Dredrebaisel, the world-famous bacteriologist, had made a scientific discovery of quite stupendously far-reaching consequence.

The general opinion was that a reorganisation of the military was expected; oh yes, indeed, perhaps even a complete transformation of the armed services as we knew them. Why else would the Minister of War have been in such a hurry to summon the famous scientist to a meeting? Hm?

And once it was known that secret stock-market syndicates had been set up to exploit the discovery and to advance Professor Dredrebaisel a large sum of money so that he could undertake an urgent study trip to Borneo (Borneo?!), there was no end of popping eyes and wagging jaws.

"But I ask you, could we bring Borneo to the War Ministry?" Herr Galizenstein, that respected stockbroker, and relative of the scientist, had replied amid gesticulations, when interviewed on the subject. "How could we bring Borneo to the War Ministry?! Where is Borneo, anyway?"

The following day the newspapers repeated every charming syllable of the words of our farsighted financier, adding that an American government expert, Mr. G. R. S. Slyfox, M.D., F.R.S., had just had an audience with Professor Dredrebaisel.

All of which, of course, raised public curiosity to fever pitch.

Newshawks used to bribe the clerks in the War Ministry to find out details of new inventions that had been submitted; in the course of their activities they would repeatedly unearth material that bore eloquent witness to man's ceaseless endeavours to perfect the science of warfare. Very innovative in the opinion of experts, was, for example, a proposed submission regarding the operation of the baggage train in both war and manoeuvres that would improve the current success rate of nought percent by five (!) times.

But the *pièce de résistance*, all were agreed, was the ingenious Automatic Honour Calibrator invented by Infantry Captain Gustav Braidiner, an officer who was famous far beyond the borders of our country for his uncommonly idiosyncratic conception of the word of honour. Just imagine, an appliance, a clockwork mechanism that any lieutenant can operate without previous experience or instruction, in brief a power-driven, water-cooled officer's code of honour which can be aimed in any direction at a touch: it does away with all the lengthy and tedious coaching in the prescribed honourable attitude for each individual situation, replacing it with a hygienic mechanical device.

Many, many such things came to light, but there was no trace of any invention or discovery by Professor Dredrebaisel.

So there was nothing for it but to be patient, to let matters ripen like fruit on the trees, and wait for the results of the expedition to Borneo.

Months passed.

All the rumours of the great invention had long since nodded off and left the field to new questions, when a European newspaper broke the news that Professor Dredrebaisel, and with him perhaps all his companions, had died a terrible death. All that was known was contained in a brief telegram:

13th May. Silindong, Pakpak District, Borneo.
(A cable from our own correspondent.)

"Last night Professor Domitian Dredrebaisel was torn to pieces in his own house by a horde of orang-utans. Many servants and keepers shared his fate. His assistant, Dr. Slyfox, is missing. The Professor's desk was smashed; the floor was covered with countless scraps of paper from his notes and articles."

A brief obituary for a glorious idea.

II

Motto:

Rear ends covered with brass buttons, fill turkey-cocks with pride.
And what makes them even prouder: they think with their backsides.

*A letter written three years later from Borneo by a certain Dr.
Ipse to a friend:*

Silindong,
Borneo,

1st April 1906.

My dear old friend,

Do you remember – years ago in Maader's "Box" it was – how we promised each other we would write at once if, in the course of our journey through life, we should ever come across anything which was beyond the experience of the common herd, anything which had an air of the extraordinary, the mysterious about it, anything, in short, which did not fit in with the banal merry-go-round of daily life?

Well, old chap, today I am in the happy position of being able to report something of the kind, something which justifies taking you away from your alchemical tomes or whatever recondite studies you are immersed in at the moment.

How will you feel, over there in Europe, if someone from

far-away Borneo should dare to use the axe of knowledge to attack your unbounded awe of all things military at its roots?

I would love to be able to eavesdrop on your thoughts for a while after you have read this letter, to see how soon it was before your patriotism had been washed clean of all pride in the uniform, just as the message written in sugar is washed from a gingerbread soldier that has been left out in the rain.

Tell me, have you never wondered why it is that educated people of the same profession – yes, even barbers – call each other 'colleagues' (which in English means 'people who read or study together'), whilst the turkey-cocks who form our officer class address each other as 'comrade' (from *camera* = room = to sleep or lounge around in the same room)? It always reminds me of a nice chapter heading used by the medieval scholar, van Helmont, "Of divers profound Mysteries that do lie in Words and Phrases."

But now I must plunge head first into the whirlpool of events.

First of all, guess whom I met here? None other than Mr. G. R. S. Slyfox, M. D., F. R. S., former assistant to the late, lamented Professor Dredrebaisel. Just imagine! Here in Silindong, in the deepest jungle in Borneo! Mr. Slyfox was the only survivor of that ill-fated expedition. In reality it was he who had directed the experiment from the very beginning, Professor D. D. was only the front man, and immediately after the Professor's death he left Borneo for Europe to offer the perfected version of his discovery, or rather, invention, to several states, above all to the one we all love and admire so much which had shown such great initial interest.

I will come to the success of his trip later. For the moment suffice it to say that Mr. Slyfox is back in Silindong, poor as a church mouse and continuing his researches.

And now, I assume, you are impatient to know what Professor D.'s, or rather, Mr. Slyfox' invention actually consists of.

Admit it. You are, aren't you? Well then:

In decades of studying the inoculation statistics Mr. Slyfox had observed that, in areas where the smallpox vaccine was no longer taken from humans but from calves, there was a marked increase in the urge to defend the fatherland, even when there was not the slightest necessity.

In Mr. Slyfox' inventive mind it was only one step from this observation to his later, epoch-making experiments.

With the unerring judgment of an American, for whom nothing is sacred, he immediately connected the above-mentioned symptom with the inferior mental capacity of calves, and this provided the basis for a series of experiments.

His very first tests, using a number of specially selected surgically treated rams (those that are normally called 'wethers'), produced outstanding results. And if, in addition, the vaccine derived from such wethers (so-called Wetherglobin A) was passed through the blood stream of one or two sloths, it became so effective that, when injected into youths with a natural low patriotism quotient, it produced a kind of primary patriotic frenzy within a very short time.

In individuals with a hereditary tendency to patriotism, this state rapidly developed into incurable, galloping patriomania.

The profound changes that were also brought about in the aesthetic sensibilities of the inoculee can perhaps best be demonstrated by the case of one of our most respected cavalry poets who, after inoculation, opened his volume of poems with the lines:

O blade at my left side – aah,
A-gleaming as I ride – aah.
etc., etc.

But to return to Mr. Slyfox: initially, as you will be aware, the government was extremely interested in the invention, which was to be put out under Professor Dredrebaisel's name, and a syndicate had advanced the costs of the expedition.

Silindong, in the middle of the most impenetrable jungle of Borneo, is the home of the orang-utan, and as quickly as possible around two hundred such apes were captured and immediately injected with Wetherglobin simplex A.

Mr. Slyfox maintained that the enrichment with lymphatic secretions, which came from passing the substance through sloths, would be, given the rarity of these animals, much too expensive for its mass use in the armed forces. He hoped that the characteristic of the sloth which produced the strengthening of the vaccine – its surplus stupidity – could be replaced, perhaps even improved, by the great ape's innate qualities.

Of course, no one could have foreseen the fateful consequences of locking up so many strong animals together.

The night of terror, in the course of which the orang-utans smashed their cages, and everything else, to smithereens and killed Professor D. D. and their Malay keepers, almost cost Mr. Slyfox his life too; it was only by a miracle that he escaped.

After they had finished destroying the camp, the orang-utans held a meeting lasting several days, the purpose of which was at first a complete mystery but later highlighted the effects of Wetherglobin and everything connected with it.

From his hiding place the American had been able to observe how the apes, after endless palaver, had chosen one of the group as leader – it was the one which, even when they were imprisoned, had struck everybody as being completely gaga – and had then taken some gold (!) paper they had found in a broken box and stuck it on its backside.

The scene which then gradually unrolled before the American's eyes was equally calculated to arouse amazement.

The orang-utans formed up in platoons with sticks and branches, or whatever they could get hold of, over their shoulders, and set off, marching upright in close formation along the jungle paths, with their leader, gold backside gleaming and full of his own importance, a short distance in front. From time to time he would bark out:

"Gwaaah-gwek! Gwaaah-gwek!"

which would send them all into a kind of black ecstasy.

An oddly grumpy expression would come over their features, they would jerk their faces to the left and stamp the ground with their heels like maniacs as they marched.

It must have been an unforgettable sight. "For a few moments", these were Mr. Slyfox' own words, "I felt I was no longer in the jungle, but somewhere quite different, on some parade ground in Europe."

And later, when I saw how an objector was arrested and one of the apes stood on a leather hat-box and gave such a deafening performance that eventually even this stubborn individualist was seized by 'primary patriotic fervour', well, the new ideas came simply flooding in.

These apes, so I reasoned, have nothing to model themselves on, and yet they have come up with the idea of decorating their rear ends with gold to make a warlike impression, and they have hit upon institutions which, in the light of my research I now know must be the result of the effect of substances similar to Wetherglobin clouding the brain, whether injected or produced by the body itself, where their development is encouraged by hereditary bigotry.

I will deliberately refrain, my dear old friend, from taking Slyfox' train of thought any farther, if for no other reason than so as not to deny you the subtle pleasure of working it out for yourself.

And would you not have to agree with me if I were to maintain that the arrogance of the turkey-cocks has nothing to do with true patriotism and everything to do with the desire to impress 'harlots' of both sexes, with a kind of capercaillie's courtship display?

Or is it really possible that two such as us, whose friendship has weathered into a union of souls, could have different opinions on such a fundamental truth, even for a fraction of a second?

And even if that were the case, would it not really be sufficient to call to mind the average level of culture of the 'turkey-cocks'; of course, I am thinking of those of a particular great power.

But away with such speculation. I was going to tell you what the attitudes of those states was to whom Mr. Slyfox offered Wetherglobin.

One gave a curt refusal; they wanted to observe the effect in other countries first.

The other replied, informally through an intermediary as usual, to the effect that, thanks to the traditional loyalty to the royal family, to quotations and patriotic songs learnt off by heart at an early age, as well as to cleverly designed and brightly coloured children's toys etc., the vast majority of its population was already in a satisfactory condition. A programme of vaccination such as the one proposed, especially since it was no longer guaranteed by the name of the unfortunate Professor Dredrebaisel, seemed, therefore, premature. Added to that, in the opinion of experts it had not been conclusively proved that Wetherglobin would not, like other toxins, after some time lead to the production of antitoxins in the blood which would have the opposite effect.

They would, however, naturally continue to follow Mr. Slyfox' experiments with keen interest and remained, etc., etc. So Mr. Slyfox was left high and dry and had no choice but to continue his experiments on all kinds of beasts over here.

And I'm assisting him.

Even if, contrary to expectation, success has so far eluded us, we are determined to catch a rhinoceros and inject it with Wetherglobin. That is certain – Mr. Slyfox would bet his bottom dollar on it – to convince all the sceptics.

By the way, old chap, I meant to say that the apes are no danger to us any more, just in case you were concerned for my safety. We too have decorated our backsides with tinsel and, as long as we are careful to suppress any sign of intelligence when the animals approach, they take us for officers and treat us with great respect, so that we are completely safe. You might feel that shows a certain lack of principle, but there are some concessions you have to make if you live among orang-utans.

But I'll have to finish quickly now, outside I can hear the patriotic apes approaching with their smart

"Gwaaah-gwek! Gwaaah-gwek!"

Hearty but hasty greetings from your old friend,

Egon Ipse.

Blamol

Gustav Meyrink

> In truth, without deceit,
> I say to you surely
> As it is below, so is it above.
> *Tabula Smaragdina*

The old cuttlefish was resting on a thick Blue Book that had come from a vessel that had sunk, slowly taking in the printed characters.

Landlubbers have absolutely no idea how busy a cuttlefish is all day.

This one had devoted himself wholeheartedly to medicine, and all day long, from morning to night, two poor little starfish were obliged to help him turn the pages, because they owed him so much money.

Around his corpulence, just where other people keep their waists, he wore a golden pince-nez: another piece of marine loot. The lenses were forced wide apart on either side, giving anyone who might look through them a disagreeably dizzy sensation.

All around was quiet.

Suddenly an octopus came lunging up, its baggy snout pointing eagerly ahead, its arms trailing in its wake like nothing so much as a bundle of sticks. It settled down beside the book, and waited for the old fellow to look up before composing an elaborate greeting and unwrapping a tin box from amongst its arms. "The violet polyp from Turbot Alley, I presume," observed old Sepia graciously. "Yes, that's right, I knew your mother well, née von Octopus. (I say, Perch, just fetch me the *Almanach de Gophalopoda*, will you.)

Now, what can I do for you, young polyp?

"The inscription – read what it says," oozed the other, embarrassed, pointing to the tin box. He had a rather slimy way of saying things.

344

The cuttlefish stared hard at the box, like a prosecuting counsel, his eyes popping out.

"What is this I see – Blamol? This is a priceless find. Surely it comes from the Christmas Steamer that ran aground? Blamol! The new miracle cure – the more you take, the healthier you get!"

"This must be opened at once: Perch, just dart off to the two lobsters over there, will you – you know, Coral Bank, Second Branch, the Scissors brothers – and hurry

The green sea-lily, who resided nearby, rushed over the moment she heard about the new medicine – oh, she *really would* like to try some, really and truly, she'd give *anything*!

And she undulated her several hundred tentacles in captivatingly languorous fashion, riveting everyone's eye upon her.

Sharks alive, was she beautiful! A big mouth, for sure, but that's often what makes a lady so exciting.

They were all gaping at her, so they missed the arrival of the two lobsters who were already busy at the tin, chattering to each other in their harsh, outlandish dialect. With a final gentle tap the tin fell apart.

Like a shower of hail the white pills swirled out and, lighter than cork, shot upwards and vanished.

"Catch them, catch them!" came the cry, and they all fell over in their haste, but none was quick enough. Only the lily was lucky enough to secure a single pill and she hastily stuffed it into her mouth.

Indignation all round: the least the Scissors brothers deserved was a box on the ear.

"You, Perch, I suppose you couldn't manage to watch what was going on? What's the point of your being my assistant?"

Everyone was left to swear and argue – all except for the octopus who, speechless with rage, was hammering away at a mussel with its clenched tentacles, enough to make the pearls squeak.

Suddenly there was a general silence: look at the lily!

She must have suffered a stroke: rigid and quite unable to move, with her tentacles stiffly extended, she could be heard gently whimpering.

The cuttlefish pulsed importantly over to her and commenced his examination with a mysterious air. With the aid of a pebble he palpated a tentacle or two and then probed further in. (Hm, hm, – Babynski's Reaction: disruption of the Pyramidal Channels.) Then with the edge of his wing he stroked the lily a few times across her cup, his eyes taking on as he did so an intense and penetrating quality.

Finally, puffing himself up, he said in a grave tone: "Lateral Chord Sclerosis – the lady is paralysed."

"Is there anything we can do? What is your opinion? Please just help her – I'll go to the chemist's" cried the good-natured seahorse.

"Help? Are you mad? Do you think I studied medicine in order to effect cures?" The cuttlefish was getting angrier. "It seems to me you think I'm a barber. Are you trying to make fun of me? Perch, my hat and stick, if you please

One after another they all dispersed. "The things that can happen to you in this life. It's awful, don't you think?"

The place emptied, soon leaving the perch grumpily casting about, looking for anything the others might have lost or forgotten.

Night descended upon the seabed. The rays of light, of which none knew whence they came nor whither they went, shimmered in the green water like a veil, tired, as though at the limit of exhaustion.

The poor sea-lily lay immobile, gazing at them with a heart full of bitterness as they rose and vanished into the distance far above. Yesterday at this time she had been fast asleep, curled up safely into a ball, and now – to have to die on the street, like a mere – – animal! Little pearls of air beaded her brow. And tomorrow was Christmas!

She fell to thinking about her husband, gadding about somewhere far away. Three months it was now since she had become a seagrass-widow. Really, it would have been no surprise if she had been unfaithful to him.

Oh, if only the seahorse had stayed with her!

She was so afraid!

It was getting so dark you could hardly see your own feelers in front of you.

Broad-shouldered night crept out from behind the stones and algae, devouring the pale shadows of the coral banks. Black shapes glided out like ghosts, with eyes aflame and luminously violet fins. Fishes of the Night! Hideous rays and sea-devils, going about their nefarious business in the darkness, lying murderously in wait amidst the wreckage of ships.

Stealthily, shiftily, mussels beckon to the belated traveller, inviting him all unwary to join in some gruesome vice amidst the soft pillows that can be glimpsed between their gently parted shells.

In the distance a dogfish barks.

Suddenly, a bright light flashes through the algal ribbons: a shining medusa appears, guiding some drunken revellers homewards – a pair of slick eels, with a couple of moray sluts twined round their fins. Two young salmon, gaudy in silver, have stopped to gaze at this scene of depraved intoxication. A dissolute verse can be heard...

Down where the green weed grew
I asked when I had met her
Did she want me to screw
Her? "Yes, oh yes, you'd better."
So down she bent
And off I went
Right where the green weed grew...

"Out of my way, bloody salmon!" roars one of the eels, interrupting the song.

Silversides bridles: "Shut your trap! You'd do well to watch your language. Just because you think you're the only lot who were born on the right side of the Danube..."

"Shh, shh," the medusa pleads, "watch your tongues, look who's over there!"

They all fall quiet and gaze with some awe at a small group of frail, colourless figures making prim progress along the way.

"Lancelets" someone whispers.

"? ? ? ?"

"Oh, very hoity-toity they are, Counsellors, diplomats and the like. Born to it. Real marvels of nature – no brain, no backbone: quite spineless."

There ensues a minute or two of silent amazement before everyone swims away, this time quite peaceably.

The noises die away. Absolute silence descends.

Time passes. Midnight, the witching hour.

Did we hear voices? Not shrimps, surely, at this time of night? It's the Night Patrol: police crabs!

What a noise they make with their armoured legs as they crunch across the sand, dragging their captives off to a place of security.

Woe betide anyone who falls into their clutches: no crime escapes them, and their lies stand on oath before the law.

Even the electric ray turns pale at their approach.

Lily's heart misses a beat in terror: here she is, a defenceless lady, out in the open! What if they catch sight of her? They'll drag her up before the beak in front of that old perjurer of a crab, the biggest crook in the sea, and then... and then...

Here they come, getting closer – they're just a step away; the cruel talons of ruin and disgrace are on the point of encircling her waist with their iron grip.

Suddenly the dark water shivers, the coral branches creak and shake like seaweed and a pale glow illumines the scene from afar.

Crabs, rays, sea-devils dart and scatter across the sand, pieces of rock break away and swirl up in the current.

A bluish, smoothly moving wall as big as all the world comes flying through the waters.

Nearer and nearer comes the phosphorescent light, the gigantic glowing wing of *Tintorera*, the demon of annihilation, comes sweeping up, stirring fiery chasm-deep whirlpools in the foaming water.

Everything becomes caught up in the spinning eddies. The

lily flies vertiginously up and down again over a landscape of emerald froth. Where now are the crabs, where the shame and dread? Raging destruction has come storming through the world, a bacchanal of death, a glorious dance for the prize of a soul.

The senses expire like a smoking flame.

Then next a frightful shuddering jolt, the eddies stand in the water, but continue to spin faster and faster, flinging down on to the sea floor everything they had previously torn up.

Many a fine armoured piece meets its Waterloo there.

When at last the lily awoke from her fainting fall she found herself lying on a bed of soft algae.

The gentle seahorse (who had taken the day off from work) was bending over her.

A cool morning stream fanned her face, and she looked up. She could hear the cackling of goose-barnacles and the cheerful bleating of a lam[b]prey.

"You are quite safe here in my little house in the country," replied the seahorse to her look of enquiry, and gazing deep into her eyes. "Please rest a little more, dear lady, it will do you good."

But she could not, for all she tried. An indescribable feeling of nausea overwhelmed her.

"What a storm that was last night – my head is still swimming from all the commotion," went on the seahorse chattily. "By the way, can I tempt you to a spot of blubber – a really nice fat piece of juicy sailor-blubber?"

At the mere mention of the word the lily felt so ill that she was obliged to clamp her lips tight shut. But it was no use. She began to retch (the seahorse turned his head discreetly to one side), and in a moment had brought up the Blamol pill which, quite undigested, floated and vanished upwards in a cloud of bubbles.

Thank God the seahorse hadn't seen it.

The invalid suddenly felt as right as rain again.

She curled herself up with contentment.

Wonder of wonders! She could curl up again, could move her limbs about, as before.

Ecstasy upon ecstasy!

The seahorse could feel bubbles of joy pricking his eyes. "Christmas, it's really Christmas today!" he rejoiced. "I must tell the cuttlefish at once: in the meanwhile you must have a really good long sleep."

"What do you find so remarkable about the lily's sudden recovery, my dear Seahorse?" asked the cuttlefish, with a condescending smile. "You are an enthusiast, my young friend. As a matter of principle I don't usually discuss medical matters with non-professionals (bring up a chair, Perch, for the gentleman), but I'll make an exception this time, and endeavour to match my mode of expression to your level of understanding as far as I can. So, you consider Blamol to be a poison, and you attribute the paralysis to its effects? What a mistake! I might add, by the way, that Blamol is now altogether passé, it is yesterday's panacea; today we usually recommend Idiotine Chloride: medical science strides eternally onwards. That the illness should have coincided with swallowing the pill was pure coincidence – it's well known that everything that happens in the world is coincidence – for in the first place Lateral Chord Sclerosis has a quite different set of causes (though discretion forbids me to name them), and secondly, Blamol works, like all such agents, not when you take it, but only when you spit it out – and then of course it's bound to be beneficial in its effects.

And finally, as far as the cure is concerned, well, here we have a clear case of autosuggestion. In reality, – and by 'reality' I mean what Kant called the '*thing in itself*' – in reality the lady is just as ill as she was yesterday: she just doesn't notice it. It is precisely in the case of those with inferior mental powers that autosuggestion works so effectively. Of course I'm not implying anything by saying this – you know how highly I esteem the little woman at home:

'Give all honour to the ladies,
They plait and weave...'

as Schiller puts it.

But now, my young friend, enough of this, it will simply upset you unnecessarily. A propos – you will of course do me the honour? It is Christmas and – I'm getting married."

"Who is he marrying, then" he asked the perch on the way out. "You don't say – – the blue mussel? But why not, though – just another one in it for the money."

When, that evening, the lily arrived, somewhat late but with a glowing complexion, and leaning on the seahorse's fin, the congratulations were without end. Everyone gave her a hug, and even the veiled snails and the cockles who were acting as bridesmaids put their maidenly timidity aside in the warmth of their hearts.

It was a magnificent occasion, as only the rich can provide – the blue mussel's parents had millions after all, and they had even organised some phosphorescent sea-fire.

Four long oyster-banks had been laid out and the feast had lasted well over an hour, yet still more dainty dishes appeared. The perch went on steadily circulating with a glittering decanter (upside down, of course) of hundred year-old air, recovered from the cabin of a sunken wreck.

Everyone had become a little tipsy, and the toasts being drunk to the blue mussel and her bridegroom were being drowned out by the popping and clicking of dead men's fingers and the clatter of razorshells.

The seahorse and the lily were sitting at the far end of the table, quite in the shadows, hardly noticing their surroundings. From time to time he would squeeze one or other of her tentacles, and in return she rewarded him with a glance full of ardour.

Towards the end of the meal the band struck up with a song:

A joke, a kiss
For a *married* Miss
Is utter bliss;
It's quite what's done
When you're having fun –
But he's got to be young...

And their table-companions exchanged a sly wink. It would have been impossible not to suppose that everyone had their own ideas about what sort of liaisons were being quietly arranged here.

The Ring of Saturn

Gustav Meyrink

One step at a time they came, disciples feeling their way up the circular stair.

Inside the Observatory the darkness came billowing up into the round space, while from above starlight trickled down along the polished brass tubes of the telescope in thin cold streaks. If you turned your head slowly, allowing your gaze to traverse the darkness, you could see it flying off in showers of sparks from the metal pendulums suspended from the roof.

The blackness of the floor swallowed up the glittering drops as they slid off the smooth surface of the shining instruments.

"The Master's concentrating on Saturn today," said Wijkander after a while, pointing to the great telescope that thrust through the open roof panel like the stiff, damp feeler of a vast golden snail from out of the night sky.

None of the disciples contradicted him: they weren't even surprised when they looked into the eyepiece and found his assertion confirmed.

"It's a complete mystery to me. How can anyone in this near-darkness possibly know what the instrument is pointed at, merely by looking at its position?" said one, bemused. "How can you be so sure, Axel?"

"I can just sense that the room is filled with the suffocating influence of Saturn, Dr Mohini. Believe me, telescopes really do suck at the stars like leeches, funnelling their rays, visible and invisible, down into the whirling focus of their lenses.

Whoever is prepared, as I have been for a long time now, to wake through the night, can learn to detect and to distinguish the fine and imperceptible breath of each star, to note its ebb and flow, and how it can silently insinuate itself into our brains, filling them with changeling intentions; will feel these treacherous forces wrestling in enmity with one another as they seek to command our ship of fortune... He will learn, too, to dream while awake, and to observe how at certain times of the night the soulless shades of dead planets come sliding into the realm of visibility, eager for life, exchanging mysterious confidences among themselves by means of strangely tentative gestures, instilling an uncertain and indefinable horror into our souls...

But do turn the lights on – we may easily upset the instruments on the tables in the dark like this, and the Master has never allowed things to get out of place."

One of the companions found his way to the wall and felt for the switch, his fingertips brushing gently but audibly against the sides of the recess. Then suddenly it was light and the brassy yellow lustre of the telescopes and pendant metal shouted aloud across the emptiness.

The night sky, which until that moment had lain in yielding satin embrace with the window-panes, suddenly leaped away and hid its face far, far above in the icy wastes behind the stars.

"There is the big, round flask, Doctor," said Wijkander, "which I spoke to you about yesterday, and which the Master has been using for his latest experiment. And these two metal terminals here on the wall you see supply the alternating current, or Hertz Waves, to envelop the flask in an electric field.

You promised us, Doctor, to maintain absolute discretion about anything you might witness, and to give us the benefit of your wisdom and experience as a doctor in the mad-house, to whatever extent you can.

Now, when the Master comes up he will suppose himself to be unobserved, and will begin those procedures which I hinted at but cannot explain in more detail. Do you really think that you will be able to remain unaffected by his actions and simply by means of silent observation of his overall behaviour be able to tell us whether madness is altogether out of the question?

On the other hand will you be able to suppress your scientific prejudices so far as to concede, if necessary, that here is a state of mind unknown to you, the condition of high intoxication known as a Turya Trance – something indeed that science has never seen, but which is certainly not madness?

Will you have the courage openly to admit that, Doctor? You see, it is only our love for the Master and our desire to protect him from harm that has persuaded us to take the grave step of bringing you here and obliging you to witness events that perhaps have never been seen by the eye of an uninitiate."

Doctor Mohini considered. "I shall in all honesty do what I can, and be mindful of everything you told me and required of me yesterday, but when I think carefully about it all it puts my head in a spin – can there really be a whole branch of knowledge, a truly secret wisdom, which purports to have explored and conquered such an immeasurably vast field, of whose mere existence we haven't even heard?

You're speaking there not just about magic, black and white, but making mention also of the secrets of a hidden green realm, and of the invisible inhabitants of a violet world!

You yourself, you say, are engaged in violet magic, – you say that you belong to an ancient fraternity that has preserved its secrets and arcana since the dawn of prehistory.

And you speak of the 'soul' as of something proven! As if it is supposed to be some kind of fine substantive vortex, possessing a precise consciousness!

And not only that – your Master is supposed to have trapped such a soul in that glass jar there, by wrapping it round with your Hertzian oscillation?!

I can't help it, but I find the whole thing, God knows, pure..."

Axel Wijkander pushed his chair impatiently aside and strode across to the great telescope, where he applied his eye peevishly to the lens.

"But what more can we say, Dr Mohini?" responded one of the friends at last, with some hesitation. "It *is* like that: the Master *did* keep a human soul isolated in the flask for a long time; he managed to strip off its constricting layers one at a time, like peeling the skins off an onion, so as to refine its powers, until one day it managed to seep through the glass past the electric field, and escaped

At that moment the speaker was interrupted by a loud exclamation, and they all looked up in surprise.

Wijkander gasped for breath: "A ring – a *jagged* ring, whitish, with holes in it – it's unbelievable, unheard of!" he cried,

"A new ring of Saturn has appeared!"

One after another they looked in the glass with amazement.

Dr Mohini was not an astronomer, and knew neither how to interpret nor to assess the immense significance of such a phenomenon: the formation of a new ring around Saturn. He had scarcely begun to ask his questions when a heavy tread made itself heard ascending the spiral stair.

"For Heaven's sake, get to your places, – turn the light out, the Master's coming!" ordered Wijkander urgently, "and you, doctor, stay in that alcove, whatever happens, do you hear? If the Master sees you, it's all up!"

A moment later the Observatory was once more dark and silent.

The steps came nearer and nearer, and a figure dressed in a white silk robe appeared and lit a tiny lamp. A bright little circle of light illuminated the table.

"It breaks my heart," whispered Wijkander to his neighbour. "Poor, poor Master. See how his face is twisted with sorrow!"

The old man made his way to the telescope where, having applied his eye to the glass, he stood, gazing intently. After a long interval he withdrew and shuffled unsteadily back to the table like a broken man.

"It's getting bigger by the hour!" he groaned, burying his face in his hands in his anguish. "And now it's growing points: this is frightful!"

Thus he sat for what seemed an age, whilst his followers wept silently in their hiding-places.

Finally he roused himself, and with a movement of sudden decision got up and rolled the flask closer to the telescope. Beside it he placed three objects, whose precise nature it was impossible to define.

Then he kneeled stiffly in the middle of the room, and started to twist and turn, using his arms and torso, into all sorts of odd contorted shapes resembling geometrical figures and angles, while at the same time he started mumbling in a monotone, the most distinguishing feature of which was an occasional long-drawn-out wailing sound.

"Almighty God, have pity on his soul – it's the conjuration

of Typhon," gasped Wijkander in a horrified whisper. "He's trying to force the escaped soul back from outer space. If he fails, it's suicide; come brothers, when I give the sign it's time to act. And hold on tight to your hearts – even the proximity of Typhon will burst your heart-ventricles!"

The adept was still on his knees, immobile, while the sounds grew ever louder and more plaintive.

The little flame on the table grew dull and began to smoke, glimmering through the room like a burning eye, and it seemed as if its light as it flickered almost imperceptibly was taking on a greenish-violet hue.

The magician ceased his muttering; only the long wails continued at regular intervals, enough to freeze the very marrow of one's bones. There was not a sound else. Silence, fearful and portentous, like the gnawing anguish of death.

A change in the atmosphere became apparent, as if everything all round had collapsed into ashes, as if the whole room were hurtling downwards, but in an indefinable direction, ever deeper, down into the suffocating realm of the past.

Then suddenly there is an interruption: a sequence of slithery slapping sounds, as some invisible thing, dripping wet, patters muddily with short, quick steps across the room. Flat shapes of hands, shimmering with a violet glow, materialise on the floor, slipping uncertainly to and fro, searching for something, attempting to raise themselves out of their two-dimensional existence, to embody themselves, before flopping back, exhausted. Pale, shadowy beings, dreadful decerebrated remnants of the dead have detached themselves from the walls and slide about, mindless, purposeless, half conscious and with the stumbling, halting gait of idiotic cripples. They puff their cheeks out with manic, vacant grins – slowly, very slowly and furtively, as if trying to conceal some inexplicable but deadly purpose, or stare craftily into space before lunging forwards in a sudden movement, like snakes.

Bloated bodies come floating silently down from the ceiling and then uncoil and crawl away – these are the horrible white spider-forms that inhabit the spheres of suicides and which with mutilated cross-shapes spin the web of the past which grows unceasingly from hour to each succeeding hour.

An icy fear sweeps across the room – the intangible that lies beyond all thought and comprehension, the choking fear of death that has lost its root and origin and no longer rests on any cause, the formless mother of horror.

A dull thud echoes across the floor as Dr Mohini falls dead. His face has been twisted round back to front; his mouth gapes wide open. Wijkander yells again: "Keep a tight hold on your hearts, Typhon is..." as all at once a cacophony of events erupts.

The great flask shatters into a thousand misshapen shards, and the walls begin to glow with an eerie phosphorescent light. Around the edges of the skylights and in the window-niches an odd form of decomposition has set in, converting the hard stone into a bloated, spongy mass, like the flesh of bloodless, decayed and toothless gums, and licking across the walls and ceilings with the rapidity of a spreading flame.

The adept staggers to his feet, and in his confusion has seized a sacrificial knife, plunging it into his chest. His acolytes manage to stay his hand, but the damage is done: the deep wound gapes open and life trickles away – they cannot close it up again.

The brilliance of the electric lights has once again taken possession of the circular compass of the Observatory: the spiders, the shadows and the corruption have vanished.

But the flask remains in shattered pieces, there are obvious scorch marks on the floor, and the Master still lies bleeding to death on a mat. They have sought in vain for the knife. Beneath the telescope, limbs contorted, lies the body of Mohini, chest down. His face, twisted upwards, grins grotesquely at the roof reflecting all the horror of death.

The disciples gather round the spot where the Master rests. He gently brushes aside their pleas to stay quiet: "Let me speak, and do not grieve. No-one can save me now, and my soul longs to complete that which was impossible while it was trapped in my corporeal state.

Did you not see how the breath of corruption has touched this building? Another instant, and it would have become substance, as a fog solidifies into hoar-frost, and the whole Observatory and everything in it would have turned to mould and dust.

Those burns there on the floor were caused by the denizens of the abyss, swollen with hate, desperately trying to reach my soul. And just as these marks you can see are burned into the wood and stone, their other actions would have become visible and permanent if you had not intervened so bravely.

For everything on earth that is, as the fools would have it, 'permanent' was once no more than mere shadow – a ghost, visible or invisible, and is now still nothing more than a *solidified* ghost.

For that reason, everything, be it beautiful or ugly, sublime, good or evil, serene though with death in its heart or alternatively, sad though harbouring secret happiness – all these things have something spectral about them.

It may be only a few who have the gift of detecting the ghostly quality of the world: it is there nevertheless, eternal and unchanging.

Now, it is a basic doctrine of our brotherhood that we should try to scale the precipitous cliffs of life in order to reach that pinnacle where the Great Magician stands with all his mirrors, conjuring up the whole world below out of deceptive reflections.

See, I have wrestled to achieve ultimate wisdom; I have sought out some human existence or other, to kill it in order to examine its soul. I wished to sacrifice some truly useless individual, so I went about among the people, men and women, thinking that such a one would be simple to find.

With the joyous expectation of certainty I visited lawyers, doctors, soldiers – I nearly found one in the ranks of schoolteachers – so very nearly!

But it was always only nearly – there was always some little mark, some tiny secret sign on them, which forced me to loosen my grip.

Then came a moment when at last I found what I was looking for. But it was not an individual: it was a whole group.

It was like uncovering an army of woodlice, sheltering underneath an old pot in the cellar.

Clergywives!

The very thing!

I spied on a whole gaggle of clergywives, watching them as they busied themselves at their 'good works', holding meetings in support of 'education for the benighted classes' or knitting horrible warm stockings and protestant cotton gloves to aid the modesty of poor little piccaninnies, who might otherwise enjoy their God-given nakedness. And then just think how they pester us with their exhortations to save bottle-tops, old corks, paper, bent nails and that sort of rubbish – 'waste not, want not'!

And then when I saw that they were about to hatch out new schemes for yet more missionary societies, and to water down the mysteries of the scriptures with the scourings of their 'moral' sewage, the cup of my fury ran over at last.

One of them, a real flax-blonde 'German' thing – in fact a genuine outgrowth of the rural Slavonic underbrush – was all ready for the chop when I realised that she was – – 'great with child' – and Moses' old law obliged me to desist.

I caught another one – ten more – a hundred – and every one of them was in the same interesting condition!

So then I put myself on the alert day and night, always ready to pounce, and at last I managed to lay my hands on one just at the right moment as she was coming out of the maternity ward.

A real silky Saxon pussy that was, with great big blue goose-eyes.

I kept her locked up for another nine months, to be on the safe side, just in case there was anything more to come in the way of parthenogenesis or budding, such as you get with deep-sea molluscs for instance.

In those moments of her captivity when I was not directly watching her she wrote a great thick book: *Fond Thoughts for our German Daughters on the Occasion of their Reception into Adulthood.* But I managed to intercept it in time and incinerate it in the oxy-hydrogen compressor.

I had at last succeeded in separating soul from body, and secured it in the flask, but my suspicions were aroused one day when I noticed an odd smell of goat's milk, and before I was able to readjust the Hertz Oscillator which had obviously stopped working for a few moments, the catastrophe had occurred and my *anima pastoris* had irrevocably escaped.

I had immediate resort to the most powerful means of luring it back: I hung a pair of pink flannel knickers (Llama Brand) out on the window-sill, alongside an ivory backscratcher and a volume of poetry bound in cyanide-blue and embellished on the cover with golden knobs, but it was all in vain!

I had recourse to the laws of occult telenergy – again it was to no avail!

A distilled soul is hardly likely to allow itself to get caught! And now it's floating freely about in space, teaching the innocent souls of other planets the infernal secrets of female handicrafts: I found today that it had even managed *to crochet a new ring round Saturn.*

That really was the last straw. I thought things through, and cudgelled my brain for a solution until I came up with two possibilities: either to use deliberate provocation, as in the case of Scylla, or to act in an opposite sense, like Charybdis.

You are familiar with that brilliant statement by the great Johannes Müller: 'When the retina of the eye is stimulated by light, pressure, heat, electricity or any other irritation, the corresponding sensations are not specifically those of light, pressure, heat, electricity etc., but merely sensations of *sight*; and when the skin is illuminated, pressed, bombarded with sound or electrified, only *feeling* and its concomitants are generated.'

This irrefutable law holds here too – for if you apply a stimulus to the clergywife's essential nucleus, no matter by what means, it *will start crocheting*; if however it is left undisturbed" – and here the Master's tones grew faint and hollow – "it *merely reproduces.*"

And with these words he sank back, lifeless.

Axel Wijkander clasped his hands together, deeply moved. "Let us pray, brothers. He has passed on, on to the tranquil realm. May his soul rest in peace and joy for ever!"

The First Hour after Death

Max Brod

The odd little incident occurred as the Minister, Baron von Klumm, was leaving the Palace of the House of Representatives at the head of a largish group of leading diplomats.

A frail man pushed his way through the ring of policemen and, in full view of everybody, ran very quickly, or rather bowled, up the steps and fell to his knees at the top, crying, "Baron Klumm, grant justice to our enemies and we will have peace!"

Baron von Klumm, not in the least put out, smiled his courteous smile and asked, "You are called ...?"

"Arthur Bruchfeß."

"And your profession?"

The man flicked a lock of blond hair, that had fallen into his face as he ran, back from his forehead, "Chimney sweep."

"My dear Herr Bruchfeß, if you were to grant justice to your chimneys, do you think they would blacken you any the less?"

By this time five, eight, fifteen policeman had run up panting and laid hold of the petitioner, who was looking bewildered.

Von Klumm had already moved on, surrounded by the throng of dignitaries, who gave a sigh of relief as they giggled belatedly at the Minister's witticism.

A gaunt, bronzed old man went up to him, followed by a crowd of eager faces. "A statement for the press?"

The Minister looked up and glanced round uncertainly for a moment.

The Head of the Secret Police had guessed what he was thinking. "Oh yes, Minister, everyone saw what happened and took note of it."

The Minister immediately began to dictate to the thin air: "Attacked by a mental defective; police on the spot; took necessary steps; would-be assassin taken to lunatic asylum; being examined by doctors; Minister carried out his duties as usual – omit my little joke, of course. And now, if you'll excuse me, Commissioner –"

"I don't know what I admire most about you", said Herr von Crudenius, the military attaché of an allied power, as they sped towards the embassy shortly afterwards in von Klumm's car, whilst the assembled populace broke into cheers. "You do make the choice difficult for your admirers. Is it the masterly rhetoric of your speech before the House of Representatives today, the ready wit of your riposte to the chimney sweep, or the remarkable tact with which you immediately suppressed the publication of your riposte."

"A matter of routine, my dear Crudenius, nothing more. Of course, not routine in the pejorative sense, with its connotations of a heartless lack of scruple. There is no point in my running myself down unnecessarily, not that I'm the most modest person in the country, anyway. What I mean is that it's something one learns, one becomes accustomed to, just as one becomes accustomed to everything. Nineteen-twentieths of our life consists of blind, unconscious habit."

"That is precisely what you said just now in Parliament, Baron Klumm. Your courage took my breath away. At the very beginning you forfeited the approval of the conservative-nationalist group by speaking out against any policy of national prestige, and at the end you threw down the gauntlet to the so-called progressive parties by your praise of the maintenance of traditional values."

"Not praise", interrupted von Klumm, whose intelligent features bore not the slightest trace of mental exhaustion, such as might have been expected after a strenuous five-hour session. "I praised nothing, I merely stated the facts; stated them, if you insist, with a certain regret. I have, as you are well aware, a fanatical love for objective facts and established truths. I feel responsible for the well-being of the Empire, responsible, in the fullest sense of the word, before my own conscience. As a responsible person, I must pursue a path of the most down-to-earth political realism, and I am a declared enemy of all ideologies, whether they come from the right or from the left, whether they rattle a jingoistic sword or wave an idealistic olive branch. To tell you the truth, my dear Crudenius, in my view it is people who hawk ideologies, utopias, irresponsible visions who are the worst, indeed, the only enemies of mankind,"

The attaché laughed. "And when you think of it, that is the kind of people you are dealing with all the time, my poor chap. That man on the steps, and all those 'men of the people' inside to whom you had to explain the true moral dignity of warfare: is it not, at bottom, always one and the same enemy you have to deal with? Woolly-headed idealism, getting everything the wrong way round, against sound common sense?"

"You are just the kind of person I could happily trust to write my biography", said the Minister, not without a hint of irony. "You know the way my mind works, so to speak. With one reservation, perhaps: I have no liking for your trade", and he pointed to the betasselled hilt of Crudenius' sabre. "Although today I said some things that might suggest I have, I said them because they had to be said. Nor do I have any liking for this war, that has lasted for twenty years already."

"But you said that people had become accustomed to it, provoking a storm of indignation from the Social Democrats."

"I said it because it is true, an undeniable fact. You have the proof: every year those very same socialists approve our war-credits without quibbling. But there's still a difference between being accustomed to something and liking it, isn't there? There are bad habits as well, and I have no compunction in describing this state of permanent warfare as Europe's bad habit. But who can seriously dispute the fact that we have managed to make war one of our so-called 'instinctive functions'? It is no surprise; most of the generation at present in positions of responsibility were mere schoolboys when the war began. We have grown up with war and will doubtless come to our ends before it does. Young people today have no idea what 'peace' means; they have never experienced it, it is a myth to them. Of course, strictly speaking, peace has never existed, and it is my firm conviction that it never will. All that we had was an absence of war, a state of mutual hostility and deep antipathy between the states, papered over by commercial hypocrisy and cleverly drawn-up treaties. This was very well portrayed at the time by a writer who was already mature when the war broke out and was therefore able to compare conditions both before and after from personal

experience; I am referring, of course, to Max Scheler, whom I
have had put on the school curriculum. According to him, the
difference between covert and open warfare, which merely
disclosed the hatred already existing, is not all that significant.
On that point I am in complete agreement with him. Otherwise
it would be impossible to explain why we endure it so well and
how we have managed to integrate it so completely into the
social fabric. It is just that war has always existed, since the
world began. War is the natural condition of mankind, only its
outward form changes. Just look around you, my dear Crudenius. Does this busy street, the crush outside the theatre, the
throng all round and inside the department stores look abnormal? After having overcome some initial disruption, which
appears child's play to us today, the economic machinery is in
perfect working order. Exports have vanished but the internal
market has developed. And with what success you can tell by
the unheard-of dividends our companies are yielding. The
material destruction is more than compensated for by the spur
to our native inventiveness and the exploitation of new raw
materials. We are approaching the ideal of a closed economy as
proclaimed by Fichte. The transformation of professional life
was as radical as it was smooth. Man is the warrior, woman is
trained for all kinds of civilian work, along with the old and
those unfit for service. Of course, there is no one who regrets
more than I do the fact that each year thousands of young men
must die defending our frontiers, but did no one ever die in the
so-called peace? We have put into effect many sensible
measures which people before the war considered a pipe-
dream: dynamic initiatives to encourage population growth, an
expanding network of state child-care, the abolition of mono-
gamy, programmed leave for soldiers for the purposes of rep-
roduction, land reform, detached houses, hostels for war-vete-
rans, garden towns, etcetera, etcetera. And the result of all this
is that the population is showing an even higher annual rate of
increase than ever before, and that the general level of health is
constantly rising. As a consequence of the drop in infant mor-
tality the number of deaths per year, including all military los-
ses, has even shown a decline, albeit a very small decline, in

absolute terms compared to the pre-war period. Those are statistical facts. Nowadays we are raising people, so to speak, whereas in earlier times the state – one cannot understand why – supported measures which were downright anti-people, such as the preservation of large estates and tax concessions to unhygienic production methods."

"But then how do you explain the general dissatisfaction? There is a rumble of discontent going round the world, dull but unmistakable, that finds expression in embarrassing scenes like that this afternoon."

"Being accustomed to something is not the same as being happy with it. Didn't I say that before? People have become used to the most dreadful conditions because they have no choice, but that does not mean they are happy with them. We have even become accustomed to death. Don't laugh; I'm serious. As a race, as the genus humanum, we have become indifferent to death. And yet when you think of it by yourself, as an individual, the thought of dying is terrible, unthinkable even, the notion that from a particular moment onward you will not feel, not think, not exist any more, not temporarily, but simply for all eternity. What will it be like inside our heads an hour after death? And five hundred thousand years after? What you must remember is that this horrifically long state of non-being is certain for each one of us, inescapable, not merely a nasty misfortune which we might avoid if we are lucky. It is this absolute, unconditional certitude of death which is the most horrible thing about the whole affair."

The young officer flushed with emotion. "I thank you, Baron Klumm. Oh, what a debt of gratitude I owe you, since you have befriended me in this alien city! You have made a human being of me. Without you I could not go on living."

"You have just become accustomed to me, my friend. Everything is a matter of habit."

"No. I love you. You are my only support", replied Crudenius passionately. "It was hard for me, harder than you can imagine, to be torn from my home, torn from my parents, whom I respect, from the company of my friends, and brought here to a court that is, let us be open about it, stiff and ceremonial and whose language I can hardly understand. You have often laughed at me for my sentimentality ..."

"Yes; and I still do today. The world is the same all over, the modern world, at least. Everywhere you will find sleeping-cars, bathrooms, underground railways, concrete, asphalt, jazz, the same elegant ladies' dresses, even the same perfumes. Modern man can find things that he is used to everywhere. Apart from latitude and longitude, I can see no difference at all between the great cities of today."

"But there must be between peoples, otherwise there wouldn't be this war."

The Minister twisted in his seat in mock horror. "Oh dear me! Is that the result of all the lectures on realism I have been giving you for the last few months? Have even you fallen for clichés such as the different character of the nations, the different genius of the races? If I have made any significant contribution, however modest, to history, it is in my protest against such suggestions. You must come to understand that the inevitability of war is based not on the differences between nations – which I allow, though in microscopic degrees that are of no account – but on the ineluctable similarity of all nations: because their needs for survival are identical, it is in their nature to compete for space, for the opportunity to develop. The simple truth is that like needs come into conflict, and will do so until the earth evolves several surfaces, one above the other like organ keyboards, until there are as many earths as there are nations. In the distant future every nation will require the whole of the earth's surface for itself. And that distant future will come all the more quickly, the better and stronger the nation is, the more powerful its development, the greater its sense of moral responsibility. And along comes some poor devil demanding vehemently that I should 'grant justice to our enemies'. I do, I do, and I always have. Do you imagine I approve of the dreadful, jingoistic, obscene language the popular press uses against our enemies? Of course, as a means of making sure the nation does not slacken in its efforts it is indispensable, just as mines and flame-throwers are indispensable, and one wouldn't describe those as particularly nice. But it really is naive to assume that we in the government actually think what we get the papers to write about 'barbarians' and 'hypocrites'. No, we are fair; we fully recognise the enemy's qualities, and the justice of their claims. But our fairness also leads us, without hatred or rancour, to a clear recognition of the fact that we have good qualities and justice on our side as well, that, as ill luck would have it, there is not one justice in the world, but two, several indeed; that our real, material interests (and they are what count, not some figments of the imagination) collide with the equally real material interests of the enemy, that the nations must fight because, and for as long as, they must breathe. It is just the same as a chimney: however fair and good-natured it is, it has no choice but to pour out soot. Are there really people so short-sighted that they cannot see that, cannot see the whole, real, irrefutable *tragedy of human existence*? I must also say that anyone who does not accept that is not a good Christian. As Luther says, the very clay from which we are formed is sinful. The essence of humanity is lust, original sin, and it seems very superficial to me to blame the wretched condition of mankind on transitory errors by the government, or on individuals' dishonesty, narrow-mindedness or megalomania, instead of on this darkness underlying all human life, even the most benevolent and best-intentioned. Let us look reality squarely in the face! The man of the church can renounce the whole world at one fell swoop, but that is not possible for the statesman, whose task it is to direct the worldly affairs of this world. He may desire to be just as good a Christian as the unworldly ascetic, but there is one thing he must be clear about: his policies can never be directed towards abolishing war, nor human suffering and misery in general, but only towards – what shall I call it? – improving the organisation of our misery. That is the most he can hope to achieve."

They had reached the ambassadorial palace. His companion took his leave. "I must say", was the Minister's final comment, "that it was precisely the war which taught me this true, this deadly earnest Christianity, this sublime religion of suffering. By the way, you're coming round after ten for bridge, aren't you? The fair Gabrielle will be there, and I've invited your Nannette as well."

In the Ministry there was a long queue of officials waiting to make their reports. After sessions in parliament, Baron von Klumm, whose industry and meticulous attention to detail were proverbial, used to make up for wasted time, as he put it, and at such times he would often work without rest until late into the night. So too on that evening there was a constant stream of advisers and clerks, telephone calls and dictation. A delegation from the annexed territories was admitted and presented their petitions and requests. The Minister made a note of a number of books and pamphlets which were mentioned in the course of the audience. Even though it was nine o'clock, he sent the messenger to the Ministry library and then, in the car on his way home, immersed himself in one of the recommended books, that dealt with the most abstruse financial and currency questions.

Gabrielle, a ballet dancer with the Court Opera, was already waiting with the other guests in the Baron's private residence; the whole company was charmed at her lack of inhibition in assuming the role of lady of the house. The company was decidedly mixed: actors who needed no encouragement to play their part in the entertainment by recounting more or less spicy anecdotes, a few provincial governors, wrapped up in their eternal hunting stories, two or three ironic conversationalists from the diplomatic corps and a Jewish writer, who was the first to get drunk, at which he indulged in revolutionary speeches, to the great amusement of the rest. Nannette, a cabaret singer who obviously came from the lower classes and had not yet been 'discovered', delighted the military attaché with her lively dialect, which he found bewitchingly natural, although each expression had to be transposed into the standard language, which he then, just for himself and ignored by the rest, translated into his own mother tongue and indulged in reminiscences of the fields and peasant girls of home. His diffidence, the result of this dawdle through the byways of sentimentality, was dispersed by a brisk observation from the Minister, and the cards soothed all passions. Gabrielle, for whom there was always a suite of rooms ready in the villa, had long since retired to bed when the last guests, supported by sleepy lackeys, crunched their way over smashed champagne glasses to the door.

Baron von Klumm had his valet make a cold compress for his forehead. He intended to do a little more work before going to Gabrielle. Throughout the dinner his mind had been occupied with ideas suggested by the book on economics; it was one of his major characteristics anyway, always to be brim-full of important matters, even in the midst of shallow entertainment. He sat down at his desk. As was appropriate for a genuine bachelor residence, his study was spacious and centrally positioned. It was more of a hall than a room and with its four windows took up most of the first floor façade. Its three high walls, covered from floor to ceiling with books and files, disappeared into the darkness, and from the windows, through which came the howl of the night wind, the snow-covered, moonlit range of nearby mountains could be seen.

"You've let some snow in, Peter". The baron pointed to a lumpy, shining white patch on the parquet floor.

His servant gave an uncomprehending shrug of the shoulders, tugged at the window handles to show that they were all shut, then quickly produced a rag and gave the floor a wipe at the place the Baron was still indicating with his finger, though with the hurt expression of one who has been given an eccentrically elaborate task and is only doing it out of good will.

Then he left.

The Minister began to read, but was soon disturbed by a soft, crunching noise. Was he still treading on broken glass? He looked up. To his great astonishment the white patch in the room, which, moreover, lay beyond the strip of moonlight in the shadow of a cupboard, had grown into a regular mound, indeed, it was still rising visibly, like a mushroom sprouting unnaturally quickly. No, that wasn't a patch of snow, it was moving. Suddenly he recognised it. It was a human head.

It took a mere second for the Baron to recover his composure, seize the revolver he always carried with him and fire a shot at the head. 'I didn't realise there were trapdoors in the house.' He fired again. Six shots, then the revolver was empty.

The shots obviously missed the head, but produced a different, quite unexpected effect.

"Ah, that's it", cried an ungainly voice, thick with phlegm

and half asleep, and with one jerk the whole, very long form of the apparition, like a tautly inflated gas balloon, floated up into the room all at once but, remarkably, without causing any further damage to the floor. It was an imposing, white-haired old gentleman who rose before the Minister, his eyes closed and his arms pressed against his sides. The liberating force suddenly seemed to weaken, so that the feet and calves of the strange being remained below floor level, without this fact particularly disconcerting either the being itself or its audience.

Beneath his cold compress the Baron's hair was trying to stand on end. He fell back into his armchair; all strength, indeed all sensation, had drained from his legs so that he felt as if he had an iron hoop round his hips, pinning him in a sitting, or half-lying position, incapable of moving a muscle. However, he was not the man to take a ghostly apparition, or, more likely, some silly practical joke, lying down. He automatically sought for a conversational opening, but the only thing to cross his lips was a small amount of spittle followed by a gurgling and babbling, not unlike a baby's first attempts at articulation. Finally he managed to produce some recognisable sounds, "Your name is ...?"

The apparition had opened its eyes by now, beautiful big brown eyes, not at all eerie, and was looking down with a quiet, friendly expression in the approximate direction of the Minister's struggles. As was his habit, the Minister returned its look with a firm, severe gaze, in spite of his helpless position, stretched out in the chair, his upper body lying between the arms, rumpled and disjointed, as if it had been thrown out on the dung-heap. "You name is ...?" he repeated, his voice steadier now, and tried to regain control over his limbs by blinking vigorously. Eventually he realised the pointlessness of the exercise and lay there quite still, since he was afraid of looking silly in front of the ghost. All the time his brain had been working furiously and had come to the conclusion that he was dealing with a genuine ghost, and not just a hoax. The size of the apparition alone suggested that. It was more that twice the height of a normal human and thus much taller even than the usual giants one sees exhibited; for all that it was perfectly proportioned, thus lacking the coarse, freakish quality which makes the fairground monstrosities seem so sinister. The only sinister thing here was that this strange figure, as if to compensate for its size, appeared to be made of some strangely loose material, through which the windows behind it could be seen and even the dull gleam of the moonlight reflected on the distant mountain ridge. A remarkable sight which, as von Klumm observed with scientific precision, could not have been produced by any kind of trickery. However, the most inexplicable fact about it was that the figure slowly and gradually began to shrink, to condense, so that the texture became firmer and firmer, without, however, distorting its outline or features in the least. Everything about it simply became more delicate, more familiar, more human, so to speak. It was now plain to see that the phantom was not at all interested in frightening anybody. On the contrary, it gave the impression (perhaps a delusion, perhaps an accurate observation of the Baron's returning senses) that it wanted to gain the Minister's confidence; indeed, it was not long before he was confronted with the incredible sight of a ghost that was most afraid of itself, that would have preferred to have cowered timidly in a corner so as not to cause any fuss, but was unfortunately fixed to the spot, to its great embarrassment and confusion.

The Minister pulled himself together and forced himself to sit upright. The first thing he did was to remove the cold compress, which he felt somewhat spoilt the tone of a private audience. Then he said, quite cool-headed once more, "But you must tell me your name, your name."

"Name", repeated the ghost, as if it were making a great effort to work something out. "Name ... name ... what is that now: name?" Its voice was not sleepy any more, but clear and high, only with a little too much vibrato to come from human vocal chords. It had an unmistakable note of great shyness and humility.

The Baron looked up at the figure again, scrutinising it from head to toe, or rather, to knee, since parts of its lower extremities were still below floor level. Again there was a pause, which the Baron used to settle himself more comfortably in his chair, whilst the apparition seemed to realise for the first time that it had arms; at least it now looked down at them in astonishment and detached them, hesitantly, incredulously, from its sides, lifted them a little and then let them fall back down again. As it did so, the movement of its head, which was the first it had made, seemed to fill it with amazement, even terror, for the expression on its face became more anxious by the second, and after these experiments in movement the rigidity of its contours became even firmer for the next few minutes.

When occasion demanded, the Baron could be 'quite tart' as his close colleagues called it. An occasion for his tartness had arrived. As if to compensate himself for the fright, which he had only just managed to overcome, he barked at his visitor, "Damn it all, man, you must know who you are, what you're called, why you're here and how you got in here at all!"

At the sound of these harsh words the apparition summoned up all its energy. An old man knitting his white eyebrows as he desperately tries to remember something – that was more or less what the apparition looked like. But all he managed to do was to twitter, "I think I must have just died into here."

"'Died into here?' What on earth is that?"

Another pause.

"Come on, man, I asked you a question; what is that?"

"If only I knew, sir", replied the old man. "Do have pity on me. I have only just died, a little while ago, and I committed so many sins. How should I know where I am? I'm all of a daze. It's not easy, believe me." And after these few sentences, the first coherent things he had said, he closed his eyes again, as if exhausted from so much exertion.

"Remarkable", said the Baron, "strange. Hmmm ... Never heard anything like it." As if seeking help, he felt around with his hand and grasped the shade of his desk-lamp. The contact seemed to give him an idea. Holding on to the lampshade for support, he twisted round in his chair until he was in the bright light of the standard lamp, thus for the first time removing the ghost from his sight. Suddenly he began to rummage desperately among the piles of papers and books: they contained his normal, everyday work, his usual thoughts and ideas. He tried to cling to the individual words and figures he read, to fasten on to them, but they went blurred before his feverish eyes, he could not decipher anything at all. However, after a while he thought he had come sufficiently back to his senses to risk a glance into the room behind him. He took it slowly as he returned to his former position. There was the room, melting into endless darkness, of which the electric lamp only illuminated his immediate surroundings, not much farther than his feet. And right in front of him was that bean-pole again who – it was grotesque – had not used the interval to arrange himself in a comfortable position, but was still standing there, stiff and in deadly earnest, apparently waiting, in complete oblivion of everything else, for the Minister's reply.

"Now, you tell me ... You say you have died ... And yet you're alive ... What is that supposed to mean? Can't you express yourself a little more rationally? Have you really died or are you here?"

"I died into here ... because of my sins."

The Baron shook his head. "Because of your sins? You've said that already. What kind of sins? You're a murderer, aren't you?"

A violent shudder of loathing passed through the ghost's body; it shook itself thoroughly then, still somewhat clumsily but with emphatic vigour, raised its arms and even clasped its hands above its head, as it cried out piteously, "A murderer!? Me, a murderer!? No, the Lord be praised, I kept well away from that all my life. However painstakingly I examine my heart, as it was and as it now is, I cannot find the slightest trace of murderous thoughts."

"So you must have been a thief, an embezzler, a black-marketeer, a swindler, or at least dishonest in some way, mustn't you?"

"Dishonest, yes, that might be it. I did not always bear the eternal truth of things in mind everywhere I went and everything I did, although I kept on making a firm resolution to do so."

"And that was the sum total of your dishonesty?" The Baron burst out laughing.

"Oh, it was a sin, the very worst sin of all! That is why my punishment is this dreadful transfer to another world, that is why my death did not lead to promotion to a higher sphere, but this terrible exile in a parallel, if not lower stage of development."

"Incredible. So you still insist that you are dead?"

"Of course. What I am going through at this moment is the thing men should stand most in fear of, or rather, since it is a sign of divine justice, most in awe of: I am going through the first hour after my death."

"That must be terribly interesting", the words had passed the Baron's lips before he had time to think about them. "That is ... I mean ... Wouldn't you like to sit down? You must tell me more about it. What is it like, this first hour after death? You must realise that I have often spent an idle moment thinking about it, or rather, trying to visualise what it must be like. Unfortunately I am always very busy. But sometimes, you know, between important matters of state, such abstruse ideas do occur to one; I feel I must call them abstruse, for how can a living person know or imagine with any degree of accuracy what will happen inside him after his death. It's a downright impossibility, an absurdity. Now, I feel I must preface my remarks by saying how close this matter has always been to my heart, I have kept it constantly under review ..." As he warmed to his subject he automatically began to use the elegant phrases with which he had been fobbing off petitioners and deputations for years, showing just how much this conversation had lost its bizarre and phantom character for him, how much he was beginning to regard it as a normal conversation and not at all eerie. "To put it in a nutshell, I imagine in that first hour that everything, if that is the right word, around one will be quite dark and empty and desolate. Nothingness, do you understand, nothingness in the most precise meaning of the word. That's how I imagine it. Of course, I wouldn't dream of putting my experience on a par with yours, or even of comparing it. You must forgive me for going on like this. I would much rather listen to what you have to say than to go blethering on myself. There, I'm all ears. But please, do sit down, over here ..."

The ghost had let its eyes wander round the room with a rather bewildered air, but now they focused on the leather armchair the

Minister was drawing up. It seemed to have understood the words, for it sat down obediently, and as quickly as the fact that its feet were still stuck in the floor would allow; it did, however, reveal a certain lack of familiarity in the use of seating as it flopped down across both armrests at once. But it would anyway have had difficulty in squeezing itself into the wide seat of the chair, since it was still of gigantic proportions.

"Off you go then, tell me something about this paradise that the preachers claim to be so well acquainted with."

"Paradise!" replied the ghost with a sigh. "How should a miserable wretch like myself be able to tell you anything about paradise. I might enter there after a billion years, perhaps never."

"Tell me about hell then, if you like", countered the Minister with a casual wave of the hand, as if he were making conversation.

"Well, unless I am very much mistaken, I do seem to have escaped hell", replied the apparition, with a not very confident glance round the room; but it seemed to feel that even that glance was presumptuous and immediately corrected itself with quiet modesty. "Anyway, you must not think it is something special. The extremes, that is complete redemption and complete damnation, are probably, at least that is my assumption, just as exceptional in eternity as in our mortal existence. The middle ground, with its thousand shades of grey, is much the commoner. Although I am not entirely sure about it, a plot of that middle ground seems to be my lot as well."

"To my mind nothingness, the absolute nothingness that follows death, would be hell enough."

"Nothingness?"

"Yes, the nothingness I spoke about before, the disappearance of all sensation, of all desire and joy and sorrow."

"I'm very sorry, but I can't have understood you properly before. You must be patient with me. I'm doing my best, but I've been so confused, so dazed by all the new things around me, that I find it difficult to follow you, in spite of all your kindness. Nothingness after death, you said? I should have contradicted you straight away there. It's the precise opposite, in fact. After death one is assailed by a wealth of fresh and unsuspected impressions. It takes a great effort to fend them off ..."

"New impressions ... at the moment of death?"

"Not precisely at the moment of death. That is accompanied by a brief instant of diminished consciousness, during which you feel nothing apart from a violent tearing, the previously unknown, quite strong but brief sensation of the soul detaching itself from the body, a tug, of which it is impossible for me to say whether it is closer to pain or pleasure. However, as I said, it only lasts for a fraction of a second, then the soul is free of physical matter, completely pure and unhampered. But that is just what is the most strenuous thing about it. How can I describe it? We spend all our days trying to saturate our physical being – which, let's be honest about it, is the main focus of our existence – with mental, emotional and spiritual life, which we extract for our own use from the streams of life flowing all around us. Suddenly our soul is free, is what you might call a non-material cavity, a vacuum, a bubble surrounded by matter. But matter, which is accustomed to feeding on spiritual life, to drinking its fill, so to speak, naturally falls on the cavity from all sides, wild with desire, and tries to penetrate it. All types of substantiality, even those of the lowest forms of life, would like to take possession of the liberated soul, to feed on it and fatten themselves up. Those first minutes are terrible. I must say that I came through it quite well, I kept a tight hold on my tiny bundle of soul. But there are many souls that are ripped apart in those first moments of their new life, simply torn to shreds. It gives me the shivers to imagine the suffering a soul that has been reduced to atoms like that must go through: in spite of everything, they retain their awareness of the self as a unity, whilst at the same time having to continue a physical existence as an earthworm, a leaf, and perhaps a few bacteria on it that are devouring each other. I assume it is this condition which people call hell."

"Could be, could well be", interrupted the Baron with the smile he reserved for opponents he had caught out. "The only thing that puzzles me, however, is where you get all this precise information not only about your own destiny but about that of other souls into the bargain? Without wanting to offend you, you are aware, aren't you, that with all this you are treading on ground which is wide open to all kinds of fantasies and delusions, especially self-delusions? Have you searched your heart enough in this regard? Are you completely sure that a little .. I won't say lie ... that a little exaggeration or distortion of the truth is quite out of the question?"

The old man was not offended. On the contrary, he seemed grateful for any admonition and, after having achieved a relatively calm tone in his last speech, now reverted to his initial abject contrition, "Oh, you are right, you are so right. Obviously you are ordained to be the judge before whom I have to justify myself, no, not justify, before whom I am to confess my sins. Yes, it is true, I certainly have not truly searched my soul, nor have I guarded against vain self-delusion sufficiently, although that was my firm intention. My insight, if I might be allowed to use that word for the wretched sum of my life, was just sufficient for me to survive the first test after my death, the attack of physical matter. At that moment I was endowed with a truly remarkable clarity of vision which allowed me to see not only what was happening to me but to all the other newly dead around me. I saw terrible things in only a few minutes and had a clear premonition of some even more terrible. Moreover, in spite of my desperate defence, I did not succeed in remaining completely pure myself. I see I have all kinds of alien matter stuck to me that should have nothing in common with immortal substances." As he spoke these words, he fingered his coat buttons sadly and pulled the jacket he was wearing tight across his stomach with a gesture that showed that he found the article of clothing incomprehensible, that he thought it was perhaps a part of the body.

"Don't worry, there's something grotesque about all clothing", the Minister graciously comforted him.

"Clothing you call it ... Ah, now I understand. Though our clothing was quite different. In the Sylphian sphere, where I come from, clothing consists of a certain very high velocity at which individuals spin round their own axes like tops."

"So you are a Sylph, a Sylphide." A vague memory of the fair

Gabrielle and her Dance of the Sylphides in the last ballet floated through the Baron's mind. "Though our image of Syplhs does not quite correspond to your figure, I'm afraid."

"They are quite different, that is true, and their mode of life is quite different from mine at this moment. At the moment I am in the middle of a transfer to your world; I'm in a half-way house, so to speak, and doing my best to behave as a human being. That is the second trial I have to go through: you suddenly find yourself in a completely different world with completely new standards. You shed all your habits, all the things you did as a matter of routine, and that is the acid test which shows how much real reality, reality that is valid for any possible world, you have managed to acquire in the course of your life ..."

"So you're not a dead human being at all, but from another world?" asked the Baron, leaning back in his chair, somewhat bewildered again.

"I have died into this world from another one", repeated the ghost patiently.

"From the moon, maybe, or from Sirius?"

"No. As I said before, I come from a completely different world system."

"From the Milky Way or the Orion Nebula?"

"However far you go in your physical world, you will not find my home. My home is a realm of different senses, or rather, it was so until today, and I still belong there a little. We Sylphs do not see, we do not hear or smell, nor are we heard or seen. We have different organs, are subject to a different gravity and different natural laws. As far as space is concerned, we live amongst you humans. There just happens to be an infinite number of worlds, but they are interlocking rather than running parallel, and despite their contiguity they know nothing of each other. Until this moment your world, with its starry sky and Milky Way and everything your senses perceive, was completely hidden from me as well. I am absolutely amazed to find myself in such an unsuspected, novel environment without moving from the spot, merely by means of an inner conversion of my organs."

"Wait a moment, not so fast! I need to digest that first", cried von Klumm, pressing his hand against his forehead, which was once more throbbing painfully. "Everything here is quite new to you? ... Well, I must say ... assuming all these things you have been telling me are correct ... I must say you show commendable good manners and self-assurance. Many people have sat there, where you are sitting now, and been so embarrassed they didn't know what to do with themselves. Perhaps I should tell you that I am – I can say this without being presumptuous – a man of some influence, and strangely enough people say of me – I have really no idea how I have acquired this reputation – that there is something imposing about my personality, so that even the boldest or most impudent citizens find it difficult to preserve their *sang-froid* when face to face with me."

At this the ghost, who up to that point had been following the conversation just as intently as the Minister, gave the first sign of boredom, a rather clear sign in fact, as it fixed its eyes on the window and began to look at the landscape outside with visible enjoyment, craning its neck and even half rising from its chair.

The Minister was too polite to notice it.

"What beautiful mountains", said the ghost, and its breast heaved with a sigh of longing.

"So you recognise our earthly mountains as well", said the Minister in a tone of coolly polite commendation. "I must compliment you on your capacity for rapid orientation. Are there things like mountains in your world too?"

"No. At home everything manifests itself – or rather, everything manifested itself – in electric waves, spinning funnels of air and whirlpools."

"And yet ..."

"In our kind of matter there is also natural beauty, sublime expressions of eternal forces, of growth and decay. It is probably because during my whole life, whenever I managed to get out and enjoy nature, which was rarely enough with my awful job – indeed, it was probably precisely the fact that it was so unusual that gave me a thirst for the glories of nature and a true delight in them – but whenever I did commune with nature, it automatically aroused in me the feeling that the joy I felt brought me into contact with eternal, general truths, with the bedrock of reality; and that is probably what enables me to respond so quickly to any kind of natural beauty, even in this new world, and to sense immediately whenever I am in the presence of anything significant in that respect here as well."

"Most strange. To tell you the truth, I couldn't match you in that. If I came from a place where the Alps consisted of nothing but whirling airpools ... that's what you said, wasn't it? ... of nothing but soap bubbles, with no rocks, no snow, no plants, no colours ... of course, without colours ... well, I must say, if I were confronted with real mountains I would be totally baffled, totally ..." The Baron fell into a brown study from which he eventually came to with a start. "In a word, I would be baffled."

"I think you are mocking me", moaned the ghost. "Am I not sufficiently baffled or confused? It is only with nature that I feel I know where I am."

"Not at all; there are other areas where you seem surprisingly sure of yourself. Even, it seems to me, the most important ones. You have a precise idea – let me be honest, an unnaturally precise idea – of where you come from and where you are going."

"But sir, I don't know, I don't know at all."

Then Baron refused to be distracted, "You are even aware of the fact that you are at a transitional stage. You have some idea of the trials that await you, of a court of judgment that you must face and of the good works you can cite in evidence before the court. Added to that, you have, remarkably, no difficulty at all with our language or our concepts in this rather complex field. You talk like a book, you talk of eternal justice as if you were related, you talk of God, and death, and hell, and the Devil knows what else ..." The Baron had worked himself up into a rage and was pacing up and down the room.

"Yes ... well ... fortunately I took something of an interest in that kind of thing during my lifetime", said the spectre, very timidly, "even if it was nowhere like enough. Not that I really understood them, but I felt a certain yearning that kept drawing me back to them; and there, too, I had the feeling that I was dealing with the foundation of reality that was valid for all places and all times ... Unfortunately it meant that I neglected other things, and I'm paying dearly for that now ..."

"Come on then", said the Baron impatiently, as the ghost paused. "That is just what I would like to hear about. What is it that you are paying for now? What was your sin?"

"I was ... I was ..." he stuttered with the shame of it, "how shall I put it, I was very clumsy about minor details. That is, I thought they were minor details, but now I see that they have their own significance and even, if you take proper care over them, contain a grain of reality which one should respect. Now is the time I need them. That is the special rule that governs us in this first hour after our death. Action and reaction are completely reversed. All the things which during our mortal lives we regarded with respect, awe and wonder are now familiar to us. But the things we treated casually, that we debased to matters of soul-less routine, appear alien and incomprehensible to us here. That is why I am having such problems with ..." again he broke off, "with my clothes. To be honest, I neglected them badly. Matters of polite behaviour I never understood at all. I looked down on them with a certain arrogance and, because of my interest in higher things, I even believed my arrogance was justified. Now I'm being punished for it. I'm sure even etiquette – civilised behaviour between creatures, moderation, keeping your distance – contains something of universal value, is part of God's design. It could be that keeping your distance is exaggerated, that it contains a grain of truth and a large amount of deception. But it was my duty to find that grain of truth; however crude the deception that concealed it, it was not a sufficient excuse for letting myself be put off by the wrapping. My punishment is that now I am totally at a loss as to how to behave. Just imagine how embarrassing it is for me that I still can't work out what form you take. I can't see you at all. I think that your voice comes from that beautiful, radiant body", he pointed to the desk-lamp behind the Baron, who at these words, perhaps for the first time in his life, felt small and insignificant, though the only effect it had was to intensify his rage, "and I take the light for the centre of the personality I am conversing with. But unfortunately, beyond that I can find no shape distinguishable from the sur-roundings. And I can't work out what to do with my own body, however hard I try to adapt to my new world. One moment I seem to wrinkle up, the next I feel as if I'm spreading in all directions. I feel uncomfortable in every pore. Believe me I have no spatial orientation at all, everything is reeling through my head in a most dizzying manner. I can't find the right level for my movements. I see everything lop-sided."

"Yes, I realise that now", said von Klumm with a mocking laugh.

"Only now do I realise how right a friend of mine was who kept telling me about his homesickness. He had only come from another city, not from another world, but he kept on complaining how alien he felt, as if it were a punishment even. An aspect of his life which at home had been concealed beneath a blanket of agreeable habits in the close-knit, almost bodily warmth of the family circle was stripped bare here: a certain inner emptiness and meaninglessness."

"That is just what the Military Attaché was saying today", murmured the Baron, and his suspicion intensified.

"If", the apparition continued unperturbed, "you spend your life under the delusion of constant activity, if you are always industrious and ambitious, concentrate on the so-called 'serious' things, which mostly concern just the bare – and banal – essentials, and waste your leisure on 'unserious' things which are just as unreal as the 'serious' ones ... in brief, if all you can see is dreary routine and necessity, never the liberating, absolute truth ..."

"That's going too far", the Baron shouted, striding over to the spectre with clenched fists, "now you're talking about me!"

"No, about my friend", screamed the apparition, pulling its upper body back as far as it could.

"Hah! So he could not see absolute truth anywhere? Listen, I take my hat off to him; he is a grand fellow, your friend, he's just my man. That's the way I am too. The bare facts of life I recognise; some things are more expedient, more reasonable than others – relatively speaking! But all this drivel you talk about the foundations of reality that are valid for all places and all times ... Damn it all, I see the whole purpose of my life – a modest purpose, but perhaps not without some significance – in combating such foolish ideas. Good grief, is there anyone so short-sighted that they cannot see that? There are no rights that are valid for all, no justice, because everyone is in the right, every single one of us. That is why there must be war without end, conflict between man and man, and warfare between the nations ..."

Scarcely had the Minister spoken these words than a transformation came over the ghost. If, up to this point, it had been one of the plaintive sort, almost entirely lacking in spirit, it now flew into a frenzy of rage equal to the Baron's. "What?! What?! That's rubbish", it shouted, putting aside all its meekness at once. "There is no such word as 'must', things that are reasonable are not so merely 'relatively speaking'. With views like that you're just blinding yourself to the true nature of reality."

"Me, blind! Me, whom everyone recognises as the most down-to-earth, most realistic of modern statesmen!? And who says so? A utopian daydreamer like you! Do you know that I consider people of your kind the worst, indeed the only enemies of mankind?" The Baron was so overcome with indignation that he had grabbed the apparition by the arm and was dragging it backwards and forwards. But the apparition had lost its temper as well. In its fury it hit out in all directions, but so clumsily that it missed the Baron. "Such an enemy of mankind, in fact", screamed the latter, jumping out of the way, "that I have no hesitation in shooting you and your silly ideas down on the spot." He rushed to the desk, opened a box and began to reload the revolver, his hands trembling. At the same time he kept on shouting and arguing, his voice getting hoarser and hoarser with excitement and rage, "You and your stupid talk of eternal justice! Don't you realise you are blaspheming against mankind's most dearly held belief. If there were one right, one justice valid for all, then what about the intrinsic wrongness, pointlessness of all earthly existence which depends on the very fact that all those who are lashing out at each other, all of them, are in the right at the same time; what about Christianity, the religion of suffering, what about the essentially tragic nature of earthly life?"

"You miserable wretch!" The ghost, for its part, now screamed with all its might, and in its voice there was a rumble of something like underground thunder, even the windows seemed to echo it darkly, and the wind outside blew with even greater force, bringing from the mountains a strange, soft, whistling, rustling sound, as if somewhere in the distance the age-old rock was cracking and preparing to trickle down in streams of fine sand. "You miserable wretch!" In its fury, the whole of visible nature seemed to be joining in the scream. "Is it any business of yours to meddle in God's affairs, to take the tragic nature of His creation under your gracious patronage, when enough, probably more than enough, is done to make it tragic if, in His infinite goodness, He allows harmful pests such as you to go on living, instead of exterminating them!" At these words the ghost bent right back, as if it was preparing to run at the mannikin, knock him down with the mere force of its body and crush him. By this violent movement, however, it unexpectedly freed itself completely from the floor, in which it had still been stuck as far as its knees. It shot up, as if through a trap door, and amazingly did not stop when the soles of its feet reached floor level but, as if with the force of its own violence, continued to rise in the air, not, however, straight up, but at an angle, as if it were floating up an invisible staircase. In the course of this it passed close by the Baron like an icy draught; that is, it missed him. "Woe is me!" it cried now, with a searing, plaintive sound, as it suddenly stopped in mid-air, almost fixed to the spot apart from a gentle pendulum motion. "My sins! My sins!"

The Baron had tumbled trembling to his knees, the gun flying in a wide arc from his hand and clattering to the floor. It was not so much what the ghost said that demolished his painstakingly erected composure, as the awful sight of its body hanging in the air, as if from an imaginary gallows, far surpassing in its eeriness all the strange things he had seen on this memorable evening. And now the trembling words from above him, that sounded as if they came straight from a tormented heart, plucked at a nerve in his soul which had not resonated for years, perhaps not since his earliest childhood. "My sins! My sins!" he started to whimper as well, and rolled his eyes, for the tears would not come; over the long years he had forgotten how to cry.

For a while their piteous moans filled the whole room, arousing an eerie echo in the gentle creaking of the furniture. The moon had set, and outside the circle of lamplight there was complete darkness. Only now did the soft glimmer of bluish-white light around the apparition become visible, like the crackle of a comb as it is drawn through the hair. It really gave the impression that every tiny fibre in the ghost's clothes was standing painfully on end and shivering in the alien, refractory medium of the earth's atmosphere, which made itself felt at the slightest movement in an unpleasant soreness.

"What is the matter with you? Lord above, what's the matter?" cried the Minister, whose fury had completely dissipated, and who now only felt pity, pity for the poor, lost, spectral apparition, and even greater pity for himself, for he was beginning to suspect that his fate in that inevitable first hour after death would turn out to be similar to that of the ghost, only much, much more horrible.

"Can't you see?" came the pitiful wail from above. "I have no sense of space, that is what is the matter. I can see that there are rooms and stories, a certain regularity in the arrangement of above and below, of right and left. But I can't integrate this peculiar arrangement into my senses, I can't feel it from within ... And now I've realised for what particular event in my life this punishment has been visited upon me."

"Oh, how terrible", lamented the Minister. "What crime did you commit? Perhaps I can help you. If it lies within my power, you can rest assured that I will leave no stone unturned ..." The usual diplomatic clichés came tumbling over his pale lips, only completely tonelessly.

The ghost did not respond to his offer at all, it seemed sunk in recollection and to be talking to itself. "Once a real gentleman, some kind of minister I think, came to visit me in my attic. He probably came with the best of intentions, full of good-will. He wanted to learn from me, he said, wanted to examine with his own senses my original way of life, my home-grown philosophy – those were his very words. Then I became puffed up with proletarian pride and threw him downstairs single-handed, crying out in exultation, 'Let that be a lesson to you that for me

386

there is no difference between high and low, superiors and inferiors'."

"No difference between high and low? And that's why you're hanging in mid-air, you poor man? Well, it wasn't a very nice thing to do though, was it?"

"Yes, that's what I shouted after him. My voice rang with conviction, I believed I had done something fine. Unfortunately I'm very quick-tempered, as you have just had an opportunity to see. It seemed the right thing to do, the obvious thing even, to grab him by the collar and throw him down the stairs. For a long time afterwards I was really pleased with myself for having had such a brilliant idea, it seemed to come from my innermost soul, I could not imagine it could have happened any other way. Now, however, I feel that it is precisely that apparently obvious and self-enclosed nature of things, their lack of love, their blatant palpability and certainty which is the worst danger, the worst temptation for mortals. It's just the way things are, we think – or rather don't think; we salve our consciences with the idea that although misery and hypocrisy and mass murder and wastage exist, that's it and we can do nothing about it. We think we can't change or improve anything, quite forgetting that we could make a start with ourselves ..."

The Baron interrupted him, his teeth chattering in an outburst of abject fear, "But my dear fellow, just think what will happen to me, if you have to suffer so much just because of one single, insignificant transgression, merely a piece of robust behaviour? I'll be well up in matters of etiquette and keeping one's distance, it's true, but what about all the other and, so it appears, more important things, which I just treated as routine and which will consequently all rise up against me? I was in the habit of saying that we had even become accustomed to death. I'm going to find everything, simply everything in this upside-down world, in the afterlife, I mean, startlingly new and inexplicable, aren't I?"

"Ah, now I can feel it", exclaimed the ghost joyfully at that moment, completely ignoring the horror-struck Minister. "Now, now the chastisement is slackening. I can feel that I am being forgiven. I can feel a sense of unparalleled harmony flowing through my every limb ..." The ancient apparition was silent, its eyes glistening with tears of joy as, with a gentle smile on its lips, it slowly floated down to the floor. It was now not much more than the normal shape and size of a human, and the prickly sparkle had disappeared from round its body. Now its feet were on the floor. Immediately they were freed from their puppet-like restraint, and it walked easily towards the Baron, whom it now seemed to have no difficulty in distinguishing from his surroundings. It noticed that the latter was kneeling on the floor. "Get up", it said in a friendly voice, and gave the groaning Minister a helping arm. "No one is entirely lost ... But I am being drawn powerfully to some other place. What other trials await me? Or are they already at an end and I have been purified, ready for the highest level? I do not know. All I feel is that my time in this terrestrial world is over and that I am about to plunge into another sphere, perhaps – oh, the mere idea is bliss! – into a purer one than this and my own are. Fare thee well!"

"No, stay!" cried the Baron in despair. "Stay with me. Speak to me still. It makes me so happy. And you mustn't think that simply means I have become accustomed to you. Your staying will be something quintessentially real."

The apparition shook its head earnestly. "I may not."

"Not even if I go down on my knees to you? Not even if I tell you that your words could be of infinite, decisive significance for my soul's salvation, that my eternal redemption is in your hands?"

"It is a higher law that compels me to go."

In a gesture of humility such as he had never before known, the minister bowed his head. Gently, the apparition held out its hand to him.

"Then tell me one thing at least. What shattering experiences and lofty studies, what scholarship and distinguished instruction did you go through in your Sylph world to achieve such a sublime level of understanding that after death your whole punishment was a mild embarrassment? You must have studied with philosophers and been a philosopher yourself, or were you a great, misunderstood artist, even an apostle, prophet, founder of a religion?"

"No", replied the apparition with a curiously restrained smile, "my life was nothing out of the ordinary. I could not stand injustice, it is true, but I had little time for study. My profession, however, was what might be called a philosophical one. You see, I was often alone, in a dark, narrow chamber, far from other people, all on my own. That kind of thing invites reflection. In your earthly world you would call me something like a chimney sweep."

The Minister started. "Chimney sweep ... chimney sweep", he repeated, gibbering.

When he looked up the apparition had disappeared without trace.

Suddenly he gave a shout and rushed over to the telephone. "Hello, is that the lunatic asylum?"

It was the nurse on night duty.

"Is Arthur Bruchfeß there? The chimney sweep who attempted to assassinate me this afternoon? Did he not die just half an hour ago?" The Minister was convinced the apparition he had just been speaking to must have been the ghost of that man.

"I will check immediately, Your Excellency."

After a while, during which the tension stretched almost to breaking point, he returned. "No, the patient is alive, even remarkably calm and cheerful. He has not gone to sleep, but is walking up and down in his cell, warbling away to himself. The doctors have not been able to find the least trace of mental disturbance, not even of any abnormal stimulation of the nervous system."

"Release the man, immediately", panted the Minister, "the whole case against him must be abandoned. We must change everything, the law, the whole world, everything ... Have you understood? He is to be released immediately."

"Yes, Your Excellency."

Breathing heavily, the Minister collapsed into his chair. All the time he was gently slapping himself on the head, as if to rouse himself to comprehension of the unutterable.

Then there was a rustling from the doorway.

It was the beautiful Gabrielle. The loud conversation had not woken her, but the ringing of the telephone had. "When are you coming?" she said, pursing her lips in a pout. She stood there, shivering slightly since she was wearing nothing but her thin, semi-transparent nightdress with just two light-blue silk ribbons over her gleaming shoulders. Her unsophisticated, young face, her delicate, rounded arms and the slight, apple-smooth curve of her small breasts: the most natural things in the world, and promising the oblivion of intimacy and the accustomed sweetness of unconscious repose. A stronger man than the Baron would have been unable to resist the gentle power of this ravishing sight. In a moment he was beside her. "How long do I have to go on waiting, all by myself?" she breathed tenderly, as he clasped her to him with a wild joy and a deep sigh of relief; he shook himself free of the horror, which with his accustomed wisdom he had already filed under the heading of 'dream', or 'temporary nervous disorder', and abandoned himself to the sweet, motherly warmth of sleep her body exuded, and the gentle touch of a loose lock of hair like a willowy wand on his cheek.

Signor Scurri
or
Herr von Yb's Strange Voyage to the Seaside

Fritz von Herzmanovsky-Orlando

The story that follows will perhaps appear a little absurd to some readers, and at one particular point it even exudes an unpleasant and mysteriously compelling potency. In spite of that, it will be found to be infinitely instructive, especially for the younger generation, since the foundations of their outlook rest on the shifting sands of logical principles which are hopelessly out-of-date and no longer sufficient for the age of cosmic tension in which we live. In my opinion, a story such as this should be included in school anthologies for the sixth form: displayed among the classical columns of worthy native prose and the plaster torsos of officially sanctioned poetry, it can only be all the more effective. As to its truth, there can be no doubt at all: my friend, Achatius von Yb, was already of mature years at the time of the experiences I am about to relate, which he confided to me in a quiet moment; moreover he was a man who was most honourable, truthful and – as this story will show – punctilious to the point of excess.

Destiny had laid him in a magnificent cradle of gold, or rather, as precision is our aim, in a cradle of ebony inlaid with the most fantastic and confusing patterns of imitation ivory, as the tyrannical fashion of the *Deuxième Empire* demanded. In spite of all this ivory splendour and in spite of the stylish matching musical chamber pot, our hero's path through life was overgrown with – and this is no exaggeration – thistles the height of houses. The Devil only knows in what conjunction the great constellations stood, which thundered out the hour of his birth! At that time no one thought of casting horoscopes. The people who do that now in those days were making their living partly by dealing in insect powders and patent remedies for corns, and partly through advertisements with graphic illustrations which promised, depending on sex, an ample bosom or luxuriant moustache. It was an age of liberalism, an age of enlightenment; rubber galoshes were the latest thing, and everyone who was anyone at all, was proud to trace their ancestry back to the ape, as was demonstrated daily and with crystal clarity by Science triumphant. Respectable families almost came to blows in the course of impassioned debates on the feasibility and advantages of horse-drawn trams, and on such occasions many an idealistic son was told never to darken the paternal door again, so that he left to seek his fortune in America or some other primitive country.

But even these luminous times still had their fortune-telling gypsies. One such forced her way to the bed, where von Yb's mother lay in the throes of childbirth, and proclaimed in prophetic tones that the child should beware of water ... of great quantities of water ... and of dung ... yes, of dung too ... in fact, of anything connected with waste products, she added, staring fixedly into the distance.

It gave Frau von Yb a terrible shock; moreover, she was furious that such common things as water and dung should be mentioned in a refined household such as hers, and refused the witch payment. At that, the rather grubby spawn of the land of the Pharaohs made her departure amid a splutter of curses.

It soon became apparent that the seed of her prophecy had fallen on fruitful ground. Age of Science or no, a family council was called, chaired by Uncle Doublear (a man known throughout the city for his caution: he even had a tiny lightning-conductor on his top-hat complete with silver chain dragging along the ground behind). Everyone was in complete agreement that, as far as little Achaz' future career was concerned, there were two things that must be avoided at all costs: he should never become an admiral, nor a member of the landed gentry. Instead, Uncle Doublear recommended a dry profession, guaranteed free from all contact with waste products: the boy should suck at the breasts of Science. The ladies leapt up in indignation and a flush of modesty ... but they were mollified somewhat when they realised that that was Uncle Doublear's flowery way of saying that Achatius von Yb should become a scholar of note, which was agreed upon.

I had the pleasure of making his acquaintance at the Congress of the Academy of Sciences, an occasion, by the way, on which more violent passions were aroused than at any other meeting of that august body. Someone stirred up a veritable hornet's nest with his question as to whether it was Archimedes or Ramon Lull who should be regarded as the inventor of the game of solitaire. It set off a furious squawking; bald-headed luminaries dashed heavy tomes to the ground in clouds of dust, or, trembling with passion, grabbed each other by the buttons of their frock coats; some even spat at each other's feet. Only the sudden appearance of a scholarly profile with an icy glint in his spectacles brought some light into the dark confusion. It was the great physicist, Ernst Mach, and my admiration for him dates from that first meeting. There was a gentleman beside me who was literally crowing with enthusiasm. We shook hands – and that was how I made the acquaintance of Achatius von Yb, whom I was to meet again so many years later and under such melancholy circumstances.

At the time of our first meeting he must have been in his early thirties, though his age was impossible to determine. His sparse, silky-thin hair was colourless, his posture somewhat hunched, his dress slovenly and, although of the very best quality, always looked crumpled and faded, even when it had just come from the tailor. His parents, who had died early – while he was still at university – had occupied a genteelly sombre apartment in a district of monumental architecture of which they had assigned to him a suite of rooms looking out onto the courtyard. Even after the death of his parents, von Yb continued to inhabit his gloomy bachelor's chambers, absorbed in abstruse studies and bizarre reflections. For all that, he was no misanthrope. Twice a year he gave great *soirées*, when his house would blaze with the light of countless candles and the salons, empty for the rest of the year, would glitter with the illusion of life. When they were over, the deathly silence would gather round him again, and for months he would not leave his quarters. It would never have occurred to anyone to prophesy that one day he would have to scurry shyly from one to another of fifty cheap lodging houses, and all because of a minor lapse that was the result of an unguarded moment.

It began one morning when Herr von Yb left his dark-panelled study, to which in the early summer only an occasional stray beam of gold penetrated (when one did, it produced a bewitching display of melancholy brevity). He went to his library, a narrow room with a row of arched windows giving onto a half-lit air-well. Suddenly the unworldly scholar realised that the room, redolent with the smell of books, was brighter than usual. He went to one of the arched windows and saw up above, in the narrow opening of the air-well, sunlight sparkling like jewels, saw a veritable orgy of glittering rays, saw a crystalline sky of that deep blue which usually only occurs over glaciers, and saw lustrous white clouds sailing across, like hosts of snowy angels in their swift flight. Deep down below at the bottom of the well, beside some mossy patches on the rough-hewn ashlar, a pitiful bird was twittering in its cage. Immediately opposite von Yb was a glassed-in corridor leading to the space where the trunks and cases were stored in the palatial house adjoining his own. In this room, with its jumble of luggage, an open gas flame burnt day and night in a frosted glass bowl; von Yb had often noticed it without paying any particular attention.

This time, however, the suggestive power of this combination of circumstances was such that he was overcome with a longing he had never before experienced for the beauty of the world outside. With a joyful feeling such as only children feel on the eve of holidays, he set about realising this moment of inspiration. He resolved to go on a voyage, a long voyage on which he would see the sea for the first time.

He decided on Genoa as the scene of the magnificent spectacle he was already looking forward to. This decision may well have been subconsciously motivated by the fact that his grandfather had fought with Radetzky in Northern Italy in 1849 and had laid down his life for his country there. Thus there was a blood-tie with the region, and Herr von Yb, the grandson, set off, drawn by a some mysteriously compelling force to this Saxony beyond the Alps, a province that was mysterious and yet equally full of bourgeois enterprise.

After a pleasant journey in the half-empty midnight express he saw Carinthia through the morning mist. The train rushed along beside huge lakes, through gloriously dark-green forests then, finally, past gigantic peaks with a dusting of fresh snow piled one above the other, to reach the Italian frontier in the early afternoon. Here a new world began abruptly: dusty stone-built houses, a noticeable lack of trees, dirty washing fluttering in the breeze, donkey-carts in deserted streets and, permeating it all, a smell that was a mixture of oil, vinegary wine, smoke and the sickly-sweet stench of rooms where a corpse has been laid out. After an unnecessarily long delay for customs – it became obvious to von Yb that he was by now the only passenger – the journey continued. The train rattled at a truly frightening speed along the rocky precipices, was engulfed in the countless tunnels by a crescendo of inexplicable claps of thunder and scattered such a shower of sparks at every curve that the passenger had to duck.

With much clunking and clanking the train stopped at a small station. One excessively elegant lady got on, sat opposite von Yb and stared fixedly at him out of mysteriously large eyes. At the next station the apparition abandoned him and its place was taken by a man in black whose skinny frame was surmounted by a tiny, olive-yellow bird's head covered in deep furrows which were filled with a dark black patina such as is found on antique bronzes when they have just been dug up. After a while spent sunk in gloomy reflections, this man took a pinch of snuff from a little box, which then proceeded to emit the strains of a hymn to the long-lost General Palafox, the Hero of Saragossa. Then two large flies, which he must have brought with him, flew out. At this he, clearly at home in polite society, began to chase after them with a blue handkerchief, stepping, as he did so, rather heavily on von Yb's toes with his buckled shoes. This quite naturally led to a conversation. He was a Spaniard, explained the man in black, and this was the fourth time he had almost reached the frontier of Austria, the goal of a lifetime's longing, and once more he had had to turn back because of a lack of money. Whilst von Yb was still wondering at the old man's disconcertingly high voice, the latter told him that he had been a priest and, in spite of his calling, had three times suffered knife-wounds, most recently and painfully whilst reading the lesson – from the *Lamentations of Jeremiah* – on the Maundy Thursday of the last Ordinary Jubilee.

Von Yb expressed his deepest sympathy and asked him why he had left the priesthood. At this the other muttered something about needing to be a whole man, shrugged his shoulders and stared silently out of the window; this he continued to do until the train drew into the station at Udine.

The station concourse echoed with noisy life. Everywhere there were bright lights, and the platform was overcrowded with people getting in the way of the porters and occasionally treading on sleeping children, who evidently regularly spent the night there. Our traveller was ushered into the restaurant, where bottles of icy sulphur-water and pungently bitter liqueurs were ranged in rows of strident colour along a gilded sideboard which resembled a church altar. Generals in magnificent uniforms promenaded up and down with fat ladies with warts sprouting black hair who fanned themselves vigorously. The throng was enlivened by the twitter of strikingly pretty girls in gaudy dresses, some with combs in their hair and lace shawls.

As he was serving some southern dish, a waiter with an eerie, fixed glass eye extolled the charms of a girl who possessed an unusual physical defect. Von Yb rejected the suggestion with indignation. Deprived of his major source of income, the *garçon* tried to avenge himself by giving copper coins that were no longer legal tender in change: *soldi* from the last doge of Venice, one of the hastily minted coins of Theodor von Neuhof, the 'summer king' of Corsica praised by Voltaire; there was even an ornate admission token to a Neapolitan brothel from the time of Casanova. Von Yb was so delighted by them that he almost missed the shrill departure bell.

The train thundered off into the night. After only a short time, however, it started a mournful whistling, which rose and fell for several minutes, after which it stopped and then puffed its way back into the station.

Scarcely had it arrived than the station master and all available staff rushed to the engine, where a loud debate was carried on by everyone at once, gesticulating wildly with the lanterns. Von Yb joined the circle but, as the discussion was in the Friulian dialect, all he could make out was that "It" had been seen, quite distinctly, and that now just the same would happen as had seventeen years ago. On no condition would they continue, neither he, Cesare, the driver, nor Pompeio, the stoker.

It did not matter whom von Yb asked, to him they were as silent as the grave. Eventually he found an old porter who, in return for an excessive tip, told him that it was the "funeral procession of the gnomes of Verona" which had never before been seen so close to Udine and which presaged disaster. And for the love of God his Honour was not to tell on him, it would cost him his job, his livelihood; the ghostly apparition was an official railway secret that was kept carefully concealed from outsiders. There was no question of the journey continuing along this stretch of the railway. And indeed, the passengers were transferred to another train consisting of antiquated carriages from the earliest days of rail-travel, which, only dimly lit and rocking gently, set off into the mild summer night.

Von Yb looked round the compartment. The atmosphere of the good old days of his grandparents struck a nostalgic chord that brought a tear to his eye. The ceiling was decorated with colourful tracery, the walls were neatly covered in wax-cloth with a pattern of grey stars, the seats were deep and comfortable, the windows, rounded at the bottom as in old coaches, had bead-work loops to rest your arms in. He was about to lean back dreamily when he noticed a concealed door, which he would not have suspected in the confined space. His scholar's inquiring mind was immediately roused. He went into the neighbouring compartment.

To his not inconsiderable surprise he saw that it seemed to be a lady's dressing-room: it was littered with women's clothes and lingerie and filled with a delicate perfume. At the farther end there was another door; von Yb – somewhat more tentatively this time, it must be admitted – opened it and could scarcely refrain from exclaiming out loud, so delightful was the picture that presented itself to his gaze:

In the middle of the room, bathed in a rosy glow from a

hanging lamp, was a four-poster bed, on which a beautiful, raven-haired girl lay sleeping in an aesthetic pose.

After a few moments of ecstatic contemplation, von Yb returned, on tiptoe and totally confused, to his compartment.

Fortunately, it was not long before the ticket-collector appeared, making his acrobatic way along the footboard. In reply to his question, he was told that it was the youngest granddaughter of the celebrated dancer, Taglioni, who had died of cholera in 1854, that she owned the Port Said Opera House and that she had hired this carriage, formerly belonging to the Sardinian royal family, for her own personal use. Von Yb was in the chamberlain's quarters, added the shabbily dressed official, proffering a hand as hairy as a monkey's.

Scarcely had the guard – was that a satyr's smile playing round his lips? – disappeared, than von Yb was overcome with an unprecedented lust for adventure. To prise a large box of chocolates out of his case and slip over to the door to the shrine of the sleeping beauty was the work of a moment. His heart was beating in time to the muffled rhythm of the wheels. He was already on his knees beside her bed, brushing her half-open lips with a fleeting kiss, when he realised that he had no idea what to do next.

Just as he was about to stand up and slip out of the room, the fair sleeper, still only half-awake, wrapped her arms around him and whispered, "*Oh ... momognone mio ...*"

Von Yb closed his eyes in rapture. He thought he was in paradise. But the very next moment his sleeping beauty was no longer half, but fully awake and shattered the spell with a scream of indignation after which he was drowned in a raging flood of Italian oaths. Von Yb was stunned; the only escape from his sheepish embarrassment that he could think of was to offer the box of chocolates wordlessly to the Fury. And it did indeed produce an effect. Pouting, the fair maid devoured the delicious confection, calmed down and demanded to know, with an accent that had a delightful Levantine tinge, what von Yb thought he was doing in her compartment?

The latter maintained he had merely been looking for the way to the restaurant car for his usual bite of supper, but had strayed

– it must have been the will of the gods – into her compartment and, whether consciously or unconsciously, he could not say, fallen down at her feet in adoration. Oh, if only he might hope! How gladly would he lay his life and his wealth at her feet! And, carried away by his unaccustomed ardour, he bent down towards her.

Once more it was his fate to be cruelly disappointed. The object of his fond desires placed a firm hand against his chest, gave him a brief, searching look then pushed him away with a toss of her fragrant locks. What on earth was he thinking! Never! She was a virginal priestess of art and wanted to have nothing to do with men. She knew all about them! Added to that, he wasn't even an artiste, one could see that at a glance; not a tenor, nor a lion-tamer, nor anything else.

Was there no hope at all? asked von Yb. Even if he could never take her hand in marriage, was there not a place – any place – that would keep him close to her, might they still not be good friends?

He was barking up the wrong tree there, was the angry reply. If that was his idea, then he would do better elsewhere, for example the Ziziani Theatre in Alexandria, Rue de la Porte, or the "Palais de Danse" in Damascus, or the "Friponnière" in Port Sudan! And so, goodbye!

It cut von Yb to the quick that he had never been trained for a real profession such as opera singing, mime, or at the very least fire-eating. Sadly he departed, casting a yearning glance back at the *belle dame sans merci*, who had already taken up a silver-framed mirror and was carrying out repairs to a portion of her gums that seemed to have aroused her displeasure. Sighing, he staggered back to his compartment, where he spent the night alone with his torment and many starving fleas, the latter presumably the property of the Italian State Railways.

A two-hour long break for lunch in Mirandola gave von Yb the opportunity of admiring his unapproachable fellow-passenger as, in full dress and clouds of perfume, she took her meal, served by a snarling Arab in a white burnous and a pubescent Levantine girl with an amber complexion.

A timid attempt to make further advances got no farther than the connecting door, which was locked. Then the obliging guard offered to cause a slight derailment of the train, in the course of which von Yb would have the opportunity of rescuing the fair maiden; it would, however, cost at least 500 lire. Von Yb rejected the offer with a shake of the head.

Shortly after sunset the guard's head reappeared against the lurid evening light with a reduced price of 300 lire, but met with the same cold reception as before. He had no more success with his final offer of 100 lire shortly before they entered the notorious Montegiove Tunnel, where smoky oil-lamps in front of decaying pictures of saints bore mute witness to countless accidents.

It was well on into the night when von Yb finally arrived in Genoa. Exhausted and alone in an exaggeratedly high-roofed, two-wheeled carriage with rattling windows, he drove through the narrow alleys that squeezed between the tall, dark houses. A ragamuffin with a coloured lantern on a long pole walked in front of his conveyance, which took von Yb to an old-fashioned hotel which, although respectable rather than luxurious, had been warmly recommended.

He immediately went to the restaurant, which was lit by a few hissing gas-lamps. He could hardly keep his eyes open as he ate his dinner; hot waves of sleep washed over him, almost obliterating consciousness, and the few weary waiters took on almost ghostly form against a background that disappeared into darkness.

When he had finished his meal he called over the *maître d'hôtel* and asked, half asleep as he was, whether it would be possible to have a quick look at the sea. The head waiter replied with a nod and ordered one of his underlings to guide Herr von Yb. They passed through several gloomy corridors before reaching a door which the boy had difficulty opening. To von Yb's surprise – he had expected to step out into the street – they entered a fairly spacious store-room where various herbs, empty wine-bottles and all sorts of other junk were kept.

Where did they go now? von Yb asked the boy, who had lit the lamp.

The answer was odd: they were there. And the youth in his black tie and tails led him over to a small receptacle with a lid.

Von Yb immediately classified it as a rubbish bin. His young cicerone took off the lid, and when von Yb gave him a questioning look he was told that the sea was in the bin.

It struck von Yb like an electric shock. He felt as if he were undergoing a dislocation of his personality, of his environment or of reality itself. What he saw beggared all description: within this mundane receptacle glowed the deepest, most luminant blue of an infinite abyss.

There was no doubt about it, that was the sea. His mind was thronged with words: Poseidon, Thetis, the sombre tones of Medusa. Just as he was about to exclaim, "Thalatta, thalatta!" an inner voice thundered, "Don't get carried away by your classical scholarship! It's crazy! That cannot possibly be the sea! Just think, infinity in a garbage can!?" "But why not, why not?" whispered Satan, whose telephone line has a connection to every human mind. "Don't listen to the voice of so-called reason; it never learns anything new and will only allow you to accept the most banal facts as true, you poor soul ..."

Unsure of himself, von Yb looked round in some confusion, and saw the ancient *maître d' hôtel* with the Franz-Josef whiskers, who had followed them on silent, if somewhat flat, feet and now, with much confidential clearing of the throat and an almost embarrassed wave of his serviette, began his tale, "Yes, Your Honour, it is the sea. I know exactly what you feel, Your Honour, even though I am only a simple waiter. It is the sea, the genuine sea. Not the vulgar *kitsch* that is passed off as the sea to your common-or-garden tourist. I would never try to cheat Your Honour with anything like that, I who had the honour of serving under Your Honour's grandfather in Radetzky's army in '49! I was Company Cook in Freydenplitz' Horse. Lively lads from Carinthia, all of them. We would have all gladly given our lives for the Colonel. But fate had decreed otherwise ..."

The old waiter wiped a tear from his eye with his serviette before he continued, "A Piedmontese bullet went right through Your Honour's late grandfather at the Battle of Mortara. It shattered my ankle whilst I was riding my steed through a hail of bullets, slicing up a Verona salami on my little portable chopping board to comfort the wounded. The bullet killed my packhorse, Schackerl, the dapple-grey who had twice been awarded the silver medal for bravery, the one that used to carry the so-called mounted coffee-urn on his broad back ... And when I was discharged, as I was a war-invalid, they gave me the sea as a kind of gratuity. Everyone was given something: one man a roundabout, another a licence for a barrel-organ, someone else the lease on a state tobacco shop, or a tame monkey in a French general's uniform. Yes. And I got the sea. The very same one the Holy Roman Emperor Rudolf is supposed to have had and that was afterwards kept in the treasury of the shrine at Mariazell. But they didn't like it there."

Von Yb's head was spinning; he had difficulty in staying on his feet.

"Would your Honour like to take a turn along the beach?" the waiter asked.

He took the unresisting von Yb by the arm and promenaded him round the garbage bin a few times. There was such a strong, fresh, tangy breeze blowing out of it that von Yb's hand went up involuntarily to hold onto his hat.

"Have a good look at it, Your Honour", said the man with the Franz-Josef whiskers. "Admiral Tegetthoff sailed his first ships on that as a boy."

The strange dread, which all the time had kept von Yb fixed in a state between dreaming and waking, now seemed to grip him by the throat and take his breath away. He had to get away from here as quickly as possible, get away from the disturbing sound of that sea, from the mysteriously compelling sight of that blue abyss in the apparently harmless guise of a rubbish bin ...

Like a man possessed, von Yb tore himself away and rushed out into the dark street. Tegetthoff ... Mortara ... Emperor Rudolf ... the shrine at Mariazell ... a blue abyss ... the impressions of the last few minutes were rushing around inside his weary brain. Or was it merely himself, rushing along between the tall, dark houses of midnight Genoa?

He was brought to a halt by a shadowy, seething mass of bodies and, against his will, forced to look on as a massive, herculean silhouette disentangled itself from the silently grappling sailors, grabbed a Chinese stoker by one leg, swung him round in the air, in spite of all his wriggling, and smashed him against a door that glistened like bronze in the moonlight; it shattered with a splintering crack, and the wretched stoker was swallowed up by a black, yawning cavity. From a dimly-lit kitchen came the sound of sizzling fat and through another von Yb could see a hunchbacked writer dip his pen in the ink and scribble away. Farther along, a contralto of mature years struck the pose of a tragic mother as she practised an aria whilst on the top floor grey, dripping washing was being hung out to dry, a task that had clearly been interrupted earlier. Suddenly a hysterical screaming rang out, a clattering and cursing, then a tangle of half-clothed figures erupted through the shattered door, and before von Yb had recovered from the shock, two pretty, full-bosomed girls with sparkling eyes had seized him and dragged him off.

Von Yb never could – or would – describe precisely what had happened next. All he would say was that he had the feeling he was being quite well looked after. He could also remember a dream that kept recurring obstinately in which he was back in the middle ages as a palfrey being gently ridden by a lady round a flower-strewn meadow full of gushing streams.

He felt he had slept for several days and finally woken in a strange house. He was still somewhat the worse for wear but decided to set off straight away to see the sights of Genoa and ... and ... His head started to spin again and it was only with difficulty that he managed to remember what it was he had really wanted to see: the sea.

But he did not get that far. The two girls would not let him leave until he had paid a certain sum of money, which they counted out for him down to the last ha'penny on their nimble fingers. A sum which seemed rather high to him.

He looked for his well-filled wallet in his coat, he searched through every pocket and found nothing, nothing at all. The smiles gradually disappeared from the faces of the two girls, to be replaced by a businesslike seriousness.

When Herr von Yb, who was punctiliousness itself in money

matters, tried to leave to fetch the money from his hotel, he found himself grabbed and detained by the two delicious creatures, who suddenly seemed to develop muscles of steel. They rolled up their sleeves and dragged the flabbergasted Herr von Yb down some dark steps and locked him in a musty cellar which smelt outrageously of sick poultry. The mildest of the insults they screamed through the bars sounded suspiciously like "Swindler". He would not see the light of day, they shouted, until he had written a letter to his bank in Vienna that they would dictate to him! With that, they disappeared.

For a while von Yb tried to escape from his gloomy thoughts by declaiming to himself Goethe's immortal poem of 'the land where the lemon-trees grow, where through the foliage dark, golden oranges glow' in a variety of intonations. In the long run, however, even the most punctilious of scholars will be seized with despair when incarcerated in a disused chicken-run, and thus Achatius von Yb ended up staring wild-eyed at the sturdy if mildewed door that shut him off from the glories of Italy.

One day, after he had stared at it for a particularly long time, the miracle occurred. The door opened and, with the graceful step of the Goddess of Love herself, in walked his fair companion from the train journey, the dream-vision from the Pullman car. With a charming smile she approached, inspected the poor prisoner from head to toe through her lorgnon and maintained both her smile and her silence.

Bright red with shame, von Yb tried to think of an excuse to explain his presence here – perhaps some reference to fascinating architectural features? But he was forestalled: the beautiful owner of the Opera House in Port Said was looking for new singers for the chorus; she had heard, to her dismay, of the unfortunate situation that had befallen some distinguished visitor and recognised her former travelling-companion through the keyhole. She had come to bring him his freedom, more than that, even, to grant his deepest wish. No, not her hand in marriage, not that, but the place close to her that he had asked for so fervently. To put it in a nutshell, she was going to engage him. There was the contract, he only needed to sign. Then, however, he would be hers for the rest of his life.

"I am yours already!" cried von Yb in wild enthusiasm as he went down on one knee before her. "But, my dearest, how can I serve you? I am a scholar, highly respected, it is true – I even have several honorary doctorates – but I am neither an actor nor a singer."

"It's nothing like that that I have in mind", was the amiable reply. "It is something else. You know that in the South we like to fill the intervals of bloody tragedies with comic interludes. In my opera house, for example, we put the torture scene from *Tosca* on the open stage; every time it is greeted with thunderous applause and has to be encored. After that, of course, we need some comic relief ... Let's not beat about the bush, any more. I want to use your undoubted talents as a buffoon to cheer up the audience during the interludes."

Von Yb froze. He couldn't believe his ears. "Buffoon?" he stammered. "No; impossible. Consider: a distinguished scholar ... honorary doctorates ..."

"Very well", replied the vision, completely unmoved. "Then you will stay here until the end of your days. Or rather, till the end of your money. They will squeeze every last penny out of you and then make sure you disappear, as has happened before to many an innocent traveller in this city with all its dark secrets. I would have bought your freedom and taken you with me, but as you don't want to come, adieu!" And she turned to leave.

What else could the unfortunate von Yb do but call back the pitiless mistress of the Port Said Opera and sign the paper which, with a smile on her lips, she held out for him.

As he put pen to paper, his brain seemed to be rent by an inner thunderclap. A buffoon! A buffoon for his whole life! And not even a chance of promotion, there was no career structure in buffoonery, no post of senior buffoon. If his grandfather had known, Arbogast Caspar Ferdinand von Yb, Lord of Upper and Lower Yb and member of the Upper House of the Estates of Carniola! Achatius gnawed at his bloodless lips.

Meanwhile the other signatory had inspected the document through the long lashes of her almond-shaped eyes; she gave a satisfied nod and handed her new recruit a banknote of a fairly high denomination: his signing-on fee. Then she indicated he should follow her; they were to go straight on board ship.

Von Yb went out into the street, with a sigh of relief, in spite of everything, keeping close behind his fair employer, who was leading him through dark alleyways towards the harbour.

Suddenly the thought flashed through his mind that now he would at least see the sea. For a few seconds he felt that fate had treated him kindly. But was it really the sea he was heading for? Was it the real sea? He felt dizzy, just as he had when the waiter with the Franz-Josef whiskers had taken him under his wing.

His companion was hurrying up. He could already hear the screech of the sirens, the clank of the cranes. At most there could be one row of houses between him and the so-called sea.

"Flee!" It was like a flash of lightning in von Yb's tormented brain. "Contract or no contract – flee!"

The screeching and clanking grew louder and louder, filling him with dread. He was still following his new mistress, who was striding along even faster. She was about to turn the final corner.

Then von Yb, that model of punctiliousness, turned on his heels and ran, still clutching, crumpled up in his hand, the large banknote, the earnest of his contractual obligation. As if the devil himself were after him, he tore up one street, down the next and came to a halt, before he realised where he was, outside the station; he rushed onto the platform, onto the Vienna coach of the waiting express, and into the lavatory and safety.

The signing-on fee was just enough to get him to Vienna. After an uncomfortable journey, he arrived there somewhat bent, having spent the whole journey crouched behind the lav-atory-pan, and hurried home. It was days before he was anything approaching his usual self again.

But that was when the torment began. Poor von Yb started every time the doorbell rang: in his imagination he could hear the footsteps of the men sent to seek him out, von Yb the swind-ler who had misappropriated his signing-on fee. Breach of contract – this he knew from the experience handed down in the family by a long line of civil servants – breach of contract was no laughing matter. On the advice of the family lawyer, a gloomy gentleman with dark spectacles who told him in no uncertain terms how serious his situation was, von Yb left his splendid apartment and rented a number of cheap rooms in different parts of the town, scurrying from one to the other like a startled animal.

His social life was non-existent. Only the night-watchmen and members of the drinking classes staggering home in the early hours would see him flit timidly round the corner with a pensive shake of their heads.

Soon he was generally known as "the scurrier" and then, when word got round that he had been to Italy, as "Signor Scurri".

The whole of Vienna, from the humblest purveyor of roast chestnuts to the Emperor himself, knew of the dreadful predicament of this once highly respected gentleman. And it was not only the metropolis that bewailed his pitiful fate, in Brno, Graz and Olomouc as well he was the subject of sympathetic comments, even the occasional tear. As he still had a considerable income at his disposal, they could hardly organise a collection for him. Austria's keenest legal brains were systematically racked to try and find a solution to this special case of a buffoon in breach of contract. Experts in international law and reciprocal arrangements, specialists in extradition treaties and theatre contracts gathered together and, under pressure from public opinion, this assemblage of illustrious minds was allocated one of the empty rooms in the Imperial and Royal Academy of Sciences, where they could meet daily to discuss von Yb's wretched situation and, it was to be hoped, his deliverance.

It gradually became the done thing for anyone who wanted to make a name for himself in Vienna to slip into the magnificent baroque meeting chamber at around four o'clock in the afternoon, whisper a few discreet words to the attendant and then join one of the groups that were concerning themselves with von Yb's situation. Here and there a hoary-locked old greybeard would be leaning against a globe, deep in thought. In the middle of the room a number of scholarly profiles were sitting around a table, brooding over piles of black folders containing all the relevant files. In the corner an expert with furrowed brow shook his head to himself as he took a wad of cotton-wool out of his ear, placed it in an amber cigarette-holder and proceeded to light it. And almost every window had a complement of four frockcoats, standing with their backs to the room, staring out into the gloomy street whilst their fingers performed silent piano sonatas behind their backs. That alone made twenty-four first-class minds, but in total it was more than that who assembled here, day in, day out. Then, amid suppressed coughs and the soft chink of coins slipped into the attendants' open palms, they all left the ornate splendour of the stucco'd hall, where nothing was resolved, apart from the occasional dispute as to which umbrella was whose.

Thus it was Signor Scurri's dismal lot to eke out his days in obscure hide-outs, sometimes even, when he felt the furies of fraudulence too close upon his heels, in rather dubious hotels; as he scurried in through the door, he would be allocated one of the rooms with a sympathetic nod.

He sank into a joyless decline, and on those few occasions when his mind was a little freer from worry and dread, they would be replaced by the torment of the great unresolved question of his life: had he actually seen the sea or not?

It was a question which von Yb, for whom there was no hope of improvement, never resolved. Given the knowledge of spatial relationships at that time, he could not know that one cosmic dimension can penetrate to within an arm's length of another.

On his death-bed Achatius von Yb, known as Signor Scurri, presented a curious sight: beneath his incredibly wrinkled forehead, his eyes were opened wide, and the yellowed index finger of his right hand, bearing the old family signet ring, was pointing fixedly up in the air – like someone who has just seen the light saying, "Aha!"

Brief Austrian Chronology

1804/1806   Emperor Franz proclaimed Emperor of Austria; the Holy Roman Empire dissolved.

1814-15   Congress of Vienna; Austria renounces claims to the Netherlands, gains Lombardy-Venetia; the main territories of the Empire, besides present-day Austria, are: Bohemia, Moravia, Slovakia, Polish Galicia, the Bukovina, Transylvania, Hungary, Croatia-Slavonia, Dalmatia, Carniola (Slovenia), Istria.

1835   Death of Franz I; Ferdinand becomes Emperor.

1848-49   The liberal and nationalist revolution, eventually defeated; Emperor Ferdinand abdicates in favour of Franz Josef.

1859   War against France and Piedmont; Austria loses Lombardy.

1866   Austro-Prussian War. Austria defeated at Königgrätz (Sadowa), expelled from Germany and loses Venetia.

1867   Austro-Hungarian Compromise; Empire divided into Austrian and Hungarian parts ('Dual Monarchy').

1878   Occupation of Bosnia-Herzegovina (annexed 1908).

1889   Suicide of Crown Prince Rudolf at Mayerling.

1898   Empress Elizabeth assassinated.

1914   28 June: assassination of the heir to the throne, Archduke Franz Ferdinand, in Sarajevo.

1918   Austrian Republic proclaimed; Habsburgs go into exile.

1919	Treaty of Saint Germain: Austria reduced to present-day territory.
1922-24	Inflation.
1933	Authoritarian régime established by Dollfuss.
1938	Austria invaded by Hitler, *Anschluß* proclaimed.
1945-55	Austria occupied by Britain, France, USA, USSR.
1955	State Treaty; Austria proclaims neutrality.
1989	Austria applies for EC membership.

For more detail on the social, political and cultural background the reader is referred to:

Carl E. Schorske, *Fin-de-siècle Vienna: Politics and Culture* published in Great Britain by Weidenfeld and Nicholson and in the U.S. by Random House.
Hilde Spiel, *Vienna's Golden Autumn 1866-1938,* published in Great Britain by Weidenfeld and Nicholson and in the U.S. by Grove Weidenfeld.
Lonnie Johnson, *Introducing Austria: A Short History,* Ariadne Press, Riverside, CA.
Alan Sked, *The Decline and Fall of the Habsburg Empire 1815-1918,* Longman's, London and New York.

About the Authors

Franz Blei (Vienna 1871 – New York 1942)
Better known as a critic and cultural historian than a creative writer, Blei was an important figure in German literary and cultural life in the 1920s and early 30s. As a vehement opponent of the Nazis, he left Germany in 1933 and died in exile.
Die Kafka, Das Meyrink, Der Schnitzler first appeared in: Franz Blei, *Das große Bestiarium der modernen Literatur,* Rowohlt, Berlin, 1992.

Max Brod (Prague 1884 – Tel Aviv 1968)
Brod is still best known for defying Kafka's wish that his works should be burnt after his death, but he was a novelist of considerable importance in his own right. His novels on Jewish and Zionist themes and his historical novels were widely read in the period between the wars.
Die erste Stunde nach dem Tod (The First Hour after Death) was published by Kurt Wolff Verlag, Leipzig, 1916.

Paul Busson (Innsbruck 1873 – Vienna 1924)
Came from the Tyrol, where some of his novels and stories are set. His most successful work, *Die Wiederkehr des Melchior Dronte* (The Man who was Born Again), is based on the idea of the transmigration of souls.
Die Kleinodien des Tormento (Folter's Gems) was first published in: Paul Busson, *Seltsame Geschichten,* Verlag J. A. Kienreich, Graz, Vienna, Leipzig, 1919.

Franz Theodor Csokor (Vienna 1885 – Vienna 1969)
The most important dramatist of Expressionism in Austria, Csokor's best-known play is his elegy for the disappearance of the Empire, *3 November 1918.* Although neither a Jew nor a communist, he left Vienna immediately after the Nazis marched in; when he returned after the war he was made President of the reconstituted Austrian PEN Club. He was a bohemian character who acted on his humanist beliefs in 1938 (unlike most of the

leading Austrian writers) and who in the post-war years encouraged many young writers.

Die steinerne Frau (The Kiss of the Stone Woman) and *Schattenstadt* (Shadowtown) were first published in:

Franz Theodor Csokor, *Über die Schwelle: Erzählungen aus zwei Jahrzehnten,* Vienna, Prasser, 1937.

Friedrich Freiherr von Gagern (Mokritz Castle, Carniola 1882 – Geigenberg, Lower Austria 1947)

Came from a very old aristocratic family; wrote a number of novels dealing with the decline of values in the modern world, set in the rural area of Carniola/Croatia. He published popular volumes of hunting stories and of tales based on his adventurous journeys round America.

The Gypsy's Prophecy and *A Fragment of a Vision* are taken from:

Friedrich von Gagern: *Geister: Gänger Gesichte Gewalten,* L. Staackmann Verlag, Leipzig, 1932.

Fritz von Herzmanovsky-Orlando (Vienna 1877 – Merano 1954)

Both Herzmanovsky's writings and his drawings are characterised by a grotesque humour. During his lifetime only the novel *Der Gaulschreck im Rosennetz* (A Scare-nag in the Rosy Net) was published, the rest appeared posthumously.

Cavaliere Huscher oder Die sonderbare Meerfahrt des Herrn von Yb (Signor Scurri or Herr von Yb's Strange Voyage to the Seaside) was first published in:

Fritz von Herzmanovsky-Orlando, *Maskenspiel der Genien,* Langen-Müller, Munich, 1958.

Hugo von Hofmannsthal (Vienna 1874 – Rodaun 1929)

Hofmannsthal astonished the literary world with the beauty and perfection of the lyrics he published in the early 1890s, while he was still at school. After an artistic crisis around the turn of the century, he devoted his creative activities almost entirely to the theatre, of which the libretti he wrote for Richard Strauss (e.g. *Der Rosenkavalier*) are the most widely known result. He founded the Salzburg Festival together with Max Reinhard. *Reitergeschichte* (Sergeant Anton Lerch) was first published in: Hugo von Hofmannsthal, *Das Märchen der 672. Nacht und andere Erzählungen,* Wiener Verlag, Vienna and Leipzig, 1905.

Franz Kafka (Prague 1883 – Vienna 1924)
The best-known twentieth-century writer in German, Kafka was born into a Jewish family in Prague at a time when the city was becoming increasingly dominated by its Czech majority. For Kafka, Czech, the language of the nursery, was replaced at school by German. The family had no close ties with Judaism and it was not until his later twenties that he became interested in the Jewish tradition of thought and religion. Most of his stories and novels are variants on the theme of not belonging; the best-known are *The Trial, The Castle, The Metamorphosis.*
Ein Landarzt (A Country Doctor) was first published in:
Franz Kafka, *Ein Landarzt: Kleine Erzählungen,* Kurt Wolff Verlag, Leipzig, 1919.
Der Jäger Gracchus (Gracchus the Huntsman) was first published in:
Franz Kafka, *Beschreibung eines Kampfes,* Heinrich Mercy Sohn, Prague, 1936.
Vor dem Gesetz (Outside the Law) first appeared as part of:
Franz Kafka, *Der Prozeß,* Die Schmiede, Berlin, 1925.

Alfred Kubin (Leitmeritz, Bohemia 1877 – Zwickledt, Upper Austria 1959)
Kubin was an important graphic artist with a particular sensitivity to the nightmare world of the grotesque and the fantastic. His main medium was pen and ink and he was in great demand as a book illustrator. *The Other Side* was his only work of fiction; it was first published as *Die andere Seite,* Georg Müller, Munich, 1909.

Paul Leppin (Prague 1878 – Prague 1945)
An admirer of Meyrink, Leppin was one of the main representatives of decadence among German writers in Prague. His

novels, especially *Severin* and *Blaugast* are suffused with a sultry sexuality which holds their main characters in thrall. *Severins Gang in die Finsternis* (Severin's Road into Darkness) was first published by Delphin-Verlag, Munich, 1914.

Gustav Meyrink (Vienna 1868 – Starnberg, Bavaria 1932)
Was famous in the first decades of the century for his grotesque and fantastic short stories satirising such things as militarism, the bourgeoisie and religious orthodoxy. His novel *The Golem* was largely responsible for popularising the image of Prague with its Jewish ghetto. He became increasingly interested in the occult, editing occult texts and using his knowledge in novels such as *The White Dominican* and *The Angel of the West Window*.
Blamol, Das Präparat (The Preparation) were first published in:
Gustav Meyrink, *Orchideen: Sonderbare Geschichten*, Langen, Munich, 1904.
Die Pflanzen des Dr. Cinderella (Dr. Cinderella's Plants), *Der Ring des Saturn* (The Ring of Saturn), *Schöpsoglobin* (Wetherglobin) were first published in:
Gustav Meyrink, *Das Wachsfigurenkabinett: Sonderbare Geschichten*, Langen, Munich, 1907.
'Night–Awake' is from *Der Golem*, Kurt Wolff, Munich, 1915.
'The Destruction of Amsterdam' is from *Das grüne Gesicht*, Kurt Wolff, Leipzig, 1916.
'Lucifer's Drum' is from *Walpurgisnacht*, Kurt Wolff, Munich, 1917.
'The Nightwalk' is from *Der weiße Dominikaner*, Rikola, Vienna, 1921.
'The Silver Shoe of Bartlett Greene' is from *Der Engel vom westlichen Fenster*, Grethlein, Leipzig/Zurich, 1927.

Leo Perutz (Prague 1884 – Bad Ischl 1957)
A very successful writer in the 1920s and 30s with his novels, many of them historical, where the action hovers between crime, mystery and the fantastic; one critic described them as the "result of an affair between Franz Kafka and Agatha

Christie". Being Jewish, Perutz was forced to flee – to Tel Aviv – in 1938, losing both his publisher and his audience. His books were republished in the 1970s and 80s, attracting both a reading public and critical attention.

Pour avoir bien servi was first published in:
Leo Perutz, *Herr, erbarme Dich meiner! Novellen,* Phaidon, Vienna, 1930.

Rainer Maria Rilke (Prague 1875 – Valmont sur Terriet, Valais 1926)

The greatest German poet of the twentieth century, from his early atmospheric poems celebrating Prague to the late, hymnic *Duino Elegies* and the delphic *Sonnets to Orpheus*. In his early period he also wrote many prose sketches. *The Papers of Malte Laurids Brigge* was written under the impression of his stay in Paris, where he went in 1902 to write a book on Rodin.

Die Aufzeichnungen des Malte Laurids Brigge, was first published by Insel, Leipzig, 1910.

Arthur Schnitzler (Vienna 1862 – Vienna 1931)

Practised as a doctor, but later devoted himself entirely to writing. His many plays, novels and short stories mostly portray the leisured Viennese upper middle classes to which he belonged himself. He reveals the social attitudes of his contemporaries through subtle psychological depiction of individuals; his concentration on erotic entanglements brought some of his works the whiff of scandal, especially the cycle of sexual encounters in *Reigen* (La Ronde).

Blumen (Flowers) was first published in:
Arthur Schnitzler, *Die Frau des Weisen: Noveletten,* Fischer, Berlin, 1898.

Die Weissagung (The Prophecy) was first published in:
Arthur Schnitzler, *Dämmerseelen: Novellen,* Fischer, Berlin, 1907.

Karl Hans Strobl (Iglau, Moravia 1877 – Perchtoldsdorf 1946)
A fertile and popular writer (he published over 100 books) who was one of the leading figures in the fashion for fantasy lite-

rature in the first thirty years of this century, both through his own novels and stories, and through his activities as editor of anthologies and of a periodical called *Der Orchideengarten* (The Orchid Garden). Probably the best-known of his magic novels is *Eleagabal Kuperus*. He also wrote historical novels of an increasingly German nationalist tone and ended as a National Socialist hack.

Die arge Nonn' (The Wicked Nun) was first published in:
Karl Hans Strobl, *Die knöcherne Hand und Anderes,* Georg Müller, Munich, 1911.
Der Kopf (The Head) was first published in:
Karl Hans Strobl, *Lemuria,* Georg Müller, Munich, 1921.

Franz Werfel (Prague 1890 – Beverly Hills 1945)
Achieved overnight fame as a twenty-year-old with his first collection of Expressionist verse, *Der Weltfreund* (The World-Friend), which was followed by further volumes of poetry and then Expressionist plays. After the First World War he won great popular success with his novel about the composer Verdi, and from then on he concentrated on prose. Born a Jew, he became a devout Catholic, although he was never baptised, and by far the most widely read of his novels is the somewhat sentimental *Song of Bernadette,* which he wrote in fulfilment of a vow he made after the Nazis invaded France that he would celebrate Bernadette of Lourdes if he should reach the safety of America.

Spielhof: Eine Fantasie (The Playground: A Fantasy) was first published by Kurt Wolff Verlag, Munich, 1920.